To Herta,

May all your winds
be tailwinds.

—— Marjorie

Bird Watcher

Bird Watcher

A Novel

Marjorie Johnson

Aero ergo sum.

ISBN 0-7414-4205-1

The cover includes a scanned version of a 12 x 16 acrylic artwork painted by the author.

Published by:

PUBLISHING.COM

1094 New DeHaven Street, Suite 100
West Conshohocken, PA 19428-2713
Info@buybooksontheweb.com
www.buybooksontheweb.com
Toll-free (877) BUY BOOK
Local Phone (610) 941-9999
Fax (610) 941-9959

Printed in the United States of America

Printed on Recycled Paper

Published August 2007

Acknowledgments

Many persons have helped me to produce this book, and I wish to thank each one here. First and foremost, my husband Frank Johnson uncomplainingly gave up evenings and weekends while I worked at my computer; he helped me to rethink certain chapters.

Edie Matthews inspired me, and her creative writing class critiqued my work one chapter at a time. They gave me advice and tore into my mistakes without tearing into me; a special thanks to Cody Lawrence, Carolyn Donnell and Richard Amyx.

My cousin Mark Baker edited and critiqued the third draft and suggested several important modifications. Several other friends read the book: David Stowell, Gerald and Shirley Bergum, Linda Hagelin, Martha Dietz, Paul Spears, Barbara Mock, Judy Stark, and my daughter, Jan Fey.

Dr. Colin P. Spears advised me on things medical. Barbara Mock, flight instructor *extraordinaire*, advised me on technical aviation matters. Martha Dietz corrected my German. Judy Stark, a fellow pilot, proofread and edited the manuscript. Kelly Harrison, also a pilot, edited early chapters and gave important suggestions. Linda Hagelin checked information on birds and birding. Jan Fey and David Argo scanned the cover. Joe Milliken helped me week after week at the FedEx Kinko's copy center.

Thank you all from my heart.

Reader's Comments on Bird Watcher

A great airport read. *Bird Watcher* is a fascinating story with a lot of plot twists. I enjoyed the descriptions of California from the air. — Martha Dietz

Wow! A wild adventure: starring a couple of incredibly brave teachers. Hooray! — Linda Hagelin

Bird Watcher is fast-paced airport reading. How many books about terrorism are charming? — Colin Paul Spears

The dialogue is hilarious. — Kelly Harrison

Bird Watcher is an enjoyable read. The author has done a lot of research and does a good job of tying everything together. — Judy Stark

You have a great story there. — Barbara Mock

Bird Watcher kept me guessing and turning pages. My neighbors want to read it. — Shirley Bergum

It's a hoot! — Cody Lawrence

1.

Cadet Kedar Khazari had thirty hours in his logbook but he knew he would never get his pilot's license. At the conclusion of this flight, his first—and his last—solo cross-country, he would meet his mother in heaven. He had joined the Guards last year, before his fifteenth birthday. Would anyone miss him? Not his foster mother; she had been glad to see him go.

Kedar pushed himself up high enough to look out over the cowling. He wondered how tall he would have been. Below him the landscape was as harsh as the sunny side of the moon. He shuddered, thinking about landing down there in the rocks and snakes. Except for a dirt road, the desert gave no clues to his location. His captain wouldn't know that he had been off course, as long as Kedar found his target.

He had the moving-map for navigation. The flight path on the blue moving-map pointed to the Daggett airport, the arrow piercing a small dot labeled DAG, the shaft crossing a military restricted area and higher terrain. Unlike his computer-based flight simulator game, the on-board GPS had no keyboard or mouse. Without the right knob twists, the machine wouldn't return to the assigned flight plan. The student pilot pushed the yoke slightly to level off at 9500 feet over a highway heading south.

When the map showed a path to Daggett clear of Edwards Air Force Base, he turned east; he could reorient himself over Daggett. He thought he recognized I-15, the interstate to Las Vegas. The aircraft cabin was cozy and he felt sleepy; last night instead of sleeping, he had looked forward to this flight: the captain had said that it would be his first solo cross-country, but he hadn't told Kedar about the explosives and the secret mission until just before take-off. Kedar drank some water but he really wanted coffee and a sweet roll. He stuffed his sweatshirt under his butt to raise himself in the seat enough to look outside without straining his neck. Then he saw clouds.

Dark clouds. How close? Some mist around his plane's wings. Thick cumulus hovered over half the sky, blocking his path. He had to alter course to avoid them—he would be unable to see. The Cessna had plenty of fuel. He turned south, away from the clouds, away from the restricted area, away from Daggett.

The aircraft engine ran with a strange sluggishness. Was something wrong? The tachometer showed 2200 RPMs; he had set it higher than that. The mags—no, it would lurch and stutter. Temperature: okay; oil pressure: okay. No problem, then: the altitude must affect the RPMs some way. Kedar glanced below a knob on the instrument panel where he had suspended his wristwatch. Airborne four hours, he wanted to pee. Why was the airplane slowing down?

The airspeed had decreased to 85 knots. The tach showed lower RPMs: only 1800. He pushed in the throttle and leaned the fuel-air mixture exactly as the captain had directed. He had never landed this particular Cessna 172, different from his familiar Cessna 152 trainer. Would it land the same way? The captain had said not to land anywhere.

"I am a soldier in a holy war, proud to be a Guard." Cadet Khazari chanted the mantra the captain had taught him: "Focus your mind on the mission, always the mission first . . . Chant 'I am a soldier in a holy war' . . ." The mantra didn't focus his mind. Kedar stared at the gray plastic barrel on the seat beside him. He couldn't land at Daggett and he couldn't land in the rocks.

" . . . Proud to be a soldier . . ." Kedar breathed faster, shallow breaths. He needed to think, not to sedate himself with chanting.

The engine knocked and vibrated. The RPMs had dropped to 1100. He pushed in the throttle as far as it would go. No change. He pushed the red mixture knob all the way in. The engine coughed twice and shuddered. Then silence,

2

except for the thump-thump, his heart pounding. He felt dizzy.

Kedar scanned the horizon, turning his head right, then left. The clouds were still there, but he could make Daggett. The captain had told him not to land for fuel, not with the explosives onboard. He pressed the alternator button and then pushed and pulled the primer. The engine was dead. The RPM needle had dropped quickly to the bottom of the dial. He felt the Cessna descending, a dropping sensation under his seat. He couldn't turn the ignition key to engage the starter—no key—because the captain had hot-wired it. Kedar needed a flat place to set down.

The wind screamed and whistled over the aircraft cabin—unnerving, unnatural—a sound like nothing he knew. The aircraft creaked and whined. Faster and faster, going down. Slow it, slow down. Where to land? His eyes darted across the terrain. Mountains. Rocks.

"I am a soldier . . . " The mantra taught to him by the captain was useless. He needed someone here, with him. He needed his flight instructor John. John would tell him what to do: *Fly the airplane, all the way to the ground.*

Lifting the nose gently and pulling the trim wheel, an adjustment that helped to stabilize the glide attitude and speed, Kedar brought the airspeed into the middle of the white arc that indicated a glide speed for emergencies that John had told him about. If he slowed the descent, he could glide a long way, but how far was that? Altitude 9000 feet, glide how many miles: John would know the calculations.

Without engine power, a Cessna turned into quite a good glider. A car with no power will coast a short distance, but an airplane can glide perfectly well with a dead engine. A stalled aircraft was something else—something fearsome. In a stall, the wings no longer flew and the plane would plunge downwards, faster and faster. John had shown him how to recover from a stall but John could give the engine power if he needed it. Stall practice was scary. Kedar tried to reason with the Cessna: "Don't stall. Oh, please, don't stall."

3

Without engine power, if Kedar pulled back too strongly on the yoke, the wings would no longer keep the aircraft flying. The plane would tumble to earth—nose first, even spinning.

"Don't crash. Please, don't crash." He pleaded with the airplane, a quaver in his voice. Fear gripped his gut. He could have flown into a dam at full throttle. The captain would kill him if he didn't. That was his mission and he'd go to heaven but he had failed. He was afraid. Falling out of the sky. Falling uncontrolled, through endless space. His worst nightmare: worse than fire, worse than drowning. He forced himself to breathe deeply and evenly.

He saw a dirt road, crooked, not straight, but the smoothest surface in the area. Could he make it? He lined up with the road. No sharp turns. No sudden changes to the yoke. He reasoned with himself: If he kept the aircraft under control, he had a 95 percent chance of survival.

Kedar's heart pounded and his stomach knotted. He couldn't tell where the Cessna would set down. There was a rule for that but he didn't remember—something about looking for the point that didn't move. Everything moved. The ground rushed by. He slowed the descent by lifting the yoke. The airplane turned left, no longer lined up with the road. More right rudder, it needed more rudder control.

The Cessna made one bounce on the road, then lurched to the ground two hundred feet to the north, off the road. The impact lifted him off his seat and bumped him back down. Rolling, bouncing too fast.

Rocks. Rocks. Everywhere. One wheel hit a rock. The plane twisted left, settled on the right wheel, and stopped abruptly. His head jerked forward, whipped back. Dazed, he looked through the yellowed windshield at brown-gray weathered granite only inches from the now-still propeller. Alive, spared by luck: he exhaled. His hands shook and his heart pounded. What would he do now? Where would he go? He saw only rock.

No explosion. A fire siren—no, the sound came from the radio. He hadn't run out of gas because he could smell it.

He staggered out of the cockpit. His knees wobbled and he couldn't think. He couldn't remember anything that had happened in the last three minutes: not the landing, not the descent to the road. Kedar had been afraid—a coward—and he deserved to die.

He had failed his mission. The captain would kill him. When the cadets had barbecued the chicken, the captain had told them all that he'd wring their necks if they failed; he had grabbed the rooster's neck in one hand and twisted its head with the other. Kedar hadn't eaten his.

Kedar stumbled away from the Cessna. The captain said it would explode, blow up at any moment. He had to get away, far away, up a steep hillside, scrambling, the loose gravel rattling down. He forced himself to breathe evenly and changed to a zigzag path to climb above the fallen airplane. Holding one hand to his forehead to shield his eyes from the intense sunlight, he scanned the terrain around him: rough ground to the west, prickly plants to the south, more rocks to the east. Kedar walked eastward on a dirt road, the sun warming his right arm and leg.

Kedar heard a loud whooshing and turned to face the fallen Cessna. Flames shot up above one wing. Sparks, likely from the hot-wired ignition system or from the radios he reasoned, caught the fumes. He watched with fascination. With another whoosh, flames engulfed the plane.

Run. Run. Get away. The fire would set off those gray barrels. His breath came in ragged gasps. His legs moved in slow motion. Move faster. Run.

The massive explosion knocked him to the ground.

2.

On Monday morning Frank Peterson stood next to the Cessna in its tie-down at Palo Alto Airport and rolled up the pant legs of the National Guard flight suit he wore, still bearing brass epaulettes. He didn't understand the military masquerade. His buddy Jerry usually wore a leather aviator's jacket and jeans. Last year, Frank had bought half of Jerry Christensen's Cessna—too expensive for one teacher's salary. Jerry had been his mentor when he learned to fly, a stronger emotional bond than he had felt with his flight instructor. Frank glanced at the mirror on the car door and removed the colonel's insignia from both shoulders. "I'm taking these off," he said. "Probably against the law to impersonate an officer."

"We're not hurting anything and it'll be fun. Here, Frank, your pants are too long." Jerry tossed him a roll of duct tape. "Turn them under and hold them up like this." With one foot propped on a fender, Jerry smoothed the tape inside a pant leg, creased the hem with his fingernails, and adjusted his aviator's sunglasses. "Don't we look cool?"

"Best-looking redheaded pilots in the county." By coincidence, they were both redheaded, both left-handed. Except Frank had the beard—his blazing red beard, as his wife Mary called it. He wondered why Jerry wanted to wear the flight suits and where he got them, but what better way to spend a week off than flying?

Frank sat in the cockpit and turned the master switch on and then off while Jerry checked the lights and the stall horn. After Jerry finished a careful preflight inspection, he climbed in to the pilot's seat and started the engine right there in their tie-down space. He listened to the ATIS and got clearance to taxi from the ground controller. After Jerry's careful run-up, he called the tower. "Cessna Three-Three-One-Eight-Echo, ready for take off, right Dumbarton."

"Cessna One-Eight-Echo, cleared for take off."

Those always were magic words to Frank. He felt the acceleration as Jerry pushed in the throttle, then a gentle rise into the sky at 60 knots. Today they could see forever—or at least fifty miles, according to the Palo Alto ATIS, which gave automated weather and landing conditions and the usual caution for bird activity on final approach. The airport bordered a wildlife refuge for waterfowl, home to 500 Canada geese. A big goose breaking a plane's windshield could kill a pilot, before or after he lost control of the aircraft.

Sitting in the co-pilot's seat, Frank surveyed the heavy traffic, like tiny ant vehicles from this altitude, on Highway 680 over Sunol Pass leading out of the San Francisco Bay Area. In the distance, the snow-capped Sierra Nevada gleamed in the bright morning sun. Past the windmill farms, the Central Valley spread out as a vast patchwork quilt of green and brown fields between areas of urban sprawl. After half an hour, Frank saw the red-clay eyebrow-shaped landmark on the bushy hill above Auburn Airport. Jerry dropped down over the familiar road until the plane was in position to turn base leg over the canyon. The Cessna's wheels nearly brushed the treetops during Jerry's descent.

On the runway, an ultra-light took off, the pilot sitting in a swing-like seat mounted under the wings. "Like riding a bicycle while holding an open umbrella," Jerry said. He landed safely with one chirp of the stall horn and taxied to a parking spot in front of The Gyro House, a little early for their installation appointment.

Jerry paused at The Gyro House door to tame his hair and to admire his flight suit as mirrored by the sun-reflecting foil on the southern-facing windows. Frank bent down and checked that the tape still held Jerry's hems.

Just inside the door of the avionics shop, an older woman who wore jeans and a gray sweatshirt leaned over a computer under a wall-length mural: a floatplane above a lake towed a red and white banner, *Freedom The Power of Flight*. Without looking up, she said, "Drop the keys here."

The FBOs—fixed-base operators–clustered together on the west side of the single runway at Auburn Airport. Frank followed Jerry next door and ducked under the half-open hangar door at Gold Country Aviation.

Ruben's shoes stuck out from under the belly of a Comanche. The feet gave a quick push and Ruben Estrada shot out on his creeper, scooting over a spotless floor. He brushed off the seat of his pants and placed a gleaming wrench in a chest with a dozen drawers, each arranged in order of size, every tool in its place. Ruben operated on engines with the precision of a surgeon transplanting a heart.

"And who do we have here?" Ruben's eyes scanned Jerry from head to foot and back up again. "A colonel, huh? I'm ready for inspection any time." Ruben clapped Jerry on the shoulder, then spit on one finger to polish the epaulettes.

Frank peered into the cockpit of the low-wing airplane behind Ruben. The instrument panel had no radios, only empty holes waiting. He patted the propeller and asked, "What's the story on this Comanche?"

"She had a hard landing; broke off her nose wheel, curled up her prop. Only thing not damaged was the GPS, the one I traded to Jerry. I replaced the propeller and flew her up from *Los Baños*."

"Isn't that iffy?" Frank said.

"Any trouble, I always have a mechanic on board."

Jerry put one foot on a stepladder and re-adjusted the duct tape on his pant leg. "Hey, we're taking you to lunch," he said to Ruben. "Those hamburgers at Wings Grill are the best around."

"I'll give you that. But their pies are only Number Two. The best pie—*numero uno*—is at *Los Baños*."

"Number two? Is that like Avis, or . . . something else?" Jerry deadpanned, except for his wiggling eyebrows.

"You've been teaching at that junior high school way too long," Ruben said. "I'm putting together an airport food guide."

"Is that airman alimentary system maintenance?" Jerry asked.

"I thought you were talking exhaust systems." Ruben slapped Jerry's back.

"Oh, come on, Ruben," Frank said, glancing at the mechanic's aircraft maintenance manuals: a good twelve feet of books. "Jerry's buying."

Next door at Wings Grill, a young blond waitress set a glass of water in front of Ruben. She almost brushed his arm with her ample bosom, barely contained by her tight red sweater.

"Ah, the lovely *Señorita* Robina," Ruben said in his soft Latin accent. He moved the water glass to the center of the table. "So beautiful today . . ."

Robina pulled out an order pad from her white apron. "So . . . what'll you have, good looking?"

"The usual," Ruben said. "You know what I like."

"What do you guys want?" She leaned toward Jerry.

"How about a ride in my airplane, babe?" Jerry moved his arm to touch the waitress. She pulled away.

"Give them what you're bringing me," Ruben said.

"Three usuals, coming up." She turned and disappeared into the kitchen.

"And what do you guys want?" Jerry mimicked her, his eyes wide open and innocent. "Boobs on rye."

"*¡Arriba!*" Ruben guffawed and slapped one leg.

"Knockers with a French roll." Jerry laughed at his own joke.

"Everyone's looking at us," Frank said. Downright embarrassing, the way Jerry carried on with waitresses. He hoped Robina didn't overhear the crude remarks.

After lunch, Jerry showed Ruben the new upholstery in One-Eight-Echo—still tied down outside, still without the GPS. As a hobby, Jerry had reupholstered and restored the interior of several vintage automobiles. Using special fabrics approved by the FAA, he had refurbished the entire cabin of his aircraft. "Next weekend," he promised, "One aircraft cabin interior for one GPS. You'll love the finished product."

Ruben's Comanche, that's the source of the navigation radios, Frank thought, standing next to Jerry and their airplane. So many wires stuck out through two empty holes in the Cessna's instrument panel that he wondered if the job would be finished before dark.

"Come back in three hours," the avionics technician called out from someplace inside the hangar. "Installing your GPS is my next job."

"He didn't know he was dealing with a colonel." Frank followed Jerry toward the adjacent golf course. The afternoon sun felt pleasantly warm through his flight suit. A crisp morning had become almost a spring day.

"A counterfeit colonel—serves me right." Jerry laughed at himself. "Even the waitress wasn't impressed. Sometimes, I'd like to wear a uniform for real."

"Then you should've joined the military." Frank sprawled onto a bench with a good view of landing traffic.

"I didn't want anybody shooting at me. And I wanted to make a difference in someone's life. Education of the young, all that." Jerry plopped down onto the grass and drew up his knees.

"How idealistic. So, then, why did you want to fly?"

"When I was ten," Jerry answered, "a Piper Cub landed in our pasture, such a marvelous event that I still remember the moment. Probably to make me stop pestering him, my grandfather let me go for a ride."

"I knew your grandparents raised you but I never heard that story," Frank said.

"That ride in the Cub hooked me for life. I just wanted to fly. I dreamed about soaring and swooping, even pretended I was an eagle."

"Why do I believe the pestering part? What about the swooping?"

"Not that much of an eagle. More a rooster with a clipped wing, running around the yard." Jerry chuckled.

Then he checked his watch. "If we had taken One-Eight-Echo to San Jose to get the GPS, we'd be home by now."

"But without Ruben's deal on the GPS. I can hardly wait to try it out." Frank looked forward to navigation with the Global Positioning System, using satellites to give location anywhere in the world. He had spent hours computing flight plans and wind corrections.

"The GPS can do all the math for you," Frank said. Not that Jerry used his computations. Jerry flew like a homing pigeon, correcting small deviations from course while watching scenery, telling stories, and making jokes. "You won't need me anymore."

"Watch out. It won't talk as much as you do. Hey, you should see the avionics shop at San Jose. Big hangar, a dozen planes parked in there, mechanics all over the place. The FBI has a whole fleet of Cessna 210s."

"Surveillance and drug interdiction."

"Yeah, spy planes. Computers instead of middle seats . . . wires sticking out all over." Jerry spread his arms like antennas and punctuated with both hands. "Sniff out drug operations, better than those dogs at the airports."

"A flying, drug-sniffing beagle." Frank laughed, pleased with his joke.

"More a porcupine with a pig's eye . . . the FBI eye in the sky." Jerry crossed one leg over the other knee. "Good thing we have a Cessna 172. Nobody steals those to run drugs."

"If it had more range, someone might try it." Frank looked at his watch and yawned. When would that mechanic finish?

Three hours later, Frank took off from Auburn just at sunset with Jerry in the co-pilot's seat. Frank pushed in the throttle and released the brake, rolling faster and faster until the aircraft lifted magically into the air. There was no other feeling like it, that first change from earthbound to unfettered, and no way to explain the thrill of it to someone who didn't fly. What a blessing, the gift of flight. The sky was the color of ripe pumpkin with slashes of fluorescent pink.

Like all pilots, Jerry wanted to try out his new toy. He put Palo Alto into the GPS to check the heading and distance and estimated time for the flight. He tried this button and that, then one marked D with an arrow through it. "Hey, Frank. I've got the nearest airport where we could go for an emergency landing. Head 260, see if we find a private airport. Isn't this cool?"

Frank changed the heading. The red-orange sky faded to blues and purples. "It won't be lighted."

"I think I see it. Head 010 and see what we get."

"We're going back towards Auburn and we haven't been home for hours," Frank said. The sky darkened, a moonless night. Sacramento came alive with light: yellow, red, and green. "I'm heading for the barn. We can learn how to use the GPS tomorrow."

Returning to Palo Alto, Frank descended past the salt ponds at 1500 feet. The air was smooth and the beacon flashed its white-green-white-green greeting. Frank relaxed and listened to the ATIS broadcast with its usual warning about bird activity on final. Landing in five minutes.

Ka-THUMP-Bump. Loud bang.

"Holy shit!" Jerry turned toward the right wing.

"What the heck!" Frank's heart missed a beat. His mind speeded up. The Cessna flew in slow motion. Fly the airplane. Think of nothing else.

A split second later, a gull flew past the left side of the airplane, so close to Frank that he thought it would break the windshield right in front of his face. Both he and Jerry leaned forward against their shoulder harnesses.

"Palo Alto Tower, Cessna One-Eight-Echo. We have a bird strike."

"One-Eight-Echo, are you declaring an emergency?"

"Negative," Frank said. "Just watch our landing."

"Those birds didn't listen to the ATIS," Jerry said. "I thought they didn't fly at night."

"We might not have landing lights." Frank was glad that they hadn't hit a goose. The engine was still running, the plane still flying. Frank turned onto final.

Under minimal airport lighting, the asphalt runway was invisible between two rows of blue lights. Frank turned on the landing lights; the right one was out. He strained to see and managed to say, "Like dropping into a black hole."

"You know how to land in the dark? Turn on the landing lights, and if you don't like what you see, turn them off again."

Frank was too busy to answer. He descended and held what he hoped was the centerline on his final approach. The Cessna touched down with a bounce, a recoverable bounce. Frank, so relieved that he could have kissed one of those geese advertised on the ATIS, turned off the runway just as the other landing light went out.

"One-Eight-Echo, clear of the runway. We lost our second light," Frank radioed. "Thanks for watching over us."

"You landed with one eye closed. Taxi to parking, this frequency."

"Roger."

Jerry hopped out with a flashlight to lead Frank along the taxiway. With no moon, Frank could see nothing beyond the light's cone of illumination. After they tied her down, Jerry beamed the light back and forth along the right wing while Frank ran his hand over the surface to inspect the damage: a large dent, surrounded by blood and feathers.

"Big Bird won't have the guts to do that again." Jerry sounded serious, then laughed at his own joke.

"Yuck. What a mess." Frank felt shaky, now that the danger was over. He needed to do something physical. "Hand me that towel. I don't see any fuel leaking out."

"I don't smell it either, only a dent in the leading edge with no noticeable damage to the fuel tank. I think it's safe to leave it until tomorrow."

3.

The birds hadn't noticed him. Moving only his eyes, Aquila scanned the parking lot at the nature preserve. At six foot eight, he towered over a group of Boy Scouts assembled near his Volkswagen van. He slammed the side door shut. Avoiding eye contact, he carried his equipment around the noisy boys toward the duck pond. Binoculars dangled around his neck and a bird-identification guide protruded from a bulging jacket pocket. Aquila thought no one would notice him. Wearing tan cargo pants and a wide-brimmed hat, he blended into the bird-watching environment.

Aquila The-Bird-Watcher heard quacks, whistles, and chirps and saw the usual waterfowl—ducks, egrets, and curlews—in the salt marsh and mud when he set up his tripod-mounted telescope near the edge of San Francisco Bay. Snowy egrets perched atop stubby palm trees and more stood at the edges of the pond. Amid a chorus of calls and cackles, a group of swimming ducks moved out of the way for two graceful blue herons.

Pretending to follow some Canada geese, he turned his telescope toward the final approach flight path for Palo Alto Airport where student pilots landed like gooney birds from the Marshall Islands. He could see most of the tie-down area at the airport beyond the fence. Two redheaded men—red-crested finches—walked around a Cessna making a careful preflight. He had watched them before, the same two men, the same khaki uniforms. With morning overcast, their shoulders didn't glitter in the sunlight as they had yesterday, but he knew they wore bright brass epaulettes with what appeared to be military uniforms, probably Air National Guard. They were men who would demand a plane in top condition, and so did he. He pulled a crumpled paper from a side pocket and recorded the tail number 3318E.

Before he drove to Los Banos for a birding session with his students, Aquila needed a closer look at Palo Alto Airport, only half a mile away. He loaded the telescope and took the van; time was short. At the Palo Alto Terminal Building, a flurry of swirling air followed him through the door and deposited a fast food wrapper at his feet.

Across the lobby, someone leaned on a broom. Aquila walked to the bulletin board, conveniently located outside the open office door and beside the surveillance monitors. He faced the bulletin board and studied the monitors out of the corner of his left eye.

Broom-man swept over and said, "I haven't seen you around. Do you fly out of Palo Alto?"

"No. I watch birds." Aquila glanced down at his baggy cargo pants and bulging jacket; he didn't blend into this environment.

"I'm Brad. I'm the airport administrator when I'm not polishing floors." Brad picked up the fast food wrapper and dropped it into a wastepaper basket. "If you need anything, let me know."

Aquila read the board and the monitors for a few more minutes, memorizing the surveillance information. He stared directly at Brad before he walked out the door and into the parking lot. He didn't say goodbye, but then, he hadn't said hello either. He threw his jacket onto the passenger's seat of his battered blue Volkswagen van and drove away.

Later on Tuesday and after a two-hour drive, Aquila pulled his VW van into the parking lot behind McDonald's in Los Banos. He waved at Cadet Kedar Khazari who had dressed for their birding session, his cargo pants rolled up three turns. His student waved goodbye to the sergeant in the truck and walked towards the van.

Aquila stepped out, zipped his many-pocketed jacket, and went inside to order coffee. When he returned, Aquila balanced a cardboard tray on a fender and dug for his keys. He asked, "Ready, Cadet?"

"Yes, Sir."

"Then fall in. Here's coffee and a sweet roll. We can eat on the way." Aquila drove north on Wolfsen Road and parked within the San Luis Wildlife Refuge. He stood next to the cadet briefly while unloading the van. Cadet Khazari's head didn't come up to Aquila's shoulder; the boy would be much taller in a year or two, if he had that much time. The captain gave the kid a pair of binoculars and unloaded a telescope with a tripod.

In the marsh, thousands of waterfowl squawked and called, competing for space—a bird watcher's paradise: cranes, coots, pintail ducks, and egrets. The sharp stink of guano hung in the still morning air. "Each call means something," Aquila said. "Close your eyes and tell me what birds are flying overhead."

Cadet Khazari squinted his eyes shut. "Canada geese. They sound like this." His honk sounded so real that two of the birds came nearer.

"Very good, Bird-Caller. Now I want you to look at a different kind of bird." The captain pointed up at an airplane.

The birds paid no attention to the Cessna descending for landing at Los Banos Airport, a small non-towered field without fences and with self-service fuel. After the bird watchers locked the telescope onto the small plane, they paid no attention to the birds.

"It's time to use those flying lessons for something." The captain pulled a map out of one bulging pocket and spread it across a nearby picnic table. He had chosen Kedar Khazari, his best student, to fly the mission.

"You will fly from Los Banos in such a plane. You will head southeast." Aquila traced the flight path on an aeronautical chart with his index finger.

Kedar leaned over the chart, studying it.

"Turn east here. Land at Daggett for fuel. Afterwards, fly to the Colorado River. Descend to 800 feet above the river and fly north, below radar. Make a delivery here . . . Boulder City, near Hoover Dam."

Kedar smiled, so excited he could hardly stand still.

Aquila stabbed at Edwards Air Force Base on the chart with his forefinger. "Follow directions—they won't scramble the F-16s. Got that?"

"Yes, Sir." Kedar's eyes danced when he looked up at the captain.

"Your flight instructor, John, said to count this as a solo cross-country."

A little after nine on Tuesday morning, Frank and Jerry taxied their Cessna to the wash rack at Palo Alto Airport to remove the blood and feathers acquired in last night's misadventure. Frank gave the plane one last scrub. Jerry repaired the landing light and tightened the final screw on the cowling, re-buttoning the metal skin around the engine compartment. Jerry waxed the leading edge of the dented wing while Frank checked the condition of both wings, especially near the big dent.

"The fuel tank seems all right—not leaking," Frank said. "That dent needs repair, first thing next week."

"Smell any fuel?" Jerry asked.

Frank gave the fuel vents a second inspection. "No eau de Avgas."

"Well, then, we should be okay." Jerry cleaned the oil off his fingers with baby-wipes. "I'm finished here. Let's see how that new GPS works for instrument approaches."

Frank climbed into the cockpit to play with the GPS while Jerry did the preflight and the run-up. The GPS chip had flight information for every airport in the United States. The Latitude-Longitude button showed Palo Alto Airport with coordinates N 37° 27.67', W 122° 06.90', accurate to 100 feet. Direct JFK, New York, showed 2235 nautical miles almost due east. Of course, their Cessna couldn't do that non-stop. Their aircraft manual, always optimistic, gave them a range of 600 nautical miles with a cruise speed of 120 knots. In car-speak, that was 700 miles with a speed of 140 miles per hour, not corrected for headwinds or tailwinds. Frank dialed in their flight plan.

Fog covered the bay. Engine running and ready for take-off, Jerry tapped his fingers on the yoke. Pilots at Palo Alto, located between international airports at San Francisco and San Jose, always waited for clearance from departure control when visibility was limited—sometimes for half an hour. "Hold, hold, hold," he said. "I'm growing moss under my headset."

The radio crackled into action. "Cessna One-Eight-Echo, change in your clearance. Ready to copy?"

"Ready to copy."

"Cleared to Stockton Airport. After take-off, turn 060 within one mile. Climb and maintain 2000 feet, expect higher in five minutes, direct SUNOL. Rest of clearance unchanged. Cleared for immediate take-off."

"Cleared for take-off." Jerry pushed in the throttle and said to Frank, "Hurry up and wait."

After take-off, the thin fog layer over San Francisco Bay reflected the salt evaporation ponds below, a pink-orange glow followed by cloudy white-out. Frank tapped the right window with an index finger. "Brine shrimp cause that orange color. They're growing food for fish and pets as well as collecting salt."

"Looks like tomato soup to me," Jerry said.

One of Frank's bushy eyebrows went up, poking above his glasses. What a peculiar simile, he thought: almost a mixed metaphor. He watched Jerry tune in the ATIS for Stockton to check the winds.

"Stockton's clear," Jerry said. "Hand me the hood. We'll see if I can find the place without peeking."

Frank held the yoke while Jerry adjusted the hood, a piece of plastic that blocked his view of everything outside the cockpit to simulate foggy conditions. Limiting a pilot's vision forced him to pay attention to instruments only and to disregard visual information. Frank watched for traffic and other danger while Jerry shot practice approaches to Stockton, a way to find the runway for landing in heavy fog.

Frank preferred *Foggles*, like bifocal sunglasses except that only the reading segment of each lens was transparent; the rest was opaque. To simulate a whiteout, Frank had only to flip them down. Shooting approaches, practice necessary to keep a pilot's skills sharp, was a great pilot game.

At Stockton, the controller cleared Jerry to ORANG for a hold—a four-minute pattern in the air around an imaginary charted point. Jerry concentrated on making the airplane glyph on the GPS moving-map follow a smooth oval-like path drawn on the jewel-like blue screen while Frank swiveled his head checking for traffic—birds or planes coming too close.

"What a wonderful piece of technology." Frank gave the instrument a love pat. "Just dial it in and go. High tech navigation, but in an aircraft still using an ignition system designed seventy years ago."

"If there weren't any birds, we wouldn't have to look outside." Jerry removed the hood and turned towards home. He tipped the wings, right and left, just for the joy of it. "A whole week to fly—our week to howl."

"Whoo-e-e!" Frank hooted.

Crossing SUNOL intersection, Frank noticed that the fog had cleared. Jerry landed uneventfully.

Back on the ground at Palo Alto, Frank tied down the left wing, the one with the dent. "I don't detect escaping fuel. We're all right unless somebody lights up."

"Smoking around fuel? Then he'd light up the whole place," Jerry said from a few steps away. He turned back towards the Cessna, his pen between his teeth, and pointed his toes way out into a flat-footed duck-walk.

"Some fat guy, smoking a cigar, waddles on over, says what's that smell? Ka-boom! He's covered with soot, hair standing on end, eyebrows singed, cigar flattened against his face. Says Whoa, Dude. Cigars only explode in the movies."

Frank ignored the show. "I turned off everything electrical."

"Tomorrow, it's Squaw Peak or Bust."

19

4.

Wednesday had no moon. Three hours before sunrise, Aquila slipped under the surveillance camera at the boundary of Palo Alto Airport. Behind him and to either side he saw nothing in the blackness. No one would see him.

Aquila walked across the ramp, directly to Cessna 3318E. He flashed a small penlight at the old Cessna lock, loose. Careful jiggling of a door key copied from a rental airplane unlocked the door. The aircraft papers in the map drawer showed a low time engine and long-range fuel tanks. Perfect for the mission.

Stealing an airplane for a weapon: the modern equivalent of using the enemy's rifles and horses. Even better, one owned by two military men, probably Air National Guard. This was a holy war. The first flight of his cadet air force would strike a blow for *Paha Sapa*, his grandmothers' holy place. He had trained four pilots; even a small plane could make a significant strike. The United States Government owed them. Aquila was ready to collect.

Out of camera range, Aquila pulled the Cessna by its propeller to reposition it on the taxiway. He stepped into the cockpit. With his feet on the newly upholstered passenger's seat and his shoulders on the floor on the pilot's side, he directed his flashlight beam into the nest of wires under the instrument panel. It took less than three minutes to bypass the ignition key.

He unfolded himself, set the brake, climbed out, and pulled the propeller through one revolution. No one touches a propeller when an engine has been hot-wired—except to start the engine—and then only with extreme care. The propeller could kill him. It took two more hand props for the engine to turn over.

Aquila kicked away a wheel chock, leapt into the pilot's seat, and closed the door. Taxiing without lights to the end of the runway, he stopped to check the panel instruments with his flashlight. In a hurry to leave Palo Alto without being seen, he did not run up the engine before he advanced the throttle to take off in the dark.

Without the moon, he had no visible horizon; spatial disorientation could make a pilot dive into the bay, but that wouldn't happen to him, not if he used careful control inputs. Aquila made a gentle turn to a heading of 060, the same routine as a departure into the fog, and flew at 500 feet. Soft light from distant highways and streets rimmed the otherwise black and featureless bay. With momentary use of the landing lights, he verified the salt pile at the evaporation ponds. He saw white headlight beams from cars crossing over the Sunol grade and followed them as far as Tracy. He turned south towards Los Banos and flew above Interstate 5 through the Central Valley, a route usual for small aircraft.

At Los Banos, Aquila used a credit card at the self-service fuel pump to fill the tanks, first disconnecting the ignition wires to avoid a spark. On the fuel tag, he recorded the tail number as 58133, reversing 3318E. Make them guess—if anyone checked. He pulled the aircraft away from the pump and reconnected the wires. One of his men—Sergeant Wamblee—ran to meet him and held the brakes while Aquila gave the prop one turn to restart. Wamblee taxied to the parking area where a Volkswagen van waited.

With the propeller turning and blowing grit, Aquila's men loaded three plastic drums onto the back passengers' seat and a fourth onto the right front seat. Wamblee set the parking brake and stepped out into the prop wash. Aquila held his hat with one hand to keep it on his head and moved the seat forward to allow Cadet Khazari's shorter legs to reach the rudder pedals.

Aquila had to shout to communicate over the engine roar. "A secret mission . . ."

Kedar Khazari—a fifteen-year-old student pilot—climbed into the pilot's seat of a Cessna at Los Banos. It was too dark to make out the trim color on the white airplane. His dark eyes glanced at three barrels on the back seat and his handsome face wrinkled with concentration. He listened carefully to the captain.

Aquila stood on the tarmac next to the open door. He spoke loudly to overcome the engine noise. "Use this GPS until you have light to see the ground. Then fly east like we went over yesterday."

"Yes, Sir." His first cross-country, equipped with a GPS and moving map: totally cool.

"Follow the Colorado River north. Your mission: take out Hoover Dam." Aquila pointed at a gray barrel on the seat next to Kedar. "You will fly these explosives directly into it."

"Yes, Sir." Kedar's eyes opened wider. Different than his briefing yesterday . . . cadets must obey orders without question.

The captain leaned close to Kedar, holding a photograph. "Now this is a secret. See this?" He tapped the photo, indicating a doorway above a black walkway. "Hit it there, the Achilles' heel."

"Yes, Sir." He saw the picture; what was Achilles' heel?

The captain reached across Kedar and taped the photo to the instrument panel. Kedar sucked in his gut, away from the captain's long arm. He saw a picture of a cement wall and a green-ink arrow. The captain moved back, beside the open door. "Lean the mixture to conserve fuel. Just turn that red knob."

"Yes, Sir." Conserve fuel? Had he studied that? What happened to Daggett and Boulder City?

"You won't need more fuel—long-range tanks. Don't land anywhere. A spark will blow up the fuel tanks. A hard landing will set off explosives."

"Yes, Sir." He glanced at the gray barrel on the seat next to him.

22

The captain yelled, "You can't shut down. It's hot-wired. Fly carefully."

"Yes, Sir." What was in those barrels? Obey orders.

"You are a soldier in a holy war, a secret mission. You must not fail."

"Yes, Sir." Holy war? This was California.

"Now, give me your wallet."

"Yes, Sir." His student pilot papers . . . his pilot's logbook was under his sweatshirt. *Obey orders without question.* He handed over only his wallet and slammed the Cessna's door, locking it.

"I am a soldier in a holy war," he chanted over the engine noise. He lingered a few moments in the run-up area and prayed. He would never return, but he couldn't stop now—with the captain watching.

Still dark, the sky began to lighten over the mountains on the eastern horizon. He had never taken off in the dark. Would it feel different?

The instrument panel was familiar from his favorite flight simulator game. He would climb at 500 feet per minute, hold runway heading to 2000 feet, and make a gentle turn southeast, just like his game.

Kedar pushed in full throttle. The Cessna rushed down the runway.

From the ground at Los Banos, Aquila watched Cessna 3318E take off down the runway and gather speed as it ascended into the predawn sky. He scanned the sky, his feet rooted in the parking area, his eyes riveted on the aircraft, until he could no longer see her navigation lights.

Haii-yee-ah. Haii-yee-ah. Haii-yee-ah. The beat of a war-dance drum cursed through his memory. Aquila could almost hear tonight's news, every channel: Small plane hits Hoover Dam. Explosion knocks out turbine, the extent of damage unknown.

Aquila pictured helicopters flying over rubble, water shooting down, but he knew that wouldn't happen, not without extraordinary luck, like the collapse of the tower in New York because the airliner hit the ideal place. Jimmy

Black Bear—he had worked on the dam in the 1930s—had told Aquila about Hoover Dam's weak spot, hollow work ways near the front surface of the dam. In a few hours Cadet Khazari would strike the belly of the beast.

Aquila's secret Wartech explosives—600 pounds equivalent to 12 tons of TNT—would open the front wall of the monolith and reverberate through the interior walkways, destroying at least one turbine. A small down payment on what the government owed to the Indians.

At first, Jerry thought he had been so eager to get into the air—a cloudless winter morning perfect for flying—that he had driven down the wrong taxiway at Palo Alto Airport. He stopped in the middle of Taxiway November and counted down the row with his eyes. Except for Frank and Frank's car, One-Eight-Echo's tie-down space N-12 was empty.

Jerry jumped to the ground and paced, still disbelieving. "Where is it?" He traced the *twelve* painted on the asphalt with his toe. "Who moved it? We did put it away here on November row where it belongs, didn't we? Think somebody stole it?"

Frank walked behind their tie-down, scanning both directions along the taxiway as if searching for clues. "They weren't satisfied with stealing our new GPS. They took the whole damn airplane. Now what're we going to do?"

Jerry punched his right hand with his left fist. "Damn, damn, damn! They'll abandon One-Eight-Echo someplace out in the weeds, steal the GPS." He gave a pebble an angry kick. He wanted to kick the thief, punch him out. "We have to find them before it's too late."

"How can we do that?"

Jerry stood still, right in the middle of the empty tie-down space. He stared skyward, as if for inspiration. "I can track it," he said.

Frank stared at Jerry. His mouth formed a silent "How?"

"Over Christmas break I rented a van from ACE—that car rental place on 101. I went skiing at Tahoe. Thought I'd run over to Reno one evening until I read through two pages of small print . . . a big fine if I crossed the Nevada border."

"So?" Frank's bushy eyebrows furrowed.

Jerry waved his hands wildly. He pointed at Frank. "Would you believe $500? I was really burned up. I called Rick—you know Rick—the mechanic at ACE? He told me how to take off the bug—they follow you in their rental cars. So, I went to Reno."

"What the heck does all that have to do with our missing airplane?"

"When I returned the van, I forgot the bug. I installed it on One-Eight-Echo yesterday, and I wanted to fly directly across Lake Tahoe into Nevada today. A rental car in two places at once. Drive ACE crazy."

"What does flying across Lake Tahoe have to do with anything?" Frank shifted his weight and put his hands on his hips. "You're wasting time. We need to report this to somebody."

"But I may know where it went." Jerry pulled out his cell phone. "Hey, Rick . . . Jerry here. Do me a favor, will you? See what your computer says about that van I used last month. It's important. I'll explain later."

In less than five minutes, Rick reported that the map showed it between Barstow and Bullhead City. "Near some place called Kelso, some place with no roads. What's it doing there? How can it be parked *here*, and be *there*?"

"Tell you later. I owe you a big one." Jerry turned off his cell phone and turned towards Frank. "Rick says Kelso. Know anything about Kelso? Or Barstow, or Bullhead City?"

Frank stood by his open trunk and fiddled with his flight bag. "I've never been there, but here's a map." An out-of-date Los Angeles Sectional showed a wasteland near the California-Arizona-Nevada border and numerous MOAs, Military Operation Areas. "Not heading for Mexico and drugs. Las Vegas? Why would they want a little Cessna, out in that desert?"

Jerry wasn't listening. He was running down the taxiway. "Maybe the controllers can help us," he called out over his shoulder. "Come on!"

At the base of the Palo Alto Airport control tower, Jerry rang the bell and yelled through the intercom, "We have an emergency and need your help."

"State your name and business."

"This is Jerry Christensen. My Cessna 3318E is based here."

"Jerry? Why didn't you say so? Come on up," boomed the speaker on the wall. The door buzzed open.

Jerry rushed up the stairs and burst into the observation room fifty feet above the runway. Without a hello and without taking a new breath, Jerry said, "We need you to call Air Traffic Control. Our Cessna was stolen this morning. We have a tip—it's east of Barstow and south of Las Vegas. Tell them to scramble the F-16s."

A few seconds later, Frank caught up. He still clutched the map. His heart pounded from the sudden exertion. Palo Alto Airport's control tower smelled of stale coffee, and walls of windows provided a bird's eye view of the field. Two controllers, each equipped with a headphone and a microphone, sat in front of computer monitors.

The bald controller turned to face Jerry. "We'll advise Air Traffic Control of a stolen aircraft in that sector, but I can tell you right now they're not going to send F-16s after a small ticket item—it's not like someone hijacked a jumbo jet. They only go after a Cessna that invades their airspace. And, they need more info."

More info . . . Jerry hurried down the stairs. How would he find more information? Maybe Brad had seen something. Jerry sprinted along a taxiway in an effortless gliding run he had developed in high school with his grandfather's coaching. He burst through the door at the Palo Alto terminal building and said, all in one breath, "Hey,

Brad, somebody just stole our Cessna, anybody unusual hanging around?"

"Hey, slow down. Somebody unusual, you say?" Brad Williams, the airport administrator, leaned on a broom and touched one hand to his head. "Strange man with a limp, a tall birdwatcher-type, the coldest eyes I ever saw, like a fish. Gave me the creeps: the irises in his eyes were almost colorless silver-gray. He didn't say hello or goodbye and seemed real interested in the surveillance cameras."

"All those new cameras, did they catch anything this morning?"

Brad fumbled with the tapes, picked out the one from the Runway 31 area, and loaded it into the video player. He ran it twice. It showed nothing—a dark night, no moon— nothing at all.

Frank arrived in time to watch the blank tape. "No clues—what a helpless feeling," he said, running his fingers through his hair. "A bird-watching stranger. Probably visiting from Palo Alto Baylands Nature Preserve next door. Have you been there?"

"Just a bunch of birds."

"And the airport's just a bunch of airplanes."

Before they left the parking lot, Brad called out the door, "Hey, Jerry, telephone for you. It's the tower."

The message boomed out from the speaker, loud and clear. "Air Traffic Control says nothing on radar in the sector from Barstow east. Two pilots reported an emergency transmitter, probably an error. Sorry. No way to help you."

Jerry asked Brad to relay a thank-you to the controller at the tower. Still standing in the parking lot, he said to Frank, "Guess if we want anything done, we have to do it ourselves."

Frank shrugged and threw up his hands.

"Wait—I have an idea." Jerry whipped out his cell phone and hit redial. "Hey, Rick, can you look again?" After a slight pause, he said, "It'll be interesting. I guarantee it."

Jerry nodded at Frank and held up one hand, then selected speakerphone. Down at ACE Car Rental, Rick raced

27

to the computer terminal. "You're not going to believe this. The second marker for the van, the one in Kelso, disappeared. Now everything's working right. Just one marker: the van in the yard. What the heck happened?"

After Jerry put away the cell phone, he said to Frank, "One-Eight-Echo sent a distress signal from Kelso."

"That could have been a false alarm."

"Come on. Let's rent a bird and head out before the trail gets cold. If we go to Barstow, we can rent a car and ask the local pilots what they saw."

Frank paused and considered Jerry's proposal. They could rent a plane, and he had looked forward to a day in the air. "Well . . . All right. We planned to fly to Reno today anyway, but we're under-equipped to fly out into the desert."

Frank stopped at his car. "I have water and some granola bars. And here's a road map for Southern California." Standing next to the open car-trunk, he unfolded the map. "Where the devil is Kelso anyway? Devils Playground, a ghost town called Calico, and look at this place name, *Zzyzx*. *Zis-icks*? What kind of insult is that?"

"Come on, Frank. You're wasting time. Just grab your flight bag and your jacket. We can get stuff when we get there."

"All right. I'll put the aircraft rental on my card and you can charge the gas." At the flying club after arranging a rental, Frank consulted their wall-sized planning chart and purchased charts for Southern California. "Looks like we're going to Daggett, nearest airport to Barstow."

"Never heard of it."

"All right. You fly down, just head for Interstate 5 and follow it south," Frank said. "I can compute the flight plan by the time you need it. The valley's clear. No time to check weather for Daggett."

Within half an hour, Frank sat beside Jerry in the cockpit of a rented airplane en route from Palo Alto to Daggett in an attempt to trace their stolen Cessna 3318E. This day—

Wednesday, February 23—would be forever etched in his memory. Why would someone steal the Cessna? His anger made him tense. He took a deep, slow breath and unclenched his jaw; his dentist said he ground his teeth while sleeping.

High in the sky to the south, three contrails zigzagged across Frank's field of vision—three military jets playing tag. On such a clear day, private pilots who avoid metropolitan areas and military zones can fly without filing a plan, but Frank felt uncomfortable. He liked to plan in advance.

Frank ran his thumb down the blue lines marked on the sectional chart and changed the frequency of the VOR navigation radio. Because Daggett was on a Victor airway, he could give Jerry headings directly from the chart. "Head East from here, 080."

"Head 080. Look at that tachometer, falling RPMs." Jerry added carburetor heat.

Frank adjusted his microphone boom. "Lots of moisture in the air today. Who would have thought— carburetor icing in the middle of the desert."

"Good old One-Eight-Echo's favorite trick. I wish we had her here now." Jerry wrinkled his nose. "This airplane stinks, worse than a wet dog. Some dirty dog smoked in here." Jerry paused and chuckled. "A pug-nosed pup puffing with the pilot."

Frank forgot the lost airplane and dissolved into laughter, Jerry's laugh as contagious as a yawn.

Jerry let go of the yoke and hooted. "Smoke coming out of their ears . . ."

"You're pretty jolly for a pilot searching for a stolen plane," Frank said. "All that fooling around, we're thirty degrees off course."

After the aircraft turned east, Frank noticed towering cumulonimbus clouds ahead on the horizon—thunderheads. The sky, black in the Daggett direction, threatened mischief.

"Whoa. Look at that wall of water. Guess we won't be touring Kelso today." Jerry tightened his seat belt as the wind increased and the turbulence bumped them around, a toy ship bouncing through rapids in a river of air. "We'll be lucky to make Daggett."

The Cessna jumped and bumped through air so rough that Frank could not tune the radios. Dark clouds—powder kegs of immense energy. Frank scanned the terrain. A spectacular lightning bolt hit close to what had to be Daggett. He called out, "Runway in sight, five miles at one o'clock."

Just at touchdown, a torrential downpour reduced visibility to fifty feet. Jerry cleared the runway but couldn't see to taxi. Which way was the transient parking area? Frank studied the map and directed Jerry, a few feet at a time.

By the time they secured the aircraft, water ran down Frank's nose and dripped off his jacket. He dried himself with paper towels in the restroom in the terminal. After he was drier and more comfortable, Frank followed Jerry to the next room, a pilot ready room with telephone and computer for filing flight plans and checking weather. A local pilot they met there didn't know anything about One-Eight-Echo; he suggested the fuel truck driver. Jerry ordered fuel by telephone and chatted with the driver. No news.

Afterwards, Jerry and Frank held their jackets above their heads and dashed through the deluge to the aircraft repair area. Beyond a half-open hangar door, Frank saw two Cessna 182s and a Duchess twin in various states of undress. The three aircraft filled most of the working area.

Ken Avery of Avery Repair Station marched through the narrow walking access to the front of the shop. His crew cut and military bearing suggested ex-marine. He hadn't seen One-Eight-Echo. He loaned Jerry a handheld GPS, rented him a Jeep, and offered advice. "You need something tough to drive into the desert. Things will heat up tomorrow. Be sure to take plenty of water."

Before they waved goodbye, Ken wished them luck and said, "Don't expect a lot of help from the Feds."

Later, warm and dry in a motel room, Frank poured over local maps and tourist pamphlets to plan their search for tomorrow morning. He inhaled the aroma of the new maps and savored the small print legends. "We're only eight miles from Calico, a restored ghost town. Rich silver mines in the 1880s: gold, silver, and borax. Just a tourist trap now," he told Jerry. "A railroad track goes through Kelso, built in 1905 for steam engines to take on water. Lots of rocks and sand dunes, but not many roads."

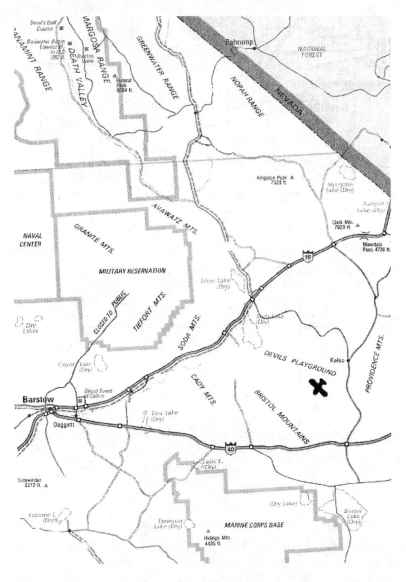

Jerry had stretched out wet socks and shirts over the shower curtain before flopping on the bed. He wanted an early start. "When we fly over the area tomorrow, you mark what we see on both the Los Angeles sectional and the road map. Later, we'll drive into the desert. Just find us a road back."

"All right." Frank enjoyed the challenge of tracing a route with his thumb. Tomorrow, he could record positions from the borrowed GPS. He drew a tiny airplane glyph, covering thirty square miles on the map. "One-Eight-Echo won't be easy to find, with no signal from its emergency locator transmitter."

"Maybe we're not looking for it. Think now, why does someone want a Cessna 172? Small aircraft: small resale value, not much speed, not good for running drugs. Not a kid joyriding—someone knew how to take it without a key. He wants the GPS and any scarce aircraft parts."

Frank turned off the light and snuggled into the other twin bed. "Then all this is a wild-goose chase?"

"Maybe, maybe not." Jerry's voice sounded more let's-party than let's-find-a-stolen-airplane. "Have you seen the aircraft bone-yard near Tucson?"

"Never heard of it." Frank consulted the map of Southern California one more time. It didn't yield any new clues, and Frank didn't have a map for Arizona or Nevada. The rental car bug had shown Mojave Desert, California, not Arizona. Surely Jerry wouldn't fly there next. "Why are you skipping off to Tucson?"

Ignoring Frank's question, Jerry said, "The government has parked miles of obsolete military aircraft out in the desert, just stockpiled there. The Mojave Desert would work just as well, and some wrecked World War II aircraft are probably still out there. We should look for an illicit aircraft salvage operation."

In bed in the dark, Frank had expected to share confidences—grief for a stolen airplane or maybe stories about wives. Why was Jerry discussing ghost aircraft? "What about the emergency signal?"

"A hard landing would set it off. When he got tired of hearing that siren through the radios, he could have turned off the ELT."

"What about the rental car bug?"

"He probably saw it when he rewired the thing."

Sure that Jerry was suffering serious denial, Frank said, "One-Eight-Echo probably crashed. What about the fuel leak? A spark from the hot-wiring could have set it off."

Undaunted, Jerry said, "We search for aircraft remains, one way or the other."

Thursday morning at Daggett dawned clear and sunny, perfect for flying grids—search patterns—over the desert. Perfect for searching for their stolen airplane. Frank had never flown a grid. Pilots in the Civil Air Patrol did that to locate downed aircraft, sometimes finding a pilot who had filed a flight plan after only a day. But not usually: with fewer clues, the search might last a week or be given up entirely. Jerry planned to start at Kelso. Frank held the maps and Jerry held the yoke.

Kelso, a ghost town, appeared as a tiny spot on the California road map along an unpaved road through an uncharted area called Devil's Playground. The aeronautical chart showed a seldom-used railroad track. Jerry flew east over the track until Frank spotted a lone water tower. Then he flew lower, over a loading dock and two ramshackle buildings, their wood siding aged light gray. Kelso: near the last recorded sighting of One-Eight-Echo as reported by the rental car company's position bug.

Jerry slowed the aircraft and flew 1500 feet above the ground: north three minutes, east three minutes, south three minutes, east three minutes. At twenty miles east, he flew farther north and moved westward until he was twenty miles to the west of Kelso. He flew north from there and repeated the pattern.

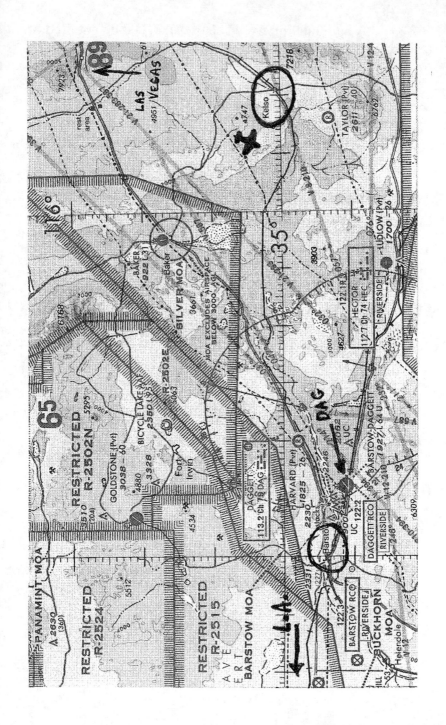

For three hours, Frank followed their flight path with his thumb on the chart while Jerry flew back and forth, scouring the region below. Jerry concentrated on desert to the north of Kelso, never to the south of it. The railroad tracks led directly to Kelso, the only landmark in an unfamiliar and featureless terrain. Below, one rock looked like any other.

Somewhere to the northwest of Kelso, Jerry said, "*Bingo!* See that blackened pit, over there at three o'clock? Like a meteorite scooped out a crater or somebody dropped a bomb."

Frank felt as though someone had kicked him in the stomach and dropped a bomb right under his heart. "That's no aircraft salvage operation."

Jerry wanted to explore the black crater from the ground. He circled twice over a dirt road and Frank marked it on the chart, recording the latitude and longitude from the GPS. The narrow road branched into trails that led nowhere and did not appear on either map.

The black area receded from view. Frank choked back tears, as though he had to arrange a funeral for One-Eight-Echo, lost forever. How would they get another airplane? They hadn't finished paying for this one.

Half an hour later, Jerry landed at Daggett. "Ken was right," he said, taxiing the Cessna to parking. "The ground is so rough out there that we'll need the four-wheel drive in that Jeep."

Frank tied down the right wing. He had to admit that he was enjoying the whole surreal adventure. "The terrain won't be the same when we return, not if those rocks walk like the ones in Death Valley."

"Oh, come on."

"On a *National Geographic* special on TV, rocks left mystery trails in the sand behind them. The rocks had to have moved."

"From the air, you'd see zebra stripes."

"Only if the rocks rolled and displaced enough sooty sand."

"Oh, when the saints come rolling in, when the saints, when the saints come rolling in—"

"You're singing off-key," Frank said. "I only said things might be different when we return."

Later on Thursday, Frank set out with Jerry in a dented olive drab Jeep rented from the same aircraft mechanic at Daggett who had loaned Jerry the GPS on their earlier trip. Jerry drove; he had an uncanny sense of direction. The Jeep labored up steep dirt roads past an area of complete devastation in the Mojave Desert near the location that Frank had recorded while Jerry flew search patterns. Jerry stopped near a blackened crater-like pit, a good thirty feet deep and at least one hundred fifty feet across.

A lone charred skeleton-tree marked the spot: rocks painted black with soot, a white scar over a new rock fall. Was it One-Eight-Echo's grave marker? Frank shivered and said only, "This has to be the place."

"Big enough for an Olympic swimming pool," Jerry said. He tipped his water bottle and sucked out the last drops. "I could drink it dry."

A wide brimmed straw hat from the drug store kept the afternoon sun off Frank's fair skin but provided no cooling. "Unusually warm for February," he said. "At least 95. The average February high is 73."

Jerry picked up one scorched aircraft tire. Frank found twisted and charred scraps of metal five hundred feet away and picked up a sample. Still legible on one melted lump of metal, he found a figure *eight* written in bubbled paint, shrunken and peeling off.

Jerry dropped the tire and studied the deformed *eight*, turning it this way and that. "Looks like this is it, all right. All that's left of One-Eight-Echo."

"How do you know that? That's only an *eight*."

"It can't be a coincidence. I just know."

"You said we were searching for aircraft salvage." Aircraft paint should be more brittle. Frank twisted the rubbery paint back and forth. Except for meeting in the middle, it could be deformed into any letter.

Jerry turned his head back and forth, sniffing the air. "Hey, do you smell that? Gun smoke, like when my grandfather took me hunting."

"It does smell like firecrackers around here. But where's the engine? It's so heavy, it should be here someplace." Frank scrambled to the top of a large boulder, a better vantage point. The rock beneath his bare hands was uncomfortably warm. If it felt hot in February, how would it be in July?

"Probably sank to the bottom of the pit, burrowed in like a meteorite." Jerry sat down on a hot rock, then jumped to his feet and rubbed his bottom.

"Burrowed in? Heavy things do sink, but we don't see it, do we? And this piece of metal could have been here for years." Frank paused, deep in thought. "Not nearly enough evidence to notify the FAA."

"I'd have to tell that I kept the rental car bug. Rick's boss would find out."

"Reporters crawling all over the place and it might not be One-Eight-Echo," Frank said.

"No trespassing while the Feds investigate for months and months while we still don't have an airplane," Jerry said. "And the thief gets away with it."

"Gets away with it? Whoever flew this vaporized."

"Maybe the thief wasn't the one flying it," Jerry said, gazing skyward as though the answer was hidden within a puffy cumulous cloud. "Maybe he sent somebody else to do his dirty work. Maybe the pilot got out before it burned. It was that Fish Eye guy Brad told us about."

"How do you know it was the bird watcher fellow?"

"It was Fish Eyes, I just know it, right here," said Jerry, patting his firm gut. "And I'm going to get him, somehow."

5.

The wind screamed and whistled over the aircraft cabin, a fearsome sound like nothing he knew. The aircraft creaked and whined. Faster and faster, dropping out of the sky. Kedar had to slow it, slow it down.

"Don't crash, please, don't crash."

He pleaded with the airplane, a quaver in his voice. Falling uncontrolled through endless space: worse than fire, worse than drowning.

A road below . . . Hit something soft. The Cessna bounced, bounced harder, and lurched across the ground. Rolling, bouncing, lurching past rocks.

"Brakes! Brakes!"

Kedar had to get away. He scrambled up a steep hillside. Gravel rattled and slid beneath his feet. He tried to run, run, run … he couldn't run. He had to get away, get away.

A massive explosion knocked him to the ground . . .

Sometime later, covered with dirt, the boy lifted his head and pushed himself up to his knees. His hair felt singed, stiff and crispy. He saw blood, lacerations on both arms. His head ached. How did he get here, face down on a dirt road? It must be Allah's will. Struck by lightning, in the middle of a desert. Would he be God's messenger?

He stumbled along the rough dirt road. This direction seemed as good as any. The wind cooled his back. It would rain soon. He smelled ozone—and something else—sulfur-stink from chemistry class. There up ahead, he saw a tall white-haired woman with a walking stick: a ghost wearing jeans.

"Hello, my son," the mirage said. "What happened to you? You're hurt."

"I don't know." He didn't mention the lightning sent from God. What was she doing here, out in the middle of the desert?

"Your shirt is shredded. Follow me to my cabin. I will doctor those bloody arms. What's your name?"

"I don't know." Who was she? She wasn't wearing a hat. He wished he had a hat. He felt sunburned, on the back of his neck.

"Then I will call you Robert. Just call me Mother."

The boy's forehead wrinkled. His mother? Had he been reborn? He fell in step behind the woman. Tall, she had a long stride. Working hard at keeping up, he followed her long white braid like a beacon. She didn't walk like an old woman. Sweat ran down his back, making it sting.

Soon she stopped and leaned on her walking stick. He glanced at his wrist to check the time. He didn't have his watch or his wallet: only a folded tissue, a cough drop, and a stick of gum. He didn't know why.

"Over there," she said, pointing to a steep path. "We had a mine. My son Robert worked there until he joined the Army. He never came back from Iraq, you know, killed by a suicide bomber."

The boy stopped and studied his shoes, sturdy brown leather. How would he know about a suicide bombing in Iraq? His memory was blurry.

"Just a little farther. Follow me."

"Yes, ah . . . Mother." He saw a shed glued to the side of a steep hill, the door framed with rough timbers, the roof flat and covered with gravel. The front wall had no windows, only a door.

The shed was really a porch. Inside and through the back wall, dark and cool like a cave, a long hallway with rock walls sparkled when Mother turned on the light—like she had pointed a magic wand. One crystal wall, the others like frozen dessert, scooped out with a big spoon and fork.

"We tunneled eighty feet into the mountain with mining equipment. Warm in the winter, cool in the summer." She handed him a glass of water and asked, "How do you like *mein haus*?"

"Cool." Did she build this mine house? Was she some kind of a wizard?

"I can see you're a man of few words," she said, smiling. "Here's a towel. Now take a shower, and clean yourself up, your hair, too. Then put on these shorts. You look like someone shot you with a shotgun loaded with rock splinters."

"Yes, Mother." He remembered his training from somewhere: *Obey orders without question.* The warm water was rain from heaven on the front part of his body, but needles of fire on his back. He lathered and splashed and admired the shower. There was no curtain or door, just a big cavity lined with pieces of rock, crystals, and white quartz with thin gold veins running through it. Like standing inside of one of those rocks, out there in the desert.

The shorts fit.

Mother spent an hour picking rock shards out of his back with tweezers and putting antiseptic on his wounds. She had a soothing ointment for burns. "We can't let this fester. You have a strong miner's back. Where are you from?"

"I don't remember." His face showed no emotion.

"What a blessing, Robert. You can think about how you want your life to be, without the clutter of knowing how things are. The desert is good for that."

He didn't answer and he didn't feel blessed. Not remembering was disturbing. He couldn't remember breakfast. He felt as though he hadn't eaten for a week. He ate a bowl of hearty soup and a thick slice of homemade bread.

"You will feel better in the morning." Mother opened the door to a small bedroom and pointed. "You sleep here."

"Yes, Mother."

He slept on his stomach in his own bed in his own room. He liked the way she smiled with her blue eyes, her

40

friendly eyes, lined with laugh-wrinkles. But could he trust her? She had a strange way of speaking: *vee* instead of *we*. Who was she? Not his mother.

For that matter, who was he?

She called him Robert. How did he get here?

Without a watch and without light from windows, the boy slept until he heard Mother-not-his-mother knock on his door.

"Yoo-hoo, Robert, time to get up. I can't wait to tell you what I found this morning."

He opened his door to the yeasty perfume of freshly baked bread. Brewed coffee. His father used to make that . . . for Kedar . . . sweet and syrupy. Kedar stirred sugar into his coffee and bit the end off of a red strawberry. Just as Mother—not his mother—had said, he did feel better, as long as he kept his back away from the chair.

"Just off the road, there's a blackened crater. A meteorite must have fallen, and it opened a pegmatite dike. We are rich, Robert, we are rich."

Kedar's eyes widened. What did she mean?

"I see from your face that you don't know what I'm talking about," Mother said. "I do wish you'd ask questions. A pegmatite dike has hidden caverns, often filled with crystals."

Kedar didn't answer. His face registered no emotion.

"Did you notice my wall of quartz crystals?" Mother asked. "That's part of a small dike. After the gold was mined out, we enlarged the cavity for living quarters."

She walked away and called out over her shoulder, "Here, I'll show you."

Kedar remembered the sparkling wall and the gold in the shower. He took another sip of sweet coffee, not as strong as his father used to make. He felt fine, as long as he didn't move his head.

Mother returned waving a geology book, open to an illustration of a pegmatite dike. "Millions of years ago," she said, "crystals formed while magma cooled. Oh, think how it must have been—glowing red lava, fire lighting up the sky, hot springs and geysers and brimstone."

What a cool book. He wanted to read it: *Pegmatite, also called giant granite, has large crystals of quartz, feldspar, and muscovite mica within cavities large enough for a man to enter.* "Cool," he said.

"We will drive past the Devil's Playground when we get supplies. Today we have to get moving."

Kedar kept his nose in the book.

"Robert, come out of there and make your bed. Always shake out your shoes to make sure you haven't picked up a scorpion. Take this walking stick in case there are snakes."

"Yes, Mother." Snakes, scorpions, devils. Was she an Infidel? He wanted to experience pegmatite dikes first hand, to discover why that made them rich. He followed her, barely able to keep up the pace. His back was tender and his neck was stiff. His thoughts tumbled and jumbled and bumbled.

"And Robert, you must tell no one. Yesterday's rain might bring out the wildflowers and the hikers from the Los Angeles basin."

Why did she insist upon ordering him around and calling him Robert? His name was Kedar.

Later on Thursday in the desert near Kelso, Mother and the boy she called Robert stood at the edge of a crater, its sides blackened as though something had burned. "Right there a meteorite landed. Under the sand it's still hot."

Mother pointed across the pit to a belt of white granite. "That opening over there, that's where we'll enter."

Kedar found the place familiar. Sitting in the cockpit, the rock ahead . . . he had landed the airplane. A shiver rumbled through his gut. Was it here? He didn't remember a black pit. Why would he fly an airplane into the desert? Why did she keep calling him Robert? He stayed silent.

42

Kedar followed Mother-not-his-mother, sliding through oily scree and loose rock and picking his way down the steep sides of the pit. The ground felt warm. He picked up a pebble; it blackened his fingers and smelled like fireworks, the illegal ones everybody exploded on the Fourth of July.

Kedar crossed the sand to an outcropping of bedrock that had a new break in it, stark white and light gray, not weathered to a dirty gray brown like the rest of the hillside. The beam from the flashlight directed into the opening reflected red and green—huge crystals—an underground wonderland. He had never seen anything so beautiful. It reminded him of Mother's shower.

When Kedar put his head through the hole, his shoulders were too broad to enter without hunching, an opening too small for Kedar to squeeze through without scraping the wounds on his back. His arms and his neck felt sore, too tender to crawl in there. He was relieved when Mother said, "Tomorrow we will go in when we have proper tools. Right now, we must hide the entrance."

Mother was already marching across the sand. She climbed the steep crater wall at an angle, staying close in and displacing no rocks. Kedar, less skilled, slipped back with each step and started several rockslides. He was panting from the exertion when he reached the top and his back stung from sweat. Following her back to the house, he hoped he could read that book.

Before Kedar could settle in with the book, Mother gave him a drink of lemonade and rushed him back outside. She backed out a large dirty-green pickup and drove to the entrance of the mine, closed by a heavy metal door painted *Argonaut Mine Private* in large white stenciled letters and *Keep Out* in irregular yellow dripping letters. The large gravel pile that she called *tailings* sat beneath a tall rough timber structure with some cables and pulleys and steps leading to the top. He wondered if her name was Argonaut.

Mother told him what to do. They took the door off its hinges and leaned some corrugated sheet metal against the opening in its place. Kedar loaded the door onto the bed of the green truck. That strong miner's back—that's what Mother-not-his-mother called it—hurt whenever his muscles bulged and pulled a scab.

"*Mach schnell.* Hurry up. We must finish before dark." She grabbed a flashlight just in case.

Mother's old pickup clattered and bumped, carrying the door as far as it could on the narrow twisty road. The hand truck wasn't much help. Kedar, glad that she had given him gloves, turned the door end to end across its corners to move it along the rough ground; Mother helped when she could. They stopped at the edge of the pit, and he set down the door. Were they going to carry it down? Kedar had trouble just climbing down before. Carrying something this heavy and unwieldy would be impossible.

"Here's the easy way," Mother said. She moved the door in the downhill direction and pushed it over the side. The door bounced and banged, thirty feet down to the sand. They slid down to meet it, then dragged and pushed the door through the pit and pulled it up ten feet or so to wedge it across the glaring white opening in the granite.

Mother erased their trail with a broom; she directed and swept and held the flashlight. Kedar moved the rocks that he could roll and shoveled scree until the surface of the crater blend into the landscape. He ached. Where did she get such energy?

"Robert, let's go make some lemonade."

She called him Robert, again. He felt annoyed and stiff and sore.

Kedar turned in early on Friday night. He ached all over and slept fitfully. He kicked out his legs and screamed, "No! No! Don't stall! No!"

He shot up in bed, heart pounding, ready to run, run.

"There, there . . ." Mother came into the dark room and sat on the edge of the bed. She pulled him over to her and cradled his head. "What's the matter?"

Kedar choked out, "I was flying the airplane and something went wrong. Crashed in the desert . . . failed my mission."

"That's the bravest thing I ever heard. You crashed an airplane and walked away?"

"I'm a coward. I failed my mission." What was he doing, talking to Mother-not-his-mother, in the dark? He pulled away.

"Nonsense. What mission?"

"I don't remember." Kedar realized he had told Mother his secret—the soldier who had been trained never to talk. The captain wouldn't like that.

"Robert, you're so brave. Get up, I'll fix you something special for breakfast."

Kedar followed her to the kitchen and sat at the table out of her way. Something smelled wonderful, coffee and something else. Mother gave them each a plate: meat, fried eggs, oranges, and toast. Mother picked up the meat with her fingers, so he did, too. He tasted a bite of crunchy salty meat: delicious. Mother put hers down and took a bite of fruit, so he did, too.

"Special occasion bacon from the freezer, Robert."

Kedar's eyes opened wide. He spit the bacon remaining in his mouth into his paper napkin and cleaned out his mouth with a bite of toast. He finished the eggs and fruit and pushed the rest of the bacon on to the side of his plate.

"Don't you like bacon, Robert? Mind if I take yours?" When he didn't answer, Mother reached over and speared his bacon with her fork.

He watched her eat it. Then Kedar knew. Mother-not-his-mother was an Infidel. And it was annoying, the way she kept calling him Robert. He was glad he hadn't told her all his secrets, about being a soldier in a holy war. What would she think if she knew he'd been on a suicide mission? Then he heard her, ordering him around again.

"This morning, Robert, you will load the truck. You must finish before that dark metal door gets hot enough to fry your hands."

He played with toast crumbs with his fork.

"*Schnell*, Robert, *schnell*. Hurry up!"

Kedar pictured snails on jet skis shooting across a wet lawn on a slime ribbon. He hurried.

Mother pointed out saws, hammers, prying bars, and other tools that Kedar didn't recognize. He helped her lift each one into the bed of the battered green Ford pickup, along with weathered timbers and the hinges that matched the door. She said he would drag everything heavy on a sledge. If his back hurt, she would try to do it herself. Kedar wasn't sure that he wanted to do this, and he didn't know what a sledge was either. His back was sore, and the scabs pulled every time he bent over.

Mother climbed into the truck on the right. "Get in. You can drive."

"But I don't have a license." He had never driven a truck, not even a car, but he didn't tell her that.

"You can fly an airplane but you can't drive a truck? Nonsense."

Kedar turned the key, expecting it to start like an airplane except without priming and with a foot pedal instead of a throttle. The truck started, jerked, and died.

"Don't forget, use the clutch. You can do it." Mother waited calmly for him to try again. "We will get you a license in Las Vegas."

Kedar tried again, grinding gears. How could she get him a driver's license? The truck lurched down the road, mostly in second gear. He stopped above the crater.

Kedar liked driving the truck, but he didn't like dragging the timbers and the hinges and the tools down and across the pit on a big piece of canvas. The sun, above the hill, scorched the sand. After an hour, he was hot and thirsty. Did she ever get thirsty?

Kedar removed the door that he had used to block the cavity in the hill yesterday and set it out of the way, shaded temporarily by a large boulder. He kept his back below the ragged edges and crawled through the opening. Red, green, and clear crystals lined the wall and the roof of a deep cave, large crystals catching the beam from his flashlight, like a gigantic geode. Kedar had seen a geode once in a museum; the Indians called them *thunder eggs*.

Mother knew just where to strike with a chisel to knock off the crystals that bordered the entrance without breaking them. She collected them in a gunnysack while Kedar knocked off some pieces of rock, practicing with the chisel and enlarging the entrance. How much longer before he could take a break?

They framed the entrance with weathered timbers and hung the iron door, Kedar doing the heaviest work, Mother directing and helping him lift. He shored up the steep wall beneath the door—ready to build an entrance platform tomorrow—and dragged tools and extra materials into the dike opening. Mother secured the door with a heavy padlock and smoothed out their trail with a broom while Kedar shoveled scree and rearranged boulders to hide all the blackened rocks.

After what seemed the longest time, Mother said, "Time for lemonade."

Kedar climbed back through the broken pieces of granite and the pebbles on the sides of the crater. He had learned how to do it without causing a rockslide. Finally, he could go back inside to read that geology book. When Kedar looked back over his shoulder, the door to the Argonaut Mine looked as though it had been there for years.

47

6.

"They'll never believe us. Finding the crash site in the middle of the Mojave Desert with only three hours of searching. I'm not sure I believe it myself." Frank sat in the pilot's seat of the rental Cessna, en route from Daggett to Palo Alto on Friday morning. Jerry, seated on his right, hadn't said a word for half an hour.

Frank's stomach growled. Coffee and a mini-muffin at the motel just didn't do it. He hoped to land in time to get a turkey sandwich at the golf course. He jiggled the switch on the intercom, needed to overcome engine noise in the cockpit. "Hey, Jerry. How do you read me?"

Jerry turned on his headset. "Sometimes I hear too many words," he said.

"Three hours. Trained search and rescue teams take three days." Frank couldn't leave it alone. Something wasn't right, but Jerry didn't seem worried. "That tracking bug only placed the Cessna somewhere near Kelso, out in the vast Mojave Desert. How did you know where to go?"

"I just had a feeling. Remember the storm? I flew where a non-instrument pilot would have gone to avoid the clouds." Jerry readjusted his headset.

"Feelings don't cut it. That blackened pit could have resulted from military training in World War II." Frank wished he had kept the curled eight. Not knowing who might need to investigate later, they had taken away nothing.

"It can't be coincidence." Jerry turned up the volume on the intercom, making a whistling sound in Frank's ear.

"Hundreds of cars are stolen every day, and most, never recovered. The score for stolen airplanes is even worse. Good thing we have insurance." The intercom crackled. Frank adjusted the squelch on the radio receiver.

Jerry didn't answer.

Frank touched the transmit button an extra time. "We should report the possible crash site. Let the FBI reconnoiter with one of those spy planes." Why did Jerry choose to ignore him?

After several more seconds of silence, Jerry said, "Then we'd never find Old Fish Eyes. It won't make any difference to the insurance company, as long as we report it stolen. Joe, that's the guy who works on FBI planes at San Jose, he said never send the Feds on a wild-goose chase. We have to catch Fish Eyes ourselves."

Jerry's answer made Frank uneasy. He called the thief Fish Eyes—a wartime hate-the-enemy tactic like calling Japanese slant-eyes in the Second World War. Why the major hang-up on Old Fish Eyes? After the weekend, Frank would notify the insurance company of the theft.

Somewhere near Bakersfield while flying the stinky Cessna towards home, Jerry's phone vibrated against his thigh. He unfastened his seat belt, dug the phone out of his pocket, and pushed the headset off of his right ear. Holding the phone firmly against his ear, he said, "Jerry here."

Frank heard a garbled voice through the speaker on Jerry's cell phone. "Ruben . . . Auburn. Just heard you lost your plane . . . real tough."

"That's right. It's hard to hear you. We searched everywhere. No leads."

Flying in the noisy cockpit at 6500 feet, Frank heard only part of the conversation. "When did it disappear?" Ruben asked Jerry. "I saw some men loading it at *Los Baños*, couple of days ago. Funny thing: they changed pilots at the last minute—with the propeller turning—didn't shut down the engine. Some people never forget a face. I never forget a tail number."

"*Los Baños*?" Jerry yelled above the engine noise, his hand cupping the phone to his ear beneath his headset.

"I drove there on Tuesday to pick up a damaged airplane and slept in my van to get an early start," Ruben said. "I saw One-Eight-Echo take off towards the southeast before sunrise."

Jerry was so excited that he yelled across the cabin instead of using the intercom. "Hey, Frank—finally a clue. One-Eight-Echo refueled at Los Banos on Wednesday. The thief wasn't flying it."

After Jerry and Frank tied down the rental plane at Palo Alto, Frank settled the bill on a credit card that was nearing its limit. Jerry paced and circumambulated the flight-planning table before grabbing Frank's sleeve. "Come on. We can grab a sandwich later, after we check out that bird-watching place."

"That's a pretty slim lead." Frank returned his VISA card to his wallet. Baylands Nature Preserve, the source of those warnings of bird activity on final, was right down the road from the airport terminal building. The thief could have walked in from there.

"We can't afford to let any clues slip by," Jerry said. "They'll do it again—I just know it—since they have this operation, whatever it is, all worked out." As usual, Jerry was moving fast, out the door and towards the road, only a quarter mile from the entrance to Baylands Nature Preserve.

"Hey, slow down." Frank bent down to retrieve his hat. The wind came in gusts. "Bird watchers do it standing still and you might miss a clue. By the way, they call themselves *birders*, and they go *birding*."

Jerry smiled. "Birders, huh? That's what my grand-dad called birddogs. He used to take me duck hunting."

"S-h-h-h. Don't say that in the Nature Preserve." Frank hoped no one was listening. An arrow-bearing sign pointed left.

Across the parking lot, several birders dressed in light tan cargo pants and jackets with bulging pockets focused binoculars on the duck pond. A cyclone fence and a path surrounded a pond full of ducks and other waterfowl amid a cacophony of grunts, cackles, and screeches. Everyone watched the birds so intently that no one seemed to notice Jerry and Frank.

Frank focused on the watchers, six of them: two petite women and four men, none of them tall, none of them in any way suspicious. He smelled guano, sharp and ugly.

Jerry sneezed and covered his nose with his handkerchief. "No wonder they call them foul."

"Maybe they don't like the way we smell, either." Frank pointed to a group of white birds—maybe twenty of them—perched atop the branches of short stubby bushy palm trees, each tree about the height of a single story house. "How peculiar—wading birds up in trees."

The birder closest to Jerry had her binoculars trained on the palm trees. Under that hat, she was a blue-eyed blond, maybe thirty, pretty.

"Excuse me," Jerry said. "Could you show me what you're looking at? I've never gone bird watching, and I wonder what it's all about."

"He means we've never been birding," said Frank, translating. "Are those herons up in the palm trees? I thought they were waders and slept standing on one foot with the other tucked up into their feathers."

"Were the birds you saw pink? You may have confused herons with flamingos, not found in the Bay Area. Over there, those are snowy egrets."

"How can you tell?" Frank asked.

The young woman pulled a bird guide out of her pocket and showed them herons and egrets. "Egrets are a type of heron," she said, "and these are unusual, because they usually nest on the ground. In the North Bay, near Bolinas, they nest a hundred feet high in the redwood trees, definitely a learned behavior."

Frank recorded her egret tips in a small notebook he carried in his pocket.

"You don't say—in redwood trees?" Jerry flirted with his eyes.

She smiled. "You should come back in May when the chicks learn to fly. It's amusing to watch them practice taking off and landing. Pick up a map at the ranger station and check out the Web site."

Jerry tipped his baseball cap. "Thanks for the info. We know about take-off and landing. We're both pilots, fly out of Palo Alto."

Just a few yards away, the door was open at the white adobe ranger station. Inside, a volunteer docent slept with his chin on his chest, snoring loudly. The bulletin board held several posted permits and an announcement for a nature walk for Boy Scouts: scheduled for the Monday just past, the day they flew to Auburn for the new GPS, now blown to bits in the desert . . . or, *gone*, somewhere. The brochure and map for Palo Alto Baylands showed fifteen miles of hiking trails, and further to the east, a sail station or boat dock and miles of boardwalks through the salt marsh.

A small flock of birds circled over the marshland. They stretched full-length, their necks fully forward, their legs strung out behind them. They swooped in, a cloud of colored feathers landing in shallow water. Frank couldn't tell if those wonderful aerodynamic shapes landed gear up or gear down. He had stumbled into a new world.

Jerry wasn't interested in what lay to the east, away from the airport.

Frank followed Jerry back to the duck pond where a young man trained a telescope somewhere behind them across the marsh. "Those ducks are geese," Frank said. "They should call it the goose pond."

"Oh, whatever." Jerry pointed to the marsh, eastward. "What do you think he's watching—way over there?" Then he turned to the opposite direction, facing westward, toward the runway, the ramp, and the tie-downs.

Jerry grabbed Frank's arm and waved his other hand wildly, pointing to the young birder who was still absorbed by something in the marsh. "I have one of those telescopes in my room at school. No one's using it over the vacation. Let's go get it."

"Now, wait a minute. I'm starved. We forgot to have lunch."

"I'll pull through a fast-food on the way."

"Why do you need the telescope? Stargazing to-night?"

"I have an idea. I'll show you, before it gets dark. Here, get in." Jerry drove out of the birding area and past the airport terminal. He noticed several small trainer aircraft in the run-up area and in the air practicing.

Three Cessnas lined up for landing at Palo Alto Airport were under surveillance from the tower and from the duck pond just across the fence: only one bounce out of three landings. Watching the 31-end of the runway, the end nearest the wildlife refuge, Aquila wondered how the kid could let his captain down like that. The plane had just disappeared. Those suicide bombers in Iraq never just disappear. He thought Muslim boys understood holy war. His best holy-warrior-cadet didn't hit his target—nothing made the news. He had to select another Cessna for the next mission.

The cold salt air, that acrid stink of guano, made his nose run. He wiped it with a handkerchief. Aquila wouldn't be here much longer, standing along the edge of San Francisco Bay at Baylands Nature Preserve. He-Who-Watches-Eagles had eyed another pampered Cessna. He chose Cessnas because they were so common and easy for a student pilot to handle. He chose Palo Alto because he could observe operations, and because it felt good to steal from the rich.

Let them finance the cause, help him make the government pay. Aquila had three replacement pilots, ready to go out in a blaze of glory.

7.

Jerry set up the astronomy club's telescope, heavier and bigger than the one used by the birders, at the edge of the duck pond in the nature preserve next door to Palo Alto Airport.

"Why the big effort to watch birds?" Frank asked. "Only the day before yesterday, you called this *just a bunch of birds*."

"Okay, they're watching birds, but I can read tail numbers with this. It's aimed right where we tied down One-Eight-Echo. Look at this."

Frank twisted his head around, trying to make sense of it. "The image is upside down. What do you do—stand on your head?"

"It just needs an adapter thing. The kids have been playing with it."

"You should have a star party and show me the constellations. I only know the Big Dipper and the North Star."

"Polaris." Jerry smiled. "You should write that in your notebook."

"Mary could make some of her famous hot chocolate."

"The magic word is chocolate, but back to my point. You can see everything from here, if you watch a different kind of bird. *Bingo*! He could have watched us preflight our Cessna—right there—at our tie-down."

Frank scanned the area through the lens a second time. "Suppose he did watch us from here. How'd he get past the airport surveillance cameras?"

"Who knows?" Jerry threw up his hands. "We have to start here, see what the airport's like at night, check out the camera coverage."

"Jerry, we haven't been home yet from Daggett. I've done enough."

"But it's our only chance—days off from school. We have to act fast."

"You really think a night shift will help?"

"Got a better plan?"

Frank shrugged, a woebegone expression on his face. On the way to McDonald's, he borrowed Jerry's phone to leave a message for his wife Mary. "Still searching for the Cessna. Found a great place to take you hiking. Back tomorrow. Love you."

Frank handed Jerry the cell phone. "You'd better call Sally."

"No, she's working at the art gallery today. I'll go home eventually."

"You should call her. You check out all the wait-resses, but with your wife Sally, you're as romantic as that rock over there." Frank pointed out the side window at an out-of-place chunk of stone floating on a front lawn.

Jerry laughed. "What's this, advice to the lovelorn?" What a peculiar phrase: romantic as a rock. Waitresses liked his attention. In fact, women loved him. He returned the cell phone to its case.

"Hey, listen. Those National Guard flight suits, they're still here in the van. We can look official, make a ramp check if anyone starts up in the dark."

"Ramp checks? What if it's the thief? What if he has a gun or something?"

"Got a better plan?" Jerry asked. "I really need your help."

"Well, I'm in it this far," Frank said, "but I'm strictly back-up."

Later and dressed for action, Jerry wasn't sleepy. When Jerry got *all wound up*, as his wife Sally put it, he lived on nervous energy. Once she had called him a *stem-*

winder, whatever that meant. He closed the door and said to Frank, "You're wonderful, backing me on this. You sleep first."

Frank stifled a yawn and wedged himself into the second seat in Jerry's van, settling in for a tedious night watching parked aircraft at Palo Alto Airport. "You could sell encyclopedias to Aborigines. Long flights in airliners always leave me with a stiff neck." Frank's voice was sharp and grumpy. "Why do I let you talk me into these things?"

"You're the one who could sell encyclopedias. When I need help, you're the one I can always count on." Jerry, wearing the borrowed National Guard flight suit, had parked his van in One-Eight-Echo's now empty tie-down space. Earlier, he had used the airport entrance code posted by each pedestrian gate—protection designed to slow down children and adults who couldn't read—and walked by each camera. Tomorrow he would check coverage on the airport surveillance tapes to learn how a thief could evade the cameras.

Jerry spotted someone pulling a Cessna onto a taxiway in the dark, 4:45 by his digital watch. Jerry was in motion while Frank was still waking up.

"Hey, Frank. Wake up, s-h-h-h. Look over there."

The aircraft door slammed shut. The pilot turned on the ignition key and ground the starter. The engine caught.

"Come on. Let's go!"

From sitting to sprinting in seconds, Jerry could have won a hundred-yard dash hands down. Chasing the moving airplane, he knocked on the pilot's door with his right hand.

"Stop right there!" Jerry yelled, competing with the engine noise.

The pilot braked and opened his window a crack. He glared at Jerry.

Without missing a beat, Jerry said, "This is a ramp check. Let me see your pilot's license and your aircraft registration papers." He looked the part in his flight suit. He sounded good, too.

A few seconds later, Frank appeared and stood behind Jerry, stern but silent. The pilot regarded Frank briefly and then focused again on Jerry.

"Hey, now, wait just a darn minute. Who the heck are you?" The pilot turned off his engine. He unfolded himself and stepped to the ground, towering over Jerry. He was angry and he was big.

Jerry stepped back a step and drew himself up to his full height. The top of his head was level with the big fellow's chin. "I'm with the National Guard."

"Then show me your badge and ID." The pilot sounded tough.

"Uh, I think they're in my other shirt."

Jerry, with perspiration beading on his forehead, tried to look cool. The only light came from the cabin of the aircraft. His sweat wouldn't show. He hoped his voice wouldn't quaver. Enough light to see the pilot's bulging biceps: a fullback bearing down, about to tackle him.

"Then I don't have to show my ID. Read your FARs. What the hell are you doing here anyway?"

"A routine ramp check—"

"At five in the morning? You're making a big mistake. Obviously you don't know what you're doing. Or who you're dealing with. I am Chuck Perry, Sunnyvale Police, and this is my airplane, and this is my badge. I should arrest you for impersonating an officer."

Arrest him? Jerry was almost speechless with embarrassment, and maybe, *fear*, too. "Look, I'm sorry. I thought you were stealing an airplane. Someone stole mine right out of its tie-down, two rows over."

"I'm sorry to hear that," said the hefty pilot in a quieter voice, "but you're doing things the wrong way. The only thing right, there are two of you. You could get hurt, trying to make a citizen's arrest. To say nothing of being sued."

"Thanks for the advice." Jerry wished the big cop would climb back into his airplane and fly far, far away. "Sorry to inconvenience you."

"Here's my card." The policeman extended his hand to Jerry before he stepped into the cockpit. "Call me at a more civilized time. We'll talk about what you can do about this. I mean it, now. Call me before you get yourself into trouble."

When the aircraft engine started, Jerry breathed a heavy sigh and turned towards Frank. "Whew. I'm glad that's over. I just didn't get it right."

"I expected him to slap on handcuffs and drag you away. I told you wearing those uniforms was a bad idea."

"I know, and you were right."

"It's time to report everything we know," Frank said. "Let experts take over before we get ourselves killed."

"You worry too much," Jerry said. "I have another plan to run by you over coffee."

"Where are you going to get coffee at this hour? Nothing's open yet."

"Just tell your stomach who is boss. Tell you what, I'll treat you this time, somewhere special."

"Okay, if you're buying," Frank said. What was Jerry's mysterious plan?

8.

Los Banos Airport, rural and unfenced: Jerry's only remaining lead. Jerry and Frank left Palo Alto Airport at sunrise—before the coffee shop opened—in a rented airplane, traveling south along Interstate 5 over a valley green from winter rains. Mirror-like, a full reservoir reflected the rising winter sun. Ruben called it *Los Baños* Airport; the maps all dropped the tilde. On a trip to Mexico, Frank had noticed that *baños* meant toilets, and *rustico baño* meant no running water. The engine almost lulled Frank to sleep. On his left, a flock of large white birds flashed past the wing. Probably gulls. Frank started involuntarily and pictured hitting a dozen of them at once.

After he landed, Jerry taxied directly to the self-service fuel-island at Los Banos Airport, passing a windsock and several crop-dusters. He charged eight gallons to see exactly how the system worked. On Wednesday, Cessna One-Eight-Echo had refueled there.

Frank helped Jerry tie down the Cessna near Mid-Valley Aviation. The mechanics always started early, before it got hot in the summer, by habit in the winter. The hangar door, rolled up halfway, covered an entrance about fifty feet wide and fifteen feet high. Frank fantasized the lid of a giant's eye, half-awake, just like him.

"Hello-o-o-o, anybody home?" Jerry called out and ducked under the hangar door. Frank followed him, his glasses darkened from the sunlight.

Three mechanics, wearing denim coveralls and holding work orders and coffee mugs, materialized from the dark. "Come on in," said the one with the gray crew cut and bottle-lens glasses.

"We're checking on a lost Cessna 172, green and white," Jerry said. "Stolen from Palo Alto—refueled here Wednesday. See anything unusual lately?"

"Actually, yes." The one with the crew cut stepped forward and punctuated his words with his coffee cup. "Had a bad fuel tag—stolen VISA card—maybe two weeks ago. Invalid tail number. A stolen Cessna, you say?"

"Stolen right out of its tie-down. By the way, I'm Jerry Christensen, and this is Frank Peterson. We're trying to collect information, but you know how it is. Without something specific, you don't get any help from the powers that be. That thief can't get away with it, stealing our airplane."

"Oh, man, that's tough. Let me know any way I can help. You could sift through the fuel tags. I'm Dick Provenski, I own the place, and here's my card."

"Good idea, Dick. Thanks."

Dick waved his cup towards the back and led them to a small office. He turned on the light and handed Jerry an envelope with fuel tags stuffed in every which way. "Give 'em back when you're done. I'll be out front."

"Okay. Thanks." Jerry pulled out a fistful of small slips of paper.

"He just met you. How does he know he can trust you?" Frank asked.

"Mechanics can tell if you're a good guy. Now how can we tell anything from these?"

"Help me sort them by date," Frank said. After a few minutes, they had a dozen Wednesday tags. "We can discard these: 40 gallons, 60 gallons—too much gas—and these, under five gallons, not enough to matter. That leaves eight possibilities. This one, 25 gallons is about right, but the tail number 58133—"

"You wouldn't expect him to give the right tail number. We don't know his name, either. Wait—I have an idea," Jerry said. "Copy them. One of them is it."

"You can't do that. Those slips have credit card numbers."

"You never know what you might need," Jerry said, turning on the copier.

"You only need one tag, 58133. Change the *5* to an *E* and reverse the five letters: 3318E."

"Oh, come on. That's just a strange coincidence," Jerry said. After he copied them all onto one piece of paper, he thanked Dick for the info.

"Think nothing of it," Dick said. "Stop by any time. Not many visitors here at Los Banos. Just pilots who want the best work and the lowest prices."

"We'll be back . . . when we have an airplane. You know, pilots always think they're hot shit. Without a good mechanic, they'd fall right on their butts."

Dick guffawed and slapped Jerry across the back.

Jerry waved both hands in the air and shifted his weight to the other foot. "I don't know where this is leading, but I do know you can always count on mechanics to help. Couple days ago, Ken Avery at Daggett loaned us his Jeep and a handheld GPS. Do you know him?"

"Can't say as I do, but I know mechanics most everywhere. You have to, in this business, fixing older airplanes. Can't find parts."

"Do you know Ruben from Auburn?" Frank asked Dick.

"Oh, yes. He's a master craftsman, can make anything fly. Comes down here, works on a wrecked airplane until he can fly it home. He restores aircraft."

"Did you know he's writing an airport food guide?" Frank asked, still thinking about coffee and hoping Jerry would get the message.

"He said Ryan's Place across the highway is best for pie," Dick said.

"Thanks for the tip. We're going there next."

Frank and Jerry returned to the rental plane sitting in the otherwise empty transient parking area and locked the door. Jerry wore a black leather flight jacket, Frank a tan windbreaker layered over a navy-blue sweatshirt. Frank felt chilled, even with the jacket.

"What would Old Fish Eyes like about it here besides no tower and no fences?" Jerry pointed out the unfenced access road and the empty parking lot and the open field surrounding the airport. He walked around the fuel pumps three times, gazing here and there. Answering his own question, he said, "He likes the seclusion here and the self-serve gas."

"Now that you're completely wound up, why don't you walk around the pump three times in the other direction? You always do that, circumambulate." Frank wrapped his cold arms around himself. "When do we get coffee?"

"You're always ready for pie and coffee," Jerry said. "Good idea to check it out—Fish Eyes could have gone there."

Across Highway 152 at Ryan's Place, the waitress taking their order was young and pretty and liked to flirt. Frank positioned his new hat at the center of the table, and Jerry hung his baseball cap off the back of his chair.

Frank felt as rumpled as Jerry looked, but the waitress here was more attentive than the one at Auburn when they had worn the cool flight suits. Frank glanced up when two men, binoculars hanging around their necks, sat down at the next table.

Jerry stepped right over there. "You guys look like bird watchers. Any good places to go around here?"

The tall one, still wearing his hat and loose fitting multi-pocketed jacket, answered. "Only one of the biggest wildlife refuges in the country, San Luis. Thousands of waterfowl are migrating right now, to say nothing about hawks and songbirds. We bagged forty different species in the first hour this morning."

"Wow, forty different species," said Frank from the next table. "And is that close to the airport?" He studied their hats and turned his upside down. *Tilley* hats, just like his, green under the brim, cotton duck, British brass, sewn with Canadian *persnicketiness*, it said so on the label. He liked that word.

"Right across the road," the other watcher answered. "We see the small airplanes taking off and landing from there. Never seems to bother the birds."

The waitress finally brought Frank his coffee and a piece of berry pie. Jerry came back to the table and dug into a big piece of chocolate cream pie. His eyes looked like his mind was somewhere else. After half a dozen bites, Jerry said, "Bingo."

"That's odd thing to say. What do you mean, *bingo*?"

"They have bird watchers, just like at Palo Alto. I just fit a big piece into the puzzle." Jerry didn't explain *bingo* or what piece in what puzzle. He did say that he had an urgent question for Ruben.

"And I have an urgent question for you. Is lunch included?" Frank asked. Too bad they couldn't rack up frequent flyer miles. Daggett, Los Banos, Auburn, where next? After coffee and pie, Frank felt more civilized and ready to accompany Jerry to Auburn to visit his mechanic friend, Ruben.

With a tailwind, Jerry made good time. He landed at Auburn at noon. Frank helped him tie down, as usual. Another of Jerry's mysterious plans. He told Frank only that he'd run *the plan* by him over lunch.

Ruben was always ready to have lunch at Wings Grill—especially when Frank told him that Jerry was buying. Once they were seated at Wings Grill, Frank said, "We tried some of the pie you recommended at Los Banos—excellent. By the way, your book should include the best chocolate milkshake in California at Hollister Airport, at the Ding-A-Ling."

"Ding-A-Ling?" Ruben looked puzzled. "I thought that's what you called somebody who's, uh, well, a ding-a-ling."

Frank noticed Robina glancing their way, but she didn't come to their table; she sent Bob instead. Just as well—Frank wasn't in the mood for baiting waitresses today, and she probably hated Jerry for his crude boob jokes.

Jerry cleared his throat and leaned towards Ruben. "How would you like some of the best pie in California for breakfast?"

"*¡Ay chihuahua!* Is that a bribe? You're setting me up for something."

"You haven't heard the plan yet. It's brilliant." Jerry put his hands behind his head and leaned back. "We're going to nab Old Fish Eyes—the guy who stole One-Eight-Echo. I stake out Palo Alto from my van. When I see a plane leave, I call you in Los Banos. You call the sheriff over there. They catch the thief in the act while he gets gas. They'll go Monday or Tuesday morning."

"Whoa, slow down, *amigo*." Ruben's voice took on a serious tone. "So, what I do is sleep at *Los Baños* Sunday night until you call me. Then I call the sheriff and sit back and watch the fun. Somewhere in there, I go and eat pie?"

"You got it."

"Why Monday and Tuesday?"

"Because the moon will be lighting up the place by four a.m. from Wednesday on. I think he likes the dark."

"How do we stay awake that many nights?" Frank asked. Pie warmed him to the idea, until he remembered his stiff neck after sleeping in the van. "We're not going tonight, are we?"

"Sorry, pal," Jerry said. "We should monitor tonight, too. Right now, I'll call Brad at the Palo Alto Terminal and ask him for a list of owners with tie-down spaces and tail numbers, just Cessna 172s and 182s."

Palo Alto was a long way from the prize-winning pie. Frank was in it because Jerry was in it. He'd be lucky to get a take-out muffin at Starbucks.

"I'm in it for the pie," Ruben said. "Let's get those *banditos.*"

There was no moon. Frank and Jerry, dressed all in black including black ski masks, waited and watched in Jerry's van at their tie-down space at Palo Alto. Frank, not a night owl, struggled to stay awake. Jerry wore goggles that covered all of his upper face; Frank thought he resembled Spider Man.

"These night vision goggles are weird. Everything looks kind of flat and green," Jerry said. "Here, you try them."

Frank peered one way down the taxiway and then the other, like viewing an old black-and-white TV through a tunnel, the whites and grays tinted an eerie lime green. The end of the taxiway seemed farther away, fuzzy images bordering a bilious viridescent center. The warmer hood on a dark sedan, ordinarily eggplant purple at night under streetlights, glowed the green of putrefied broccoli without the smell. "These take some getting used to, a little hard to stomach. Where'd you get them, anyway?"

"Don loaned them to me. He's a mechanic at ZP Maintenance right here on the field. He's the guy who found those flight suits we wore to Auburn."

"So that's where they came from. My legs are bald from that duct tape," Frank said. He plumped a pillow and settled in. "You take the first watch."

Three hours later, Jerry banged Frank's shoulder. "Hey, something's happening."

Frank pulled down his black ski mask. "What? Where?"

"Over there in Lima row. He's hand propping a Cessna."

"Is it Fish Eyes?"

"I can't tell. He has a ski cap pulled over his hair and he's wearing black."

"Everybody wearing black—uniform of the day." Frank yawned.

The aircraft engine caught.

"Come on. Stay behind him so he can't see us. He can't hear us either with all that engine noise." Jerry jumped out and slammed the door and ran toward the turning propeller, waving his hands and yelling, but the Cessna was already in motion. Frank caught up with him at the now empty tie-down L-9, right in the middle of Lima row.

The Cessna took off without lights.

Back at the van, Jerry used a flashlight to read Brad's list of tie-down spots and owners. His cell phone got Jack Peacock out of bed.

"Hell, no," Peacock said. "I would never loan my airplane to anybody. I'll be right down there."

"Better confirm with Air Traffic Control that a plane is heading for Los Banos," Frank said. "It's a big coincidence that the thief does the exact same thing."

"Good point," Jerry said. Before calling Ruben, he called ATC: the controller reported a target moving toward Los Banos. "See—what did I tell you?"

"Better call Ruben then—this must be it."

Ruben answered his cell phone on the first ring. "*¡Ay chihuahua!* I'll round up the sheriff. Those guys are in for a big surprise."

Brad, the Palo Alto Airport administrator, said he was out the door. He arrived within ten minutes later and met Jerry, Frank, and Peacock in the parking lot in front of the Palo Alto Terminal Building.

"This is a sorry story. Four pilots needing to get somewhere in a hurry and none of us has an airplane," Brad said. He called the after hours number for Palo Alto Flying Club. In half an hour, someone delivered the keys to a Cessna.

The sun was rising when Frank landed at Los Banos.

"Red sky in the morning, sailor take warning," Jerry said from the back seat. "This good weather won't hold much longer."

Frank taxied to transient parking. "You can't tell from that, and everybody's heard it. How about the rest of it: Red sky at night, sailor's delight?"

"Aha. The sheriff sent someone to pick us up," Brad said. He hopped out to wave the deputies over. Peacock stood watching, his hands on his hips.

Jerry helped Frank secure the aircraft. "I want to get a gander at Old Fish Eyes," he told Frank. "Make sure he gets what he deserves."

Before Frank tied the last knot to attach the Cessna to the tie-down ring, a black and white sedan with Merced County Sheriff painted on the doors screeched to a halt directly in front of the rented Cessna. Frank wondered why policemen always burned rubber like that. Must go through a set of tires every month. The deputy driver left his engine idling and rolled down a window. "Get in, guys. We've got your man."

"Super," Peacock said. "Can I fly my airplane back to Palo Alto?"

"Why not? After a little paperwork downtown." The deputy without a name looked rumpled, as though he had been up all night. Frank hadn't realized Los Banos had a downtown; he had seen only Ryan's Place across the highway.

At the sheriff's office, a lanky deputy named Leonardski interviewed the four of them and had them sign some forms. They all shared coffee from a pot that had been brewing all night.

Afterwards, Leonardski leaned towards Jerry. "I hear you're the leader here, the one with the plan. We nabbed that thief right in front of the fuel pump, as soon as he shut down the airplane. He must have asked me three times how we found him so fast. So, just how *did* you do it?"

"I just expected someone to take it, exactly like he stole our airplane last week," Jerry answered. "I hope you caught that same guy."

"Just a minute. I have his photo." Leonardski passed around a mug shot still warm from the printer in the booking room and asked, "Do any of you recognize this man?"

The man in the photo wasn't smiling: one front face photo, one profile. East Indian or maybe Middle Eastern. Jerry didn't see the cold eyes and gray hair that Brad had described.

Brad's brow wrinkled in puzzlement. "No. This isn't the suspicious man I saw hanging around at Palo Alto."

"Did you nab anyone else, maybe someone who came to meet him?" Jerry asked the deputy. The thief had had helpers when he refueled at Los Banos.

"No. He seemed to be working alone."

"But it had to be Mr. Fish Eyes." Jerry knew that the bird watcher did it. He just knew it. The thief was still out there, and he'd be back.

"Who's Mr. Fish?" Leonardski asked, his pen poised midair, ready to write a name on his clipboard.

"Oh, I just call him that—the jerk who stole our plane. The bird watcher with cold eyes that Brad saw hanging around."

Frank banged down his coffee cup. "Come off it, Jerry. You caught an airplane thief red-handed—he's already under lock and key."

"Maybe Fish Eyes just planned it this time." Jerry crossed his arms over his chest. Fish Eyes had to have something to do with it, . . . perhaps a whole chain of aircraft robberies. His coffee cooled on the table, forgotten.

"This is just a coincidence," Frank said. "What do you use for proof?"

"Then we make our own bulletproof plan."

"No bullets," Frank said. "No more ramp checks."

"What's this about ramp checks? Not at Palo Alto Airport," Brad said.

"One of my ideas that didn't pan out," Jerry said. "However, I know a Sunnyvale policeman who will advise us about setting up a pilot watch program to beef up Palo Alto's security. Okay to meet with you next week?"

"Good idea," Brad said.

"Count me in," Peacock said.

"I'm already in," Frank said.

Jerry paused. His plan needed a few days to crystallize, especially since he had just thought of it. "In any case, time is of the essence. We can't twiddle our thumbs waiting around for proof that is harder to find by the hour while Fish Eyes gets away with it."

9.

"Guess what? The insurance company won't pay us." Frank leaned back in his chair behind the desk in his study, holding the policy in one hand and the telephone in the other. Just off the line with the claims representative—he had waited until the first of March to call him—Frank filled Jerry in with the latest. "Without proof of loss, we have to wait six months. Looks like, no wreck, no check."

"Bummer. We pay that big premium every month, and now they won't pay us? How the heck will we get the money to buy another airplane?" Jerry sighed and shifted his cell phone to the other hand.

"It might be worse than that," Frank continued. "Did you ever read all that legalese in our insurance policy? They can deny the claim." Frank had read through ten pages of small print: no coverage if the aircraft carried explosives or did crop dusting. No coverage for damage from a hurricane or a nuclear blast.

"All those policies read like that. They have to pay."

"Not if there were any explosives—that crater in the desert is *colossal*. Along the same line, it says right here, due to the Terrorism Risk Insurance Act of 2002, the policy won't cover claims for losses caused by acts of terrorism."

"Some terrorist creep steals it, we don't get paid?"

"Exactly. It doesn't seem right."

"Do they pay anybody for anything?" Jerry remembered the small print in the ACE rental car contract and how he had narrowly avoided a $500 fine.

"Pretty confusing, all right. The policy says theft of an entire aircraft represents a total loss, but it also says loss means physical damage, with no coverage for disappearance in flight. And, worse—the agent didn't say they *pay* in six months—he said *review our claim* in six months."

"What if a wing falls off while I'm flying it?"

"Covered. Damaged when it hits the ground."

"But you have to die to collect. What good is that?"

"Jerry—a wing never just falls off."

"That's not the point. They like one-way money: lots going in, none coming out. We did our part: police report, FAA notification of stolen aircraft. But we have to wait to report the location of the crash. If we say explosion, they don't pay," Jerry said, still stubborn. He wanted resolution. The only way to get something done right was to do it himself. Some way, he would find Fish Eyes.

"We have to work within the system. We have to report the crash site." Frank voice was so loud that Jerry moved his cell phone two feet from his ear.

"But Old Fish Eyes did it and he gets off scot-free. I'd like to wring his neck." Jerry remembered his grandfather with a rooster that had crowed once too often. Big fish eyes, the neck growing longer, red and bare and ugly . . . He reached out to grab that turkey neck, and realized that he didn't know what the thief looked like. He heard Frank, still there, on the cell phone.

"Don't worry—he's dead for sure. The only good thing coming out of this is the Pilot Watch Program. No more aircraft will be stolen, now that someone watches every night."

"The pilots will get tired of that in a few weeks. Somebody won't show up just when something happens," Jerry said.

"If school weren't in session, you'd pitch a tent at the airport and stay there night after night. Months, maybe years."

"Whatever it takes. You remember how big that crater was? A chemist I know said an Olympic-pool-sized crater was too large to be made by a burning Cessna. He said explosives were involved. Analyze that greasy black stuff, and we'd at least know what blew up. Can you fly back down there Saturday?"

"Daggett . . . again?" Frank finally said he'd go, just one more time, against his better judgment. "Why do I always agree to whatever fool thing you dream up? Daggett, dog nab it, dag nag it."

"I hope that means Daggett Saturday. We've got to get him."

Jerry pushed the off button and listened to the cell phone chirp the shut down tones. He was tense. His stomach churned. His jaws were clenched. He took three deep breaths and then chewed a handful of antacid tablets. No help from search and rescue. No way to make an insurance claim. Jerry pounded his open hand with a closed fist. Whatever it took. He would catch that damned fish-eyed thief.

Armed with a digital camera and a handheld GPS and plenty of sunscreen, Frank and Jerry flew south from Palo Alto in a rented airplane on Saturday morning. At Daggett, Jerry rented the same Jeep that he had driven on the previous trip. This time, he drove into the desert near Kelso from the north, through fields of sand dunes painted gold by rose quartz particles.

Frank, enjoying the scenery, tapped a *Mojave Desert* pamphlet with his index finger. "It says here, these are *booming dunes*. When it's windy, they make strange rumbling sounds like a Tibetan gong."

"No way." Jerry twisted and bumped the Jeep eastward along rutted roads.

After several false turns, Frank sighted the skeleton tree. Something was wrong. The handheld GPS showed the same position, but he saw a different landscape. Still a pit on the north side of the road, but not blackened and not as deep as Frank remembered. The Argonaut Mine hadn't been there before, and neither had the pickup truck.

A three-quarter ton Ford truck blocked the dirt road, wide enough for one vehicle at best. It might be green under all that dust; too dirty to see into the cab. Frank didn't see anyone around. He picked his way down through loose gravel towards the blackened tree, the only familiar landmark.

"See, rocks do walk," Frank said to Jerry over his shoulder. "Just like that TV special I told you about."

"No way—" Jerry stopped mid-sentence and mid-step.

"This is private property," someone yelled. "Belongs to the Argonaut Mining Company. You can't go in there."

A tall woman dressed in faded jeans and a long-sleeved red plaid shirt stood next to the Ford truck. She had a weathered face and a long white braid.

"Argonaut Mine? That wasn't there the last time I was here." Jerry turned to face the woman. "I don't see any No Trespassing signs around."

"Here's my son Robert. We've been mining out here for years. What are *you* doing here?" Their jeans and red plaid shirts were the same. Otherwise, they looked nothing alike. She had blue eyes and a tan and was tall for a woman. The boy was dark and short, his too-long jeans rolled up.

"We're searching for a lost airplane." Jerry, facing the truck, moved forward and shaded his eyes with one hand.

"Haven't seen one of those. You won't be finding it here, so just leave the way you came in." She stood with her hands on her hips. Her son glanced over at her and put his hands on his hips. The kid seemed about fifteen, not much older than Frank's middle school students.

"Okay. We just need five minutes over there." Jerry pointed toward the other side of the road and hurried away from the woman. Frank walked south and watched her out of the corner of one eye. She stayed near the truck.

"At least she's not packing a pistol," Jerry whispered, wiping his forehead with his handkerchief. He picked up the scrap with the figure eight written in bubbled paint but left the aircraft tire.

Frank recorded the scene with the digital camera and noted the coordinates from the handheld GPS. "Why do they call these *tail numbers*? They're usually painted on the fuselage."

"S-h-h-h. Pistol-Packing Mama will hear you."

"I thought you said she didn't have a pistol." Frank stole a glance over his shoulder. She was still there, next to the green truck.

After coming all this way, Jerry couldn't leave without some gravel samples. He needed to walk down into the pit and to search around the tree skeleton. The mine and the tree were to the north. Eastward, he saw the truck and higher terrain.

Jerry moved the Jeep a quarter of a mile to a better viewpoint and parked out of view of the green truck. Its engine hadn't started.

Frank followed Jerry and climbed the western rocks. He scanned the area with binoculars and shook his head. "Nothing useful in sight."

"Too hot," Jerry whispered, sweat dripping off the tip of his nose. "Let's get out of the sun."

Back at the Jeep, they poured water on themselves and on top of their hats and waited silently, shaded from the sun. When the green truck drove away stirring up yellow dust, Jerry pointed to the pit and put a finger over his lips.

Frank tiptoed towards the pit. Little heat currents danced in front of his eyes. The skeleton tree shimmered.

Jerry found oily gravel just below the surface under the hot sand. He held a blackened pebble above his head to show Frank and said, "Greasy like soot, stinks like a day-old firecracker."

"Somebody wanted to hide the black stuff. Why?"

"Beats me." North of the burnt tree, Jerry found two more aircraft scraps. He took one piece of bent and charred metal, and Frank photographed the site from the top of the hole.

Jerry scraped oily sand off his shoes with a stick and brushed off his pants before getting back into the Jeep. "A lot of work for two pieces of bent metal and some gooey black gravel."

"You got what you came for." Frank took a turn driving on the return trip to Daggett. The hot air moving past

73

his face gave no cooling. Even at their slow speed, dust boiled up.

"What I really want right now is to jump into a swimming pool full of ice cubes." Jerry wiped his forehead with his handkerchief and fanned himself with the road map.

After a few more miles, Jerry shook the bag of black gravel and examined the contents. "Maybe this will tell us what Old Fish Eyes used for explosives."

"Why do you call him Fish Eyes? Fish don't see that well. They're near-sighted but have superior eyesight in low-level light. That's why lures that rattle work well in dirty water, and why game fish prefer to feed at daybreak and dusk."

"Why are you telling me all this? My ears are burning up, listening to all those words."

"Because you should call him Eagle Eyes," Frank said. "But, of course, Fish Eyes is more insulting."

"Eagle Eyes? He has cold eyes, cold like a fish."

"Eagles can see for miles, then swoop in and grab prey. A bird's eyes sometimes weigh more than its entire brain."

"Well, a bird's brain isn't much."

"An eagle's eye is the same weight as a human eye, even though a full grown adult Bald Eagle weighs only about fourteen pounds."

"You're feeding me way too much stuff. Where do you get all that?"

"Surfing the Web. I keep notebooks. Eagles can change the shape of their lens and also the shape of their corneas," Frank continued. "They can focus much more precisely than humans can."

Waves of heat rose from the road—a mirage of palm trees and cool water. Frank's eyes didn't seem to focus. He needed an eagle for a hood ornament to point the way.

"Well, I guess the eyes have it, but he's still Fish Eyes to me," Jerry said. "Until we find him. Then we'll see. Fish eyes or eagle eyes."

"It's my turn to make like an eagle. My flight home."

"Deal." Jerry put his feet up on the dash and fanned himself with the map.

Two hours later at 7,000 feet on the return flight to Palo Alto, a sudden loud screech startled Frank and threw him into panic mode. Frank, flying the rented Cessna, turned his head right, left, up, down. His eyes scoured the sky outside and scanned the instrument panel. Except for that awful noise, everything seemed normal.

"What's that noise? Is the engine going to seize?" Frank's heart beat faster. His ears magnified the cockpit roar.

"No problem. I can fix it." Jerry unbuckled his seat belt, hung his knees over the back of the front passenger seat, and swung his head under the instrument panel.

Frank took a deep breath and swallowed. Jerry's non-problem was near panic for Frank; would he have the right stuff to handle a real emergency? He held the aircraft level.

The noise stopped as abruptly as it had started. From his inverted position, Jerry said, "Tachometer cable. Same sound if the speedometer cable goes out in an automobile."

"The rental company won't like that," Frank said, acting like *Mr. Cool* for Jerry's benefit, his heart beating double-time. "No record of the flight hours."

"Well, good. Then they'll fix it for sure." Jerry refastened his seat belt. "I hate renting airplanes—always something wrong with them. That Fish Eyes . . . stealing One-Eight-Echo. I'll find him and he's going to pay."

"How do you know who did it?"

Jerry had a habit of answering questions that Frank didn't ask and not answering the ones he did ask. Jerry said, "We'll know soon enough what exploded. I know a chemist; he'll tell us what that black stuff is that I collected."

After a pause, Jerry said, "I know who did it. I just can't prove it. If we find out what's in those explosives, we might have a new lead."

On Tuesday, Jerry forgot his half-eaten sandwich after he answered his cell phone. The chatter in the faculty lunchroom faded to background noise. His chemist friend Al had analyzed the oily residue from the crater.

"Yes, I tested it," Al said. "I have results for some of it, but I'm unable to determine every ingredient from your sample."

"That's what you said in the first place, before I brought you the stinky sand. Why'd it make such a big hole then?"

"Like I said, I don't work miracles or read minds."

"Are you sure, nothing more? My hands stank like used firecrackers for three days after getting that stuff."

"You mean you used your bare hands?" Al sounded surprised and concerned. "Don't you know, chemicals go right through your skin, straight to your liver."

"Any worse than booze?" Jerry shifted the phone to his other ear, like he didn't want to hear that.

"A lot quicker. Next time wear gloves."

"Really stank out there. Smelled like gunpowder. Would that mean a recent explosion? Or would the odor fade, say, after a year?"

Al hesitated. "Probably recent, that strong a smell."

"Well, at least let me take back my sample."

"Sure," Al said. "I'll leave everything in a bag with the receptionist in the lobby, as well as a copy of my report."

After Jerry hung up, he turned towards Frank, seated next to him at the table in the faculty lunchroom. "Basically, Al says he doesn't know what the stuff is. How could a homemade explosive make such a big pit? And make One-Eight-Echo do a disappearing act?"

"The rocks all blackened, then swept away. What do you think, why the cover up?" Frank asked.

"It points to the aircraft's final resting place. Has to. What else can I say?"

"But what was it? All we know—not nuclear."

"Don't ask me. You should investigate, maybe use the Internet, and learn how to make explosives."

"That's dangerous," Frank said. "I don't want any part of it."

"Only read about them. Don't make them."

"The FBI could find out what exploded with such force. We need their help. Will you tell them?"

"How would I explain where I got the stuff?" Jerry asked. "Then the insurance company won't pay for sure. They'll either get us on carrying explosives or on an act of terrorism."

10.

Scissors in hand, Mother bent over and cut five inches from the legs of Kedar's faded jeans that used to belong to Robert, who didn't need them any more. "Now stand still," she said. "We need some No Trespassing signs before the flowers bloom and bring the hikers. You can practice driving all the way to Las Vegas."

Kedar stood patiently. He liked to drive the truck.

"We'll get you a driver's license first stop, and then we'll show the gem and mineral dealer the tourmaline crystals."

Kedar didn't answer. A driver's license meant a test and preplanning.

Mother pulled out two new white T-shirts with Argonaut Mine printed in large black letters. "Do you know what an *Argonaut* is?" He didn't answer, as usual. She pulled *Greek Myths* off the shelf and pulled two chairs nearer the lamp. Kedar had not heard about Jason and the Golden Fleece; no one had read to him before. He enjoyed it.

"Robert, don't you get curious about things? Ask me questions."

Kedar didn't reply at first. He was confused. He could follow orders without question, but was that an order—to ask questions? Finally, he asked, "What is Achilles heel?"

Mother's eyes widened with surprise. "Why, . . . it's the weak spot. Achilles was the bravest hero in the Trojan War. When he was born, his mother tried to make him immortal by dipping him in the magic water of the River Styx. She held him by one heel, and that part, untouched by the water, stayed mortal."

More magic. He answered with a second question, one he had wanted to ask for weeks. "Why do you call me Robert, Mother? My name is Kedar."

"Then I will call you Robert-Kedar. I have always called my sons Robert."

What did she mean by that? Kedar decided to ask her that later. Say, in another three weeks.

Dressed alike in faded jeans and *Argonaut* shirts, Mother and Kedar left for Las Vegas in the big green truck and bumped along a back road—the roughest one so far. Kedar gripped the wheel with both hands and slowed.

"This area is called the Devils Playground. Those tangled rough lava formations would tear your shoes apart."

Mother had mentioned the Devils Playground on the day she had shown him the pegmatite dike. Before he learned to drive the truck. He didn't smell any sulfur stink. He glanced out to the left, half-expecting a devil to appear with a flash of light and a puff of smoke. Instead, Kedar saw only sand and rocks.

"Don't worry. This Ford truck is tough," she said.

Kedar was glad that she knew the way. Whenever the road or trail branched, both ways looked the same to him. There were no signposts.

After an hour and twenty minutes, Kedar pulled into a rest area at the entrance to Interstate 15. Glad for a comfort stop, he watched the traffic whiz by while he waited for Mother. When he restarted the truck, she reminded him to fasten his seatbelt before the fast traffic.

He had expected her to admonish him to drive carefully. Instead, she said, "Now, Robert, when we turn onto the Interstate, blow off some dust."

"Snails," he said, remembering the peculiar way she had told him to hurry.

Mother cocked her head as though she hadn't quite heard him, then clapped his shoulder and guffawed. "*Nein, nein*, Robert. *Schnell*."

Kedar didn't smile. After a few minutes, he said, "Mother, did you forget? My name is Kedar, not Robert."

She didn't answer.

Traveling at 80 mph in the truck felt like flying. Kedar felt at home behind the wheel, his first time driving the Interstate. It was hard to think of Mother as an Infidel. He had not prayed since he landed in the desert. Was he God's messenger? His other life seemed far away.

He heard Mother say, "Have you ever been to Hoover Dam? Everyone should visit it once. It's an engineering marvel. It weighs over five million tons and holds back water over 500 feet deep in Lake Mead."

Mother held a colored brochure picturing a dam and pointed to the turn-off for Boulder City. "Hoover Dam is that way. No time today. If we got lost after dark, we would spend the night in the truck."

It might be fun, camping in the truck. They could have a hamburger and fries and a milkshake. Kedar concentrated on the road until Mother directed him to pull into a parking lot on the outskirts of Las Vegas: the Nevada Department of Motor Vehicles. He parked behind a large building with glass doors.

Inside, Mother took a number. Kedar swept his eyes across the building: a line for vision tests, private booths for written tests, waiting areas for the driving test. He wondered how he would pass. He had no idea about the driving test: maneuvers of some sort with the truck. Aircraft turns-about-a-point and ground reference maneuvers wouldn't help him park a truck.

When her number flashed onto the information board, Mother grabbed his arm and strode to the window, almost dragging him along. She slapped the numbered slip and a wrinkled orange wad of paper onto the counter in front of a tall skinny clerk with a beard and a ponytail. "This is my son Robert."

The clerk smoothed out the orange form and tried to read it. Then he glanced at Kedar, looked back at Mother, and shook his head. "Expired."

"There's a small mistake on that paper," Mother said. "He's a good driver and he can pass the driving test today."

"What do you mean—a mistake on the application? Does he have an appointment?" The clerk tapped on the counter with his ballpoint pen.

"A small clerical error." With a flick of her pen, Mother changed the year and Robert B to Robert K and handed the paper to the clerk, who ran his index finger down the schedule book.

"He's not there. You have to make an appointment and come back later. How about tomorrow?"

Kedar's face fell in disappointment. No driver's license today after all. Mother would have needed witchcraft to carry that off anyway.

"No, we cannot come back later."

Mother leaned over the counter and raised her voice. "What do you mean, we have to wait for a driver's license, when people can get married in an hour?"

"You make an appointment, then take the test." The clerk's face flushed.

"Robert could pass your test. Right now."

"There isn't any examiner on duty right now," the clerk said, studying Kedar's Argonaut Mine shirt. "Wait—you said he drives for your business? No problem." He started to type something but stopped at the address line.

"No, no street address. We don't have one. Our rural location has no mail delivery. We have a mine. I can give you a crystal." Mother gave him the smallest, but still very beautiful, tourmaline crystal.

Kedar watched with his mouth open.

"Okay, I'll add a note to the file. He's awfully young looking. He's twenty years old?"

"*Ja, Ja,* he does seem younger. He's twenty, and I should know—I was there. Don't you have any records in this place?"

The clerk saw a line forming behind the boy and his mother. He said he would mail the license for Robert K. Herold to Mother's Las Vegas post office box. No problem, and no test. He snapped Kedar's picture.

Afterwards in the parking lot, Mother said, "Did you see his face when I changed that B to a K?"

"A small clerical error."

Mother guffawed and clapped his shoulder.

She did it. He had a driver's license. Robert Kedar Herold. Kedar: the herald. For the first time in a year, Kedar laughed.

Kedar the licensed driver stepped into the truck. He felt six inches taller. He wasn't sure where they were going, but Mother would tell him.

"Head for the big city, Nevada driver. We'll get you a wallet to keep that license in when it comes in the mail, a nice leather one."

Kedar thought he'd ask her for a hat. Mother needed to start wearing a hat for sun protection. Maybe she'd follow his example.

"Just turn to the right and do what the other cars do," Mother said. "I'll tell you where to turn."

"Okay." Kedar had never been to Las Vegas. The captain would never find him now.

Aquila parked his Volkswagen van in the sandy parking lot near the beach at Oceano. He handed binoculars and a baseball cap to one of his students, ready for a birding session. He heard gulls, the noisiest of seabirds. Too bad about Kedar Bird-Caller: Once he had imitated a gull until it took food out of his hand.

Kee-yah, Kee-yah. Peep-peep-peep. Gulls circled above the beach, dipping in and out of the lifting fog. Two crabs scuttled across hard-packed sand. Sandpipers, gliding on Russian-ballet-dancer legs, scurried in and out of the froth of the incoming tide. Aquila and his cadet, Amjad Hamide, walked to the edge of the sea and stood just above the foam beneath seabirds calling and squawking and cackling.

"Close your eyes and tell me what birds are flying above your head," Aquila said.

Amjad squinted his eyes shut. "I hear the gulls laughing."

"No, no. Laughing gulls live along the Atlantic coast, not the Pacific. You can't get this by reading that book." Aquila pointed at the bird guide in Amjad's hand and kept his voice low and patient. Amjad never seemed to get it. "Kee-yah. Open your ears and listen."

"Peep-peep-peep. But they *are* gulls, Sir."

"Better. California gulls. That's easy to remember—you're in California—although large numbers breed near the Great Salt Lake in Utah."

"Yes, Sir."

Aquila glanced upwards and over his shoulder. When the sun came out, small airplanes would land and take off from the small landing strip, just above the beach. He asked his cadet, "How are your flying lessons coming?"

"John said I would fly solo soon, Sir."

"I thought you had fifty hours."

"Yes, Sir. John says I'm not ready to solo."

"You will show me soon." Aquila had located another Cessna. Time to collect the government payment: *past due.*

11.

Aquila exchanged his light-colored bird-watching attire for a black sweatshirt over dark jeans. He left his van near the duck pond and carried an aluminum ladder through the deserted parking lot. The tall cold-eyed bird watcher knew the exact placement of the cameras ahead.

Aquila slipped the ladder beneath the surveillance camera at the east entrance gate at Palo Alto Airport. He stepped behind the mechanical eye and spread the ladder legs. A double joke, he thought. He-Who-Watches-Eagles takes out the watcher and becomes He-Who-Soars-With-Eagles. He climbed two steps up and covered the lens with a black dress sock.

After Aquila blinded the cameras at the gate, he took care of the one scanning the Runway 31 run-up area. He discarded the ladder near the camera with the unseeing eye and walked to the center of the ramp, where he had noted a particular cherry of a Cessna.

He felt high as an eagle, almost the same rush as when he took off in Cessna One-Eight-Echo. This time, his routine was faster, guided by the light of a full moon. Jiggle the key in the door, hand-prop the plane, underway in five minutes. He taxied directly onto the runway without lights.

Aquila the Eagle gave the engine full throttle and roared down the runway and pulled the plane off the ground before midfield. The eagle spread his wings.

Shaking, thumping, bumping. At 500 feet, the engine stopped. Silence.

He turned back. He couldn't make the runway.

In the moonlight he could see the black surface of the bay. He had to ditch. No wind, no waves, an easy swim to shore. He unfastened his shoulder harness and unbolted the door, leaving the seat belt until the last moment.

The Cessna hit the surface of the water—harder than cement. His head struck the knobs on the radio panel. The momentum from the sudden stop carried the tail up and over. Inverted, Aquila dangled below the seat. He didn't feel the plane sinking to the bottom, twenty feet below the surface.

The murky cold water filling the dark cabin shocked him to awareness. He hung head down, cold water against the top of his head. It took precious seconds for him to unfasten his seat belt. He stood on the inside of the cabin roof. Pulled off heavy boots. Took a deep breath.

A shrinking air pocket at the cabin floor, now above his head. Air. He needed air. He leaned against the door. Heavy. He pushed against the water. Open, part way—a last gulp of air.

Lungs bursting, Aquila made the surface. He swam to the muddy margin of the bay and sank when he tried to stand in the muck. He spit out briny water and half-swam, half-crawled through the mud, a large, slimy salamander emerging from a swamp into a sunless Wednesday morning.

On Wednesday at lunchtime, Jimmy "Doolittle" Jones rented a small Cessna trainer from the Palo Alto Flying Club. He chose the one with the climbing propeller: excellent for landing practice. He needed three more hours of solo cross-country time before his practical exam for the pilot's license. After a careful preflight inspection and engine run-up, he called the tower.

"Palo Alto Tower, Cessna 2134X, request touch and goes, pattern work." Jimmy didn't have to wait long for clearance, not on a weekday. The sky was clear enough if he stayed at Palo Alto; he couldn't see the tops of the hills over Sunol where Highway 680 cut through the foothills. He had wanted to fly a solo cross-country but not today, not with those overcast conditions. No matter. He would have a turn flying and that was enough.

"Cessna 2134X, cleared for take off."

Jimmy gave it full throttle. He loved the way the Cessna performed as it accelerated and lifted off . . . perfect landings today . . . log another hour of solo work. At 400 feet he turned crosswind, then downwind at 800 feet over the bay. The aircraft engine sounded strong and rhythmic. The maneuver felt comfortable. He felt like singing. He felt like the *Student Prince*.

A gull circled beside him, and he hummed to himself. At low tide, the mud below arranged itself in intricate drainage patterns. His eyes followed a pronounced and deeper channel and focused on something sticking up just above the water on his left, maybe half a mile off shore, probably just a piece of junk dumped in the bay.

"Palo Alto Tower," Jimmy radioed. "Request left 360 to investigate an unusual object."

Circling left, he saw two aircraft wheels, their struts leading beneath the surface, and the shadowy outline of an airplane. "Looks like an airplane, wheels up, below me."

"Thanks for the report. The tower will handle it."

The student returned for landing, his last of the day; the airport closed for a few hours for rescue and salvage operations. Jimmy grabbed a sandwich and watched the excitement from the instructor's bench.

By mid-afternoon, a helicopter had hauled the ditched Cessna up through the muck and deposited it in a weedy area near transient parking. Palo Alto Tower notified the aircraft owner, who said a magneto was shot. "And what happened to that Pilot Watch Program?" he asked the controller. "Who was on duty last night, and why didn't they report anything?"

"Call Jerry Christensen: He's in charge. Palo Alto Tower will contact him, too."

During the Wednesday afternoon commute, Jerry fought traffic on the Bayshore Highway while he listened to *Romanza* on a CD and balanced a cup of coffee between his knees. When his cell phone rang, he pinned it against his shoulder, leaving two fingers on the wheel.

Don at ZP Maintenance, Palo Alto Airport: His voice came through so loud that Jerry almost dropped the phone. "Why the heck weren't your pilots on watch last night? Cessna 84MMM was my first job today—Triple Mike's owner said he wouldn't fly it until I fixed those mags. He left it, right in front of my shop, and someone took it."

"Gosh, I'll have to check into that," Jerry answered. "It won't go far with bad magnetos."

"You've got that right. It didn't make the first mile. They hauled it out of the bay with a helicopter."

"I'll get right on it," Jerry said and signed off. How did that happen? Stopped in traffic, Jerry juggled the phone and punched in Mid-Valley Aviation at Los Banos. "Hey, Dick. Jerry here. I was there about the stolen Cessna a few days ago."

"I remember. What can I do for you?"

"Any unusual activity in the last day or two?"

"No, not that I noticed," Dick said. "What's up?"

"Another Cessna disappeared from Palo Alto this morning. A helicopter hauled it out of the mud."

"The thief must have drowned, probably the end of your troubles," Dick said before he signed off.

The traffic opened up and Jerry continued homeward. He forgot to drink his coffee. He couldn't get the missing airplane out of his mind.

Later on Wednesday night, Jerry couldn't sleep. He tossed and turned, his thoughts racing out of control. The pilots hadn't watched the airport last night. Another Cessna was stolen: This one ended up in the bay. He needed to call a meeting, all the pilots . . . no, call each one individually. The surveillance cameras at Palo Alto were wearing dress socks, blinding them: Someone had watched him adjust the cameras. And that someone—it couldn't be a coincidence—had to be Old Fish Eyes.

What was he missing? Jerry replayed everything that had come down since 3318E disappeared. When he returned to the crater—the most likely crash site—he had seen the door to the Argonaut Mine. It hadn't been there before. The old lady said she and the kid had been there for years. He looked young, fifteen or maybe sixteen tops, not much older than Jerry's students.

Bingo. The pants. They didn't fit. Whose were they? Why were the faded jeans turned up six inches . . . if the kid had been working there for years? Oily rocks swept under a carpet of sand. Something wasn't right.

He recalled Frank's strange call: the GPS was wrong. "The Argonaut Mine moved. What'd I tell you? Rocks do move, even whole mines."

"Surely you jest," Jerry had answered. "You mean some gnome went in there, stole gold ore in the mining car, pushed it off the rails and down those rough roads—hopping pot-holes and jumping up and down with glee—then hid the gold somewhere else?"

Frank had sounded like he was choking, then said, "No, no, no. The mining site is two miles from where I marked the chart. Could the handheld GPS be that inaccurate?"

"Of course not: accurate to a hundred feet. Why is it wrong?"

"I found their mining claim on the Internet—using *Google*—but it's two miles away, unless they filed an amendment recently. All they have to do is take samples from the new site to the county assayer, if no one gets there first." *Blah, Blah, Blah* . . . How many claims near Kelso . . . how much gold and silver taken out before 1980 . . . way too many details: Frank's usual information dump.

Jerry sat up in bed, pulling the covers off Sally, who moaned and grabbed the blankets. That's it: the important thing from Frank's Kelso mining report. Either they made a new filing, or the GPS is wrong. Either way, they haven't been working in that location for years.

Double bingo!

He slipped out of bed—careful not to disturb Sally this time—and tiptoed in the dark to the next room. He turned the small flashlight from his flight bag, the one with the red filter to preserve night vision in the cockpit, onto his cell phone. The red glow was enough to hit automatic dial.

"Hey, Frank. It's the pants. They're too long."

"Huh, what? Who is this? Is this a joke?"

"It's me, Jerry."

"I should have known. You're waking me up in the middle of the night, telling me somebody's pants are too long? Just get him some stilts, and go back to bed." Frank sounded grumpy.

"That mine wasn't there the first time we saw the crash site," Jerry said. "We have to go back to Daggett."

12.

Like a homing pigeon Jerry drove past the rough lava rocks in the Devil's Playground—barren as a moonscape in the harsh midday sun—directly to Frank's mark on the map: the crater in the Mojave Desert near Kelso. The glare from the warm desert sun made Frank sleepy, more sleepy than arising so early to fly to Daggett with Jerry. The metal Argonaut Mine door still perched on the hill.

From the blackened-but-now-cleaned-up crater, Jerry continued to the east beyond where the dirty green truck had been parked on their last visit to track the location of the Argonaut Mine as filed with the county. Five minutes later, Frank reported mine workings above them, tailings and heavy machinery. A piece of corrugated metal leaned across the entrance to what the GPS said should be the Argonaut Mine.

Jerry stopped in the middle of what passed for a road, jumped out, and scrambled up the hill. Frank followed, picking his way and panting. Jerry pulled the leaning metal to one side and tried to cool his hands by flapping them. "*Yeow!* I should have worn oven mitts." He stepped inside and cooled his hands on the wall. "Too dark to see."

"Take off your shades. I'll get the flashlight." Frank turned downhill. Between him and the Jeep: the old woman. Where'd she come from?

"You're trespassing. Get out!" yelled the woman with the long white braid. The boy was with her. She had a shotgun this time, and she meant business.

A shotgun blast peppered Frank with quartz shards. Rock chips stung his neck and shattered a lens on his glasses. He peered at the world through a spider's web of cracks. His heart pounded. His ears rang.

Jerry stood statue-still in the quiet world after the blast. From the mine's entrance, he had the higher ground—the position of authority—but she was taller than he was. He pulled himself up to his full five feet eight. A stare-down.

In his best take-control teacher voice, he bellowed, "Ma'am, you don't want to do this. I am Captain Jerome T. Christensen, investigating a case." The words rolled off his tongue in measured cadence. He stared at the woman.

Frank stood completely still, frozen in place. A *captain* now, Jerry was; maybe for touch football.

"We traced a stolen airplane to that crater down the hill." Jerry stood tall, arms folded over his chest—the angry father pose. "Your boy knows something."

"Robert, what about this?" The mother turned to the boy, who had taken a position behind her. "You said you flew a plane. You didn't steal it, did you?"

"No, Mother." He moved closer to her and farther from Jerry.

"Well, what about it? The boy knows something. Either he will tell me now, or I will file a mining claim." Jerry stood feet apart with his hands on hips and held a blank poker face. "My airplane was in the crater before you put that Argonaut Mine door there. I can prove it. I can show a prior claim."

"Robert, what about this?" The woman grabbed the boy's shoulder. "We will lose the crystals. Tell what happened."

"I landed a Cessna, right where the crater is." He spoke slowly, turned towards his mother. "It all looked different. There wasn't a crater. I almost hit a rock wall." He paused. His face flashed panic and his words rushed out. "A meteorite hit there and made the crater."

"Why did you land there, Robert? Tell them. We could lose the mine."

"Because the engine stopped and I didn't want to crash and blow up." The boy held a hand over his mouth, as though he wanted to keep the words inside.

"Blow up?" Jerry asked, his puzzled expression hidden by his aviator's sunglasses when he glanced at Frank.

The boy looked at Jerry, looked down at his feet, and looked at Frank, like a trapped fox looking for escape. He drew in the dust with the toe of one shoe. In a muffled voice he said, "Because they put explosives in there."

"Oh, Robert! What a *terrible* thing. Why would anyone do that to you?"

"Because, because, . . ." His shoulders drooped. "I was a soldier in a holy war," he said, lifting his head, as woebegone as a boy who had lost his last friend. He blurted out, "Is the captain going to take me?"

"No one's taking you anywhere," his mother said in a loud authoritarian voice. "Now tell us. What war? Why did they give you explosives?"

"Because, because, . . . I was supposed to fly into a dam and blow everything up," he said, his voice almost a whisper, one hand still covering his mouth. He dropped his head and studied his shoes.

"Blow up a dam?" Frank asked, alarm and surprise written on his face. No one answered him. Even Jerry seemed to be without words.

"But you landed here instead," his mother said. "You are *so brave*."

"I failed my mission. The captain will kill me," he said in a small voice.

"Look, this is too serious to discuss out here. Let's all get out of the sun, have some lemonade. This way." The woman swung the shotgun, pointing to the path behind her. She held her shotgun barrel-up against her shoulder and fast marched up the rocky hill away from the abandoned mine. Her son, as much at home as a mountain goat, ran ahead. Frank and Jerry obediently followed the white braid-beacon guiding them like a siren's call.

"He blew up our airplane," Frank whispered to Jerry. "She greeted us with a shotgun. Why are we following them?"

"S-h-h-h. Yes, I know. But the kid is telling the truth. Fish Eyes did it. He must have given the kid the plane."

"How do you know that?" Frank asked.

Jerry didn't answer.

"Those suicide bombers never give up," Frank said. "They're fanatics."

Again Jerry didn't answer.

Frank's legs complained about the steepness. At the top of the path, a dirty green truck guarded a pile of metal discards—a spool of barbed wire, a large barrel lying on its side—across a steep gravel road from a sun-bleached wooden building of some sort. The woman opened the door to an entrance porch, not the small cabin Frank had expected. She leaned the gun, butt resting on the floor, against the wall. A small caliber rifle—maybe a 22—hung on the wall.

"*Kommen Sie herein*," she said, pointing down a hallway. The interior had been carved out of the heart of the hill, making an area far larger than it appeared from the outside. The living room, a bulge along a long and narrow hallway, contained three overstuffed chairs and a loveseat, a coffee table and a floor lamp. Frank saw an electronic organ, no TV. Bookshelves lined an irregular rock wall.

So fast that it could have been a magic trick, Mother reappeared holding a pitcher of lemonade. "Please, sit down," she said. The boy she called Robert juggled four tall ice-filled glasses and set them on the coffee table.

"We don't know your names. I'm Jerry Christensen, and this is Frank Peterson." Jerry gave their real names and dropped the captain-title.

Lemonade—*lemon-aid:* in an underground room. Frank had read about an underground hotel in Australia. Who were these troglodytes? How did they get here? Where did she get the ice? She stood there, still holding the pitcher.

Kedar noticed the dropped title right away and perked up. "I am Robert Kuh-DAR Herold." He spoke with pride, rolling each syllable off his tongue just as Jerry had done a few minutes before, like a school principal announcing graduates. No longer the scared kid, he smiled.

"You can call me Mother. That's been my name for so long that I almost don't remember any other." She set the pitcher on the coffee table in front of Frank and stood with her arms folded across her waist.

"All right, Mother. Just call me Frank. Here—I'll pour for you." Pouring lemonade over ice at the Mad Hatter's tea party, for a terrorist's mother.

"Thank you, Mother," Jerry said, taking a sip of lemonade. "We still need to find out what happened. How did the boy get here? Is he Robert or Kedar?"

"Of course." Mother turned to the boy, her hands on her hips. "Robert, how did you get here, and where did you get the airplane?"

"At Los Banos. I'm Kedar." The boy, his eyes opened widely, appeared serious, maybe surprised.

"Why were you at Los Banos?" Jerry asked, leaning closer to Kedar. "Who gave you the airplane?"

"I had to fly a mission." Kedar started to tap one foot and shifted back and forth on his chair. "The captain got the plane."

"Fly a mission, fly into a dam? Where was that?" Frank asked.

"Hoover Dam." The kid tapped faster.

"That blunder-head. He gave you a suicide flight, an impossible target," Frank said. Why would the boy do such a thing? He would have died.

Kedar didn't respond. He seemed unconcerned.

"What color was the airplane?" Frank asked. Hoover Dam, not far from Daggett. Was it their Cessna?

"White, I think. It was dark outside." Kedar trained his eyes on Frank.

"The captain who gave you the airplane, who was he?" Jerry asked.

The boy didn't answer.

After a slight pause, Jerry asked, "What did the captain look like?"

Frank had expected to hear: Was it Fish Eyes?

"He was just, The Captain," Kedar answered, facing Jerry. He turned towards his mother. "He was very tall, taller than you, Mother."

"What color was his hair, his eyes?" Jerry leaned forward in his chair.

"Gray hair. And funny eyes," the boy said, wide-eyed again. He stopped tapping, but he didn't pick up his lemonade.

"Funny? Did he make you laugh?" asked Mother, standing and holding a half-empty glass.

"No. Weird eyes—silver gray, kind of flashy. Just, *weird*. He scared me when he stared at me." Kedar paled, just describing those eyes.

"Sounds like Mr. Fish Eyes," Jerry said to Frank.

"Who's Mr. Fish?" Mother asked.

"Just somebody with scary eyes. Don't worry. He's not coming here."

Mother shot Jerry a silent question and put one hand on the boy's arm. She asked in a calm voice, "Where did you come from, Robert?"

"Los Angeles." His words rushed out. "I lived there with my father since I was five and my mother died. He came from Iraq and he called me Kedar. My father drove a taxi but he got in the way when there was a bank robbery and somebody shot him by accident. I was ten. Then I had to live in foster homes." The boy seemed more comfortable, even though telling such a sad story.

"How did you learn to fly, Kedar?" asked Jerry. "How'd you get from Los Angeles to flying at Los Banos?"

"Four of us got to do it," Kedar said. "A recruiter came to our school. We stayed in boot camp for three months."

Sounded like the army—but he looked too young. "Boot camp?" Frank asked. "How old are you, Kedar?"

"Fifteen."

Only fifteen? Pilots have to be sixteen to fly solo. Silent and thoughtful, Frank tried to put the pieces together:

boot camp, Los Angeles, Iraq, flying a stolen airplane, an old lady who called him Robert. He said his name was Kedar.

After an uncomfortable silence, Mother moved to the doorway. "I will cook some supper. You must spend the night because you can't make the highway before dark," she said over her shoulder.

The boy stayed in his chair and studied his shoes.

Frank consulted his watch. "If we leave right now, we could make it," he said. Then he leaned closer to Jerry and whispered, "We don't know these people. We can't spend the night. The kid's a *suicide bomber*, after all."

"Don't worry so much. It's not polite to whisper." Jerry turned back to Kedar and tried to continue his interrogation. "Where did you learn to fly, Kedar, and who was your instructor?"

"San Luis Obispo. John." Back to short answers.

With a lot of pumping, Kedar said he had joined the Guards as a cadet-warrior. They trained in the mountains with a strict routine that included vigorous physical exercise and no talking. The captain said he would be a soldier in the holy war. He flew with John, "just John," who was young and had brown hair and rented airplanes at San Luis Obispo. The cadets were driven—a long ways—one at a time to flying lessons by a sergeant. Kedar had thirty hours logged.

Jerry paused.

Kedar squirmed in his chair. Then he popped up like a jack-in-the-box and said, "Mr. Christensen, I'm sorry that I trashed your airplane. Please excuse me, sir." He ran out of the room.

Frank turned to face Jerry. "Are you sure you want to spend the night," he whispered, "with a suicide bomber and a woman with a shotgun?"

"We have to, have to find out everything we can. Too late to leave."

"That captain is evil, pure evil," Frank said, forgetting to whisper. "Teaching impressionable young people to steal airplanes. You should call him Captain Evil Eye."

"Shush, they'll hear you. Using kids for suicide missions is worse, worse than stealing airplanes." Jerry kept his voice down. "We have to catch him. Whatever it takes."

Jerry and Frank had more questions than answers. While they waited for dinner, they paged through Mother's books: *Greek Myths, Geology of California, Identification Guide for Rocks and Minerals, Mining Methods, Guide to Desert Flowers*; engineering textbooks and books by Emily Dickinson and Mark Twain.

"No bird identification guide," Jerry noted. He picked up a quartz crystal, fully a foot long, and held it to the light.

"Here's a Bible." Peering through a cracked lens, Frank opened Mother's family Bible, written in German script. On the page headed *Familie*, the earliest entry—dated 1888—was in German. Later entries were in English. Frank had to close one eye to read:

> Reinhold Gunther Herold married Inge Isolda Karlson, July 2, 1970.
> Robert Reinhold Herold: Born Jan. 2, 1974. Died May 1, 1974.
> Robert Gunther Herold: Born Apr. 5, 1978. Died Dec. 10, 1981.
> Robert Bernard Herold: Born Apr. 15, 1984. Died May 3, 2004.
> Reinhold Gunter Herold: Died April 2, 2002, aged 63 years.

Frank pulled off his spider-web glasses and squinted at Jerry. "That's why she's called Mother: three sons, all named Robert, all dead."

"Another mystery. Sounds almost creepy."

"Definitely creepy. We won't sleep soundly on this granite floor. I'll watch for the first two hours and you can watch after that."

"Shush. She's coming," Jerry said.

Frank heard Mother announce dinner. A last meal before execution at dawn—what a morbid thought. He and

Jerry had found the Argonaut Mine, all right, along with the pilot of the missing airplane and a woman with a shotgun, who now was calling them to dinner.

Early the next morning after spending the night with Mother and Kedar, Jerry bounced the Jeep towards Daggett along a hiking trail fit only for goats or boots. "Mother was right. We needed daylight."

Frank gripped the edge of his seat with white knuckles. The road shook his grogginess away. "I felt so apprehensive that I only catnapped."

"But it turned out okay just like I told you."

"I feel better now that we are on the road. Here's a puzzle for you. Would this route be shorter than yesterday's if you added the jumps up and down to our forward progress?"

"Too early for all that heavy thinking," Jerry said.

"The coffee helped." Frank felt stiff after a night on a rock floor with only a sleeping bag beneath him. "I guess I'm glad we stayed."

"That coffee really warmed you up. What about the suicide bomber part?"

"That captain's the villain," Frank said. "Not Kedar, not Mother."

"Be glad she's not a pistol-packing mama. At least, if she knows you."

"Right, only a shotgun. I'm watching the scenery through a cobweb."

"She probably adopted Kedar at first sight," Jerry said. "In spite of everything, I can't help it, I like the kid. His first solo cross-country, he found his way across the desert. You know how one rock looks like another, flying over it."

Jerry hit an exposed rock. The Jeep lifted into the air and bumped back down. "Blow up Hoover Dam, blow himself up with it. What a set up."

Jerry honked the horn, sending a buzzard away from carrion on the road.

Frank hoped bits of blood and fur wouldn't stick to the undercarriage, like the gull under One-Eight-Echo's wing.

"Old Fish Eyes should be tarred and feathered." Jerry gave the horn three more bursts. Tarred. And. Feathered.

"A Cessna blasting Hoover Dam is like a wasp stinging a hippopotamus," Frank said. "One-Eight-Echo weighed 2300 pounds at max gross. That's like one ton attacking five million tons of concrete."

"But the size of that crater. That explosive would have damaged it."

"Who knows? One-Eight-Echo could have made Hoover Dam without refueling with those long-range tanks," Frank said.

"Maybe, maybe not. Easier if it refueled someplace before the river."

"Do you think Kedar would have flown into the dam?"

"That's irrelevant," Jerry said. "The diabolic mission proves Fish Eyes is a terrorist. Will he steal more airplanes? Blow something up? We have to stop him."

"How will you do that?"

"Don't worry. I'm incubating a plan."

13.

Already Wednesday—time to set up *the plan* for Saturday. Jerry, his feet up on his classroom desk, finished a sandwich during his lunch break. He leaned back in his desk chair, almost too far back. At the chair's first roll, Jerry straightened up and juggled his cell phone. He punched the send button.

"Hey, Ruben. Jerry here. What's new at Auburn Airport?"

"Sounds like something's about to be. *¿Que pasa?* A new plan to blow up Mr. Fish Eyes, maybe catch him in a bear trap and then barbecue him?"

"Oh, come on. I'm still working on it. Say, listen . . . do you know anybody at San Luis Obispo Airport?"

"Can't say that I do." Ruben's voice sounded flat.

"I have to find somebody there I can trust, and mechanics are the best," Jerry said in his smooth-salesman voice.

"You say nice things like that, I get suckered in. If nobody has to stay up all night, I'll ask around, see if anybody knows San Luis Obispo."

"Thanks a mil." Jerry turned off his cell phone. He knew someone every place Captain Fish Eyes had been, all except San Luis Obispo—Kedar said he flew out of there. Jerry needed to check it out.

After school Jerry sauntered across the hall to Frank's classroom and studied the bulletin board while he waited for Frank to finish explaining an algebra problem to a puzzled youngster. He erased Frank's board and cleaned yellow chalk out of an extra-long sponge and emptied the wastepaper basket. Jerry followed Frank to the teachers' parking lot and, without explanation, asked, "Can you help me out one more weekend?"

"Again? No wonder you're so nice today."

Jerry laughed. "I really need your help."

"I'm ready to hide your cell phone," Frank said, an annoyed frown on his face. "You're always getting me to do something weird."

"That's why I'm asking you in person. We need to poke around at San Luis Obispo Airport. They have two flight schools. You check out one, I take the other one. Bring your hiking boots and a sleeping bag."

"Well, Kedar flew out of there, but the sleeping bag part makes me suspicious. Not another all-nighter?" Frank deposited his briefcase next to his car and held the keys in one hand.

"Here's the plan," Jerry said, ignoring Frank's question. "You go to a flight school, tell them you're interested in flying lessons for your sixteen-year-old nephew. Say you heard John's real good. Take an introductory flight with whoever has time. You go north, I'll go south. Look for clues."

"Only looking, right? Mary will shake her head in disbelief, but it does sound adventuresome. You're on for Saturday morning."

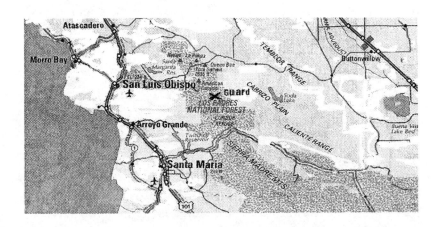

Frank had wanted to fly, despite his sizable credit card balance, all aircraft related. Instead, he rode south towards San Luis Obispo on Highway 101 in the SUV—just in case they explored the backcountry, according to Jerry. Frank wondered what he had gotten himself into this time.

While Jerry drove, Frank studied the LA sectional aeronautical chart. He loved maps: their smells, their colors. He put his index finger over an area outlined with small blue dots. "Flight restrictions, a nesting area for the California condor, not far from San Luis Obispo. A good place to watch birds, maybe near the captain's camp that Kedar told us about."

"I'll wave when we fly past."

"We're driving, remember? If you thought hitting a gull with One-Eight-Echo was fun, you should try a California condor. They're huge broad-winged soaring birds, larger than eagles, with a wingspan of ten feet; One-Eight-Echo's was thirty-six feet." Frank tried to illustrate by stretching out his arms. He bumped Jerry's shoulder.

"That's big, I'll give you that. One-third of a Cessna."

"Condors are an endangered species."

"Geez—where do you find all this stuff? No, don't tell me. Maybe you're about to be an endangered species—a red-bearded encyclopedia-hatcher."

"But you wanted me to check the Internet. There, on the right, see that steep hunk of exposed rock sticking up? The plug of a long-extinct volcano: the Nine Sisters chain. Except you can only see eight of them. One is under water."

"Okay. Westward, you run into the ocean, they drowned their sister. What is south and eastward?"

"Lopez Lake. They fish for bass," Frank said. "A wilderness area just beyond, Los Padres National Forest—"

"I don't need a doggoned travelogue. Just which way to go." Jerry pulled into a parking lot at San Luis Obispo Airport and turned off the ignition.

"Remember: Don't talk too much. Take an introductory flight. Try to find John, discretely. Then meet me here."

A little later, Jerry walked into U-2-Can-Fly Aviation, a flight school, aircraft rental, and maintenance operation: the best place to find Kedar's flight instructor John, unless he worked independently out of a smaller place.

"I'm shopping for flying lessons for my sixteen-year-old nephew. I'd like to take a demonstration ride," Jerry said to the young man sitting behind the front desk. "I heard you have somebody really good with kids. John . . . I think that was his name."

"First let me see your ID." A routine request at all flight schools. "We have three Johns here, but Eric's here now. Would you like to go with Eric?"

"Sounds good. John was young with brown hair—I could meet him later."

"I don't think he works here. Our youngest instructor named John is in his forties. Last time I looked, his hair was gray. Do you want to schedule with Eric? You could go up now."

"Okay. Flying with beginners would give anybody gray hair." Jerry pulled out a chair and waited at the flight-planning table.

Only five minutes later, Eric—an enthusiastic tall blond youth—said he would be happy to show Jerry the sights on the thirty-minute demo ride. Eric's flight crossed Lopez Lake, a wilderness area without buildings or roads. Two small compounds or private campgrounds lay in an area bordering national forest lands. Jerry marked his map and asked, "What's that down there?"

"Just wilderness—a bad place for an emergency landing. Mostly, I fly over the rocks and enjoy the view. I take the Cessna where there are lots of places to land, and I stay away from the condors' preserve. Bring your nephew over. I'll teach him to fly safely."

After the flight, Jerry helped Eric tie down the Cessna. Everybody used Cessnas for flight instruction these days. He thanked Eric and bought them each a Coke from the vending machine. Eric had flown over two possible locations for The Guards. Jerry drank his soda while he waited back at the SUV. Maybe Frank had found Kedar's flight instructor, John. Maybe Frank had seen something suspicious from the air.

After he left Jerry, Frank walked two buildings farther down the line of FBOs from U-2-Can-Fly. Inside at Aviation West, two young men held plastic-foam cups and bent over a chart at a table that filled most of the room. The operation seemed too small to employ full-time flight instructors. Kedar's teacher John probably was a freelancer using such a flight school for renting aircraft.

Frank stepped in the door and stood politely by the reception counter until the young woman working the desk hung up the phone and turned his way. "What do I have to do to arrange flying lessons for my sixteen-year-old brother? Could I talk with one of your instructors?"

"Sure. Which one—Jim, Fred, or William?"

"Well, actually, I'm looking for a John."

"Why didn't you just say so?" The young Asian receptionist, dressed in jeans and a Flying Mustangs T-shirt, pointed wildly into the air. "The john's right over there." She turned away and answered the insistently ringing telephone.

"No. I want to find a young John."

The young woman seemed annoyed. She put her hand over the mouthpiece and stared ice at Frank. "Exactly what is it that you're looking for? We're not that kind of a business."

"I heard about somebody named John, flying out of this airport. Supposed to be good with kids. If he works here, I want to look him up. If not, I want to speak to another flight instructor." Frank was annoyed now. How did they expect to stay in business, treating customers like this?

"Could I see your ID?" Without waiting for a reply, she pushed her feet against the floor and rode the chair across the room to answer the other phone. From over her right shoulder she said, "We don't have any instructors named John. I'm Susan. I could take you if you want to go up now."

"Oh, you're a flight instructor?" Frank's bushy eyebrows shot above his glasses and his eyes widened.

"You're surprised that I'm a flight instructor, because I'm a woman? Lots of women are pilots. Some are airline captains. So do you want to go, or not?"

"Yes, I like the idea." Susan was pretty. Jerry didn't know what he was missing.

"Okey-dokey. Sightseeing is so much more relaxing than instructing." Susan took Frank north and west over the Nine Sisters, above some oil tanks and tall smokestacks and along the coastline.

Frank recognized the area from pictures. A huge chuck of gray rock jutted out of the bay, as tall as a tanker but not as long. "Is that Morro Rock out there?"

"Yes. A good landmark from the air."

"Did you know it was an important landmark for naval navigation? And part of a chain of volcanic plugs: the Nine Sisters."

"Can't say I know about ships, but I do know that we stay away from that nuclear power plant. That's what I use the rock for."

"What's that, down there?" Frank pointed at a large complex of austere gray buildings, completely surrounded by sturdy fence, like a prison.

"That's Atascadero State Hospital, a maximum security psychiatric facility. Some of their customers are criminally insane."

"Oh, I've heard of that place. Did you know that *atascadero* is Spanish for muddy place or a place one gets stuck?" A good place for Captain Fish Eyes, Frank thought.

"Look. You said you wanted to talk about lessons for your brother. I'm going back. Your half-hour is up."

Susan landed and taxied behind the flight school. She left the airplane in the taxiway for someone else to refuel and put away. "That's how Aviation West does things," she said.

Frank thanked Susan and bought her a soda at the vending machine. He didn't see any coffee; he chose a canned iced tea and hurried back to meet Jerry at the SUV. Now he had a mental picture of the local geography, but he hadn't found John . . . or anything useful.

North: Morro Bay. West: the Pacific Ocean. South: beaches and highways. The Guards, the private military school Kedar attended, had to be in the wilderness area to the east, a location as imprecise as somewhere in the Mojave Desert. He hoped that Jerry had seen something and knew where to go. Where to go: that turned out to be the problem of the day.

After Frank reconnected with Jerry, they took the SUV east from San Luis Obispo towards Lopez Lake and the possible location of The Guards that Jerry had seen from the air. Frank had grabbed two deli sandwiches, a bag of granola, and some bananas at a convenience grocery, provisions for an overnight backcountry search. He didn't look forward to cold instant coffee—no Starbucks tomorrow, out there with the rocks and dry brush.

"You still haven't told me the plan," Frank said. "Where are we going?"

"That's what you're going to figure out. We're searching for Old Fish Eyes' training camp." Jerry handed Frank a map. "I've marked the sectional. From the air, I saw several possibilities in the wilderness area. Start with the most northern spot—it had buildings. Try to find us some good dirt roads."

The road wound through areas of chaparral and across a shallow stream. The SUV straddled deep ruts until the narrow road forked. Frank compared the road maps printed from the Internet to the sectional chart. He wasn't sure where they were. "Wait—stop. Which road?"

"The one on the right looks traveled. No sense driving a fire trail." Jerry turned right. Someone had smoothed the gravel and widened the road.

After a fifteen-minute meander, they stopped to check out a log building. Jerry knocked on the door: no response. Through a window Frank saw a stone fireplace in a cavern-like room, empty except for folding chairs leaning against a wall and a leaf rake lying on the planked oak floor.

Jerry tried the back. "Hello-o-o! Anybody home?"

Behind the building, a man atop a ladder threw down a handful of debris from the gutter. A broom lay on the half-swept roof. "Hello. I heard you drive in."

"We're lost," Jerry said. "Can you help us with a map check?"

"Gladly." Ladder-man climbed down and pointed at Frank's map. "You're at a summer camp for the Boy Scouts, right here. Where are you going?"

"We're looking for a private school, some kind of military academy."

"I haven't seen anything like that. Why don't you try this other place you marked? Just go back to the fork in the road. Then go right about half a mile, then left, . . . like, maybe ten, fifteen miles."

"Thanks a mil." Jerry tipped his baseball cap. After a navigational discussion with Frank, he crunched through the gravel to the unmarked road.

An hour later, the SUV passed an area posted against trespassing and bordered by cyclone fence topped by strands of barbed wire. Jerry stopped in a forested area with room for two vehicles and parked off the road.

"Why are you stopping? We're not at the second X."

"Why a cyclone fence out in the wilderness? This is it, our home for the night. Time for hiking boots, buddy."

Jerry, with Frank two steps behind, followed the ruts back and traced the fence away from the road across rough ground. The more interesting plants seemed to be inside of the wire; where they stood was almost barren. In fact, the flora and fauna seemed different on the other side of the fence.

"Rattlesnake grass, Jerry. I haven't seen any of that for years." Frank pointed at several tufts of blue-green blades a foot high with telltale pendent ovoid spike-lets waving above dry straw-colored stems.

"Rattlesnake—where?" Jerry's eyes shifted back and forth in a desperate attempt to avoid the snake. "I hate snakes."

"No, no. It's a type of grass. Dry seedpods from last season quiver in the slightest breeze and make a rustling sound, not at all like a rattlesnake buzz. Papery pods, shaped like rattlesnake's buttons."

Jerry relaxed.

"Those tree mushrooms on the white oak, like horizontal ruffled composition shingles with bands of yellow, orange, and brown—they're huge." Frank grabbed the cyclone fence for a closer view, leaning against a No Trespassing sign.

"So is that oak tree. Huge," Jerry said. "Must be 300 years old. See that white puffball mushroom—big as a soccer ball? The ones my grandmother picked were more like baseballs."

"Over there . . . rotten logs, each with a different kind of mushroom, all extra large, one like big pink ears. Those logs, their barks don't match."

"How'd they get so many kinds of mushrooms, all in one place?"

"Who knows? The mushroom is only the flower of the fungus. Those logs are filled with tangled white fibers, like an old-fashioned telephone switchboard."

"Fungus flower, whatever. I want a closer look."

"Better not. See that *Keep Out* sign? The last time we saw one of those Mother had a shotgun." Frank, rooted like a mushroom, faced the field of fungus.

Jerry grasped the fence with both hands and pressed his face against the wire. His nose fit through one of the loops.

After a short pause, Frank asked, "Why aren't there any mushrooms on this side of the fence? No rattlesnake grass, either."

"I'm more interested in the buildings over there." Jerry waved his hand and pointed at two structures built of corrugated galvanized steel, half-cylinders with closed ends. "Have you ever seen a Quonset hut?"

"The Navy used hundreds of them: all-purpose, light weight, easily assembled. After World War II, they sold those things as war surplus."

"Okay, Encyclopedia Man. I have to see this." Jerry jumped up on the fence and hoisted himself over, clearing the strands of barbed wire that ran inside the fence and above his head.

"How are you going to get out of there, with that wire over your head? Come back out of there." Frank paced back and forth. "It says Keep Out."

"Come on, Frank. We can find a way out later." Jerry walked completely around the live oak tree, the one with the shingle-mushrooms—enormous ones, in scale with the tree. Jerry stooped to pick up an acorn, three inches long and a quarter of an inch thick, curved like a fishhook. The dried leaves beneath the tree had spines. Not a good place to walk barefooted.

"Stinks like guano," Jerry said. "Are you coming?"

Against his better judgment, Frank used the No Trespassing sign for a handhold, then a foothold. He wobbled atop the fence, astride it. "Help me! I can't go either way."

"Don't fall. You'll either land outside and start over or shred yourself on the barbed wire."

"You're a lot of help. How'd you do it?"

"Bend over and grab the wire between the barbs. Swing out and jump."

Frank heard *jump* and landed on Jerry, breaking his fall. He brushed himself off and walked closer to the tree mushroom area and the hundred-foot-around oak. "Believe it or not, a live oak tree with a girth of 150 feet owns legal title to the land on which it grows in North Little Rock. Grant deed and all."

"Back to normal, telling me everything I don't need to know. But I guess, if in Roman times, Caligula could appoint a horse to the senate, the government could grant land to a tree in Arkansas." Jerry, for once, topped Frank's trivia. "Gotcha this time."

A hundred yards later, a soldier wearing camouflage fatigues and carrying a rifle yelled, "Halt! Who goes there?"

Frank stopped with one foot in the air, almost losing his balance. "Just admiring the mushrooms. It's hard going back over the fence from here."

"You should have thought of that before you came over the fence. Hands above your head." The soldier gestured with his rifle and then poked it into Frank's ribs.

"You, too." He waved his rifle at Jerry. "That way."

The soldier kept them at a fast march. Frank turned to watch him over one shoulder and stumbled. Several Quonset huts bordered a paved parking lot, home to three Volkswagen vans, a black pickup, and a Jeep. The closest one, marked HQ with a small plastic sign, resembled half an oversized tin can and had one door in its wooden semi-circular end. Several smaller huts clustered around HQ like chicks with a mother hen.

Inside Building HQ, an older man sat behind a heavy metal desk with an outdated desk phone and an overflowing file stack of white paper. His gray hair was pulled back with a leather thong; a loose strand brushed two silver bars on the collar of his tan uniform, a captain's insignia. An iMac gurgled as sharks circled a rowboat on its screen-saver. A poster advertising *The Guards Academy* depicted two young men wearing battle fatigues and leaning on rifles, above a bulleted list: •Courage; •Discipline; •Excellence; •Fidelity.

Jerry's eyes riveted on the captain, almost as tall as Frank even while seated behind his desk.

Frank stared at an ant colony in a sixty-gallon terrarium. The ants resembled stout wingless wasps, reddish-black and about an inch long. A sign warned caution: bullet ants. Frank didn't see a gun, only a box teeming with insects.

The soldier saluted. "Captain, I found these two trespassing."

Captain-no-name appraised Frank with steel-gray eyes. "Have I seen you before?" he asked, almost spitting the words.

"No, Sir. I'm sure we have never met." The captain, not the cockatrice Frank had expected from Kedar's description, had unusually pale coyote-eyes.

"Why are you here?" The captain studied Frank's red beard so intently that Frank imagined it sticky with gravy dripping down.

"The mushrooms—" Why didn't he ask Jerry?

"Didn't you see the signs? We have a fence for a reason: we don't allow visitors. Sergeant, take them back out to the road."

Escorted by the soldier with the rifle, Frank and Jerry climbed into a Jeep. The sergeant waved at a sentry and drove through a gate beneath a curved wrought iron sign—*The Guards*—a few yards from the road. He stopped outside the fence.

"End of the ride." The soldier stepped out, propped his rifle against the side of the Jeep, and opened the door.

Jerry and Frank jumped out onto the road and scrambled out of the way. The Jeep spun a U-turn and covered them with dirt as it sped back into the compound, where the captain waited.

The captain met the Jeep outside as soon as the driver turned off the engine. "I have a job for you. Follow those two redheaded hikers. Find out where they go, but don't let them see you."

Where had he seen that pair before? The one with the red beard—like a red-throated finch. The other with unruly hair—like the crest on a zebra finch—two finches hiking in the woods. Palo Alto Airport—yes. He remembered seeing two redheaded aviators preflight an airplane. But these were two hikers.

Jerry and Frank said nothing on the walk back to the SUV from their interview at The Guards. They sat there in the dark, eating granola and bananas and waiting for the moon to rise. Jerry put his banana peel into a plastic bag and leaned back. "So that's the place. We don't have to check the other spot I marked."

"First you find the crash site, then you find The Guards right away. How long is your luck going to last?"

"Just science and skill. What can I say?"

"What do you think . . . Is he Fish Eyes?" Frank brushed away an insect.

"Those eyes: Kedar said *weird*, Brad said *cold*. He's a captain at The Guards. Has to be him," Jerry said. "That's Fish Eyes."

"Now we can tell the FBI—"

"They'll put him away for good."

"We can go back to our normal lives." Frank swatted the air around his ears, fending off a buzzing mosquito. He smashed another one against the windshield with a map. "My wife says I'm a mosquito magnet."

"Any mosquitoes, I know where to send them. We could make a fortune selling pollywogs to eat all those larvae. As many mosquitoes inside as outside."

"Where are you going to find pollywogs? Did you know that mosquitoes can breed in two inches of standing water in a flowerpot after a rain?"

"Rattlesnake grass, mushroom fungus flowers, overweight oak trees. Don't tell me—let me guess. Coming next: the love life of mosquitoes."

Frank choked on his granola.

"The love life of mosquitoes," they chorused, laughter rocking the van, all thoughts of silence forgotten.

"The love life of mosquitoes . . ." After dark in the woods, the sound carried to the captain's surveillance detail.

"Listen to that, two crackbrains in that van."

"No, just those two geeks. The ones looking for mushrooms."

Unseen, two cadets dressed in camouflage fatigues jotted down Jerry's license number for the captain.

Frank washed down a handful of dry granola with a cup of cold instant coffee. He saved the banana for last. A miserable breakfast after a cramped night in Jerry's SUV, parked somewhere in Los Padres National Forest—somewhere overrun with mosquitoes—near the perimeter of The Guards. Jerry wanted to explore the western side of the captain's encampment before driving home.

Frank slathered his face with sunscreen. "Are you sure this is a good idea? Yesterday, they kicked us out. Today, we'll get ourselves shot."

Jerry poured the remainder of his cold coffee onto the ground. "We came all this way. We have to know what the captain's doing in there."

"Promise you won't jump the fence?" Secretly, Frank felt the exhilaration of doing the forbidden: That was why Jerry could lure him into outrageous situations. He hoped he would learn from this flash of insight.

"You have my word, as a gentleman and a scholar," Jerry said from the driver's seat.

"We stay out of sight." Frank sat down and slammed the door.

Jerry moved the SUV to the west, past the entrance to The Guards. Frank turned his head to follow the wrought iron sign over the gate.

"It's backwards, the sign is backwards. You need a mirror to read it."

"You don't say. No signs along the road either, just like Bolinas. Every time the county puts up a road sign there, someone pulls it down." Jerry pulled off at a wide place in the road within sight of the western fence.

"I'd rather be in Bolinas than here. What if they see us?" Frank pointed out a path twenty feet from the fence surrounding The Guards. Far enough outside, he hoped.

"We won't see them either." Jerry grumbled but he crossed the road.

A six-foot barren area bordered the cyclone fence. Beyond the firebreak, Frank struggled through brush and held branches back to avoid slapping Jerry. Bees buzzed around Frank's face through gnarled red-barked manzanita. He brushed one away. "Did you know that the berries are edible? They resemble miniature apples—*manzanita* means little apples in Spanish."

"Thank you, Professor Britannica. I tried one once. They taste terrible. You try one, see if you think they're apples."

"I'll take the gentleman's word for it." Frank brushed the ground with a fallen pine bough and parked himself beneath a thorny bush with a view through the fence. Normally, accustomed to California, Frank wouldn't have noticed the flora. Scrubby gray blue-green bushes, rocky soil, gray-barked Digger pines, live oak, foxtail grasses—just standard scrub. Inside the fence, however, he saw an oasis from a Hollywood movie set: five palm trees around a pond. Farther north, Frank noticed several different varieties of palm: coconut, date, and unnamed others with green and orange nuts and smaller fronds.

"That coconut must weigh 40 pounds." Jerry pointed to a tall palm tree with an unusually thick trunk, bearing a Siamese twin coconut.

Frank studied the shadow of a fence post. "Palm tree must be eighty feet tall." In one fluid motion, he peeled off his belt and held the ends together, forming a loop. He held it up, compared it to the coconut, and extrapolated. "Circumference at least three feet."

"Big deal. Why does that matter?"

"Last week at school, I found the volume of a coconut by displacing water in a glass aquarium. My class ate the meat later."

"So?" Jerry stared at Frank.

"It weighed 1.5 pounds. That coconut up there is three times as thick, more than 27 times 1.5, forty pounds for sure. It doesn't belong here."

"Forty pounds, what did I tell you? You'll burn out a circuit, man."

Frank continued along the fence. He took turns with Jerry holding back scotch broom; they narrowly avoided a wasps' nest. The sweat streaming down Frank's face attracted a swarm of blue insects. He brushed them away from his face and slapped his arm, knocking one bug to the ground. "Flying thumb tacks."

"The mosquito magnet strikes again."

"Balderdash." Frank stopped in mid-step and cocked his head, hearing the distinctive buzz of a coiled rattlesnake.

"Freeze, Jerry! Rattlesnake."

Jerry went immediately pale.

"You'll be all right. Just watch where you put your feet. It won't leap for your jugular—its mouth is too small. It's only a baby."

"What about my ankles then?"

"Just step where I step." Frank swept the ground with a stick. The west fence ended amidst a dense cluster of poison oak at the edge of a steep canyon. Along the north fence, high clumps of pampas grass grew as far as he could see. "You'd cut your pants to shreds getting through that pampas grass."

Frank, more than ready to leave, saw movement beyond the fence.

Rifle shots.

Jerry and Frank dove to the ground behind some scrub bushes.

"Stay down. I told you we'd get shot." Frank crawled behind a stand of dry grass. He felt the rush of danger, as though he straddled a fence between a lion's lair and a crocodile infested swamp.

"Probably a rifle range along the back fence." Jerry raised his head.

"Stay down." Frank peered out from behind a particularly scratchy bush. Behind the fence, young men in combat fatigues and carrying rifles ran toward one on the ground. Someone had been shot. Shot!

Frank's heart pounded—a tragedy, right before his eyes. He didn't see any blood but the soldier didn't move. The other soldiers surrounded the one on the ground. They were going to drag him away. Then the wounded soldier sprang to his feet, and the others clapped him on the back.

"What's going on?" Frank whispered and kept himself flat to the ground.

"A military war game, the kind where the losers are shot with paint."

"They shoot trespassers with more than paint," Frank said." Let's get out of here."

Two hours after leaving The Guards and back in San Luis Obispo, Jerry and Frank fortified themselves with the 747 Captain's Burger at the Spirit of San Luis Restaurant. "I'm glad we're heading home and I'm glad we weren't shot, paint or not," Frank said between bites. "Gone too many weekends."

Jerry dipped a French fry into catsup. "Right, except part of me is intoxicated with adventure. We need to turn this over to the FBI, now that we know the location of the captain's camp. Fish Eyes is training terrorists."

"Why do you think they're terrorists?" Frank wiped catsup out of his beard with a napkin. "Only playing a game, shooting paint. No munitions depot."

"Well, for starters, he stole our airplane and blew it up and wanted to blast Hoover Dam. Captain Fish Eyes is a terrorist. We have to stop him."

Later on Sunday, Aquila sat by the gurgling iMac in his office at The Guards and watched the screen-saver shark swim across, swallowing multi-colored small fish. He leaned back in his desk chair and held the telephone receiver to his ear. The cadets' flight instructor, John from San Luis Obispo

Airport, had just reported, "Some guy with red hair and a red beard inquired about a flight instructor for a sixteen-year-old. Said he was looking for the john so Susan pointed it out but then he said, 'Looking for John.' He was so *nerdy*. He said Atascadero State Hospital was a place one gets stuck, a Spanish muddy place. Weirdo guy, huh?"

"Wonder what he really wanted." Aquila ran his fingers through his hair and tightened the leather thong holding it back. Hikers . . . Palo Alto Airport: the red-throated finch.

"Say, what happened to Kedar—you know, Cadet Khazari?" John asked. "He's the most promising student you sent me. Haven't seen him for weeks now."

"A pity. He went AWOL," he told John before he hung up.

Aquila slammed the desk with his fist. The iMac flashed to life. After a short investigation on the Internet, he found the aircraft registration for 3318E. He rolled his chair back and said aloud, "They're the ones, the pilots from Palo Alto. *Pesky finches.*"

Why'd they show up here? Asking about sixteen-year-olds . . . it can't be coincidence. They must know— Kedar must be alive. Where was Kedar?

Aquila started planning another trip to Palo Alto.

14.

The wall phone in Frank's classroom rang just as he reached the punch line in a tale about giant coconuts. It was Jerry. Who else called him every day?

"Hey, Frank. I set up an appointment after school, with the FBI."

"Look, I'm right in the middle of things." Frank stood at the front of a classroom filled with active adolescents. He saw a paper airplane, about to fly out the window. "In the basket with that, Brian!"

After a pause, Frank said, "Today? Are you talking this afternoon?" Not a convenient time, but the FBI could fly surveillance aircraft over The Guards and pursue the perpetrator—*perp* in FBI jargon. Jerry would be done with the whole affair; he'd stop chasing aircraft thieves.

"All right, then," Frank said, pointing his finger at the wastepaper basket. "Four o'clock. FBI."

Despite having an appointment with an FBI agent to report acts of possible terrorism, Jerry and Frank waited forty-five minutes in the outer office. Frank picked up a copy of *The Police Science Journal* and read an article about lie detector tests—or *polygraphs*, the more professional term.

"Listen to this. Lie detectors don't work if the person is a pathological liar and believes his lie. Or answers with something that is true, working around the question. The trick is, say something that you believe."

"They're not going to give us a polygraph. We won't need one," Jerry said, tapping one heel. He had a bad case of the fidgets. "I made a list of what to tell them. Did you read up on bullet ants?"

"They're used in manhood initiation rites by primitive tribes in the Amazon Basin. Bullet ants have the most painful sting of any insect—feels like being shot with bullets, hence the name. The boys have to let them crawl on their arms and can't cry out when they're stung. A tribal proof, they're men—"

"Unless the things sting them in the wrong place. But where the heck did Fish Eyes find them?"

"Search me. It's illegal to import insects. Those ants are worse than killer bees. What if they escape into the environment?"

The receptionist opened the waiting room door long enough to announce, "Mr. Christensen and Mr. Peterson, Agent Matthews will see you now. Come into his office," before popping back out of sight.

"The Army game. Wait an hour, then hurry up." Jerry jumped up like a jack-in-the-box.

Frank rose slowly, straightened his tie, and followed Jerry down the hall. He read *P. W. Matthews, Special Agent* on the front of the window, reversed like in a mirror on the open door, like the wrought iron sign at The Guards.

Agent Matthews wore a suit with a white shirt and a dark blue tie. His full head of black hair was cut short, a flattop. Peering out from under shaggy black brows, he rose from his desk to meet them and shook hands. He seemed to be in a hurry—all business. He waved at two chairs in front of his desk.

"Please sit down. Now, what did you fellows have to report?"

"First of all, we had a four place Cessna at Palo Alto Airport. It was stolen six weeks ago." Jerry sat ramrod straight and faced the agent directly. "They loaded it with explosives at Los Banos and planned to fly it into Hoover Dam."

"A Cessna, to blow up Hoover Dam? Do you know how big that dam is?" asked Agent Matthews, picking up a pen that he flipped between two fingers. "That plan wouldn't

119

fly—forgive the pun. Now, the explosives at Los Banos: Did you see that happen?"

"No. We pieced the story together."

"Did you find the aircraft?"

"No, but we found the person who stole it. He has intensely cold eyes and he has bullet ants in his office and exotic tree mushrooms and coconut trees with forty-pound fruits." Jerry's words raced out of his mouth.

"He's training young men to fly on terrorist missions. We saw them playing a military war game with rifles. They shot one another with paint."

"Let me see if I have this right." Agent Matthews leaned back against the back of his chair, hands behind his head. "They have bullet ants, and their rifles fire paint. They have forty-pound coconuts. This captain, who has cold eyes, trains terrorists. Does the captain have a name?"

When the agent crossed his legs and swung one foot, Frank thought he might topple over backwards, but in such a small office, he would only slide down the wall.

"We couldn't get his name." Jerry swiveled his chair towards Frank. "But we know he's training terrorists and that he'll steal more airplanes."

"Where did you see them training?"

"We went hiking in the Los Padres National Forest and found their camp. It's called The Guards and the sign is hidden." Jerry started to sweat.

Frank realized that, without Kedar's testimony, they had no case. But they wouldn't have a case with a dead witness, either. He crossed his fingers that Agent Matthews wouldn't ask Jerry why they went to The Guards.

"So you went hiking, just happened to see young men shooting paint, and you know they're terrorists." The agent straightened his chair and moved to the edge of his seat. "Is that all you have?"

"But he stole our airplane," Jerry said, his face a plaintive question mark.

"You have no names, no proof. How do you know that the captain, whoever he is, stole your airplane?"

"Paint. They shot paint. It was his eyes. Everybody noticed them." Jerry face turned red. A vein in his temple pulsed.

"I see. No names, no proof, no way for me to proceed." Agent Matthews sat quietly for a minute. Then he reached across the desk to shake their hands.

Class dismissed, Frank thought. Jerry had created a serious credibility gap.

While waiting for the elevator in the hall, Jerry said, "That was fast. What did he give us, three minutes? Somehow everything came out wrong. The words caught in my throat and spilled out differently than they sounded in my mind—that ever happen to you?"

"Spilling words, no. Spilling coffee, yes."

"Sorry, pal. I couldn't expose Kedar. The FBI wants explosives and terrorists. Our Cessna is too small to be a priority. Guess we're still on our own."

"A pity," Frank said. "One of those FBI Cessna 210s with all that surveillance equipment could check out The Guards from the air."

"All we need is the captain's name," Jerry said.

Friday evening and into the night, Jerry played over and over in his mind the unsuccessful visit to the FBI agent, like videotape caught in a repeating loop. Still thinking about it on Saturday morning, he skipped breakfast and nursed a cup of coffee—heavy on cream, light on sugar.

The only way to solve this . . . Do it himself. This was war, all out war. Jerry spun his cell phone on the kitchen table and leaned the chair back onto two legs. Go back to The Guards, get a name for Fish Eyes. He needed a diversion. *Bingo.*

When Jerry hit the speed-dial on his cell phone, his mechanic-friend Ruben at Auburn answered right away. "I've found a great new place for the $100 hamburger, San Luis Obispo," Jerry said. "Could you meet me there in two weeks, and bring me an ELT?"

"An Emergency Location Transmitter, when you don't have an airplane? Sounds like another of those plans, when I deliver something to get a hamburger," Ruben said. "Still after Mr. Fish Eyes?"

"Well, actually, I need two ELTs, . . . and a ride in your airplane, too." Jerry kept his voice low and pleasant. "You're always so clever. Can you make one of those radios have a ticking timer?"

"Oh, I get it," Ruben laughed. "You plant the ticking ELT somewhere, and Old Fish Eyes panics when he hears it, like Captain Hook in *Peter Pan*."

"Sure. I'll tell you the whole plan when I see you."

"No way, *amigo*," Ruben said. "If I'm taking you somewhere in my airplane and making a fake ELT, I better hear the plan—all of it."

"Well, it's complicated. The FBI won't help without a name for Fish Eyes. I need to drop an ELT at his training camp as a cover story."

"Not from my airplane." Ruben's voice came through, loud and alarmed. "You can't send search and rescue on a wild-goose chase."

"The signal's only good for about ten miles. Nobody reported missing, they'll think it's a false alarm. The search will stop right there, before it starts." Jerry paused. He sounded cool and logical.

Ruben didn't answer.

"Captain Fish Eyes needs to see some activity while I'm at The Guards."

"You're *loco*, man. You'll be busted for sure, crying wolf like that," Ruben said. "But you gave me an idea. I'll fix one up with a different frequency and get you a direction finder. That arrow pointing at the signal, that great siren sound—you'll look cool."

"How about we drop one, plant another with a loud tick?" Jerry asked.

"*¡Ay chihuahua!* You talk me into the darnedest things."

"Saturday the twenty-third, then," Jerry said. "We'll storm the gates at The Guards Academy and bring back the captain's name for the FBI."

Kedar felt safe, living in a crystal cave in the Mojave Desert far from the captain and The Guards. Mother-not-his-mother seemed to have adopted him. She called all her sons Robert. His driver's license listed him as Robert Kedar Herold. For three weeks, Kedar had pondered his new name and whether she was now his mother. While helping with the dishes, he asked, "What does our family name *Herold* mean?"

"It's time I showed you." Mother walked to the bookshelf and took down a large book bound in black leather with pages gilded with gold around the edges.

"This is our family Bible, Robert, and the entries go all the way back to 1888. You belong in it now." She added *Robert-Kedar Herold, reborn February 23, 2005* in careful ink script beneath the entry: *Robert Bernard Herold, born April 15, 1984, died June 3, 2004.* "He would have been your brother."

Kedar turned pages randomly. Every page had a decorative design in gold leaf and colored ink, or an elaborate capital letter, but the lettering itself was unfamiliar. He couldn't read any of the words. Pointing at the picture of a saint, who wore a large round halo in gold leaf, he asked, "Is this an idol?"

"No, just illustrations. I think that one is Saint Peter, but I can't read it, because it's written in German script."

"The *Qur'an* is written in Arabic, the true words of God." Mother was an Infidel, with a Bible.

"Oh, my, Robert. Can you read Arabic?"

"No." He hadn't thought about that before. He didn't need to read Arabic to pray at the mosque. The only Arabic he knew was his full name, a long name that meant son of Ahmed and grandson of Altair; *Altair* was a flying eagle.

"The Bible is a translation from Greek," Mother said. "I can't read that either."

"You forgot to tell me. What does *Herold* mean?" Surely it meant *messenger*, like the lightning from God.

Instead of answering his question, Mother went to her electronic keyboard, opened a hymnal, and played through two verses of *Hark the Herald Angels Sing*. "This hymnal is how I pray. If you want to learn to play the keyboard, we will buy a music book in Las Vegas. Want to try singing it?"

After hearing the song only one time, Kedar sang correctly and on key in a clear tenor voice. Mother tried *A Mighty Fortress is My God*. He sang that effortlessly as well.

"Oh, my, Robert! Where did you learn to sing?"

He answered her question with another of his own. "Are we praying?"

"Yes, and I pray every time I walk outdoors in this beautiful desert, especially when the wildflowers come out in the spring."

"Are you an Infidel, Mother?" Kedar the messenger, living with an Infidel, praying with an Infidel.

"Of course not. Are you?"

"But you eat pork, and you don't pray right."

"Everybody prays in his own way in this country. When I was a girl, my family was Catholic and we went to Mass every Sunday, but I pray in my own way now. It's believing in God and living a life where you care about other people. That's all that really matters. The word *infidel* means someone who doesn't believe in God. Do you pray?"

"I used to at the mosque."

"You should pray, Robert. It's good for your soul. Some people call it meditation."

"Then I wouldn't fight you in a holy war?" She said she wasn't an Infidel, but she did eat pork, and she had strange ways.

"Of course not. What is a holy war, Robert?"

"It's where you fight against the Infidels."

"I think you need to pray, Robert. If you teach me one of your prayers, I'll teach you one of mine."

"It's in Arabic and you need a prayer rug." Kedar decided not to tell her about the lightning sent from God.

15.

"This is war, all out war." Jerry, loitering over Saturday breakfast buffet at San Luis Obispo Airport with Ruben and Frank, held a coffee cup in one hand and a croissant in the other.

Frank brushed crumbs away with his napkin. He hoped he hadn't made a mistake, coming along. Ruben had flown in from Auburn to deliver two special ELT radios he had built for Jerry. Aside from that, Jerry hadn't shared today's plan for a spying operation at The Guards. It was too late to pull out.

"Okay, what's the plan, Colonel?" Ruben had called Jerry *the colonel* since the day Jerry wore a certain borrowed National Guard uniform to Auburn.

Jerry put his hands behind his head and leaned back. "We fly over The Guards and drop one modified ELT. We tell the sentry at the gate that we're searching for a bomb, and he takes us to Captain Fish Eyes."

"Set off an emergency signal? Count me out on that one. You can't send Civil Air Patrol on a wild-goose chase." Frank pictured the ELT in One-Eight-Echo, an orange four-inch cube found beside the battery, that transmitted on the emergency radio frequency after a heavy impact—such as an airplane crashing. "Satellites sense even an old ELT these days. I don't want to lose my license."

"The new ones communicate directly with satellites, those black boxes you hear about on the news whenever an airliner crashes," Ruben said.

"Why black box if they're orange?" Jerry asked.

"Ask Frank—he always knows all the odd details."

"He's a formidable opponent playing *Trivial Pursuit*," Jerry said.

"Come on, guys. I just don't want to set off an emergency signal."

"Don't worry. I neutered them." Ruben opened a gym bag beside his chair and displayed two orange Cessna ELTs and a black electronic box.

Jerry grinned. "I'm glad they're not a breeding pair."

"Be serious for once, *amigo.* I changed the frequency and they tick like bombs on a timer. See the pointing needle? It's tracking the signal."

"Pretty slick." Jerry picked up one to admire it.

Frank cocked his head to one side, listening. "No siren noise, just ticking."

"*No problema.* Except for the delivery. How are you going to drop it out?"

"That's easy. Just open the door, reach down, and drop it below the belly to avoid scratching the aircraft." Jerry stretched. He sounded sure of himself.

"Just slow down, open the window, and toss it away," Frank said.

"Wrong, and more wrong." Ruben didn't smile. "Even as slow as I can go safely you're at 75 mph. The passenger door will open only a crack. The window is too small, plus the box would ruin Foxy Lady's paint on its way down."

"The cargo door, then," Jerry said.

"You got it," Ruben answered. "I had to remove it, and I brought a canvas drop-tube. We're going to hear lots of wind noise."

"All right. The canvas tube releases the ELT beneath the aircraft body. How low are you going to go?" Frank asked.

"I won't go below 500 feet. We're supposed to be higher than that over buildings, but they're not supposed to have any buildings. I call that even."

"We'll be so careful that we'll even let you drop it out," Jerry said.

"You should sell snake-oil . . . or pollywogs to Captain Fish Eyes."

"What's that about?"

"The Guards had a huge mosquito hatch. Jerry proposed getting rich by selling pollywogs."

"You should drop some of those out, too, as a good-will gesture. By the way," Ruben said, "I ran into Jeff—he's an old Army buddy—at a maintenance shop here at San Luis Obispo. I stashed my cargo door in his hangar."

Ruben put the instruments back in his bag and zipped it closed, and Jerry paid the bill. Frank followed them away from the restaurant.

On the way to Ruben's plane, Jerry stowed one ticking ELT beside the hiking boots and the sleeping bags in the rear of his SUV. Ruben tossed his red canvas flight bag over one shoulder, and Frank held the other modified ELT close to his body and under his jacket.

Crossing the ramp, Frank noticed the red tail.

"So this is the Foxy Lady." Jerry admired Ruben's freshly painted Cessna 172 and its powerful engine, new radios, and refurbished interior. She had red wheel pants, a red belly, and racing stripes running down her body. "She's absolutely gorgeous, better than new. I love those red, gold, and blue stripes."

"That's clever," Frank said. "Tail number 167FL— Foxy Lady's initials."

Frank climbed into the back and cradled the orange cube in his lap. Jerry sat in the co-pilot's seat. Ruben flew eastward towards The Guards.

Frank watched the ground race by and slipped the ELT into one end of the canvas tube. He felt sand in there. In a few minutes, he recognized The Guards below. He thought the roofs on the Quonset huts would shine like beacons but the metal had weathered dull and dirt-like. The captain's camp blended into the landscape except for the foreign colors of his exotic plants. Circling two thousand feet above the encampment, Frank had a good view of the rifle range, the ponds, and the palm trees. He spotted his target area: the back fence.

Ruben descended to 500 feet and slowed the aircraft.

Frank unbuckled his seat belt and leaned over the back seat. Gripping the ELT, he put the canvas tube on the floor, the open end by the missing cargo door. Frank had to lean way over to let the ELT rest on the floor. He tangled his headset cord. Holding the top of the tube with his left hand, he opened it into the slipstream and gently pushed the ELT over the side. It bulged through the canvas tube like a meal in an anaconda and fell well beneath the Cessna's belly.

"Bombs away," Frank said into the headset, its wires wrapped around him. The orange cube dropped into the poison oak in the canyon outside Captain Fish Eyes' north fence.

"Hurry up, Frank! Too much weight towards the tail," Ruben yelled into the intercom. He rammed in full power. The engine screamed. Foxy Lady shuddered.

"Oh! Oh! Oh!" Frank turned and yanked the cord out of his headset. A cramp. His butt. He couldn't stand. He couldn't sit. He grimaced and closed his eyes. The airplane bucked.

"Move forward!" Jerry shouted. "It's going to stall!"

"I can't lower the nose. Move forward." Ruben pushed forward on the yoke against the tail-heavy forces. The stall-warning horn shrieked.

Frank leaned over the back of Jerry's seat, moving his weight forward. He massaged his cramped anatomy with both hands and opened his eyes. The Quonset hut marked HQ at The Guards filled the entire window. "No! No! Don't hit the roof!"

Under that roof, the captain sat correcting chemistry exams at his desk and listening to background music. "They do the experiments, but they never get how to balance a simple equation," he said, talking to himself and shaking his head. In his mind, he structured a thorough review, something to capture their lively imaginations.

The roar of a small plane—low and overhead—drowned out Bach and demanded his attention. Aquila grabbed his binoculars and stepped outside. What a beauty: a little Cessna with gold, red, and blue stripes on the body and a red belly and red tail. Did it lose its cargo door in flight? How peculiar: someone stood between the seats.

Flying too low—only fifty feet above the roof. Buzzing his school.

He heard its stall horn. For a moment, he thought it would land on his head or crash onto the roof. Aquila ducked behind the building and jotted down the tail number.

The stall horn squealed. The Cessna shuddered.

Jerry braced himself against the instrument panel and moved his body weight as far forward as possible. Frank leaned forward over the back of Jerry's seat. Ruben gave the Cessna full right rudder and pushed down on the yoke.

Ruben righted the airplane. Low enough to count the ribs in the corrugated roof at The Guards. Low enough to cost a pilot his license.

His voice loud to mask his fear, Jerry said, "Everything's fine. Nobody's down there."

Frank reinstalled his headset and refastened his seatbelt. It hurt to sit. For a moment, he had thought Ruben would land on top of a Quonset hut.

"Passengers okay?" Ruben asked, leveling Foxy Lady.

"Good to go." Jerry readjusted his seatbelt.

"Fine," Frank lied. He had thought they'd buy the farm. His butt still hurt.

"Everything's A-OK." Ruben turned back toward San Luis Obispo.

Jerry dialed the modified emergency frequency from the ELT just dropped into the aircraft radio, blasting Frank's ears with a fire-engine siren sound. The little fake was doing its job—the arrow on the direction finder pointed towards the drop zone.

Jerry turned off the emergency signal. "Hey, Frank, the last time we used that canvas bag we sprinkled Elvis' ashes over the mountain."

"What was he doing here? He's buried at Graceland in Tennessee."

"Don't listen to him," Ruben said. "That canvas tube is for releasing *cremains*—that's what they call the ashes. If you throw them out the window at these speeds, you sandblast the tail and take off all the paint."

"So that sand I got on my hands was—somebody?" Frank's stomach flip-flopped. He found an airsick sack and held it at the ready. Definitely a mistake: going with Jerry.

Jerry had a second ELT to deliver to The Guards.

An hour after Ruben landed his Cessna at San Luis Obispo, Jerry and Frank departed to the east in the SUV for a two-hour drive over rough roads. Besides water, they carried deli sandwiches and apples and their signature breakfast—granola, bananas, and instant coffee. Frank hoped they wouldn't need the picnic supplies; he felt queasy when he thought about returning to The Guards. He worked on controlling his breathing.

Too soon Jerry parked the SUV out of sight near the west boundary of The Guards. Frank didn't want to be here. They wore camouflage fatigues and hiked silently along the fence toward the double palm oasis. Jerry and Frank stood sheltered by scrub brush, the same place as three weeks ago.

"Are you sure we need two fake bombs?" Frank whispered, his voice more a croak—not an omen, he hoped. He saw no one and heard no voices.

"Makes the plan fail-safe." Jerry's voice showed no anxiety whatsoever.

Frank didn't want to do this. He held a canvas bag close to his body and crept to the fence. Two small Cessna trainers, their engines whining, circled overhead. Practicing maneuvers and stall recovery. Only this morning, Frank had thought Foxy Lady would stall for real.

Jerry pointed up. "Circling like that, the aircraft could be searching for a bomb. Perfect for our cover story."

"Well, we're in it now." Frank stood up and brushed himself off. He turned on the second ELT and packed it into a 40-gallon black plastic refuse bag while Jerry assembled his fifteen-foot swimming pool hook.

Jerry suspended the little orange ticker on the hook and lifted it over the west fence. He slipped it off in bushes near the palm pond and retracted the sections of the pool hook. The direction finder had a second target.

Frank scrambled through the brush to the relative safety of Jerry's SUV. His heart hammered near panic and beat as fast as a hummingbird's. Someone could have seen them. The captain would recognize them immediately.

Back at his van, Jerry changed into his flight suit, still bearing the colonel's epaulets on the shoulders. This time, the pant legs were hemmed, and Frank had removed the insignia from his matching suit. He was strictly back-up—he hoped. Let *the colonel* look good one more time, for the sentry at the gate.

"Well, this is it, buddy," Jerry said. "Ready?"

Frank shrugged. "Here we go, ready or not." He wasn't ready. Jerry's chimerical plan was dangerous and absurd.

"The captain knows us from last time. Are you sure this will work?"

"Why not? The National Guard does all sorts of searches."

Frank followed Jerry down the driveway to the gate, the one beneath the mirror image *Guards* sign. Jerry held the direction finder box, its antenna standing up proudly. Frank held an official-looking envelope addressed *To Whom it May Concern,* a recycled envelope he had addressed yesterday in a burst of brilliance. Just the envelope: for appearances.

The colonel in the National Guard flight-suit strutted like he owned the place and addressed the sentry. "We need to speak to the captain. We need permission to walk through The Guards."

The sentry stood at attention and said nothing.

"The satellite system shows a radio signal in this area, a possible bomb." Jerry flipped on the audio, producing a wailing siren-sound. He stood tall as though he expected to be obeyed.

The sentry didn't ask any questions before he used his wall phone.

Jerry moved a few feet away from the gate and faced the Quonset huts. "See, what did I tell you? We'll get the captain's name in ten minutes and be on our way."

A sergeant arrived in two minutes. "This way. The captain is waiting."

16.

Jerry and Frank followed a sergeant too young for his uniform but carrying a rifle to a Quonset hut sandwiched between two other identical buildings and facing the large one marked HQ. The Guards: the same buildings as three weeks ago. Surreal, Frank thought; he had an anxiety attack while Jerry seemed ready to picnic. He felt like a compressed spring with no release button. He wanted to ask someone the captain's name and leave this place.

Inside the corrugated-metal half-cylinder, Frank saw a bare gray metal desk, a bare wall opening into a bare hall with padlocked doors on either side. More like a brig than a school. Frank didn't like the looks of it but Jerry seemed unconcerned.

The sergeant directed them to put cell phones, digital cameras, wallets, wristwatches, and pocketknives—all their loose objects—into a gray plastic tray, like security at the airport. "Captain's orders, security measures," he said.

He patted them down and had them sit beside a table, hands on top, under a hanging bright bulb. Not like security at the airport.

The temperature dropped ten degrees when Captain Fish Eyes strode into the room. His unblinking eyes focused on Jerry's face. With no preliminaries, he said, "Where is KAY-der?"

"What is KAY-der?" Jerry countered, moving his hands into a more comfortable position and slouching in the chair. A soldier with a croquet mallet took a position behind his right shoulder. A second soldier held a rifle.

"Hands on the table. You will tell us about KAY-der or the corporal will soften your thumbs. Show him."

The sledgehammer-croquet mallet bounced off the metal table with a resounding bang. The table bounced and vibrated. Startled, Jerry pulled both hands back.

Frank jumped at the sound and put his hands in his lap. A game of chicken played with a hammer and an amplified kettledrum.

"Hands on the table. Where's KAY-der?"

A rifle muzzle rested against Jerry's ribs.

"I don't know."

"Show him, just a little rap on the knuckles."

The sledgehammer came down across Jerry's right hand, a glancing, bruising, stinging blow. He pulled away reflexively. He didn't cry out. When the sergeant nudged him with a rifle, Jerry flattened his hand against the table. His face registered pain.

"You're supposed to rap students' knuckles with a ruler, not a hammer. I don't know anything about KAY-der. And if I did, I would never tell."

This time the sledgehammer came down on Jerry's right thumb. Jerry screamed in agony and almost passed out.

Frank, hearing the crunching, crushing of bone, almost fainted.

"Why is this envelope empty?" The captain waved To-Whom-it-May-Concern at Frank and froze him with a glacial stare.

"Uh, uh, . . . They must have forgotten to sign the letter." Frank's cheeks flushed heat. He felt his fair skin redden. Caught, caught in a lie. He sat ramrod straight, poker faced with his hands in his lap.

"Why did you plant a *bomb* at my school?" The captain's eyes held Frank captive.

"Uh, uh . . . I didn't. We followed a signal from a satellite."

Cold sweat beaded on Frank's forehead. He lifted a hand to point. "The direction finder—it's over there—in the tray . . ."

"Hands on the table. Why did you come to my school . . . with a *bomb*?"

The captain spit out the words, like sand in a picnic hotdog. He beckoned the sledgehammer bearers to close in on Frank's side of the table and asked, in cold and measured tones, "Why would a school hide a bomb?"

Frank, mesmerized by those reptilian eyes, said nothing. He shifted his gaze to the captain's lips.

"I'll leave him for you," Captain Fish Eyes said when Frank didn't answer. Frank thought he heard " . . . dream mushrooms . . . call me when he decides to talk . . . make that red-throated finch sing."

After the captain left the room, the corporal tied Frank and Jerry to their chairs with plastic lock strips and stood behind them with a rifle.

The sergeant focused on Frank. "What do you know about KAY-der?"

"Nothing." Frank made eye contact with the questioner. He hoped his direct gaze signaled he was telling the truth.

"You will tell us, *now!*"

The hammer wielder smacked Frank's knuckles, a warning blow that bounced his hand off the table. Frank screamed. No sense pretending to be brave. His hand throbbed and sent little pain needles up his arm.

"But don't you want to know about the bomb?"

The corporal and the sergeant stepped back and held a whispered conversation, glancing back and forth at Frank and Jerry. Then the hammer-wielder started towards the table—homing in on Frank's thumb.

"Wait!" Jerry cried out. "He doesn't know anything either. I'll tell. Let me tell the captain, anything he wants." Jerry sounded in control. He worked his jaw muscles and his upper lip glistened with perspiration.

The sledgehammer-bearers marched out of the room and left Frank and Jerry tied upright with their arms straight out.

"Try not to move," Jerry warned. "If we struggle, that plastic band will cinch in, ever tighter." Rhythmic waves of pain swept up Jerry's right arm to the shoulder. "Hurts. I feel nauseated."

Fifteen minutes later, Captain Fish Eyes appeared in the open doorway. His head just cleared the frame. "I knew it wouldn't be long," he said, icicle words, his gray hair like hoarfrost, his eyes frigid, piercing into Jerry.

"Look, I'll tell you whatever you want to know. That sledgehammer isn't doing either of us any good. Why don't I tell you my story, you get a lie detector?" Jerry, unmoving, stared directly into those unyielding eyes.

"That won't be necessary." The captain stood silently. After a long pause, he asked in a normal voice, "Where is KAY-der?"

"My geography isn't very good." Jerry's hand, now numb, ached. The nausea had passed. "What is this really about? It's about the Cessna, isn't it?"

The captain showed no emotion and didn't answer.

"Our airplane was stolen from Palo Alto Airport. The insurance company won't pay without proof. We tried to find it, but nobody knew anything."

"So what were you doing, *here*? We certainly have no airstrip."

Pokerfaced, Jerry sat straight and proud. "We were camping in the wilderness area and wanted to see your mushrooms."

"That was last time. Why did you come back?"

"It was your eyes. We described you when we told our friends about your mushrooms. They said you sounded like someone they knew."

"What about my *eyes*?" The captain moved nearer. Loud. Angry. "Why did you bring a *bomb*?"

Jerry didn't flinch. "Because you stole our airplane, Captain. Someone saw you around Palo Alto Airport. We want to know why."

The sledgehammer came down again on Jerry's tender knuckles and his thumb. His hand flew into the air. He screamed. Out of pure stubbornness, he sat still on the chair.

"I ask the questions here." Captain Fish Eyes pointed to two men carrying rifles. "Cut them off the chairs. Take them to my office."

The knife that cut Frank free sliced through the sleeve of his flight suit and nicked his upper arm. A fine line of blood filled the red indentation in his flesh as the feeling returned to his arms and hands. Escorted by rifles, Frank and Jerry walked to the Quonset hut marked HQ.

"Here you go." One soldier pushed them through the doorway. The other locked them in. Frank stumbled and caught himself with his injured hand. He thought his whole arm would explode.

Jerry groaned and sank onto a chair with his head between his knees.

Frank recognized the office from before. This time, the captain's desk was bare. No computer, no telephone, no outbox, no untidy pile of papers. The overhead light blazed harshly and the room was too warm.

Jerry opened the door to the toilet with his left-hand and fumbled with his trousers. "Hey, Frank, this is embarrassing. Can you help me unzip my pants?"

Frank stared at Jerry's right hand with its purple thumb. "Could be worse. The KGB would have pulled out your nail. Good thing we're both left-handed."

Frank's hand hurt but he could function. After he re-zipped Jerry, Frank opened each drawer and cupboard, searching for anything useful. In the right top desk drawer, he found an engraved nameplate mounted on a piece of polished wood.

"Captain A. V. Wachter. *Wachter*—that's guard in German, or watcher, give or take an umlaut. I remember because *Wachter* and *Watcher* are anagrams."

Jerry eyes appeared vacant.

After a few seconds of silence, Frank said, "If the V stands for *Vogel*, then his name means 'A Bird Watcher.' Trivia takes your mind off your troubles. Now we know his name for the FBI."

"Watch—did you find a clock? What time do you suppose it is?" Jerry face had a dazed expression. "Where's my phone? I didn't call Ruben."

"Don't you remember? They took everything. No, I haven't found a clock. Only a cough drop, some Tums, and a ballpoint pen."

Frank studied the bare bulletin board. "The cupboards are bare. Even the walls are bare."

"Here's the plan. That lie detector thing was a play for time."

"Plan? Always the damned plan. Where did that get us?" Frank slammed the door to the john. "Down the toilet, that's where."

"But if it comes to that, we can pass the test. We don't know any *KAY-der*. We met a Robert *Kuh-DAR* Herold."

"They aren't going to give us any test . . . just shoot us at dawn."

"We didn't find the airplane. Brad told us about the birdwatcher—"

"They'll never let us go, you know. We know too much. When they get tired of asking questions, they'll just dig a deep hole in the wilderness."

"Think positive. Inventory the office. Make a back-up plan. Start by flushing these cigarette butts down the toilet."

"That's not good for the septic tank."

"The septic tank? You're worried about their septic tank? It probably has an alligator in it, and they'll chop us up for alligator snacks."

Frank flushed the toilet. The butts went down. "Geez—they turned the water off. No more water."

"No cups anyway."

"They left two bites of donut and half a cup of coffee. I could sure use a cup of coffee. And an aspirin." Frank poked the donut scrap with a spoon.

"That's it. A coffee cup with a saucer." Jerry dumped the stale coffee down the sink. "Here. You take one of these ventilator covers off, reach down in the terrarium, and trap one of those ants."

"Jerry—they're bullet ants. Remember? What if one stings me?"

"Just don't touch it. Trap it in the cup with the saucer, like this." Jerry set the saucer on top of the cup with his good hand. "I'd do it myself if I could use both hands."

"Nothing doing. Let's search some more." Frank methodically opened more drawers and cupboards. Under the terrarium, he found a pair of tweezers. Against his better judgment, he put the long tweezers into the ventilation tube and captured one inch-long stinging ant. He pulled the ant out carefully and dropped it into the cup, covering it quickly with the saucer. Then he put the cup on the desk, replaced the ventilator cover, and returned the tweezers to the cupboard.

"Now use that napkin and put the donut scrap on the floor." Jerry pointed to a spot in front of the door. "Rub it around with the napkin. Don't touch it with your hand and don't step on it."

"What good is that?"

"When we hear them unlock the door, you dump the ant onto the donut crumbs and jump back here. We'll see if they like ants in the pants."

"I'll sprinkle a few drops of spit on the donut," Frank said. "The bullet ant likes sugar but he takes it in liquid form. In the Amazon, he eats small insects and drinks nectar."

"I hope this one likes donuts. It'll be confused and mad, and it'll climb up a leg. Then *ants in the pants*."

They convulsed with laughter, the gallows humor of convicted men.

Before long, Frank heard someone fumbling with the lock. He unleashed the ant in front of the door by the donut crumbs and jumped back. Two soldiers with rifles opened the door and stood by the ant.

"The captain wants to see you," said the sergeant. The soldier with no rank stood next to the ant. He shifted his weight from one leg to the other, then stepped forward one step, squashing some sweet crumbs with his heel.

Would he step on the ant? Frank held his breath.

"Can I have some water first—you've got some in that canteen." Jerry looked pleadingly from one soldier to the other.

Soldier No-Rank unsnapped his canteen and unscrewed the lid.

"Put that away, Cadet. The captain has orange juice for the captives."

"I need to pee." Frank moved towards the toilet, glancing at the ant over his shoulder. *Hurry up, ant!*

"Come on—let's go."

Frank saw the ant climbing up on the cadet's shoe, the one covering the sugar from the donut. "Just a second. I have to zip."

The cadet hooked his canteen onto his belt and brushed his pant leg.

Frank's mind blanked out. Where is that lazy ant?

The soldiers turned toward the door. The one on the right shrieked. He slapped his leg, dropped his rifle, and rolled on the floor—still screaming. The standing soldier—the sergeant—propped his rifle against the desk and leaned over to help the cadet.

Jerry grabbed the rifle with his good hand and swung the butt against the sergeant's head. The young soldier crumpled to the floor like a paper wad headed for the wastepaper basket. Then Jerry hit the screamer for good measure.

"Come on, Frank." Jerry leaned the rifle against the wall, opened the door and held it with his foot. Hoisting the gun over his left shoulder, he said, "Steal the ball from the opposing team."

Frank picked up the other rifle and followed Jerry out into the moonlight, dark behind the buildings. "Which way? What if they see us?"

"We'll walk out the main gate."

Frank studied every shadow. He saw no one. Jerry crept up on a single sentry who leaned against the wall with his chin on his chest, asleep on duty.

"Help him take a longer nap," Jerry whispered. With his good arm, he hit the sleeper with the butt of the rifle. The sentry folded up and fell to the ground in slow motion—just like in the movies.

Frank picked the rifle up from the ground—just in case. Then Jerry handed him the one used against the sentry. Now Frank had all three rifles, heavy and hard to hold. He banged his sore hand. He bit his lip to keep from crying out.

"Freedom," Frank said, when he walked under the arched sign, *The Guards.* "For a while, I thought we wouldn't leave alive."

"Amazing what a little adrenaline can do."

Moving over the rough ground, they stumbled down the road to Jerry's SUV, Frank juggling all those rifles, Jerry walking slowly behind Frank.

"What time do you have?" Jerry asked. "I have to call Ruben."

"They took it away, remember? Not morning yet. Too dark to drive."

"There's a spare key in the wheel well. I'll walk with the flashlight, help you stay on the road. Don't turn on the lights."

Twenty minutes seemed like two hours. Frank moved the SUV a mile down the road and stopped, sheltered from view by a few trees.

"I'm about done in." Jerry sagged into the seat, his right thumb as big as his wrist. Frank fashioned a sling out of a towel and a bungee cord to hold Jerry's hand above his heart and close to his chest. Before he passed out, Jerry muttered, "Finally, finally, somebody's going to get Old Fish Eyes."

Frank turned the key in the ignition. The engine died. Frank's heart hammered. This couldn't be happening.

After three anxious minutes, the engine caught. Frank expected to see a vehicle from The Guards on his tail at any moment.

At dawn on Sunday after a sleepless night filled with worry about Jerry and Frank, Ruben sat on the edge of Jeff's couch and tied his shoelaces. He never could sleep on couches, but it was better than a motel. He smelled coffee brewing in Jeff's kitchen, and he really needed a caffeine jolt. No telephone message from Jerry to verify that he was safe. Before he said good morning, Ruben called the sheriff.

After a bowl of cereal, Ruben and Jeff set out for The Guards in Jeff's red four-wheel-drive truck. Forty minutes later, a dark and dusty SUV approached on a road so narrow that Jeff backed up for half a mile before he was able to turn around. Both vehicles stopped.

It had to be Jerry's SUV—who else would be out here in the wilderness so early on a Sunday morning? A slumped over passenger, his eyes closed, leaned against the right front door. Ruben opened the truck's window and yelled, "What happened to you guys? Jerry looks like a coyote carcass."

Frank opened the door of Jerry's SUV and eased his way out onto the deeply rutted dirt road. "Jerry's wounded. We thought they were going to *kill* us."

Jeff leaned out of the truck's opened door. "Climb in here with me. Ruben can drive Jerry to emergency in the SUV."

Ruben hopped out. "See you later, alligator."

"Wise ass. We'll watch your tail, make sure you can find the place."

Frank climbed into Jeff's truck. Jeff was Ruben's old Army buddy, an aircraft mechanic at San Luis Obispo. He met Jeff briefly once—it seemed two years ago but it must have been Saturday morning—was it only yesterday? Frank was glad to let Jeff drive, following Jerry's SUV over the dirt road.

In a few minutes, both vehicles pulled over to make way for the sheriff's caravan: two sedans and a prisoner transport van. Frank said, "I hope they throw those sledgehammer guys into the slammer."

Jeff swerved away from a pothole. "Yeah. What happened in there?"

Frank filled Jeff in on the way back to San Luis Obispo. " . . . The captain stole our airplane and he's training terrorists."

"Out there in the sticks? Doesn't make sense. If you want to steal an airplane, why go to a towered airport?"

"Good questions. We're going to the FBI as soon as we get back."

Somewhere along the road back, Jeff loaned Frank his cell phone to call Mary. "Honey, I can't tell you everything over the phone. Jerry's been hurt, broken fingers and thumb—"

"What happened? Are you okay?" Mary's voice, soothing and concerned, made Frank want to hold her.

"Yes, I'm fine. It's a long story." No sense worrying his wife—his hand throbbed with every lurch and bump.

"Part of this misadventure, we both lost our wallets. Can you cancel the credit cards? Tell the school we won't be there tomorrow. I'll give you an update tonight." Frank closed the cell phone and rested his right elbow above the open window on the truck, keeping his right hand above his head to ease the swelling and pain. He wanted a handful of aspirin. He needed a nap, or a cup of coffee, . . . something. His scratchy eyes stung.

Before long, Jeff pulled into the emergency room parking lot and walked into the hospital with Frank. Even though the swelling across Frank's knuckles prevented finger movement, the x-ray showed nothing broken. Only deep bruises. The doctor wrapped Frank's hand with fluorescent pink tape, gave him a prescription for pain, and admonished, "No driving or operating heavy machinery."

Frank felt almost normal, but his sore hand had taken away his appetite. A cup of hospital brew and a doughnut patched him together. Afterwards, he followed Jeff six floors up to find Room 617.

The antiseptic hospital smell hit Frank, like whatever his mother had used to wipe off doorknobs combined with chlorine bleach stink. He swallowed down a nearly ejected doughnut and followed Jeff two halls down.

The door to Room 617 was open. Jerry, pale and tired looking, wore the usual open-in-the-back hospital gown and had a needle in his arm with a plastic tube leading to two bags of liquid. Ruben slouched in a straight back chair.

"The sheriff's on the way," Jeff said.

"Then they got him—got Old Fish Eyes?" Jerry waved his lime-green bandage. "Oh, ouch—that was a mistake."

"We don't know yet if they caught him," Jeff said. "How's that hand?"

"How do you like this bright green? It was lime green, or hot pink." Jerry almost made sense, even though he spoke through a morphine haze. "They're going to rebuild my pollex on Tuesday in Palo Alto. Reconstitute it, just like Ruben's broken airplanes."

"I got the pink kind." Frank displayed his hand like a badge of honor.

"Easy for the sheriff to find you, with those glowing bandages," Jeff said. "They booked the soldiers who slammed your hands, but they can only hold the others for twenty-four hours."

"That's all?" Jerry said from the bed. "The ELT will stop transmitting before they get back to camp."

"That's right. It was a used one," Ruben said, standing by the bed.

Frank fell asleep in the only chair in the room, his pink bandage resting on a wooden arm, until someone opened the door.

A nurse's aide escorted two uniformed officers into the room. "Visitors," she said. "I'll bring more chairs."

Deputy Jones hid behind a bushy beard and an oversized blue clipboard. Deputy Evans dropped his hat on the bed and unfolded two chairs.

"You missed out on all the excitement at The Guards," Jones said from the foot of Jerry's bed. "We went in with two sedans and a prisoners' van. Lucky it wasn't raining . . . those rough roads. Nobody at the gate."

"You passed us on our way out," Frank said. "I hope you nabbed the one with the sledgehammer."

"We arrested everyone in camp: fifteen cadets, three sergeants, and three disabled sentries. Two of them have concussions. Lucky thing you didn't kill anybody."

"Kill somebody? We thought somebody was going to kill *us*," Jerry said. "What about the captain?"

"No captain." The deputy glanced back at his clipboard.

"Old Fish Eyes got away?" Jerry shot straight up, and a piece of plastic tubing popped out of the drip system.

"Guess so. We didn't find him. He could have driven east somewhere."

"What about the rifles?" Frank asked. "They all had rifles."

"You mean the three 22s in your van? They weren't loaded, and they hadn't been fired."

Frank frowned. "They looked like cannons to us."

"You only lock them up overnight?" Jerry sank back against the mattress.

"Sorry. We'll keep the one who slammed your thumb until trial after we take your sworn statement. We'll represent you in the Prelim." Jones handed Jerry pictures to identify the culprit.

"Don't worry, Jerry," Frank said. "We have the captain's name for the FBI."

On the Tuesday afternoon after the trip to The Guards, Frank sat at his desk at home and stared at the phone. Unlike Jerry, he hated the telephone. He had to report the captain's name to the FBI. He drew a beard onto a basketball player on the sports page before he dialed Agent Matthews.

"This is Frank Peterson. I was in your office three weeks ago." Frank squinted his eyes shut and pictured the agent's shaggy brows and blue tie to give an identity to the talking head on the other end of the line.

"Jerry Christensen and I went to The Guards to find the captain's name, as requested. He is A. V. Wachter. That's W-A-C-H-T-E-R—"

"Three weeks ago?" Agent Matthews interrupted. "I sent you to some guards? Who the heck are they?"

"But, you said you needed the captain's name." Frank scribbled madly with a ballpoint pen on one corner of the newspaper.

"He's a terrorist, and he stole our airplane. His school isn't licensed by the State, either."

"Say, weren't you the ones with the ants?" The agent muffled a laugh.

"Yes—and that's how we escaped." Frank frowned, remembering. "This time, they tortured us with a sledgehammer."

"You went to a school and they tortured you?" Agent Matthews sounded like he was choking.

"Yes. They smashed our hands." Frank started to perspire. "You can call the county sheriff. They arrested several people from The Guards on Sunday."

"Humph . . . a sledgehammer. Unbelievable. Sounds like the sheriff has everything under control. What does all this have to do with a stolen airplane?"

Frank's heart beat faster and blood rushed to his head. He felt helpless, the interview out of control. "But we got his name—he stole our airplane. The FBI has to help us!"

"This case is closed. Closed!" Agent Matthews sounded loud and angry. "In fact, I haven't opened it, so there's no case number."

"Case closed? No, wait—"

"I don't want to know about ants that shoot bullets and rifles that shoot paint." Clank-buzz. Buzz, dial tone.

Heat flashed across Frank's face. "Buzz off, you jerk."

Frank felt weak, ineffectual, and insignificant. He put his head down on his desk and pulled his hair with one hand. The other hand hurt.

Frank scratched out the bearded basketball player—tearing a hole through the paper—before he made his daily call to Jerry. "How's that thumb? Still big enough to need its own cell phone?"

"Hey, you're the one who needs a cell phone. My thumb's fine—as long as you call it *sir*. No . . . really . . . it's sore as a boil."

Frank crumpled the torn paper and threw it into the wastebasket. "Say listen, I just hung up with Agent Matthews from the FBI. I gave him the captain's name and told him about your thumb. He said the case was closed."

"FBI not interested in terrorist activity? Unbelievable," Jerry said. "What are we spending our taxpayers' dollars on?"

"Unbelievable—that's what he said, too." Frank sighed.

"Okay. No help from the FBI. We have to catch Fish Eyes ourselves."

17.

Jerry couldn't fly with the cast on his thumb, a lime-green cast that ran halfway up his arm with wires protruding from each finger. He sat next to Frank in a rented Cessna and tried to scratch his encapsulated wrist. Approaching San Luis Obispo, Frank pointed out three tall smokestacks and Morro Rock out in the bay. Frank's wife Mary, her dark brown hair tucked under a headset, perched on the back seat behind Frank and followed their flight on the San Francisco Sectional Chart with one finger. She showed The Sisters and the butte right in downtown San Luis Obispo to Sally, who sat quietly behind Jerry. Sally gripped the armrest and didn't smile until after Frank landed.

The special Mother's Day brunch at Spirit of San Luis rivaled that in a cruise ship. When they were down to savoring the coffee and watching the airplanes land, Jerry pushed his chair away from the table. "I need to thank Jeff over at Coast Aircraft Maintenance for helping us after Captain Fish Eyes roughed us up."

"Save my coffee, honey," Frank said. He followed Jerry out the door.

Mary pushed Frank's chair out of the way and made herself comfortable. "After what happened two weeks ago, Frank felt a bit anxious coming here. I was surprised that Jerry would want to come back, even with the lure of terrific food."

"I told Jerry the place had bad karma, but he didn't listen." Sally opened her sketchbook and a small backpack containing watercolors, pens, brushes, and a small bottle that she filled from her water glass. She made a fast sketch of the toddler at the next table and tinted his face and hair.

Mary reached for the sketchbook and admired the drawings: delicate portraits in watercolor on paper half the size of a business letter. Sally herself made a lovely picture with the light falling on her long honey-blond hair, like a Vermeer painting. "These are good. You should try a self-portrait.

"A drawing of myself wouldn't be interesting."

"Why not?" Mary asked, handing the book back to Sally. "You have good bones, and those hazel eyes are striking. You don't have to cut off one ear."

Sally laughed and sketched Mary. She caught her green eyes with the watercolor. "It's the eyes," she said. "They express personality more than any other facial feature. When I get them right, the portrait's good. I'd like to see that captain's eyes for myself."

"Now there's a scary idea." Mary frowned and shifted in her chair. "Jerry told Frank he'd recognize those eyes anywhere. The other kids probably made fun of the captain at school."

"So . . . you'd like to see them, too."

"Like opening Pandora's box." Mary laughed.

"See the old woman with the hat? She has wonderful eyes and laugh wrinkles." Sally made another three-minute sketch and tinted it.

"Are you drawing me?" The woman with the hat jumped up and rushed to their table. "I love it. Can I buy it?"

"Here—I'll give it to you." Sally tore out the page.

The white haired gentleman from the next table leaned over Sally's shoulder. "Could you do my wife for Mother's Day? We've been married 55 years." Several other people surrounded Sally and watched her work.

An hour later, Sally closed her sketchbook and checked her watch.

"He'll be back," Mary said. "That's just what pilots do—talk airplanes, fly airplanes, dream airplanes, land once in a while when their bladders are overfull."

"Don't they ever stay home? That airplane is more competition than another woman. And I'm not comfortable riding in the things. Jerry's always gone longer than he says and I worry the whole time and he never calls me."

"He should call—that's only polite. He teaches with Frank—couldn't afford that plane if you didn't work—and you clean and cook while he plays. He has it way too easy. You should have a Vesuvius. Throw a royal fit."

Frank and Jerry had left their wives in the restaurant at San Luis Obispo Airport to look up Jeff, who had taken them to the hospital after the debacle at The Guards. The maintenance hangers and other aviation businesses lined up at the far end of the runway; Coast Aviation was locked. Jerry banged on the door and peered through a small window. "I'm sure this is where Jeff works."

"Well, it is Sunday," Frank said. "Let's go back."

"Look, Jeff's over there." Jerry waved his good hand wildly and raced towards a moving aircraft, a Cessna on the taxiway.

The aircraft stopped. Jeff yelled out over the engine noise, "I brake for glowing green bandages, lime-green casts, too. How the heck are you?"

Frank, moving slower than Jerry as usual, couldn't hear the answer.

"Hey, hop in," Jeff said. "I'm going up."

Frank climbed into the back seat. Before he buckled in, he reached over the seat to help Jerry fasten the seat belts and lock the door. Jerry and Jeff used the intercom; Frank held his hands over his ears to block out the engine noise. He saw no movement when Jeff circled over The Guards. Nothing seemed to have changed in two weeks.

Fifteen minutes later, Jeff landed and taxied to the self-service fuel-pump. When he shut the engine down, Frank could hear again.

"Exactly how does that thing work?" Jerry asked Jeff. "Do you close it down, like, at night?"

"We just leave it on. You have to put in a credit card before it will pump." Jeff demonstrated, filling the tanks.

"Can you turn it off, disable it?" Jerry walked behind the pump, looking for something or other.

"Sure—why? Takes less than three minutes." Jeff rolled up the hose.

"Just wondered," Jerry said. Frank couldn't imagine why Jerry would want to disable a fuel pump. Then Jerry spread out Jeff's California charts right there on the tarmac, and Jeff highlighted every airport where he knew a mechanic.

"This is amazing," Jerry said, squatting down and tapping the map for Northern California. "If you add airports where Ruben knows somebody, you could connect the entire state with a mechanics' network like a big spider's web."

"Don't be so surprised," Frank said. "You only need six degrees of separation to be connected to anyone on earth, by a friend-of-a-friend relationship. I know Jerry, that's one degree. Somebody Jerry knows, makes two degrees."

"Okay, Doctor Arachnid," Jerry said. "Maybe a spider's web will net Captain Fish Eyes."

"Say, that's what you call the thief, isn't it," Jeff said. "I know how he got in to steal One-Eight Echo. You can open most locks on older Cessnas, using the key of another one of similar vintage." Jeff used the key from the Cessna he had just fueled to open one tied down for maintenance, with considerable jiggling in the lock.

"Easier than stealing a car, I guess," Frank said. "I had never thought about breaking into someone's Cessna."

"That's it, how Fish Eyes did it for sure." Jerry folded Jeff's maps, not easy while wearing a cast. He used the cast to balance a clipboard and recorded Jeff's phone number and e-mail address with his good hand. "I don't have a plan yet but having a network of mechanic-friends is sure to help."

"What—no plan? That's a first," Frank said. He pictured Captain Fish Eyes, low on fuel, caught red-handed in a stolen Cessna . . . but he knew stopping the crafty captain wouldn't be that easy. What preposterous plan would Jerry propose next?

Sunday mornings were busy at Wings Grill at Auburn Airport, especially on a clear, warm day, more especially on Mother's Day. Aquila relaxed at a table with a good view of landing traffic, outside near the taxiway by the fuel-island. He had tucked his gray hair under a baseball cap and hidden his eyes behind aviator's sunglasses. Behind those glasses, he could be anybody.

People remembered his eyes. Even those loony redheaded pilots brought up his eyes. *Pesky finches.* How Aquila had hated it, when the other boys called him *ghost eyes* at school.

How did the red-throated finch and his buddy know about the explosives? A bomb at The Guards: *indeed.* They knew something about Kedar, his AWOL cadet. He had liked the kid, but Cadet Khazari failed his mission. He had thought that Muslim boys understood holy war.

The waitress—small, blond, and personable—brought him a stack of hot cakes, two fried eggs with bacon, orange juice, and coffee. She said her name was Robina and she already recognized him as a regular.

"Good morning Auburn Sunday," she said. "Here's extra syrup and if you need anything else, just trip me as I run by. If you ever come for breakfast on a weekday, I'll sit down and have coffee with you."

From the way Robina's eyes appraised him, he knew she'd go bird watching with him if he asked her. He wished she looked more like Dancing Dove. He had come to California for better weather for his special plants and with a secret dream: a woman to love, someone like his mother Dancing Dove. Or Califia, the Amazon warrior-queen from the mythical island of California—tall, her shiny black hair braided, hunting prairie grouse.

Aquila balanced a bite of pancake on the tip of his fork. He noticed more people at Wings than usual for Sunday. That's right, Mother's Day today. Yes, his mother. He hadn't seen her for years, since he was a boy. Not since he was five . . .

Hidden behind his grandmother's overstuffed chair, Aquila had heard his mother say, " . . . keep Aquila, just for a while. I registered him as a Warchet, a tribal member. He belongs here."

"I raised my family. It's your job to raise yours," his grandmother said.

"His father says he won't raise a half-breed with wild eyes . . . I'm dancing in a show in a big club in Las Vegas."

"So Dancing Dove is dancing, but there's no place in her life for kids."

Dancing Dove sat on a kitchen chair with her legs crossed at the knee and swinging one foot, wearing her red high-heeled shoes and a short tight black skirt. Peering around the chair, Aquila saw his mother's long fingernails painted red to match her lipstick. He had watched her rub rouge on her cheeks and draw her eyebrows.

The boy backed around the big chair on all fours, butt held high, in new jeans already too short. He noticed that one shoelace was untied. Glancing up from his shoes, he stared at two white-haired women standing silently outside the open door. They wore shirts decorated with beads and feathers. Aquila had wanted a shirt like that.

"Ak-wi-la, Ak-wi-la," one of them said, holding her arms wide in welcome. Then, pointing at herself, she said, "Ku-an-shi." Like an echo, the other one said, "Ku-an-shi."

The first old one bent down and took his hand. From outside, he heard his mother's voice, "Do they still insist upon sleeping in that teepee? He can't sleep out there on those dirty skins."

"You want to leave him here or not?" His grandmother sounded angry.

What was a teepee? *Ak-wee-lah Ku-an-shee* meant hello, how are you. Then he heard "Red warpaint" and "Dance a war dance" and they laughed.

Out behind the house he saw the *tipi* like an ice cream cone set upside down and made of skins. Inside were two sleeping places, furs set down neatly. One of the twins spread out three buffalo skins *ta-tan-ka*. They all sat cross-legged and drank bottles of flavored soda water *ka-pop-a-pi-da*.

"Ka-pop-a-pi-da," he parroted, and pointing at them, "Ku-an-shee." Slapping both hands against his chest, he said, "Ah-KWILL-ah." He liked word games, and he liked teepees. They spoke the Old Language in the *tipi*. They knew English but they weren't twins: one was his grandmother's mother, and the other, his grandmother's grandmother. With so many grandmothers, he couldn't call them all *Ku-an-shee*. The talkative one was Story Teller, and her daughter, Medicine Woman. When they used English, they called his grandmother Buffalo Mother because she had once saved a buffalo calf, but they scolded him when he called her *tatanka*, buffalo bull. Aquila spent most of his time with the old ones except for meal times when they all ate with Buffalo Mother in her kitchen. Sometimes he pretended that his mother was there, seated next to him at the table. He knew she'd come back for him soon because she hadn't told him goodbye.

That first summer Story Teller made him a pair of beaded moccasins to wear when he walked with Medicine Woman gathering herbs. She taught him to walk quietly and to listen to the forest and to call *zit-ka-da,* the small birds.

One night, Story Teller showed him the constellation Aquila the Eagle—its English name, learned from the wounded soldier she had saved, Medicine Woman's father, when she was young and pretty like Dancing Dove. She told stories about the Battle of Little Big Horn and the Winter of Big Cold and Hunger, when her *O-ji-jit-ka* Rosebud was born and when her parents and the soldier had died.

She called Aquila *Wam-bdi* Little Eagle, or *Wam-bdi-upi* Eagle Feather.

Aquila had loved Story Teller. His mother never came back . . .

At the table behind Aquila, someone sang, "Happy Mother's Day to you, happy Mother's Day to you," followed by laughter and without finishing the silly song. Aquila didn't feel like singing.

When Robina came back to refill his coffee cup, Aquila gave her one of his rare smiles. She was tiny. Would her chin be higher than his belt buckle? He liked her musical voice and her laugh.

Aquila had noticed that she flirted with Ruben. His Cessna had buzzed The Guards two weeks ago, the red-tailed Cessna always parked inside the hangar at Gold Country Aviation. Ruben had the women and the airplanes. That woodpecker Jerry did, too. Maybe he should send Jerry a message to register his disapproval.

Aquila dropped some bills on the table and stretched, then walked through the open patio. He strolled through a line of tied-down aircraft, admiring. Those for sale always parked outside.

18.

Jerry plopped Thursday's mail onto his kitchen table. A plain brown envelope beckoned from the top of the heap: hand-addressed to Jerry, postmarked Auburn, no return address. Something lumpy. Jerry had fallen into the habit of letting Sally open the mail; the cast made him clumsy. He tapped the envelope against the table. The lump shifted. He tore the package open using one hand and his teeth. White tissue paper padded a zip-lock bag holding . . . two bullet ants.

Jerry shot to his feet and shook the hand that had held the ants as though one crawled up his arm. Inch-long wasp-like ants, menacing even in death.

Fish Eyes—he sent the ants. He knew Jerry's address . . . of course: Fish Eyes kept his wallet. Fish Eyes was watching him.

Jerry's stomach roiled. He poured his fresh-brewed coffee down the sink and chewed an antacid tablet. Not wanting to upset Sally, he hid the ants in the back of his dresser drawer.

Later that evening, Jerry's new cell phone rang. This one incorporated a digital camera and video. Jerry laid it on the table to turn it on, using his left hand only: Ruben's number on the caller ID. He tossed the phone into the air and caught it on the way down.

"Hey, Ruben. What's up? Found any good planes lately?"

"For you, *amigo,* waiting for the worst crash I can find. There was one this week: a Cessna stolen from Auburn Airport Monday night."

"No kidding? Did they find it? Catch the guy?"

"Civil Air Patrol found it right away. Crashed going east, too low to clear the summit." Ruben paused, his voice serious. "The pilot's dead, only a kid."

"Captain Fish Eyes. He did it." Jerry's voice, and his blood pressure, rose. "He sent that kid into the mountains."

"His mother lives down the road. The pilot forgot to take his keys."

"That damned Fish Eyes set him up. A student wouldn't go that way, not over mountains, not at night." Jerry yelled into the phone. "We have to stop him."

"Calm down, *amigo*. Fish Eyes didn't do it. By the way, just last week someone stole a different Cessna. Abandoned it at a private strip."

"No kidding, two stolen within a week. That's more than in ten years."

"You got it."

Jerry signed off and put the cell phone back on the table. He was tired of reading its instruction book, tired of asking someone else to take him everywhere.

Not flying, Jerry had lots of time on his hands—or hand, as the case may be. He reviewed everything he knew about Captain Fish Eyes, still out there. Planting that lovely ticking orange cube at his home base . . .

Frank had been so careful, not scratching Foxy Lady. Flying low and slow . . .

Bingo! The captain had seen Foxy Lady. He could have read her tail number, traced her using that iMac on his desk. Foxy Lady was safe in Ruben's hangar at Gold Country Aviation. Only those aircraft in for service or for sale were tied down outside. Suppose Fish Eyes stole Foxy Lady. Where would he go? Not east. Not over the Sierras. Why did the student pilot go that way?

What if Captain Fish Eyes stole Foxy Lady, flew somewhere to get fuel, couldn't get any. All the fuel pumps closed down—a spider-web network of mechanics . . .
Double bingo!

Tomorrow at school he'd talk Frank into flying to Auburn for lunch with Ruben. Saturday would be good.

On a bright Saturday morning perfect for flying, Frank gave Jerry a ride to Auburn Airport in a rented Cessna. Frank hadn't seen Ruben since the fiasco at The Guards. One step behind Jerry as usual, he ducked under the half-open hangar door at Gold Country Aviation and watched Jerry wave his green cast in greeting.

Ruben was tightening a clamp on red hoses leading to the engine of a Piper that needed paint. He turned toward the door, still holding the wrench. "It's the colonel. Let me button this up."

Ruben reattached the cowling, then unzipped his shop coveralls and wiped a speck of grease off his nose. Finished, he clapped Jerry on the shoulder. "How's your hand, *amigo*?

"Better, thanks." Jerry glanced through the open door, making sure that they were alone. "Let's go into your office. This is top secret stuff."

"Top secret, huh? Why does that sound bad?"

"Watch out. He didn't tell me either," Frank said. "Just say no."

"You haven't heard the plan. This time it's brilliant."

Oh, oh, here we go, Frank thought. Another bingo moment and another outrageous plan.

Jerry dropped an aeronautical map of Northern California onto Ruben's desk. "First, mark all the airports on this chart where you know somebody. Go ahead—you'll be surprised. Frank said that a friend-of-a-friend relationship connects everyone on earth, with only six degrees of separation."

"What's that about?" Ruben asked.

"Well, you know Jeff at San Luis Obispo, and I know you, so that's two degrees of separation."

"Then mechanics only need two degrees of separation, *qué no*? We're a close-knit bunch."

Jerry added all the places where Ruben knew mechanics to Jeff's list from San Luis Obispo: someone at every airport within 150 miles. Enough to close down every fuel pump if they organized.

"Why turn off the fuel?" Frank raised a bushy eyebrow.

"Standard operating procedure: stolen aircraft. Call Northern California Approach Control to get the direction of flight. Then call every mechanic in that direction. Each one turns off a fuel pump and alerts a sheriff." Jerry sounded logical and smooth.

After a pause, Jerry said, "Perfect plan. Except for one thing."

"Somebody lives at the airport permanently." Ruben slouched in his chair and twiddled a pencil.

"I'm afraid I didn't tell you all of the plan. We need Foxy Lady for bait."

"No! No! No! *Not Foxy Lady*!" Ruben jumped to his feet, mouth opened wide, face frozen with horror.

"Jerr-rry—that's way too dangerous." Frank hit Ruben's desk with one fist and jumped up, knocking over his chair. "Wa-a-ay too far out."

"But here's why." Jerry, his voice low and calm, remained seated. "Do you remember when we dropped that ELT into the poison oak behind The Guards? Low and slow. Our bird-watching captain saw Foxy Lady and traced her to Auburn. He's sure to show up."

Frank had known dropping that orange emergency transmitter would get them into trouble, but he hadn't pictured giving Foxy Lady to Fish Eyes.

"Okay, then." Jerry's patient voice continued. "You said an aircraft is stolen once in ten years. What's the chance of someone else trying it? It's Fish Eyes specific. He'll land for fuel and we'll catch him before he knows what hit him. Your close-knit mechanics, they'll all want to guard Foxy Lady. We can't lose, and Fish Eyes can't win."

Ruben glared at Jerry. "I don't want him touching my airplane."

"Jerr-r-ry . . ." Frank's voice rose. "What if he wrecks it? Foxy Lady's too beautiful to use as a pawn." Frank was more worried by the minute. "This is a bad idea. Wild, dangerous, and completely outrageous."

"Situation under control. We can do it, catch Fish Eyes. Don't you want to make him pay for what he did?" Jerry sounded logical, controlled.

"Sure, I want to catch him, but I'll lose my airplane." Ruben's voice rose.

"Look—we *have* to do it. If something happens to Foxy Lady, I'll pay for it myself," Jerry said in a reasonable and confident manner. "I guarantee it. I'll guard her myself."

Jerry and Ruben haggled for an hour. Calm and insistent, Jerry repeated the same points over and over. Ruben would park Foxy Lady outside with a *For Sale* sign, but only daytimes unless Jerry watched all night. She had a barrel lock on her cabin door, not the original easy-to-spring Cessna lock. Each mechanic on the list would have to agree.

Frank recognized the broken record technique from his unsuccessful days selling vacuum cleaners. He knew Jerry had won when Ruben sat down.

"If you talk the mechanics into it . . . *all of them*."

Jerry divided the mechanics into three lists: one for Ruben to call from Auburn, one for Jeff at San Luis Obispo, and one for Jerry to do himself.

"You have north, south, and west covered. What if Fish Eyes flies east?" Frank, worried now, couldn't think of another counter-argument.

"He's not that crazy. Say what, I'll treat us to lunch." Jerry stretched and reached into his jacket pocket: the extra ACE Car Rental tracking bug, left in his SUV after his last misadventure. "Frank, you can put this onto Foxy Lady."

"No, I'll do it." Ruben reached out and grabbed the bug. "Nobody's opening the cowling on *my* baby."

"After all that work, I'm ready for pie and coffee," Frank said. "Do you think Captain Fish Eyes will take the bait?"

On Saturday morning Aquila leaned on his elbows and stared into space from his favorite spot in the patio at Wings Grill just off of the Auburn taxiway. He didn't drink his second cup of coffee. He didn't watch the experimental aircraft take off. *Robina.* She said her name was Robina. Her smile, warm and real, not like his daydream lady Califia, not like bright-lights-and-action Las Vegas women.

His coffee was cold. His grandmothers had called it *Black Medicine* in the Old Language. He remembered his beloved Story Teller, his great-great-grandmother, still lively when he was five. She lived to be a hundred. After all these years, he still felt sad whenever he remembered his grandmothers. Aquila had been ten years old when Story Teller died . . .

In Aquila's mind, he saw Story Teller wrapped in her buffalo robe, her snow-white hair neatly braided. She lay on her ta-tan-ka bed in her tipi. Little Eagle—afraid her spirit would fly away through her toothless mouth—knelt by her side and held back tears. She put her hand on the boy's head and looked at him with milky, blind eyes. He liked to watch her hands when she told stories, but this time her hands were still. In the Old Language she said, "He-who-watches-eagles will soar with eagles . . . high in the sky . . . close to the Great Spirit in *Paha Sapa* . . . a brave warrior chief."

A story told just for him. Touching one cold hand, he said, "Ku-an-shee."

When Story Teller pushed herself up and announced that she needed to go to *Paha Sapa*, he

161

thought she was better—until she said that her grandparents had gone there and she would die there, too.

Die there? Buffalo Mother explained that *Paha Sapa* was a sacred place, where the old ones used to go to die. *Ku-an-shee* was old. She wouldn't come this way again. Aquila had to be brave.

Maybe Medicine Woman would tell the old stories, over and over, like Story Teller. Maybe Buffalo Mother would remember about Spotted Face the raccoon, Red Claw the crawfish, Yellow Eye the coyote, *Unktomi* the spider, and Eagle Feather the brave warrior.

Story Teller called him *He-who-watches-eagles* and *Little Eagle,* but Buffalo Mother called him Aquila, the name his mother had given him. He called himself Aquila Vide-supra Warchet: AVW, Eagle Watcher. He had seen *vide supra* in a book. He liked the way it sounded and no one at school knew what it meant. He liked that, too.

Aquila wondered why his mother didn't come for him and if his father was in Las Vegas, far away; he hoped he'd stay there because he was mean when he smelled like whiskey. His father was a white man and very tall and Buffalo Mother didn't like him.

Ten-year-old Aquila was already the tallest boy at his school. They didn't like him much and called him Ghost Eyes—and Coyote Eyes—but Story Teller said a great chief had once been called White Eyes, and eagle eyes could see everything. Coyotes had yellow eyes. His eyes were gray.

Aquila had watched Buffalo Mother get the ponies ready, three ponies only. Buffalo Mother was the strongest and larger than his other grandmothers. She would walk and ride Story Teller's pony back. They would go there at night. *Paha Sapa* was their holy place but the white man had taken it away and named it The Black Hills. And that was why they had the Battle at Little Big Horn. The mighty Sioux Nation won but they lost *Paha Sapa* anyway because you couldn't trust the Great Chief in Washington.

Aquila Vide-supra Warchet had wanted to be a great warrior. He would give his grandmothers the gold the Great Chief had stolen . . .

Aquila lifted his coffee mug. Cold. His grandmothers never drank coffee.

From behind him in the patio, Robina said, "How about a refill? That's cold—I'll bring you a fresh cup."

"Thank you." Aquila turned and smiled. He watched her walk toward the Wings Grill kitchen—nothing like his mother or his daydream lover, but there was something about her. *Robina*: Little Robin Rosebud. He wondered if she would like his mushrooms, if she'd fix his coffee and talk to him at breakfast. Would she like him if he took off his sunglasses? Would she like him?

Aquila wanted to touch her hair, hold her. He thought he'd cuddle her on a cold South Dakota night and tell her stories, the ones his grandmothers told. He would take her into the tipi and they would lie down together on the white buffalo robe. He would feel her smooth skin with his hands and touch her breast, her warm breath against his face. He wanted Little Robin Rosebud to fly away with him.

Aquila didn't hear her come up behind him with the coffee. Robina leaned over and placed a mug on the table in front of him. She wore a tight red sweater profiling her ample bosom. "Here's your fresh coffee, Bill. I brewed some for you."

"Thank you." Aquila blushed and couldn't say anything more, glad that she couldn't read his thoughts. He usually struck up a conversation but not today.

"You're getting pink—too much sun. Want to move inside?"

"No, thank you. I'm fine."

163

"Just yell if you want anything." Robina walked to the next table with her order pad and a pen.

Aquila shifted in his chair and sipped the fresh coffee. Movement caught his eye over by Ruben's place. He was instantly alert as though watching for birds in the forest with Medicine Woman. He recognized the red-throated-finch pilot Frank with that woodpecker Jerry right behind him. They didn't notice him.

Aquila put a twenty under his coffee cup on his favorite outside table, walked through Wings Grill, and slipped out the back door. He unlocked his van, parked down the road.

Aquila had to drive back to The Guards for a court date to bail out one of the cadets, the one who had had all that unpleasantness with his pesky woodpecker friend last month. Sergeant Wamblee hadn't followed orders: Aquila would deal with him later. Such an unfortunate turn of events—Jerry knew about Kedar but he wouldn't talk. The preliminary hearing was set for Tuesday.

On Tuesday at the San Luis Obispo Court House, the case against Raymond Wamblee—the cadet who had struck Jerry Christensen's hand with a sledgehammer to scare some answers out of him—was next on the docket. Aquila sat in the back.

The judge called Raymond to the bench. "Do you swear that the testimony you are about to give is the truth, the whole truth, and nothing but the truth?"

"I do." Raymond wore his school uniform, his shoulder-length black hair tied with a leather thong. Clean, neat, and respectful.

"Take the witness stand and state your name for the record."

"Raymond Wamblee."

"The charge is felony assault with a deadly weapon. How do you plead?"

"Innocent, Your Honor."

"Bailiff, bring me the sworn statement. Are Deputies Evans and Jones present?"

"Yes, Your Honor."

"Be seated. Raymond Wamblee, you are accused of torturing Jerome T. Christensen by breaking bones in his hand with a sledgehammer."

"Yes, Your Honor." Raymond sat tall: quiet, polite, and pensive. "He hit me with a rifle butt, Your Honor. I had a concussion and I could have died."

"Did a captain direct you to torture Mr. Christensen?"

"No, Your Honor."

"Bailiff, escort Raymond back to the defendant's table."

"The court calls Quill Rethcaw. For the record, state your name and how you know the defendant."

Aquila, exuding confidence and dressed in a navy blue suit with white shirt and blue tie, took the stand. His shoulder length gray hair was pulled back with a leather thong. He wore tinted glasses. "I am Quill Rethcaw from South Dakota. I founded The Guards, a private military academy and part of a high school belonging to a Sioux Indian tribe."

"Why are you in California, and how do you know the defendant?"

"At The Guards—a temporary facility here in California—we teach the elite of our tribal high school, stressing courage, discipline, excellence, and fidelity. Raymond Wamblee is a student there." *Wambdi:* Little-Eagle.

"What special testimony do you have that has a bearing on this case?"

"This box, Your Honor." Aquila held an orange four-inch cube. "Mr. Christensen planted this at The Guards. He said it was a bomb."

"A bomb." The audience rustled. On the floor of the courtroom, two women turned back towards a man seated behind them. "Did he say *bomb*?"

Two men near the door leaped to their feet. "How'd he get past security?"

"Order! Order in the Court!" The judge rose and pounded his gavel. The bailiff turned towards the audience and put his hand on his pistol butt.

"A bomb scare, at your school. Continue."

"Let me show you, Your Honor." Aquila reset the ticking mechanism and displayed the orange box at the rear of the room. "You see, this direction finder points at the orange box."

"And someone found this at your school?"

"Yes, Your Honor. This was only a scuffle with trespassers. We are willing to forgive the trespasser's transgressions if you can send Raymond home. He is hotheaded. We will discipline him. He has missed three weeks of school."

"Thank you. You may be seated. Raymond Wamblee, step forward."

Raymond Wamblee stood contritely in front of the judge's bench.

"With special circumstances, I am reducing the charge against you to misdemeanor disorderly conduct, suspended sentence, probation for one year."

"Yes, Your Honor."

"If you ever hit someone with a sledgehammer again, or come into my court for any reason, you will stand trial for the felony charge and receive the maximum sentence allowed by law. Do you understand the terms of the court?"

"Yes, Your Honor."

"Case dismissed. You are released to Quill Rethcaw."

In the back of the courtroom, Deputy Evans turned to Deputy Jones. "Would you believe it? The judge let him go!"

"We drive for hours to bring him in, keep him locked up three weeks. He lets him go. Like a revolving door."

"Innocent, Your Honor . . . What a crock." Evans shook his head and threw up his hands. "Some scuffle, to mash Christensen's thumb like that. Wasn't he a teacher, Sunnyvale or someplace?"

"Mighty strange. Come on. I'll buy you a coffee."

"Who do think that Quill Rethcaw guy really is?"

19.

"Oh! Oh! No-o-o!" Ruben projected panic through Jerry's cell phone. "How'd he get past the barrel lock? You said you'd watch all night!"

"I heard the engine start. Air Traffic Control said he went east." Jerry's first night, guarding Foxy Lady from Ruben's office at Auburn Airport—he had fallen asleep on a lumpy cot. "Know anybody in Truckee or Reno?"

"East? You said he wouldn't go east—*not that crazy.* He's *loco y tonto.*"

"You call the county sheriffs. I'll call Reno and alert Nevada. I can check the tracking bug." Jerry had planned this as a telephone job. He counted the hours on his fingers: . . . 6, 7, 8, . . . just barely eight hours since wine at dinner with Robina. He had a smaller cast—he couldn't move his thumb or his wrist, but he could use his fingers. The doctor had not cleared him to fly.

"You get me up, tell me not to make phone calls, then tell me to call sheriffs. This whole operation just fell apart, like your head's gonna do." Ruben's voice reverberated across the office.

"What else can I do now?" Jerry kept his voice low and calm.

"*Fish Eyes specific—Huevos del Toro!* If you're foolhardy enough to fly in the dark, Cessna 289XT has full fuel, keys in my top desk drawer. When you get yourself killed, send back my airplane."

"Okay. I'm going." *Yikes!* Chase a stolen airplane . . . over the Sierras? Wine, thumb—two good reasons not to fly. Jerry didn't want to go. He called the controller at Mather Field to check the winds and the flight path of the target. Winds light and variable. A hurricane would be better—he could stay here. No. This mess was his idea. He had to follow Foxy Lady. He had to go.

Jerry was out the door seconds later with his flight bag. He fumbled with the key to unlock the rental airplane, then hoisted his flight bag and climbed into the pilot's seat. It started easily. He needed both hands to lift off.

Jerry pushed in the throttle with his cast and took off into the dark. He could follow the ribbon of lights on Interstate 80 leading over the Sierras—as long as he stayed higher than the hills. The air was smooth and the Cessna climbed well. He checked in with Approach Control on a special frequency—the other pilot couldn't listen in.

So far, flying with one hand wasn't too tough, except for a little pain in his right thumb, pushing the throttle. He memorized the next frequency in case he lost radio contact. He had to reach across with his left hand to tune the radio— no autopilot. He stabilized altitude with the trim wheel. Pay back time for using that cast on the throttle: his thumb throbbed.

Outside the cockpit, the terrain was enveloped in black: invisible. The Cessna was only a thousand feet above the highway at Donner Summit—Squaw Peak was higher. Jerry hoped he was missing all the rocks.

The lights came on at Truckee, ahead on the right and below Jerry's plane. The other pilot must have activated the runway lights by clicking the radio switch three times—he would need fuel. From Truckee, down in a bowl and surrounded by mountains, no one could hear the radio from Reno. Jerry clicked his push-to-talk switch and called Reno-Tahoe International Airport for a landing clearance. He asked them to track an airplane about to leave Truckee.

Descending over the east Sierra, the lights at Reno— the Biggest Little City in the World—glittered straight ahead. The gambling casinos never slept. With all that neon, Jerry had no trouble finding the airport. When Reno Tower cleared Jerry to land, they reported his target heading south.

Jerry ordered fuel and ducked into the restroom. Afterwards, he called Ruben from the pilot ready-room at

Reno Airport to make a position report. He carried bottled water from a vending machine and some cookies to the table and spread out the charts for Nevada. Las Vegas and Tonopah to the south. No places to land or get fuel out in the desert.

He memorized what he could: difficult to handle the chart in the air. Frank would love the Nevada chart, showing the Mustang VOR—a radio signal used in navigation and named for the infamous Mustang Ranch, and LUCKY intersection—an imaginary point in the air near Las Vegas over a suburb called Paradise. He wished Frank were here.

Jerry entered navigational points into his handheld GPS and stored numbers in his cell phone for the sheriffs in Tonopah and Las Vegas. He ate a final cookie and repacked his flight bag.

As ready as possible, Jerry taxied into position for take-off from Reno. He pushed in the throttle with his left hand and steadied the yoke with his elbow. Not recommended technique, but easier on the thumb. When he leveled out on course, Air Traffic Control showed Jerry's target 70 miles ahead, southbound. Between military restricted areas, only two narrow air corridors were possible: east toward Tonopah or south toward Las Vegas.

"How far can you track him?" Jerry adjusted his microphone boom and wiped his wet palms on his pants.

"About another hour before he leaves Reno radar coverage."

An hour: long enough to answer Tonopah or Las Vegas, if his luck held. Could he track Foxy Lady with the rental car bug? Jerry called Rick, his mechanic friend at ACE Car Rental. *No answer.* Of course—ACE wasn't open this time of day, and a holiday weekend to boot.

Jerry had a home number for Rick, somewhere. He trimmed for steady flight and dug into his jacket pocket. No. He tried his shirt pocket. No. He unbuckled his seat belt and lifted his butt to dig into a lumpy pants pocket. *There.* Descending—re-trim the airplane. He punched the phone's keypad. *No answer.*

After Jerry had been airborne for an hour and a half, Reno Center lost radar coverage. The target headed south: Las Vegas. Jerry pulled out his cell phone to try one more time. He needed information from the rental car bug, the only way left to track Foxy Lady.

A grumpy and groggy Rick answered. "Who *is* this—calling me so early? Better be important."

"Sorry . . . Jerry here . . . matter of life and death."

"Can't hear you . . . too much noise."

"Jerry Christensen . . . where's that bug . . . the bug in the airplane . . . remember?" Jerry held the phone close to his lips and yelled over the engine noise. "Please hurry! I'm desperate!"

"You mean you want me to get up and drive all the way down there?"

"I'm flying south at two miles per minute. Where am I going?"

"Well, in that case . . . All right. Twenty minutes."

"Thanks. You're a life-saver."

Eighteen minutes later Jerry dropped the ringing phone. He was glad that he had smooth air and could trim the airplane to hold altitude. He unbuckled his seat belt and leaned down to the floor to answer his cell phone.

"It's at—" Rick laughed and tried again. "It's at . . . Pahrump," Rick whooped. "Ever been to Pahrump?"

"Pahrump? Never heard of it." Jerry held the phone with his chin and returned to the pilot's seat to re-stabilize the aircraft.

"Oh, man. The whole town: nothing but prostitutes, a cathouse on every corner, more cathouses than casinos, unless they have slot machines for when you're waiting. Right outside of Las Vegas, towards the west of town."

"Thanks a mil. I'll tell you the whole story later." *If I come back in one piece,* he added to himself.

Jerry struggled with refolding his chart to center on Las Vegas. He found Pahrump and entered L57 into his GPS, holding the map between his knees. He had to trim again to straighten out his heading. When he stabilized the aircraft, he called Ruben.

"You're going where . . . *Pahrump*? That runway is dirt and gravel. You'll mess up Foxy Lady's paint. Why did I let you talk me into this?" Ruben's voice, too loud, carried over the engine noise.

"Have you been to Pahrump?"

"Uh, . . . No. Just heard about it."

"Yeah. *Su-u-ure*. Thanks for warning me about runway conditions. I'll fill you in when I can. Don't worry— I'm taking good care of your airplanes."

On Sunday morning the telephone rang at Your Lucky Day Locksmith in Las Vegas, ding-ding-ding-ding like the payout bell on the slots. Jackson loved that sound; he was playing blackjack on the computer. He ran his hands through his kinky brown hair and let it ring again. The clock over the wall phone said eight o'clock. Who could be locked out so early? Most of Las Vegas slept it off on Sunday. He answered after the third ring to a gruff voice.

"I'm locked out of my airplane. Can you make me a new key?"

Locked out of an airplane? Jackson could do a car. This shouldn't be that different. "Sure. Where are you?"

"Pahrump. I can't let my wife find out."

"I understand entirely." Jackson chuckled. Before the housing boom, the main enterprise in Pahrump had been prostitution. "Where do you land a plane there?"

"At Pahrump Hidden Hills, the old airport. Not the new one in the residential airpark. I have a Cessna 172 with a red tail. You'll see it. I'll pay you in cash."

"Where are you, exactly?"

"Just go south on 15 to Jean. Take 161 right on in."

"Got it. 161, right on in." Jackson checked that he had a complete set of ignition key blanks and raced out the door to Pahrump.

20.

Jerry landed his white rental Cessna at Pahrump, gentle with the controls to avoid dings in the paint. An aircraft could pick up a rock with its propeller, chipping one blade and unbalancing it. Ruben would yell if he scratched the paint.

Jerry recognized Foxy Lady's red tail in the line of parked aircraft. No pilot in sight. He taxied to parking and turned the Cessna so that it could be pushed straight back into the line; he couldn't have turned the plane with the tow-bar. Six aircraft parked between him and Foxy Lady.

His hand throbbed and sweat stung his eyes. When Jerry pulled off his baseball cap to wipe his brow with his handkerchief, his eyes fixed on his electric blue Watsonville Air Show T-shirt. *Geez.* He might as well have worn a flashing neon light—San Francisco Bay Area. Good thing, no one's around. He hadn't planned to be alone on the ground with the pilot of a stolen airplane. Jerry pulled off his bright T-shirt and climbed back into the cockpit to watch Foxy Lady.

A tall gray-haired man, dressed in generic pilot garb—jeans and a Reno Air Races T-shirt—left the green chemical toilet. He walked with a slight limp. Was it Fish Eyes? Jerry sucked in his breath. *It's really him.*

Jerry turned toward the back seat and leaned way over between the seats, fiddling with his flight bag. He didn't want to be skewered by those piercing eyes.

The captain wasn't more than three feet from the spinner on Jerry's rented airplane when he walked by, returning to the Cessna with the red tail. His eyes searched all around the tie-down area before he retrieved a brown paper bag hidden behind some weeds. He pulled out a pair of scissors and a roll of tape, crumpled the bag, and dropped it on the ground. With careful application of black tape, the one became a seven, the six an eight, and the seven a nine, transforming Foxy Lady's tail number 167FL to 789FL.

Not so fast, my fish-eyed friend, Jerry thought, seeing the one change to a seven. He pulled the blue shirt back on—inside out to hide the silk-screened label—and covered his red hair with his baseball cap. Partially disguised by his aviator sunglasses, Jerry captured the metamorphosis of Foxy Lady's registration number with the digital camera in his cell phone.

Fish Eyes checked the time with his wristwatch and waited under a wing. Too tall to stand beneath Foxy Lady's wing, he leaned over a strut to catch the shade.

A few minutes later, a silver van marked Lucky Day Locksmith pulled up in front of Foxy Lady. The young driver opened the back doors and stepped out with a tool kit. Inside the vehicle he had a complete workshop. He parked close enough for Jerry to hear conversation through the open window.

"I don't do barrel locks, man." The locksmith gestured wildly and pointed at Foxy Lady's door. "You didn't say barrel lock."

"Then can you unlock the cargo door and make it a key?"

"Piece of cake."

After three minutes with a set of lock picks, the locksmith opened the cargo door, a small door towards the rear of the aircraft. The captain pulled it open as far as it would go, backed up to the opening, and stuck his head inside. He wriggled on his back and pulled his butt onto the cargo floor. Then he twisted around and, stomach down, raised himself on his arms and pulled in his knees, his back almost against the roof. Stretching out over the back seat, he moved a large cardboard box out of the way, slid over, and unlocked the door on the pilot's side. Amazingly agile for such a tall man with a limp, he continued his slither, rearranged himself across the front seats, and stepped out of the cabin door onto the tarmac.

Jerry could hardly believe what he was seeing. He filmed a two-minute video from his hidden vantage point. Then he captured a full-face view of Captain Fish Eyes emerging from Foxy Lady.

A few minutes later, the locksmith exchanged the barrel lock on Foxy Lady's cabin door with the lock from the cargo door. The cutting machine whined and spit out new keys in his portable workshop.

Speaking softly, Jerry called the sheriff to find out what was taking them so long. They were twenty-five miles away at the new airport in Pahrump, Calvada Meadows, the one in the residential airpark. "But the thief is here, now—at Hidden Hills. He could take off at any moment."

Jerry had no idea that a place as small as Pahrump could have two airports. His handheld GPS had shown only this destination—the old Pahrump, under LUCKY intersection. Two airports: no fuel at either one. He read 1700 Zulu—Greenwich Mean Time, used in navigation—on the aircraft clock and 35 on the outside temperature gauge. He translated mentally: only ten in the morning and already 95 degrees.

Jerry had just finished his third bottle of water when he saw Captain Fish Eyes pull out a handful of bills to pay the locksmith, who stirred up the dust on his way out. The captain pulled Foxy Lady onto the taxiway to check the oil and spilled some on his shoes. Fish Eyes tried to wipe it off with a paper towel, then threw the crumpled towel under a scrubby bush. He looked both ways and, leaving the cabin door ajar, sprinted towards the chemical toilet. He rushed by just in front of Jerry's spinner. Jerry ducked down below the instrument panel.

Jerry peeped out the aircraft window until he saw Fish Eyes slam the toilet door shut. He grabbed his flight bag with his left hand, set it on the ground, and locked the rented aircraft. Tucking his flight bag under his left arm, he ducked down behind the line of parked airplanes and hurried to a path connecting the tie-down area and a rustic hotel. Glad to see a few bushes, he urinated on the ground—too dangerous to walk to the Port-A-Potty. He hoped anyone watching would think he was returning from the hotel.

Jerry edged closer to Foxy Lady. If the captain took off with Foxy Lady and a new tail number, he could buy fuel anywhere and elude the sheriff entirely. Or get shot down when someone called Nellis Air Force Base to report a stolen aircraft. Ruben would be even madder if Foxy Lady were shot down than he would be when he found out that she had landed in dirt and gravel. The rental plane was too low on fuel to follow.

This close, Jerry had to peek inside—just a peek. He pulled Foxy Lady's door open. A flight bag marked *AVW* and a large cardboard box on the backseat. Jerry eyes locked on the new key, left in the ignition. *Bingo! Steal the ball from the opposing team.*

In front of the Cessna, the taxiway was clear all the way to the runway. A black pickup truck sat parked on the far end behind Foxy Lady. Captain Fish Eyes, still out of sight, could return at any moment. Jerry threw his flight bag aboard, climbed into the cockpit, and fastened the seat belt.

Jerry's feet wouldn't reach the rudder pedals. The seat wouldn't slide forward. He unbuckled the seat belt and hopped out. A disposable cigarette lighter jammed the seat-track. He threw it onto the ground and used both hands to move the seat forward. His heart started to pound. The captain could appear at any moment.

Jerry remounted Foxy Lady. *That stink!* He emptied the ashtray onto the ground beneath the airplane. No captain, but the black truck was coming up behind. He slammed the door shut. *Get out of here, now!*

The black pickup pulled to a stop behind him. Jerry turned the ignition key. Fortunately, the Cessna started immediately. No time to deal with vapor lock.

Jerry taxied onto the runway. It was a hot day, hotter than he liked and hotter than the Cessna liked. He would need more runway length for take-off than at Palo Alto. The Cessna would climb slowly—or not at all. He threw his baseball cap over the seat and advanced the throttle while holding the brakes, prepared for take-off on a short field.

The black pickup appeared on the other end of the runway. It drove towards Foxy Lady and spun sideways, throwing up a dirt cloud. Stopped, it blocked the airstrip. Two men jumped out. They held rifles.

Jerry recognized the sledgehammer wielders.

Would he clear the truck? Jerry released the brake and spun through the gravel. He heard the pop, pop, pop of three shots and a bang and a ping. Not shooting paint. *Firing, at him*!

A bullet: through the passenger's front window. Small cracks radiated around the hole. A second shot hit the tail. He pulled up. Would he clear the truck? More shots.

The gas tanks—nothing leaking. *No fire.* Shots—from behind him. The aircraft had moved out of range, but the box on the back seat bounced around like a living thing. What unpleasant surprise waited there?

Jerry leveled off. Waited for more airspeed. Climbed slowly. He wanted speed, distance from Pahrump. Foxy Lady was sluggish in the hot air.

As Foxy Lady lumbered away from the ground, cracks curled across her glare-shield surrounding the bullet hole and limiting visibility on the right. The washboard afternoon air dropped her fifty feet and shook her, a cat with a mouse, lifting Jerry off his seat and knocking his fingers off the radio dial.

After long minutes, he tuned the radio to Las Vegas Approach. He was too busy trimming for maneuvering speed and controlling the airplane with his good hand to put on his headset. He tried to ignore his aching thumb.

With so much engine noise, Jerry had trouble hearing over the cabin speaker. He asked the controller for vectors to North Las Vegas, a nearby towered general aviation airport.

Foxy Lady was traveling slower than the truck that passed under her on the freeway. Perspiration trickled down Jerry's forehead, stinging his eyes. He couldn't see the runway. "Damn! Flew past it!"

"Say intentions," the radio crackled.

"Land North Las Vegas. I'm lost."

The controller vectored him back. He did a go-around. Almost out of gas, Jerry landed at North Las Vegas. He taxied to transient parking, following directions from the tower. He would have cheered if he weren't so tired.

By habit, Jerry turned off the magnetos and the master and set the ignition key on top of the instrument panel. He had to push Foxy Lady back into the tie-down space. Push against the propeller—standard one-man parking. Sweat ran down his face. His chest heaved. He rolled the tires across asphalt, easier than the gravel at Pahrump. Left foot forward, right foot forward, push. His cast felt tight. His thumb and hand throbbed all the way up to his elbow.

While securing the aircraft, Jerry found a bullet hole through the rudder fin and a second one through a rear window. Counting the spider-web front, two shots through windows. Two bullets imbedded, somewhere.

Jerry reached into the cockpit and grasped the keys—hanging with a bright yellow Lucky Day Locksmith medallion—to put them into his pocket. "A lucky key ring. Maybe that's what saved me." He spoke aloud, dispelling tension. "Or maybe flying through LUCKY intersection."

Jerry wanted to sit down. Leaning against the pilot's seat with the door open to the furnace-like air, he grabbed his cell phone from his flight bag and called the deputy sheriff, now at Hidden Hills outside of Pahrump. "There's been a change in plan. The stolen aircraft has left Pahrump. I have it with me at North Las Vegas Airport—along with three bullet holes and two bullets."

The deputy said he was on his way, but he needed an hour.

An hour. Jerry needed some answers, *now*. And he needed an aspirin and a drink of water. He opened the back door with a handkerchief to avoid smearing anything or adding his own prints. He hoped that the captain had left a few traces.

When Jerry opened the big box on Foxy Lady's back seat, he wished he hadn't. He jerked his arm back and jumped away. An eighteen-inch baby alligator, so eager to climb out that it scratched its claws along the sides of the cardboard box, snapped at Jerry's good hand. He re-closed the flaps. The alligator from the septic tank at The Guards: no, a silly idea. He hoped it wouldn't bite a hole through the cardboard with those teeth. Why would Captain Fish Eyes want an alligator?

Next to the alligator's box was a leather flight bag with the gold initials AVW on one corner. Jerry used his handkerchief again to hold the bag and unzip its pockets. One front pocket held a cell phone, the other the captain's handheld GPS—storing flight plans from Los Banos to Boulder City. An aeronautical chart showed Hoover Dam highlighted in orange. The rear pocket held a handgun—not licensed, Jerry hoped. Fish Eyes was guilty, guilty, guilty.

After re-packing the bag, Jerry tucked his handkerchief into his rear pocket and settled into the pilot's seat to wait. His thumb throbbed, his head ached, and he felt weak. He needed to call Ruben. He needed a drink of water.

He nodded off instead.

On Sunday afternoon after the Cessna with the red tail—and a few bullet holes—had taken off from Pahrump, the driver of the black pickup and his helper stood ramrod straight and reported to the captain. Aquila shook his head with disgust. His cold eyes reflected anger. His thin mouth tightened.

"So, he took Foxy Lady—the pilot with the red hair but no beard—and you couldn't stop him. You're both grounded until further notice." Aquila stabbed the air in front of their faces with his right index finger. "Why did you fire the rifles? I gave no permission for that."

"We had to stop him, Sir," Sergeant Wamblee said.

"You didn't follow orders. This is the second time. First, you hit Christensen with a sledgehammer. Then you shoot at him. Wamblee, as of now, you are demoted to private first class."

"Yes, Sir. I fired the rifles, but Corporal Whitehorse only loaded them," Wamblee said.

"We'll discuss this tomorrow back at The Guards. Use that half-brain of yours. Do I have to do everything myself? I send a cadet to Auburn to bring a Cessna to Truckee. He leaves it at the wrong airport. I send a cadet on a mission to take out Hoover Dam, and he disappears."

Aquila slammed his open hand with his closed fist. "Now all you have to do is deliver some boxes to the Cessna with the red tail, and you wave bye-bye instead." He scowled and stood with his hands on his hips. In a cold and measured voice he said, "Let's see if you can find the airport. The big one: where the jets land. That should be simple enough."

Aquila had time to cool down while riding in the black pickup truck to the terminal at Las Vegas-McCarran. Mercenaries in his cadet air force: his biggest mistake. Amjad ran away. Kedar—such tragedy. He would send the other two Muslim boys back to Los Angeles. His air force needed elite Sioux warriors.

The redheaded pilot with no beard, he thought, that's Jerry. How'd he track Foxy Lady so fast? How'd he steal back the airplane? How'd he make that raid? Jerry, that red-crested woodpecker *kan-ke-tan-ka*. In the old days, an Indian would have scalped somebody over less than this.

Chief Woodpecker. Chief Eagle Feather owed Jerry a warning. Aquila booked a flight to San Jose from Las-Vegas McCarran.

179

21.

At North Las Vegas Airport on Sunday afternoon, a white and black car marked Clark County Sheriff squealed to a stop in front of Foxy Lady's propeller. The sound of the approaching vehicle awakened Jerry, sleeping in the hot aircraft cabin. In a groggy voice, he muttered, "They must go through a lot of tires, driving like that."

Two deputies piled out and walked around the Cessna. They both wore short-sleeved khaki shirts and holstered pistols on their black belts. Three crisp creases on the back of each shirt and no wrinkles—even in this heat. The driver was tall and dark haired and wore a serious expression on his face with a slight frown. The shorter one, blond and red-faced, spoke to Jerry.

"Hello. You must be the pilot in the stolen plane with the red tail. I'm Deputy Iverson, Clark County Sheriff's Department, and this is Deputy Garcia."

Garcia nodded his head. Iverson smiled and held out his hand.

Jerry held out his cast. "Jerry Christensen. Sorry I can't shake."

"You flew that thing all the way here, with one hand? Holy Moly!" The two deputies admired Foxy Lady and the bullet holes.

"Just lock it up and come with us," Iverson said. "Manny's has a great Sunday brunch."

Jerry hadn't eaten anything except a few cookies. But then he remembered the hitchhiker on the back seat. It would cook in this heat. "What'll I do with the alligator?"

"Say again?"

"A hungry baby alligator, in the big box on the back seat. Have to leave the windows open." Jerry leaned over the front seat and loosened the flaps atop the box, keeping his hand well away from those teeth. He stepped out, closed the door, and put on his baseball cap. "Don't want to leave any blood."

"Better call for back-up." Iverson called the dispatcher with his police radio to arrange for another car to meet him at Manny's. "Have them buy some raw fish on the way over, something marked down for quick sale. Bring a screened-in travel carrier for a cat. Just do it."

Containing his laughter, Iverson turned towards Jerry. "Now that I've ordered lunch for the alligator, how about ours? Let's cool off at Manny's."

Jerry rode with the deputies to Manny's Landing Lights, an air-conditioned oasis near the North Las Vegas Control Tower. Stepping inside, they pointed out Major Blakely from Nellis Air Force Base. He wore civvies: shorts and sandals. His sunglasses peeked out of his baseball cap, skull side up, lying on the table. His dark brown hair had a dusting of gray across his temples and his brown eyes crinkled at the corners with smile lines.

"We asked the major to meet us. He's off duty today," said Deputy Iverson. "He knows more about stolen airplanes than we do."

Jerry hadn't heard one word from the other deputy.

Major Blakely rose to his feet and greeted Jerry and the deputies with a warm smile. He was about Jerry's height and build and moved with an athlete's natural grace.

Jerry added his hat to the pile on the table and went to wash up. He refreshed himself by splashing cool water on his face.

Later, after wolfing down a heaped plate of mixed buffet and guzzling two iced teas, Jerry tackled telling his story. "I had a hunch that Foxy Lady might be stolen—that's Ruben's Cessna 172—so I was sleeping on a cot in Ruben's maintenance hangar at Auburn Airport. When I heard Foxy Lady start up, I followed her, all the way to Pahrump." Jerry paused for another sip of iced tea.

Iverson snickered. "Pahrump!"

"I parked near Foxy Lady. Captain Wachter—the guy who stole my airplane in February—I've been chasing that guy for three months. I saw him change the tail numbers. When he left for a pit stop, I jumped into Foxy Lady and flew her here."

Iverson was the first to speak. "Holy Moly! We'll just take in the alligator. Stolen airplanes: a job for the FBI."

Jerry, revived by a gallon of iced tea, had his second wind. He had left Auburn well before dawn, recaptured Ruben's stolen Cessna, and met Major Blakely who would investigate the thefts. He stepped out of Manny's Restaurant into the oven that was North Los Vegas Airport and climbed into Deputy Garcia's police car.

Deputy Iverson, yelling and swinging both arms, waved over the Clark County Sheriff's black and white—the back-up officers he had requested. "Over here."

The sheriff's car screeched to a halt. An officer dangled a dripping package from the window in front of Iverson. "Here's your lunch—riper by the minute."

"Then I'll save it for you," Iverson said. The dripping fish could have come out of yesterday's garbage: that sharp, nasty smell. Jerry gagged. He and Major Blakely sat behind Garcia, who was driving. Iverson hopped in and yelled, "Follow us."

Both police cars parked in front of Foxy Lady. Jerry and the major stepped outside into air that felt as hot as a glory hole for blowing glass. From inside his car, Iverson directed, "Take care with that alligator."

Jerry unlocked Foxy Lady and watched from the shade beneath an aircraft wing. A deputy set the cardboard box onto the tarmac and lifted the lid. The alligator stuck its snout through the opening and scratched the sides of the box eagerly. The officer pushed it back down and jumped back. "Look at those teeth! How can I get him out?"

"Here—wear these." The fish-bearer handed him a pair of leather gloves, still clipped together with the price tag, from the soggy shopping bag. Then he emptied the alligator snacks into the cat carrier, turned the cardboard box onto its side, and jumped back. The glove-wearer opened one flap and yanked his hand out of range. The small reptile scrambled to the ripening fish in the cage.

"Okay, he's all yours. Take him in." Iverson rolled up his window and waved. Both black-and-whites sped away, leaving black tire marks on the taxiway.

"Whew. That car's going to stink for a week." Jerry turned toward Major Blakely. "Let's go somewhere cool."

"I'll take you and Foxy Lady home with me." The major had ordered fuel before leaving the restaurant. "The aircraft will be impounded at Nellis Air Force Base while I investigate—this is my airspace."

"All those restricted areas on the charts?" Jerry climbed into the passenger's seat and wiped perspiration from his forehead with a handkerchief. He needed water, again. The major looked crisp and cool, even while checking out the aircraft in the full sun.

"That is affirmative. All of Nevada, Northern Arizona, and Hoover Dam. I coordinate with the FBI. I'll add this theft to the case involving your stolen aircraft."

"But there isn't one. The FBI didn't investigate."

"You can tell me why tonight." Before he turned the ignition key, the major said, "The FBI will be interested this time. My investigation will be strictly by the book."

From the roadway, Major Blakely's house was unimpressive. A desert tan single story, rectangular and blocky, guarded by a twenty-foot saguaro cactus wearing strings of Christmas bulbs. Inside, cool and spacious: High ceilings, floors tiled in light colored natural stone, an interior patio beyond a double paned glass door. Two handsomely framed Georgia O' Keefe prints hung beside a Frederic Remington rodeo scene over an off-white leather couch. Above a petrified wood fireplace reigned the focal point of the room: an irregularly shaped woven artwork—pieces of yarn, feathers, and bits of wool—vaguely reminiscent of a spider's web with a hole near the center.

Jerry spread his hands towards the fireplace. "What a magnificent piece."

"That's Betty's dream catcher. Navajo legend has it that bad dreams get tangled in the webbing and perish with the first light of day, but good dreams slip through the small center hole and slide down the feathers to fill your room with pleasant feelings."

"I've never seen anything like it." Jerry turned towards a collection of Navajo Kachinas displayed inside a glass case, each carved out of seasoned cottonwood and decorated with fine leather and fabric. Jerry recognized a buffalo hunter and a white wolf.

"Betty loves those Kachinas," the major said from behind Jerry. "Let me show you around."

Jerry admired Betty's partially completed copy of a Navajo rug on a loom near a glass door that faced north and framed a cactus garden—she must know Indian lore.

Later, Jerry followed Major Blakely into his study. A mahogany desk sat beneath a window overlooking the patio. A framed diploma from the Air Force Academy hung on one wall. Sitting on a leather executive chair and holding a glass of iced tea, Jerry told his story while the major took notes. "I already told you about the theft of Foxy Lady. I probably should start on February 23rd, when the Cessna I owned with Frank was stolen from Palo Alto Airport."

"You said the FBI wasn't investigating that theft. Why?" Major Blakely shifted in his desk chair and sorted the papers on his clipboard.

"It was the bullet ants. The agent thought I was a nutcase."

"What?" Surprised, the major's eyes widened.

"They're vicious. Like an inch long wasp with no wings and a bite like a burning cigar held against bare flesh. The captain had a whole colony of them."

"Incredible." The major printed *bullet ants* with a ballpoint pen at the top of a blank page, upside down from Jerry's across-the-desk viewpoint.

Jerry set his empty glass on the edge of the major's desk and leaned forward in his chair. "As soon as I said *bullet ants*, I could see from the FBI agent's face that he was thinking, *Uh-huh . . . Sure*. He got rid of us right away. Actually, they turned out to be important, because Frank and I used them to escape."

"What do you mean by that?" The major drew circles and then flipped his pen back and forth.

"Let me start at the beginning. We had a tip and searched for our Cessna near Daggett in the Mojave Desert—Kelso—a ghost town. Found the probable crash site, nothing left, black gravel that stunk like explosives."

"Please go on." The major tapped the pen against his thumb.

"The insurance company needed proof to pay our claim. No wreck, no check. So we went back." Jerry paused and watched a bead of condensation run down his glass.

"When we returned to the location Frank had marked, the crater was different—like we had walked into a time warp—the rocks rearranged, nothing blackened. Some woman with a white braid— her boy right behind her—told us to get out."

The major wrote *empty crater* with such force that the ballpoint pen tore the page. "If nothing was left, then how did you find out who stole your Cessna?"

"The kid told us, the fifteen-year-old with the old lady."

"Only fifteen?" The major scratched his head. "That can't be right."

"A student pilot." Jerry continued in such a matter-in-fact way that he could have been discussing last night's dinner. "The kid—Kedar—said the captain sent him on a mission. Cessna loaded with explosives. Supposed to blow up Hoover Dam."

The major jumped to his feet, his face rigid with shock, clipboard clattering onto the tile floor. "Say again? Guarding that dam is my primary mission."

Except for his swinging foot, Jerry could have been watching a televised baseball game. "We didn't report the crash site. The captain would kill the boy if he found him."

"Who is this captain?" The major added *Captain Who* to his notes.

"I didn't know for a long time." Jerry stared at the ceiling and controlled his swinging foot. He wiggled when nervous—that probably turned off the FBI agent when he told this story before. "Early April, San Luis Obispo and The Guards, that's where Kedar said he trained. A training camp for terrorists disguised as a high school. We climbed over the fence and a soldier met us with a rifle."

"At a school?" The major sat back down, on the edge of his chair.

"Right." As in Alice-in-Wonderland mushrooms, forty-pound coconuts, exotic bugs, Jerry thought. "Bunch of Quonset huts. Kicked us out for trespassing. He was the captain, because of his eyes."

"What about his eyes?" The major drew a large eye etched into his notepad like an Egyptian hieroglyph.

"Creepy reptilian silver-gray eyes. I didn't tell the FBI about the suicide bomber."

"So that's why the FBI wasn't interested?"

"He said he needed the captain's name." Jerry tried not to squirm in his chair.

"So?" Major Blakely swiveled in his chair—never still, just like Jerry.

Jerry swung one foot and rotated his chair from side to side, then focused his eyes on Major Blakely. "This interview is confidential, isn't it?"

"I told you by the book. What you tell me will be used only for this investigation. Unless you confess to a bank robbery or a murder."

"Okay." Jerry wiped perspiration off his forehead with his handkerchief. "We dumped a fake bomb over the captain's fence."

The major's eyebrows shot up, making horizontal exclamation marks.

"We told the captain the National Guard was searching for a bomb, but he didn't buy it. We wouldn't talk so his sergeant rapped my knuckles with a hammer. That's how I got this." Jerry pointed to his cast, stood up, and walked around his chair three times, discharging nervous energy.

The major cleared his throat. "You've just circled that chair three times. Don't tell me you're going to lie down and take a nap before continuing."

Jerry laughed. "Hey, I've had a dog, too. They always do that. But don't worry. I'm seriously wound up. Well, where was I? The bullet ants."

"Not those again. What was the captain's name?"

"Wachter. A. V. Wachter. That's German for watcher. They're anagrams."

The major wrote *Wachter Watcher watcher wachter.*

"Look," Jerry said, trying to make the major understand. He couldn't goof up his story this time. "If you want a job done right, you have to do it yourself."

"Say again, what this has to do with Foxy Lady."

"It was the same guy. The captain stole both Cessnas, Foxy Lady and One-Eight-Echo. I have proof."

"And you said you had more evidence at home. I'll need that as well." Major Blakely checked his watch and stretched. "It's dinnertime. We both need a break."

After dinner with Major Blakely, Jerry called Ruben to fill him in. Ruben's airplane was safe and sound, and the FBI would investigate the aircraft thefts.

Ruben's angry voice answered right away. "So where are my two airplanes? Bring back that rental airplane, dead or alive. I'm afraid to ask which it is."

"They're both alive and well . . . sort of. The rental plane is tied down at Pahrump Hidden Hills. I didn't ding the paint but I used most of her fuel. Foxy Lady is at Nellis Air Force Base. Has a bullet hole in her rudder."

"What?" Ruben shouted something in Spanish.

Jerry pictured Ruben's red face and clenched fist. "Everything's okay." Jerry made his voice smooth and soothing. "She's only impounded while the case is investigated. I'll come to Auburn tomorrow and tell you everything and show you my pictures. Buy you lunch at Wings."

"*Loco y tonto*, buying forgiveness with lunch. You *guajalote!*"

"I'm sorry, Rube," Jerry said. Crazy, foolish, turkey—he had deserved much stronger Mexican swearing, asshole or egg of the bull or son of a whore or some other colorful expression.

"But it's done now," Ruben said before he hung up.

Jerry called Frank next. "Can you come to Auburn Airport for lunch tomorrow? And take me home afterward? I caught the captain stealing Foxy Lady."

"You caught Fish Eyes? The FBI has him?"

"No, I didn't catch him, only on camera. But I saw him steal Foxy Lady, and Major Blakely will coordinate the FBI investigation."

"Well, at least you caught an FBI investigator," Frank said. "What happened to Foxy Lady?"

"Impounded at Nellis. Ruben's mad but still speaking to me, in between Mexican swear words."

Frank promised to meet him at Auburn tomorrow.

Jerry didn't mention the bullet holes.

22.

Shortly after sunrise on Monday morning, Major Blakely and Jerry took off from Nellis in the major's sleek red and white Mooney Rocket, modified for extra speed and climbing power. Like pilots always do, Jerry had admired her during pre-flight: her new paint, her glass panel, her bigger engine. Mooney 331BB was almost twice as fast as Cessna One-Eight-Echo and cruised at a much higher altitude. Rocket-like, One-Bravo-Bravo climbed easily at 1500 feet per minute—nearly three times the usual rate of climb for a Cessna 172.

"There's something I need to show you, a detour on our way to Auburn." Major Blakely had no trouble getting permission to maneuver over Hoover Dam. From 2,000 feet above the surface of Lake Mead, the silvery water spread across the landscape as far as Jerry could see—navigable water upstream for a hundred miles, the dam and the generating plant below too large for Jerry's eyes to put into scale. Usually, no aircraft of any size were allowed so close to power generating plants or to dams.

Mooney One-Bravo-Bravo swooped into the canyon beneath the dam. Several miles downstream the terrain flattened into a high plateau. After circling, the major turned upstream and descended to 800 feet above the surface of the river. Hoover Dam loomed huge through the windscreen. "Think a Cessna 172 could damage that dam?"

"Captain Wachter thought so, with some kind of powerful explosive."

"A Cessna weighs a little more than a ton dripping wet and loaded to the gunnels. Hoover Dam is enormous, more than four million tons of reinforced concrete just in its main section, enough concrete to pave a two-lane highway

189

coast to coast. What explosive—short of nuclear—could dent that dam?"

"My chemist friend couldn't tell what was in the stuff."

Climbing and turning southeastward, the Mooney circled over Kingman, Arizona, a training area for military pilots during World War II. Restricted areas still carve up airspace on the aerial charts for Southern California, Arizona, and Nevada. "The desert near Edwards Air Force Base is under constant satellite observation. The Air Force has pictures before and after 23 February. You did record the exact location?"

"Absolutely." Before he donned the oxygen mask, Jerry asked, "Look, nothing to do with all this—does your wife go flying with you? Sally hates flying."

"We seldom fly for pleasure. Betty loves it when we fly to Santa Fe or Sedona—you saw her Kachinas. Sally may be afraid."

Jerry adjusted his oxygen mask and tightened his seat belt.

Major Blakely pushed in the throttle and the Mooney shot upwards. "We'll climb to 25,000 feet and leap over the Sierras in a single bound."

When the Mooney landed at Auburn, Frank and Ruben waved and cheered. Jerry introduced the major, and Frank helped him tie down in front of the Gold Country Aviation hangar, Foxy Lady's vacant place. After bantering and greetings, they retired to Ruben's office with cans of cold soda.

"I told you that I stole Foxy Lady back from Captain Fish Eyes at Pahrump," Jerry began. "Major Blakely is handling the investigation. The bad news is, Foxy Lady has been impounded at Nellis Air Force Base. Now the good news: Foxy Lady is scheduled for cosmetic surgery. She'll be just as pretty as she was when she left."

"Why the cosmetic surgery, and where's my rental airplane?"

"Sorry, Ruben. I forgot about your airplane. Here's the key. I left it parked at Pahrump when I stole back Foxy Lady. It's tied down close to the cathouse."

"Out in that gravel?" Ruben frowned and his voice rose.

"You can fly the rental plane back tomorrow morning," Major Blakely said. "When we finish here, I'll give you a ride to Las Vegas."

"If it's still there." Ruben glowered and sounded edgy.

"Oh, come on—the cathouse, or the airplane?" Jerry shifted his weight from one foot to the other and continued in his smooth-salesman voice. "Everything's just fine. I locked your airplane when I left. Nobody can steal it—it needs gas."

"Sure, wise guy—that's what you said before your friend Fish Eyes stole Foxy Lady," Ruben said. "How'd he get around the barrel locks?"

"Through the cargo door. I watched him do it." Jerry fumbled with his cell phone. "I have it on video, and I caught him modifying her tail numbers with black tape." Everyone laughed when Fish Eyes wiggled through the cargo door and slithered over the back seat.

"After that, things weren't too funny," Jerry went on. "The captain spilled oil on his shoes and ran to the chemical toilet, and I jumped into Foxy Lady. A black truck tried to block me—two guys shot at me—the sledgehammer guys from The Guards."

"Real bullets?" Frank's bushy eyebrows shot up above his glasses.

"Well, it wasn't paint. Oh, there was a hitch-hiker on the backseat, a baby alligator."

Ruben flopped onto a folding chair. "Are you sure you're not making this up?"

"Where'd he get an alligator?" Frank sat forward on his chair.

"Who knows? I got his flight bag, too, with his cell phone and a handgun."

"It's a wonder that you got away without a bullet hole in your head," Frank said. "What did you do with the alligator?"

"Oh, darn, I knew I forgot something at Vegas."

Pointing at Jerry, Ruben said, "He always has some new plan—*loco y tonto*. Gets into trouble, every time."

Major Blakely rearranged papers on his clipboard. "Anything to add, Frank?"

Frank scooted his chair closer to Major Blakely. "Jerry must have told all of this. We worked on the case for weeks, chasing a suspicious person dressed like a bird watcher—Mr. Fish Eyes. When we went to the FBI, the agent laughed us out of there."

"Yes, Jerry told me." The major packed the clipboard into his flight bag. "On Thursday, I'll fly to Palo Alto to collect Jerry's pictures."

"See you then," Jerry said. "Don't forget to bring some gas to Pahrump."

After the major left for Las Vegas with Ruben, Frank returned to Palo Alto in the Cessna he had rented with Jerry sitting in the right seat like a talking piece of luggage. Flying away into the sunset—without gulls, Frank hoped. Knowing that he had to teach school tomorrow, after a weekend like this one, brought him back to earth—figuratively, of course. "Tomorrow, back to reviewing for finals."

"I have to give a bunch of tests myself," Jerry said. "Fill-ins, mostly. Students write some really funny answers."

"So that's where you get your terrible jokes."

"Yeah, I'm found out," Jerry said. "Teaching tomorrow, though, I don't know, after all this excitement."

Frank turned the Cessna towards Mount Diablo, silhouetted against coral clouds. "Only two more weeks. Then you can go into hibernation."

"In the summer, you have to estivate." Jerry grinned. "Gotcha!"

"Snails do that when it's too hot."

"Oh no, don't tell me, I can't take it," Jerry said. "The love life of snails."

"Did you know that snails are hermaphrodites—both male and female, producing both eggs and sperm?" Frank asked. "They can't self-fertilize, have to fire love darts."

"That beats the love life of mosquitoes. I could've sworn they were doing something else—all stuck together like that. I'd better fire a love dart of my own."

Jerry hit the home button on his phone. "Sally honey, I'm on my way home. Can I take my favorite girl out to dinner?"

After a subdued hello, Sally sobbed, "Oh, Jerry, I'm so glad you're on your way home. I really need you now. Somebody killed Samantha."

"Oh, no. Poor cat!" Jerry said with such emphasis that Frank heard him over the engine noise. "What happened, honey?" His eyebrows puckered with worry.

"It was so awful. Someone put her body on the front porch, wrapped in a pillowcase from Motel 6, with a note written in Spanish or something. Maybe Frank will know. It said: e - n – g – a – r – d – e."

23.

Jerry had to wing it at school on Tuesday. He gave a pop quiz in each class after a short review, a good plan after a three-day holiday, extended by most of his students to four days by cutting class on Friday. That meant 150 papers to read on Tuesday evening, and he had promised Sally a funeral for Samantha.

Early that evening, Frank—always his faithful friend—dug a small grave in Jerry's backyard. Mary brought pink and white roses from her garden. Samantha lay on a scrap of white satin in a tiny casket that Sally had fashioned from an empty hiking boot box. Jerry, with a cast on his hand, couldn't play *Romanza*, the only piece he knew by heart, on his guitar; instead, he played a CD. Mary held one arm around Sally, and Frank bowed his head. Jerry read the Twenty-third Psalm. Afterwards, they each tossed one shovel full of soil over the box, and Frank tamped it down. Mary laid her floral bouquet on top of the rounded earth.

Jerry stood, head bowed, regarding the sad little mound under the apple tree. He hadn't mentioned how Samantha had died. Strangled, her neck broken. Who could have done such a cruel thing? Jerry wanted to shake him, choke him, and wring his neck.

After Samantha's funeral, Mary gave Sally a lace handkerchief. Sally tucked it into a blouse pocket and dried her eyes with a paper tissue. Then Mary served coffee and cherry pie at Sally's kitchen table.

Jerry sipped the coffee and picked at the pie. Although he dreaded it, Jerry knew he couldn't put it off any longer. He pushed his chair back from the table.

"Okay, here is the unexpurgated story of my long weekend," Jerry began. "If the doctor hadn't put a smaller cast on my hand on Friday, I couldn't have done any of this. The plan was to catch the thief in the act when he landed for fuel, a telephone job for me. On my turn for guard duty, I heard the Cessna's engine start. But she flew east—over the Sierras—where we had no mechanics covering. I followed her in Ruben's rental airplane."

"You flew in the dark, with that cast?" Sally frowned with concern. "I thought you couldn't fly until you had two good hands."

"I had to." Jerry looked at the ladies and slapped his right arm. "I used this wonderful cast when I pushed in the throttle, a painful reminder that I hadn't flown in a while. I traced Foxy Lady to Pahrump."

"Pah-RUMP? What a name," Mary said, laughing. "Sounds pornographic."

Jerry saw Sally smile. "Yeah, just outside of Las Vegas." He punctuated the air with his cast. "Nothing but cathouses, honest Injun."

"So you go away all weekend, go where they have cathouses," Sally said, an edge to her voice, "and you fly 400 miles with one hand to go there?"

"But I didn't leave the runway environment," Jerry said, on the defensive. "Captain Fish Eyes was there with Foxy Lady."

Sally gasped. "You met Captain Fish Eyes—by yourself?"

"Here, I'll show you. It's all here, on my cell phone." Jerry paused to show the video clip on the two-inch screen. After they laughed at the captain slithering his way through Foxy Lady's cargo door, Jerry continued in a bold voice. "The captain left the new keys in the ignition and ran to the chemical toilet. Then—my usual impulsive self—I jumped in and flew away."

"Sometimes you scare me to death," Sally said, grasping her chin with her left hand. "That Captain Fish Eyes is crazy, dangerous, and hates your guts."

"Somebody had to stop him," Jerry answered, eager to finish his story. "The sheriff turned over the case to Major

Blakely from Nellis Air Force Base. You'll like him. He's coming here Thursday."

"Coming here?" Sally asked. "Should I fix dinner?"

Mary fluffed her hair with one hand. "Are you going to introduce me?"

"Have to play it by ear," Jerry said. "He flies a Mooney."

"And we're just Cessna pilots." Frank played with piecrust crumbs with his fork. "He's a modern-day Ulysses, suave in that uniform and charismatic."

All at once, nobody had anything to say, all sitting quietly in a somber and meditative mood. Finally, Frank interrupted the silence. "Sally, I know what the note said, the one with Samantha in the pillowcase. *En garde* is a French fencing term, meaning on guard. And *Wachter*, in addition to meaning watcher, means guard."

"Captain Fish-Watcher," Sally said. "He did it, I know he did. He killed Samantha."

"That's impossible. In all fairness, I saw him in Las Vegas." Jerry wondered if Fish Eyes could have come here, that fast.

"I can't have another kitten until he's really gone." Sally's lips trembled.

"Don't worry. The FBI's on his trail." That damned fish-eyed turkey vulture: Jerry wanted to knock his teeth out.

"You used another of your nine lives—"

"It's okay. I have at least seven left."

"It's *not* okay, and Samantha used *all* of hers." Sally burst into tears and covered her eyes with her hands.

"Sally, don't cry." Jerry sat like a wooden Indian. "Don't worry—the major will take care of Fish Eyes now."

"I hate that awful man." Sally wailed from behind her hands.

"Come on, Sally. Let's make another pot of coffee." Mary took Sally's hand and led her to the kitchen.

By the time Jerry smelled the coffee, he heard Mary say, "Ask Jerry about love darts," and Sally giggled.

"Watch out, Jerry," Frank said. "The women are laughing about love darts. Did you know that snails were the origin of Cupid's arrows?"

"No-o-o," Jerry groaned. "No kidding? But candy's safer. Sally's touchy today." Yesterday, he thought, Frank's useless tidbit—the love life of snails. Those silly love darts. How can Sally laugh at a time like this?

"Here comes the coffee." Mary burst out of the kitchen and set a steaming mug of java in front of Frank along with a heart-shaped cupcake skewered by a white plastic arrow fashioned from a stirring-stick. "You don't have to wait for Valentine's Day."

Sally sat on Jerry's lap and held his love dart cupcake out of reach. "You don't get this until you promise not to chase that captain. Let the major reel in Fish Eyes."

The next afternoon, Jerry needed to tie together some loose ends from the stolen Cessna investigation. What a relief to let Major Blakely bring Fish Eyes to justice. Jerry wanted to thank people who had helped him, especially Rick. On the Wednesday after he returned from Pahrump, Jerry stepped inside ACE Car Rental to talk to Rick.

The maintenance department at hadn't changed since Christmas. The same automated carwash, lube-oil change pit, red Ford atop the tire-change platform. Jerry spotted Rick through a sliding glass window.

"Two-for-one special on tracking bugs today," Rick called out from his office.

"Where's that computer that saved my life? I can't thank both of you enough." Jerry handed Rick a package wrapped in bright colored paper and tied with a red ribbon.

"What's this—Valentine's Day?" Rick examined it top and bottom, then tore off the paper: *Ruben's Guide to The Best Airport Cuisine.* He opened the book randomly, to the space station restaurant between runways at Los Angeles International. "Thanks. This looks like fun."

"My friend Ruben—he's an aircraft mechanic at Auburn—wrote that. Pick a place. When I have an airplane again, I'll take you there for lunch. You and that bug saved my life—and Ruben's airplane, too."

"What the heck did you do with all those tracking bugs?" Rick asked.

"Caught an airplane thief."

Rick's eyes opened wide with surprise. "You're kidding. How'd you do that?"

"Show me where the bug is now—then I'll tell. Where's that computer?"

The computer room looked like a war strategy room from a World War II movie. Red lights and license numbers dotted a wall-sized map of California, mounted horizontally.

"Why did you turn the map sideways?" Jerry asked. "East on the top, instead of North."

"It wouldn't fit turned the other way. We only need California. We keep our prices down that way—no insurance bills from driving in Nevada," Rick explained.

"What happens in Nevada? It's not on your map," Jerry said. He hadn't had guidance flying across Nevada— too late to worry now. "How'd you find Pahrump?"

"I used the mileage scale. I measured how far off the map the red marker was. I climbed on a chair to reach it."

"All this high tech, then you guesstimate with a plastic ruler?" *LUCKY* intersection, Jerry thought. *Doggone lucky.* He could have missed Pahrump entirely—Fish Eyes could have left with Foxy Lady. His stomach muscles cramped. Jerry had to take a deep breath. After a few seconds, he said, "Show me where the bug is now."

"Right here, in the yard, but it's flashing on the monitor like it's in Nevada. See it there?" Rick pointed at a red spot on the wall above the map.

"Okay, I'll help you out. I know it's at Nellis Air Force Base near Las Vegas. Where's your map of Nevada?" Jerry showed Rick how to use the latitude and longitude numbers on the monitor, like locating a street on a city map.

"Cool," Rick said. "How can I erase that flashing one? I never told the boss about your missing bug. He won't like that."

"I'll ask Major Blakely to disable it." A lot of people had helped him chase the thief and now Rick could be in trouble—Jerry hadn't thought about that. He owed them all, and more than just a good story.

"You didn't tell me the juicy part," Rick said. "What about Pahrump?"

"We bugged Ruben's airplane, used it for bait to catch our thief. If you hadn't come down here in the middle of the night, I would have lost him. The thief changed tail numbers in Pahrump. I stole it back from him."

"Wow. Sounds like a made-for-TV movie."

"Starring Rick. We owe you a bunch," Jerry said. You saved Ruben's airplane."

Later and stopped in traffic on the way home, Jerry juggled his cell phone into position to call Ruben. "I got your book in the mail yesterday. Thank you. After I teased you about writing it. Say—it's good. I like the way you work in interesting things to see near the featured airports."

"All that praise. Trying to make me forget Foxy Lady?" Ruben sounded edgy.

"No. Just want to apologize for all the grief I caused you." Jerry pictured himself, holding his hat in his hands.

"*De nada*. You sent the rental plane home and Foxy Lady's safe. "

"I gave my copy of your book to Rick, you know, the guy from ACE who traced the bug and told me to go to Pahrump. He liked it, too." Jerry stepped on the accelerator. "And you did stick a loose order form in there?"

"Why—you want another one?"

Jerry shifted the phone to the other ear. He needed one of those headset gadgets. "Rick's company rents exclusively to California drivers. The book gives them some places to go. You'll get some orders, guaranteed."

"You think so?" Ruben sounded surprised.

"Why not? It's good. And send me a list of your group of mechanics. They helped solve the case. I want to thank each and every one. And could you FedEx me 80 copies of your book?"

"Eighty copies—you can't read that many, even with one in each hand."

"I mean it. Send me an invoice, too. I want to give each mechanic your book," Jerry said, holding the cell phone against his shoulder with his chin. "A way to thank everybody."

Jerry had to keep everybody interested. He knew Fish Eyes would be back.

24.

When Jerry mentioned Major Blakely's name, the sentry waved him through as though Ali Baba had commanded *Open Sesame*. Moffett Field, operated as NASA's federal airport, was five miles south of Palo Alto Airport. Jerry had never landed at Moffett; he had attended an air show there once. He asked directions and drove to visitor parking.

The major stood at the curb. He wore dress blues and held a leather briefcase. "It was nice of you to invite me to dinner," he said, getting into Jerry's SUV. "A pleasant mix of business and pleasure."

At Jerry's house, Sally waved a welcome from the front porch. The handsome major admired their home and enjoyed dinner, complimenting and charming the hostess—just as Frank had predicted.

After dinner, Major Blakely opened his briefcase and dropped a thick folder onto the table. "Before I forget, I recall that you were having trouble getting payment from your aircraft insurance carrier. Just send them this."

Jerry held a letter on official military letterhead, reading in part: Nellis Air Force Base is coordinating an investigation of several stolen aircraft. Cessna 3318E, stolen from Palo Alto Airport on 23 February, was completely destroyed after an emergency landing and the resulting fire. Its wreckage is scattered over a square mile in the desert near Death Valley. Please have your claims adjuster close the file.

Jerry shook the major's hand, a stiff shake with the cast. "Thank you so much." Maybe he and Frank could get one of Ruben's airplanes after all, or, at least stop the monthly payments on an airplane they didn't have.

"The least I could do. Now, you promised me a metal scrap marked with a figure eight and some sand samples."

Jerry slid a shoebox across the table. "Everything's here, and something I didn't mention before—the thief's gas tag, from fueling One-Eight-Echo at Los Banos."

Major Blakely frowned with puzzlement. "How do you know it's his tag?"

"Ruben saw him fill the tank from the self-service pump. We copied all the tags dated 23 February. Right here, Frank circled the most likely one, the one that matched his calculation of fuel usage."

"Good job. Pretty amazing, actually," the major said. "I still need a deposition from Kedar. You need to tell him. And collect more explosive residue. The Air Force wants to know what Captain Wachter thought could blow up Hoover Dam."

Major Blakely secured the shoebox with rubber bands. Then, with a devilish grin, he said, "I want to show Sally my airplane. Just drop us at Moffett. You can pick her up after you do the dishes."

"Okay." Jerry was too surprised to make a longer answer. Dishes? Sally always did those. Why did the major want to show Sally his Mooney?

At Moffett Field, Major Blakely escorted Sally to the same parking area used just last month by Air Force One. "My aircraft is somewhat smaller than the president's."

Sally admired the red and white paint job and watched him carefully preflight a four passenger, low-wing airplane. "One-Bravo-Bravo—that's a cool name."

"Would you like to take a ride? I could show you some of my favorite things."

"No, thanks. I think I'll pass on that. I should get home to clean up the kitchen." Sally should have said, because she hated little airplanes. Death seemed so close, so soon after Samantha's funeral.

"Oh, come on. It's good for Jerry to wash the dishes once in a while—I wash them sometimes myself. I'll show you something special."

Sally still wanted to say no, but it did sound interesting. Something special, he said? She climbed in after the major because the pilot had to get in first—the Mooney had only one door. He had to reach across her to drop the bolt, closing the door. One wavy brown strand of hair dropped down on his forehead. She smelled her favorite after-shave.

The major told her that his airplane was the Mooney Corporation's personal airliner, a Porsche of the air. The headset he gave her—a Bose—had different colored wires beneath the clear plastic case. It was beautiful, and it blocked out engine noise.

"I want to show you the sunset." The major reached over to check that her seat belt was fastened properly. The tendons on the back of his hand stood out under tan skin; his nails were perfectly groomed.

He taxied the Mooney to the end of the runway. She heard, "Mooney One-Bravo-Bravo, cleared for take-off."

The ground sped by Sally's window for a few seconds. She didn't feel the airplane lift into the air—it was climbing. The only instrument Sally recognized was the vertical speed indicator, showing 1500 feet per minute, a much faster rate of climb than Jerry's Cessna. The instrument panel was a bewildering array of knobs, dials, and indicators, and a large colored map on a flat panel screen.

Through her headset, Sally heard, "Cleared . . . two-five-thousand . . . direct ducky . . . expect one-zero-thousand in two minutes." She must not have heard that right.

After the major engaged the autopilot, he handed Sally an oxygen mask. "Be sure to breathe in through your nose and out through your mouth. There isn't much oxygen at 25,000 feet, so it's important to know if we are getting enough." He showed her how to monitor the level of oxygen in her blood with a special finger clip. It slid over her fingertip and looked like a clothespin with LED read-out showing her heart rate and the percentage of oxygen in her blood. Just like being in the hospital, she thought, her heart hammering.

"It's your job to check both of us every ten minutes." The major put on his own mask, hiding any expression on his face.

From the air, California was a relief map. Brown coastal hills, snow-capped Sierra Nevada peaks, and a patchwork Central Valley—small squares of different greens and browns, even some yellows and oranges. The San Joaquin River and the San Pedro Reservoir glittered, bright mirrors of light. Sally saw Half Dome in Yosemite Park, waterfalls, running gold from the sun. Sally wished she had her watercolors.

"If you feel uncomfortable, tell me, and we'll go back. And please call me Paul."

Sally felt fine. In fact, she enjoyed every minute, picking out things she knew from the ground and marveling at how they looked from so high up. She heard a voice on the radio say, "One-Bravo-Bravo, cleared to hold at *DUCKE* as published, two minute legs. Expect further clearance, zero three four zero *Zulu*."

She could understand some of the words, but she wondered if the controller was speaking English. She asked, "What's *ducky*?"

"It's an imaginary point over the valley."

"What does all that mean?"

"*Cleared to hold* means to make my airplane fly a race track shape in the sky, flying slowly, to enjoy the view," explained the major, making a wide, smooth turn.

"Flying slowly? How slow is that?"

"The airspeed indicator shows 120 knots. That means, after each turn, I fly four nautical miles, then make another turn."

"Naughts? Like naughts-and-crosses?"

"No," Paul said with a friendly chuckle. "Ships and aircraft use knots instead of miles per hour. I should have translated. We are traveling at about 140 miles per hour."

More than one hundred miles per hour, she thought, this is slow? After the turn, Sally had no sense of motion whatsoever. She could be sitting in the living room in an easy chair, except for the remarkable view.

"But it feels like we are standing still."

"That's because you have no frame of reference, no scenery flashing by."

A few minutes later, One-Bravo-Bravo turned west to face into the setting sun. A few clouds radiated red, then gold. Then the fireball sank over the coastal range, silhouetting Mount Hamilton and Mount Diablo, the clouds bottom-lit with orange, dark on top as purple as an ornamental plum. Below her, the water ribbons had stopped shining. As Paul turned to the east, she could see night behind them over the Sierras and the stars were coming out. The snow-capped peaks turned salmon-pink.

The major asked Sally how she liked the sunset. "I asked my wife to marry me, watching a sunset and holding at Paradise, an imaginary navigational point over Riverside. I had to ask her again, after we landed—so I could kiss her—and our oxygen masks got all tangled up."

"That's so *romantic*." Sally looked down at the plastic tubing hanging below her chin and said, "Like kissing wearing braces."

His laugh was so contagious that Sally's oxygen connections popped apart. She readjusted them and checked her blood oxygen level with the thumb clip.

Paul made one more lazy turn over Yosemite before starting a slow descent back into the Bay Area. Sally watched the valley cities light up like a magician had waved his wand, white and yellow bright patches.

Passing through 15,000 feet, Paul said, "You've been flying at 25,000 feet in a non-pressurized aircraft. You need to clear your ears. Just hold your nose and breathe against it gently, or swallow while yawning."

"Hold my nose—like jumping into the deep end of the pool." Sally's ears popped, relieving pressure she hadn't known she had. She couldn't master the yawning and swallowing.

"Are you okay? You can get an earache if the pressure in your ears builds up."

Her ears felt fine.

"I'll take you as my co-pilot again, any time."

Sally hoped that would be soon. It sounded devilishly adventuresome. Flying definitely had possibilities. Except for the credit card bills.

One-Bravo-Bravo descended into Moffett Field in the dark. A magic carpet riding a slide over red and white lights—glide slope lights, Paul called them. The Mooney touched down between rows of blue lights, like blue candles set out in greeting.

Afterwards, Jerry met them in the parking lot at Moffett Field. Sally, still aglow from the flight, had no idea what time it was. Major Blakely looked pleased with himself.

"Where the heck have you been?" Jerry scolded Sally. "You were gone so long, I was worried sick."

"It's my fault. I took her for a ride. She wasn't afraid."

"I was just with Major Blakely." Sally laughed behind her hand. Jerry sounded just like she had when he came home late after flying.

"You went flying with him but you won't go with me?"

"Oh, I know. Riding in the Mooney was marvelous, exhilarating. I wore an oxygen mask at 25,000 feet and checked our blood oxygen every ten minutes with a little finger-clip-thing. The sun dropped over the mountains at the same time night was behind us."

"And I only have a Cessna. Does that mean I have to get a Mooney before you'll go with me?"

Sally laughed. "We'll see what we'll see, when you can fly again."

"Take Sally somewhere soon, as soon as that cast comes off, and let her show you what she learned," Major Blakely told Jerry. "She's not afraid."

Before he left, Major Blakely shook Jerry's hand. "I need your help as liaison on the stolen aircraft investigations. You're the only one who could find The Guards. The United States Air Force wants those explosives."

The next morning Jerry bent over the breakfast table, engrossed in the newspaper and sipping from a mug of coffee. The paper was too large to hold with one hand. He had spread it over most of the table.

Sally, a faraway look on her face, stirred cream into her coffee. "Paul took his wife to Paradise and asked her to marry him while they watched the sunset."

Jerry frowned and set down his empty coffee mug. "Who's that? Do we know anybody named Paul?"

"Well, it's your fault. You're always gone someplace. I can't just sit here and do nothing all the time."

"Who is this Paul? Some French fly-boy?"

"Why, I do believe you're jealous. That's Major Blakely—he asked me to call him Paul. Why didn't you ever take me to Paradise?"

"I thought I did . . . last night."

"You're absolutely crude."

"I thought that was why you married me. I'll think about the Paradise thing, okay?" Jerry dashed out the door for his 8:30 class, kissing Sally on the cheek. She liked flying with the major but not with him, Jerry thought, and she called him Paul: Major Blakely, always so formal and proper.

Stuck in traffic again, Jerry wondered how he would unearth explosives for the major. Taking him to the Guards: easy. Visiting Kedar, collecting black sand samples: easy. Catching Fish Eyes, finding the captain's explosives: not so easy.

25.

The heat shimmered above the Mojave Desert sand near Kelso. On this trip, Frank drove the rental Jeep towards Mother's cabin because Jerry, still wearing a cast on his hand, couldn't manage the manual transmission. Frank was sure that Mother would ask them to spend the night. He hoped to have to some of her coffee, and maybe some fresh homemade bread. This time, they brought sleeping bags and inflatable mattresses. Jerry needed to convince Kedar to testify that the captain had given him the stolen airplane.

From the road below Mother's place, Jerry leaned out and cupped his hands around his mouth like a megaphone. "Hey, Mother! Hello-o-o!" It wouldn't pay to sneak up on any woman with a shotgun.

Frank wiped sweat off his brow. It was hot—must be 120 degrees. He was surprised to see Kedar outdoors in this heat.

Above them in the driveway, Kedar peered out from behind one fender of Mother's dirty green truck. Recognizing them, he stepped out and waved his hand. "Oh, Mr. Christensen. I'm so glad to see you and Mr. Peterson. Come on up."

Inside Mother's dark hallway, the air was pleasantly cool. Kedar set out glasses of ice and Mother appeared with a pitcher. An inexhaustible supply of lemonade, Frank thought. Just right for such a hot day.

"Look at you, Kedar. You're two inches taller," Jerry said, putting his good hand on the boy's shoulder. "That's an inch a month."

"That's because all he does is eat and sleep and eat," Mother said.

"And dig."

"He's so smart, too. Robert helped me sell crystals in Las Vegas. I displayed some premium ones, but the dealer offered me peanuts."

Frank noticed that Mother still called the boy Robert.

"And I just stood there and didn't say anything." Kedar smiled broadly.

"You're good at that," Jerry said.

"I picked up a crystal and held it to the light. Using a voice just like yours," Kedar said, looking at Jerry, "I told him it was flawless and worth at least twice as much. He met us halfway. Mother stuck to twice as much. When he said he'd pay, I took back the two-colored one."

Kedar jumped out of his chair. "I told him it wasn't for sale. I'll show you."

"Enough money to live on for a good three years. And Robert's been poring over those dry mining textbooks my husband left on the shelf, wants to learn more about it."

Kedar burst back into the room. He handed Frank a nearly transparent tourmaline crystal about eight inches long, a superb specimen that changed with the light and graduated from red to green. "How can I tell if this crystal is flawless? What is it really worth?"

Frank turned the crystal to see it from different directions. "This is wonderful and worth a lot to a collector. Tell you what—I'll look into it and let you know."

Just then, Mother called them for dinner: a pot of beans with bread and butter. "Strictly vegetarian—Robert doesn't eat pork," she said. "Plenty to share. I would have frozen some for later."

Afterward, Frank washed dishes. Jerry sat with Kedar at the table a few feet away.

"A lot has happened since we last saw you," Jerry said. "Our insurance company wouldn't pay for a stolen aircraft, only a wrecked one. I couldn't send them out here. The investigators would have been worse than buzzards around a dead donkey."

"You still don't have an airplane?"

"That's right, but we'll get one soon, I hope. Remember, you said you went to school at The Guards and you didn't know the captain's name?"

Kedar cocked his head to one side. As usual, he didn't say anything.

"So we decided to look around at The Guards. I climbed over the fence. Right away a soldier with a rifle showed up and marched us into headquarters. It was the captain, all right. He kicked us out for trespassing."

Kedar leaned forward in his seat and ran his fingers through his hair.

"Then we got into a big fight. That's how I got this." Jerry held up his cast and pointed to it with his other hand.

"Did you tell him about me?" Kedar perched on the front edge of his chair.

Jerry put his hand on the boy's arm. "Of course not. He doesn't know about you."

Kedar, his eyes big and frightened, stared at Jerry.

"I told him a bird watcher at Palo Alto saw him watching our airplane—remembered him from his distinctive eyes. That was like hitting a nerve. The captain yelled, 'What's wrong with my eyes?' and locked us up in his office."

Kedar's mouth made a big silent, "Oh-h-h."

Jerry knew Kedar would like the story about the bullet ants. Everyone laughed, the part about 'ants in the pants' causing howls of laughter every time someone repeated it. Then, to everyone's amazement, Kedar announced that he knew about bullet ants: They belonged to the science classes at The Guards.

"You know how you ward off the evil eye." Kedar held his hand in front of his face, palm forward and five fingers spread out. "Like this? Well, once a cadet did that to the captain. He had to run a bunch of laps, and he found a bullet ant in his bed."

Frank stood listening with a dishtowel in one hand. He knew that students disliked teachers who were strict disciplinarians. Kedar's story was only a school legend.

As to the mushrooms—and the giant coconuts and other unusual flora—Kedar said that The Guards made money from studying mushrooms, a lot of money for the school. He only shrugged when asked about the coconuts.

"What about alligators? Did The Guards have an alligator?" asked Jerry.

"No, but we were going to study reptiles next in science. Science was totally cool. The captain had some red and black frogs, and a black, red, and white banded coral snake, and a Gila monster lizard with beads all over it."

Still holding a dishtowel, Frank spoke up. "All poisonous, dangerous animals. Usually the brightest colored small reptiles and insects are poisonous."

"What else can you tell me about The Guards?" Jerry asked. "Like, what did you study, and how many cadets did they have?"

"There were about thirty cadets when we had classes, you know, English, math, science, but no P. E., just drill and push-ups and marching. We had our own dormitory, because we had secret missions, just four of us, the ones who learned to fly."

"Four of you? Who were the others?" asked Frank.

"You'll never tell, will you? The other three were Yassar Obeid, Khaled Baraket, and Amjad Hamide. They were orphans, too."

"I'll never tell. By the way, Mr. Christensen hasn't told you everything that's new. He caught the captain stealing another airplane. Now that we have proof, the FBI will bring him in. He needs to tell you how he stole back the airplane from the captain."

Mother guffawed and slapped Jerry across the back. "I love it."

"Yeah, well, first, back to The Guards," Jerry said, clearing his throat. "After we knocked out the soldiers with their own rifle butts—just like in the movies—the sheriff raided the camp, but the captain got away."

Kedar frowned, a question etched into his face: Was the captain coming here?

Mother, worried also, said, "Oh, no. You mean he's still around?"

"Oh, I'm afraid so." Jerry leaned forward. "That's why we need your help."

"We need you to go to Las Vegas to make a deposition to set up the case against the captain," Frank said. "It's really important."

"Don't worry, Mother. No one will find out where you live, and you won't have to appear in court." Jerry finished by saying, "The captain can't get away with this."

"I couldn't bear it, if I lost a fourth son."

Kedar bit his lip. "He won't be there, will he?"

"Don't worry," Jerry said in his calm super-salesman voice. "The captain won't know about it. Major Blakely will take care of us—he's from Nellis Air Force Base and he's in charge of the investigation. You can trust him."

After several minutes of discussion, Mother agreed to meet them in Las Vegas. Kedar listened with worry wrinkling his forehead throughout the entire conversation. "What is a deposition, Mr. Peterson?"

"It's lawyer-speak for a signed and notarized statement, in which you tell what you know about the captain and about the Cessna and about the explosion," Frank answered. "You won't have to appear in court, and then they can legally arrest the captain. When you finish telling your story, we'll all have a good dinner."

Kedar seemed to buy that. Before turning in for the night, he asked Mother to show their guests the electronic keyboard. She took out her music book and played his favorite, *Hark the Herald Angels Sing*, even though it wasn't Christmas time, and asked them all to sing along. Everyone except Kedar dropped out on *A Mighty Fortress is My God*. He soloed in a strong and true tenor voice.

"Robert has a fine singing voice, doesn't he? He has perfect pitch, and he's learning to read music," Mother said. "I'm so proud of him."

Kedar blushed and said in a quiet voice, "I can do bird calls, too."

The next morning at first light, Jerry, Frank and Kedar revisited the crash site. Frank picked up a metal fragment. "That was some explosion."

"Where's the engine?" Kedar asked.

"Explosions rearrange things in strange ways," answered Frank. "The engine could have been blown into the air, and then, being very heavy, fallen straight back down and burrowed into the sand. We might never find it without a steam shovel."

"You could use a metal detector."

Frank paused. "You're right. Why didn't I think of that?"

"Okay, Dr. IQ," Jerry said, laughing.

Kedar was the first to find anything of value—his charred logbook, with two pages still legible. "See, Mr. Peterson, my thirty hours."

"I'll bring you a new one," Frank said. "I'll give that one to Major Blakely, when we see him in Las Vegas."

26.

On the prescribed day, Frank and Jerry walked under a domed ceiling circled by small high windows, the lobby of a federal court building in Las Vegas. Frank spotted Mother and Kedar, both wearing new jeans with white Argonaut Mine T-shirts, Mother with her usual white braid. He and Jerry settled down on the next bench. Frank thought Kedar looked worried.

Frank and Jerry snapped to their feet when Major Blakely, dressed in his summer uniform with crisp creases, strode down the hall. Mother and Kedar stood up, stiff and hesitant, until Jerry introduced them to the major. Kedar seemed to relax after the major smiled and shook his hand.

Major Blakely led them down a marble walkway to a room with a fifteen-foot ceiling, the walls lined with somber portraits, larger-than-life unsmiling faces above tight collars. A male court reporter, waiting behind a dark polished wooden desk, offered Frank and Jerry comfortable chairs next to the wall.

Kedar sat ramrod straight in a too-large leather chair. He stared at a portrait behind Frank and turned toward Major Blakely when the questions started.

"For the record, state your full name and tell what you know about events that occurred on 23 February of this year." The major sounded relaxed and matter-of-fact.

"Yes, sir. My name is Robert Kedar Herold." Kedar spoke in a loud, clear, and proud voice. "I flew on a mission. I was a soldier in a holy war."

"What war was that?"

"I don't know." Kedar looked the major in the eye.

"Has Robert Kedar Herold always been your name?"

"No sir. When I lived in Los Angeles, I was called Kedar Khazari."

The major glanced down at his notes. "How did you become a soldier? Did you join the Army?"

"No sir. A recruiter came to my school. He said I could learn to fly."

"What did your father say, and how old were you?" The major stared at Kedar.

"I was almost fifteen. My father was dead. The Guards gave me a full scholarship because I'm an orphan." Kedar sounded matter-of-fact but his eyes looked pained.

The major stroked his chin and leaned back. "How did you learn to fly?"

"I took lessons from John at San Luis Obispo." Kedar almost smiled.

"And how many learned to fly?"

"Four of us." Kedar swung one foot, sitting to the back of the chair.

"What were their names?" The major sat forward ready to record the answer.

"It was a secret." Kedar studied the ceiling.

"Okay." The major had an edge to his voice. "What was John's name and did he ask to see your birth certificate?"

"I don't know. All the cadets were registered." Kedar scooted forward and rested his toes on the floor, like a runner waiting for the gun.

"Registered? What is that?"

"I don't know, sir." Kedar spoke in a louder voice, like to a deaf person.

"Okay. And what happened on 23 February?"

Kedar shifted in his chair and paused for a few seconds. "The captain gave me an airplane, its engine already running, a secret mission in a holy war. I saw big plastic barrels on the seats. The captain said not to land for fuel because the plane would blow up—hot-wired."

The major sucked in his breath.

Kedar leaned forward, his eyes wide and sad and frightened. "The captain ordered me to take out Hoover Dam, to fly right into it."

The major wrote something on a yellow legal pad. In a gruff voice, he asked, "What happened after you took off?"

"After a while, the engine wasn't running right. Sounded rough. I gave it more gas and the engine stopped." Kedar let out his breath in a silent sigh. "I couldn't land at Daggett—it would blow up. I landed out in the desert, but the airplane didn't explode. Or, not right away. I couldn't shut it down, but it wasn't running anyway. I don't remember what happened then, until Mother found me."

"What airplane was that, the one you flew?" The major twiddled his pen.

"A Cessna 172."

"There are a million 172s. Which one?"

"I don't know." Kedar squirmed and looked at the floor.

"This captain who gave you the airplane, do you know his name, and do you recognize any of these photographs?" The major slid three photos across the table.

"No sir. He was just, *The Captain.* That picture, that's him, but he's wearing jeans." Kedar pushed the pictures away and covered his mouth with his fist. He sucked back a sob. "That's him. He'll kill me for telling."

Turning to the court recorder, Major Blakely said, "Enter this picture of the captain into evidence. This concludes the deposition of Robert Kedar Herold, also known as Kedar Khazari."

Jerry, listening from the rear of the room, turned to Frank. "He didn't say he flew One-Eight-Echo, and he didn't know anybody's name." Jerry watched Kedar and Mother trade chairs: Mother's turn on the hot seat.

"My name is Inge Isolda Karlson Herold." Mother sat straight and tall and confident, one foot pulled back under her chair. Kedar watched her every move.

"I have lived in the desert near Kelso for more than thirty years. Since my husband's death, I am the sole

216

proprietor of the Argonaut Mine. On February 23rd, I was taking a shower when I heard a loud noise like an explosion. After I cleaned the bathroom and braided my hair, I went outside to investigate, towards the Devil's Playground area. I smelled sulfur like the Devil had just appeared."

"Yes, yes. We don't need all that," the major said. "What did you find?"

"An injured boy, covered with black oily stuff, his back and arms bloody." Mother looked at Kedar and flipped her head. Her braid fell forward, against her neck. "I picked rock splinters out of his back. Robert has helped me run the mine ever since."

Mother began to twist her braid. "Please, don't let that captain find him."

"The injured boy you found on the road. Is he here now?" The major looked as stern as the portrait that stared at Frank.

"He is Robert Kedar Herold, there," Mother said, pointing at Kedar.

At lunchtime after the depositions, Major Blakely took Frank and Jerry, and Mother and Kedar, to the courthouse cafeteria. Jerry had a music book for Mother, *All Time Favorites for Piano and Voice*. Frank had information on gemstones for Kedar.

"I decided to bring this instead of mailing it." Frank handed Kedar a package wrapped in white tissue paper and tied with a blue bow. A small gold biplane ornament rested in a nest of curled ribbon. "My wife Mary wrapped this for you."

"Thank you, Mr. Peterson." Kedar turned the package around and studied it from every direction.

"Go ahead, open it. You don't have to wait for your birthday. Guaranteed to be more fun than those mining books."

Kedar untied the ribbon and pulled off the tape without tearing the paper. He folded the tissue paper around the piece of ribbon and the gold ornament before he held up *The Rock Book* by Fenton. Kedar paged through the book and looked at the colored plates until the waitress brought his hamburger and fries.

After Kedar had finished eating, Major Blakely ordered a chocolate milkshake for him and told him he had flown so well—landing in the desert without hurting anyone—that he would like to show him his airplane.

"It's a Mooney, One-Bravo-Bravo. Fast and sleek. Want to see it?"

Wide-eyed and feeling uncomfortable, Kedar studied the major's Air Force uniform before answering. Were majors higher than captains? What did a Mooney look like? They'd come back for dinner. After a long pause, he said, "Yes, Sir."

At the airport, Kedar watched the major preflight his airplane. The tail appeared to have been put on backwards; he didn't ask why. He answered questions yes or no, followed by sir, of course, but he didn't volunteer any information. After taking off from Las Vegas-Mc Carran International Airport, Major Blakely pointed out the sights. Kedar liked the Bose headset; it screened out the cabin noise, and he could hear what the major said. Major Blakely liked to talk.

"Down there, that's Hoover Dam," the major said. "An engineering marvel. It backs up water in Lake Mead for 110 miles. If it suddenly burst, there would be a catastrophic flood. Kill thousands of people. You lived in Los Angeles, didn't you?"

"Yes, Sir." The dam looked different from what Kedar had seen with Mother from the ground: so large and so much water.

"You drank water from the Colorado River and ate fruits and vegetables irrigated from its water. It provides water for 14 million people. In fact, the dam is so important to this country that it's my job to protect it."

"Yes, Sir." Kedar was glad that he hadn't blown it up. The captain had tricked him; he had changed his mission from an exciting cross-country flight to something wrong and dangerous and deadly. He didn't tell Major Blakely that. In fact, he said nothing at all.

Major Blakely's Mooney flew southeast to Kingman, then westward towards the Mojave Desert. "There's Kelso, up ahead. Do you see it, alongside the railroad tracks, by the water tower?"

"Yes, Sir." He didn't know where to look for the Argonaut Mine.

"Down there, somewhere, is where you live, and now this is how the rest of your mission would have looked." Major Blakely circled eastward towards the Colorado River and descended.

Kedar remained silent. The major flew lower and lower and close to the dam.

"Down there is the river. You wouldn't have blown up the dam—only yourself and a beautiful little airplane."

"Yes, Sir." Kedar saw the Achilles' heel, the doorway on the cement surface. He pictured an explosion— pieces of metal flying up and raining down. Smoke and fire. *Dead.* He would be in Heaven. No, because it wasn't really a holy war.

"The F-16s would have shot you down before you got there."

"Yes, Sir." Does he really shoot people down . . . in California?

"Especially since September 11, we guard Hoover Dam around the clock. It's secret stuff, but my men would have found you, even if you flew low to the ground. My conscience would bother me forever—shooting down a small aircraft, the pilot just a kid like you. Thank God that didn't happen."

Kedar's face was expressionless and unreadable. He wished that he could fly one of those F-16s. The part about being shot down sounded like a TV movie.

Major Blakely turned to look at him. "Now that you have a whole new life, I hope you'll make something out of it. Go on to school. Study something you're good at. I'm not a religious man, but maybe God spared you for a reason."

"Yes, Sir." How did the major know about the lightning from God? He hadn't told anyone about that, not even Mother. Still awed by the uniform, he said nothing more until they landed. He remembered to thank Major Blakely.

"And thank you, Kedar," the major said, "for making a deposition to help us build the case against Captain Wachter. That was a brave thing you did."

Kedar felt six inches taller. Major Blakely said he was brave. Someday, maybe someday, the major would teach him to fly F-16s.

After the depositions were signed and notarized, Major Blakely had dinner reservations for five at Kokomos. The three men, with Mother and Kedar, sat surrounded by waterfalls and a sparkling interior lagoon within a tropical rainforest at The Mirage. The volcano erupted and spewed smoke and fire 100 feet above the waters below, transforming the tranquil waterfall into a spectacular stream of molten lava.

"Only in Las Vegas," Major Blakely said. "This goes on every fifteen minutes."

After they ordered, Major Blakely positioned a black and white 8 x 10 aerial photo dated 2 June on the table in front of Kedar. "Do you know what this is?"

Kedar studied the first aerial photograph he had ever seen—just like the desert had looked from the major's airplane. He found Mother's mine. "I can read the letters," he said, tapping the picture with one finger. "That's the Argonaut Mine."

"Oh, no!" Mother raised her voice and frowned. "You promised no one would know where our mine is."

"Don't worry, Mother," the major said. "It's from a satellite 200 miles straight up with nobody home."

Jerry and Frank were amazed at the clarity of the photo. They had seen satellite photos from the Internet, but never as clear and detailed as this one.

Major Blakely pulled out a second photo dated 20 February showing no mine and no crater. "We can photograph any place on earth from satellites. This is where you landed, Kedar. The crater you made is thirty feet deep."

Kedar arranged the pictures side-by-side and looked from one to the other. "Does it watch us all the time?" Like the eye of God?

"No. It tracks the earth's surface and the weather."

"What about navigation—GPS—and television and communications? I can read Argonaut Mine on that door," Frank said.

"They don't track people." The major rearranged his napkin and inspected breadcrumbs on the tablecloth.

"Yet," Jerry said. He moved his water glass and the waiter served his dinner.

Kedar sat quietly for a few minutes. Then he asked Jerry if he ever gambled.

"No, not since I found out that the house always wins," Jerry answered. "Besides that, the smoke gives me a headache."

Frank added that it was all a clever application of mathematics, making casino owners wealthy, and asked Kedar if he had studied probability in algebra.

Kedar didn't answer. Gambling, in algebra? He hadn't seen that in his math book.

"You don't have to gamble to enjoy all this glitz and good food," the major said.

"I'm glad you don't gamble," Kedar said. "Do you know what the Miraj is?"

"Okay, I'm your straight man," the major said. "What is it?"

"It's an optical illusion, often seen on a hot day in the desert," Frank answered. "Distant objects are reflected, often upside down, caused when the air close to the ground is more dense than the air above."

"No," Kedar said. "It's the miraculous journey made by Muhammad from Mecca to Heaven."

"He got you this time," Jerry said. "Can anybody top that?"

Kedar, his eyes wide and serious, looked from Jerry to Frank. "Is he coming back? Will the captain find me?"

"Not to worry," Jerry said. "The FBI will catch the captain."

The next morning, on the long ride home from Las Vegas, Mother told Kedar that Kelso was a ghost town. "Thirty years ago, it had a post office. Now, there's only a drop-off railroad dock. On Friday we will exchange propane tanks there."

"I flew over the railroad tracks with Major Blakely." The pickup whooshed by a truck and trailer laden with cement sewer pipe. Rising heat made the asphalt highway shimmer: a mirage. Last night, the major's aerial photo . . .

"Do you think the captain can find me?" Kedar squeezed the steering wheel until his knuckles turned white. He smelled diesel through Mother's open window.

Mother closed her window. "Mr. Peterson said the FBI always gets its man."

Her calm voice made him relax. Kedar liked these long drives when they could talk. The pickup's engine hummed. He told her that he wanted to fly F-16s.

"You can do anything you want, after you finish high school. Parents owe their child a birth certificate, a driver's license, and a high school diploma."

"Do I have a birth certificate?"

"You can use Robert's. He doesn't need it anymore."

Kedar looked towards Mother, a big silly grin on his face. "Do you know what day this is? It's my sixteenth birthday."

"Sixteen. Well, what do you know?" Mother patted his arm.

"How did Mr. Peterson know today is my birthday?"

"No one mentioned that. He helped me buy the books you need to finish high school at home. Just think of it as a whole bag of birthday presents."

Some interesting books, Kedar hoped. He had read most of Mother's books: Mark Twain, the Greek myths, geology of California, but not the German Bible. He missed school. Science at The Guards had been *the best*—except for the captain, of course.

Kedar's heart started to pound. He had told. The captain would find out. His forehead wrinkled with worry. Could the captain see him from a satellite?

27.

"Here's an unexpected clue." Frank placed a charred object on Major Blakely's kitchen table, his offering to the FBI oracle, and cleaned his fingers with a paper napkin, blackening the image of *Thunderbird*. Frank, Jerry, and the major huddled in a hushed planning session to prepare for the raid on The Guards scheduled for Monday. In the next room, their wives admired Betty Blakely's Kachinas and her weaving project, a copy of a Navajo rug from a photograph taken in Taos, New Mexico. "Kedar said to give this to you. It's his flying logbook."

"Good job. We'll trace his flight instructor." Major Blakely slapped a thick folder onto the table. "Too bad we don't know the names of the other student pilots."

"Oh, but we do, except Kedar asked me never to tell." Frank felt a need to protect the boys. He also needed to help Jerry to sift through any information the major might give them. Jerry worried about his *nutcase* reputation with the FBI; he wanted nothing to go wrong collecting evidence—and maybe arresting Captain Wachter—on Monday.

"We'll need those names." The major frowned.

"What about the February 23rd fuel pump tags from Los Banos? The one I circled had to be the thief refueling One-Eight-Echo," Frank said. That was the name the major really needed. "Did you trace it?"

"Led nowhere. No aircraft owner available from the tail number entered. The card belonged to a dead woman but someone paid the bill."

Then, who was that someone? Frank wondered if the FBI knew more.

"What about this then?" Jerry plunked a plastic package onto the tile floor; it sounded like a bag of marbles against cement. "Kedar helped us to collect some blackened gravel."

"How did you carry that suitcase filled with rocks?" The major pointed to the bag and chuckled. "Do you always travel light?"

"What about the captain's flight bag? I'm dying to know," Frank said. Was the major going to tell them anything at all?

"We're dying to know, too. We can't concentrate on weaving with all the excitement in here," Betty said from the kitchen door. Betty was small like Mary and had platinum hair like silk yarn and swimmer's muscles in her upper arms. The other two women stood behind her.

The major waved towards the other side of the table. "Okay, sit down. Now, I cannot share everything in the FBI file with you, only things that are public record, and only to give you background on the case."

Jerry and Frank glanced at each other. The women pulled up chairs.

"First, what we didn't find out. No logbook: we don't know the captain's flying history. The handgun was a starter's pistol loaded with blanks. The cell phone was new; he ordered pizza and called a locksmith. He left fingerprints but no hair or spit for a DNA sample—too bad Jerry emptied the ashtray. However, the FBI is working on it."

"Finally, the FBI's interested." Frank craned his neck and tried to read the papers.

"The FBI checked his background previously in connection with the 1995 Oklahoma City bombing: thought he was the third man. Dismissed him as a nutcase."

"They do that a lot," Jerry said.

"Wasn't that the Federal Building?" Mary asked. "I recall only two men."

"Yes, that's right—the biggest story in the news that year." Major Blakely handed her a public press release file, describing the terrorist attack on April 19, 1995, in which the

Alfred P. Murrah Federal Building in downtown Oklahoma City was destroyed, killing 168 and injuring as many as 800 people. A twenty-foot Ryder truck filled with two-and-a-half tons of agricultural fertilizer mixed with motor-racing fuel had exploded in the street in front of the building. The CIA searched international sources for possible leads among foreign terrorist groups, especially extremists committed to Jihad: holy war. Timothy McVeigh and Terry Nichols, active in anti-government militia movements, were convicted of the bombing."

"Holy war—he's a terrorist," Jerry said. "What did I tell you?"

"Or a just a fruitcake. Here, read for yourself." Major Blakely handed his thick folder to Jerry.

Frank leaned over Jerry's shoulder and read the first page aloud: "Quill Rethcaw, V. A. Age 43. Occupation: Manager, Little Eagle Casino. Residence: Eagle Creek Reservation, near Rapid City, South Dakota."

"He's an Indian. Sounds like a Sioux." Betty fingered her necklace, small animals carved out of shell and bits of turquoise. She knew the legend behind each *fetish*.

"Listen to the rest," Frank said. "Subject arrested 1 May 1995, Las Vegas. Attended meetings of anti-government groups with McVeigh and Nichols. Suspected of manufacturing explosives. Subject dismissed for lack of evidence 5 May 1995."

"Homemade explosives," Mary said, looking up at Frank.

"He's making explosives. We have to stop him." Jerry pushed back from the table, spilling his coffee. Sally handed him a roll of paper towels.

"There's more, listen up." Frank held up a second page: "Rethcaw denied making the explosives used and boasted that he would have made them ten times more powerful, using wartech and a handful of arbadacarba, special chemistry techniques. Under further questioning, he failed to explain the two terms."

"That's it, the huge black hole. We have to catch that maniac," Jerry said.

"There's more: Subject testified that, as a Sioux Indian living on a reservation in South Dakota, he would never support the white supremacist groups favored by McVeigh and Nichols. During the entire time in question, he wore war paint and feather headdress as Chief Eagle Feather and greeted guests at Little Eagle Casino."

"He's lying." Jerry's voice rose in anger. "He's a terrorist."

"No proof," Major Blakely said.

Frank studied the paper he had just read. "Why did the FBI think he knew something about explosives?"

"Lost in that mountain of paper is a report from South Dakota School of Mines and Technology. He was suspended for a semester for conducting experiments with explosives on campus." Major Blakely said. "He has a different name for every day of the week, but Wachter is a new one. Nowhere is he called Captain Wachter. His college transcript shows Aquila Vide-supra Warchet with a B. S. in chemistry."

"Wonder he graduated, blowing up things at school." Frank frowned.

Jerry jumped to his feet. "Bombs. That's what upset him so much. We're lucky he didn't strap us to a tree with rawhide and ants and leave us in the sun."

"A. V. Wachter. Warchet and Wachter are ana-grams—and Wartech, too," Frank said, a far away look on his face.

"What was that name again?" Frank focused on *Rethcaw V A*. "Read it backwards: A. V. Wachter."

"His name is Aquila," Jerry said, calmer now. "Aquila the Eagle is the constellation containing Altair."

"In the military, we have Aquila RPV—eyes for the battlefield—Aquila Remotely Piloted Vehicle."

"*Vide supra*. Latin: see above." Frank's eyes focused on the ceiling. "*Wachter—Watcher*. Watch the eagle above? Betty, you know about Indians."

Betty paused for thirty seconds. "My guess: *He-Who-Watches-Eagles*, something he may have named himself after awakening from a mushroom-induced dream."

"He has cold gray eyes. He can't be an Indian." Jerry rumpled his forehead into a frown of concentration.

"Probably part Caucasian," Betty said. "You become a member of the tribe when your mother registers you."

Frank raised his hand and waved it at Betty. "That's it. The captain said they were registered. That's why Kedar's flight instructor let him solo before he was sixteen."

"The Indians found a way to get even for the theft of their lands," Jerry said, laughing. "Gave us tobacco and gambling."

"Back to explosives," Major Blakely said without humor. "A diesel-fertilizer explosive alone couldn't inflict that much damage."

"I've got it, I've got it," said Frank, so excited that he leapt to his feet. "He used *abracadabra*. The words are backwards."

"Give me a break," said Jerry, one hand covering his mouth.

Betty leaned over the arrest report. "Look at that—Frank's right on. Written backwards." She and Frank laughed and spelled aloud Rethcaw and Wachter, forward and backward.

"This is important." Frank waved his arms wildly and focused on Jerry. "Aquila: eagle. Quill: an eagle feather. Wachter means watcher. Rethcaw means something, I'm sure of it, and Warchet, too—something in the Sioux language."

"That'll keep you busy for a while." Jerry tapped his fingers against the table.

Major Blakely looked at his watch. "The day is getting away from us. We need to plan Monday's visit to The Guards."

"We're ready." Jerry sat forward in his seat.

Frank sank into a chair next to the major. Finally. The FBI will get him—they always get their man. No, that was the Mounties. Frank couldn't remember the FBI slogan.

"Remember, now, you are liaisons because you know the way to The Guards. Let the FBI agents do their jobs." Serious and stern, the major looked hard at Jerry, then at Frank. "Your solemn promise: both of you. Don't talk too much."

"On my best behavior, honest Injun," Jerry said. Frank only nodded.

"Here's the plan. Two FBI agents will meet us at San Luis Obispo Airport. Jerry, you'll bring your SUV. The San Luis Obispo County Sheriff will send a prisoner transport van. We'll have search warrants. So, what should the FBI look for?"

"Follow the money," Frank said. The major sounded like Jerry: *the plan.* "If we find his source of money, we can trace his affiliations."

"Look for explosives," Jerry said. "Find out what lease The Guards has for that land in the middle of a federal wilderness area."

"See if he pays his income tax." Frank slapped the table. "That's how they nailed Capone in the 1930s. Get the IRS to audit him. Now, there's a way to inflict pain and suffering."

"Question those sledgehammer wielding soldiers." Jerry banged the table with the remnants of his cast. "The ones with the rifles."

"The school isn't licensed," Frank said with a gotcha-look on his face.

Jerry sprang to his feet. "*That's it!*" he said, pointing to the ceiling. "Check out that casino in South Dakota."

"No, absolutely not." Major Blakely frowned, then pushed away from the table. "Let the FBI send someone undercover. You absolutely must not go there."

28.

About time the FBI investigated, Jerry thought. Agent Matthews thought he was a nutcase. He wished Matthews were in the back—he'd show him the bullet ants and let him hold one—Ha! Jerry bounced over the dirt road in his SUV towards The Guards. Clear and dry, as usual for June. It would be hot inland. The rugged hills, not high enough to be called mountains by anyone who had hiked in the Sierra Nevada, were dressed in summer gold.

Major Blakely sat next to Jerry. Frank sat in back, wedged between two FBI agents wearing suits. A novel Jerry had read referred to them as "suits" and described their spats and turf wars; he wondered if that was true. Jerry glanced over at the major, looking so crisp in his tan summer Air Force uniform. The major believed in him. Jerry wanted to point out the captain's terrorist training camp and the strange flora and fauna. What would happen to the environment if those things got loose? Jerry shivered and said, "Hey, I'll show you the bullet ants."

"Should be interesting." Major Blakely didn't look up from his clipboard.

Jerry drove on in silence. Illegal to import those ants: another crime committed by the captain. It made him nervous, nobody talking. In his rear view mirror, he saw the van sent by the San Luis Obispo Sheriff, eating dust behind him. He pictured Captain Wachter, led away in handcuffs. No, that's too easy, it'll never happen. Who knew what they would find today?

Half an hour before they reached ground zero, Frank broke the silence. "Agent Dale, where is your home office? Did you come over from Las Vegas last night?"

Dale, hiding behind sunglasses with green lenses, seemed relaxed and looked like a man who smiled a lot. He answered Frank in a smooth, low voice, "Yes. We work out of Vegas, but we frequently travel."

Frank, sandwiched between the two burly agents, turned his head towards Agent Dale. "Did you find John, the flight instructor from Kedar's logbook?"

"No. He seems to have moved without notifying the FAA." Agent Dale sounded polite and perhaps bored.

"Can't you track him down?" Frank asked, making conversation.

"We always get our man. Just like in the movies." Agent Dale chuckled.

"What about the sledgehammer wielders, the guys arrested in April?" Frank sounded excited. He didn't have room to talk with his hands.

Jerry wanted to hear this. Surely they were locked away for a long time, by now.

"The judge ruled it a scuffle with trespassers. The Sheriff let them go." Agent Dale's face in Jerry's mirror showed no emotion.

Frank's eyebrows shot up. "Isn't torture a felony?"

Jerry's hand, still tender, tingled. "They just walked?" Jerry forgot the road and turned to the back, bouncing over a pothole.

"The Sheriff said he had to let them go," Agent Dale said, as though explaining to a small child.

Jerry recognized the turn coming up. As soon as the entry gate came into view, he would see the backward sign— The Guards—on the arch over the driveway, illegible from the road. He decided not to mention it.

Jerry stopped at the gate, and Major Blakely flashed the search warrant. The young sentry waved them through immediately. At the parking lot, a sergeant hurried out of building HQ and invited them in. This seemed too easy. Not many people around. No soldiers playing war games.

Major Blakely, Jerry, Frank and the FBI agents followed the sergeant, but the deputies preferred to wait in their air-conditioned prisoner transport vehicle.

"We need to see the captain," Jerry said.

"He's not here." The sergeant smiled without showing his teeth.

"Then we need to look around," Agent Dale said.

In the captain's office, an older iMac stared with a gray eye. This time, no sharks swam on a gurgling screen saver. The *Proud to be Guards* poster was still there; the rest of the office was bare. Jerry looked back and forth. The terrarium with its wingless wasp warriors was not in its usual place. Jerry pointed to the empty wall. "What happened to the bullet ants? They were right there."

The young sergeant—undeterminable age, no sign of a beard—shrugged. "What bullet ants?"

"Then we need to see your classrooms, your science room," Jerry said. Those ants have to be here, somewhere. Jerry, Major Blakely and Agent Dale followed the sergeant whose long black hair was held back with a leather thong.

Jerry felt uneasy. Why did Agent Dale give him the lead?

The sergeant unlocked the door to the science room, half a small Quonset hut, and stepped out of the way. Jerry stepped inside and swept his eyes around the room. No bullet ants. No poisonous frogs. No coral snake. Just a white rat that wanted out, two garter snakes wrapped around each other. A saltwater aquarium flashed with color from tiny swimming fish. A skeleton stood in the corner, or the closest thing the room had to a corner with its curved ceiling, and guarded a large collection of books. Nothing appeared out of the ordinary or suspicious.

Jerry's stomach roiled. The FBI agents would think he was a nutcase—again.

Desperate now, Jerry pointed to an adjacent Quonset hut. "What's in that building over there?"

The sergeant shrugged a silent "whatever" and unlocked the door. "P. E. in here when it rains," he said, stepping aside to let Jerry look inside. A rolled up volleyball net, basketball hoops on the end walls, a folded ping-pong table. *Empty*.

The next building, a dormitory, smelled musty and faintly like stale sweat. Jerry saw army cots, blankets and sheets folded atop each one, and footlockers, standing open. This time, the story was, "Everybody goes home for the summer." *Vacant*.

Jerry felt his stomach lurch and sweat beaded his forehead: *Nothing to show the FBI*. Then he remembered Captain Wachter's degree in chemistry and that he had manufactured explosives. "What about chemistry classes? Do you have a chem lab?"

"No chemistry lab. This is summer break, man."

Jerry wished he wore a uniform. That punk kid should say *sir*. Jerry couldn't think of anything else to ask. He could get answers for anything, but only if he knew the question in advance. Agent Dale hadn't asked a single question. Neither had Major Blakely. Why didn't they help him?

"What about rifles, explosives?" Jerry was out of questions.

"I can show you a rifle range in the back."

Agent Dale frowned and looked at his watch. His smile was gone. "Agent Allen will check for explosives."

Major Blakely face looked pinched, like he wore shoes two sizes too small. He said nothing, nothing at all.

"Take us back to the office," Jerry said, frowning. He wanted to punch that kid. No bullet ants, no terrorists, and no evidence. Jerry had never felt so humiliated.

Frank had stayed in the captain's office at The Guards with Agent Allen, who so far had said nothing beyond an introductory handshake before the drive in the SUV. Frank planned to pull the files for the four student pilots, the ones named by Kedar, and compare them to four random files. All the files were in a single drawer because transcripts were

233

issued from the school's main office in South Dakota. The sample files all had the same reservation address and progress reports on courses taken. At the beginning of the drawer, Frank found Khazari, Kedar, a folder containing only one slip of paper: AWOL, February 23. He couldn't locate Yasser Obeid or Khaled Baraket, but he found Amjad Hamide: AWOL, May 5. Did he fly the Cessna stolen from Auburn, the one that crashed crossing Donner Summit? No, Ruben said that happened after Mother's Day, May 9. But Ruben said another airplane was stolen the week before. Was this it? He would have to ask Ruben. Frank didn't want to confuse the investigation with guesses.

When Agent Allen left with a sergeant-guide to search for explosives, Frank stepped outside with a cell phone. *Phew*, it stank behind Building HQ. He smelled guano: sharp, like ammonia—a good-sized poop pile. How much did the captain need for explosives? Or, maybe he had found only the secret to the captain's giant mushrooms.

Frank used the cell phone to call Ruben at Auburn. Ruben verified May 5, *Cinco de Mayo*, that was how he had remembered the date. Only coincidence? Jerry would have one of his *bingo* moments.

When Frank returned to the captain's office, he saw Agent Allen close the door to the toilet. What was that—a five-minute search for explosives? Frank shivered, remembering: Jerry had flushed cigarette butts down that toilet—using the last of the water—when the captain had locked them in.

Frank's eyes locked on the iMac. Agent Allen would seize it for evidence. Frank had a flash drive in his pocket. He plugged it into the USB port on the keyboard and copied files. Such a descriptive name: *flash drive*. It was still copying when Frank heard the handle rattle on the door to the toilet.

Allen, wiping his hands on a crumpled paper towel, walked back into the office and stood behind Frank. "Why'd you think a school would store explosives?" he said. "We didn't find any."

Frank palmed the small object. Did the agent notice? Frank said, "The FBI investigated the captain regarding explosives before."

"Found a rifle range. Twenty rifles—only 22s, small inventory of bullets. Bows and arrows, archery targets. No secret munitions stash."

"You weren't gone long. Did you check out the guano?"

"Not enough to worry about."

Frank looked at his notes. Financials next: good. He opened the spreadsheet folder. Maybe the captain forgot to file with the IRS. "The records, here on the iMac—"

The agent shrugged. "Here goes nothing. This place has been cleaned out. If anything ever was here."

It didn't take long for Frank and Agent Allen to study the records. There were none. No income tax records: The Guards, the western campus of a high school on an Indian reservation, wasn't required to file with the IRS. No lease to use federal land: all the buildings were temporary. Income: an allotment authorized by Quill Rethcaw from Little Eagle Casino, owned by a Sioux Indian tribe in South Dakota.

Agent Allen sat down in the captain's oversize desk chair and leaned back. "They're a sovereign nation, by government treaty, you know," he told Frank, "with their own police and governing councils. A high school like this one doesn't seem like a place to train terrorists. Too far from a big city, for one thing."

"Where is Captain Wachter?" Frank asked. "I haven't seen his name anywhere." Frank found it curious that no one seemed to know anything about Captain Wachter.

Frank and Agent Allen finished before Jerry returned to HQ. Jerry looked red-faced and flustered when he came in the door followed by Agent Dale.

Jerry turned to the surly sergeant, the one who liked to shrug, and asked, "Where is Captain Wachter?"

The sergeant cocked his head to one side. A frown rippled across his forehead. After a few seconds, he said, "Captain Who?"

"Where is your captain?" Jerry asked in a louder voice. He stood with his hands on his hips. His face reddened to deep plum.

The sergeant jutted out his chin and put his hands on his hips, mocking Jerry. "A captain doesn't tell a sergeant where he goes."

Just for a moment, Jerry wished he had a sledge-hammer. Insolent puppy. "Give the captain my regards when he returns."

Jerry walked out behind Major Blakely and Agent Dale. Frank joined them from behind the building, where he had found a second source of guano stink: a small pile of white bird poop beside a growth of soccer-ball-sized white mushrooms.

"P-s-s-s-t, Jerry. Come back here. Guano."

Jerry followed him behind the building. "Just bird shit, like the rest of this. Shit. Shit. Shit."

"No, I wanted you away from the agents. Look what I have." Frank pulled the flash drive out of his front pants pocket.

"Way to go."

By the door to HQ, Agent Allen stood with the captain's iMac tucked under his arm. He said that the FBI would attempt data retrieval from deleted files. "What a wasted morning," he grumbled.

Agent Dale leaned into the window of the sheriff's van. "No captain, everything calm and normal here. Thanks for coming." The deputies left before everyone fastened seat belts in Jerry's SUV.

Riding back to San Luis Obispo, Agent Dale said, "Case like this drives you nuts, doesn't it? No evidence here. The FBI has no authority on an Indian reservation. Don't worry—we won't give up."

"I, for one, won't ever give up, not until Captain Wachter is apprehended," Jerry said. Sure, they won't give up—won't work hard, either, he thought. If you want a job done right, you have to do it yourself.

Jerry knew that they didn't have much to go on, without visiting the reservation in South Dakota. The sergeant made it seem like the whole thing had never happened: his visit to The Guards to find the captain's name, the sledgehammer smashing his thumb, the training camp for terrorists. *Nutcase. That's what they think.* Jerry fumed inwardly throughout the tedious drive back to San Luis Obispo.

The FBI agents slept in the back seat.

As soon as Jerry parked his SUV at the motel in San Luis Obispo, the FBI agents jumped out the side doors and waved a hurried good-bye. Not even a thank you. Jerry, glad to see them go, popped open his cell phone and called the sheriff. "Those Quonset huts, at The Guards. How'd they get there?"

"Sprang up in a matter of days, like a stand of mushrooms. Say, three years ago, I think," the sheriff's voice answered. "Who would think that a school would squat on government land?"

"What about that sledgehammer wielder, the one who smashed my thumb? I had had to have three surgeries." Jerry raised his voice and frowned. "You let him go."

"What else could we do? The judge released him to Quill Rethcaw. That jail's like a revolving door."

"Why the heck didn't anybody tell me?" Jerry said loud enough for the sheriff to hear him without the cell phone.

"Beats me. The judge should have notified you about the hearing."

"Well—I really appreciated your help. I'll let you know when we catch that captain fellow." Jerry, his face a red frown, turned off his phone and punched the horn twice, beep-beep. "They got away with it."

Jerry's stomach churned. At this rate, he'd have an ulcer by next week. In a controlled voice, Jerry said to Major Blakely—still seated on his right, "I never showed you a live bullet ant or cadets playing war-games. No evidence at all. It's like the whole thing didn't happen."

"A definite credibility gap," Frank said.

"You gave me a dead ant and a dead end. I thought you'd lead me to the captain's secret explosives." Major Blakely swung one foot out of the SUV.

"They were here—I know they were. The captain cleared everything out. How'd he find out we were coming?" Jerry's face turned a deeper shade of red.

"You don't interview well, do you?" The major looked at the ground.

"You're right. That means the FBI won't work very hard on this case." Jerry was mortified. He was glad that Frank pilfered the files before the agents seized the iMac, the one good thing that had happened today. He could depend upon Frank to ferret out any new clues. However, the situation seemed so unpromising to Jerry that he said to Frank and Major Blakely, "You know what this means, don't you? Our only other leads are all in South Dakota. We have to drop in on the captain's home base."

Frank stood feet apart, his arms folded, and said, "No way, partner."

29.

Quill Rethcaw, dressed in buckskin jacket and pants, his long gray hair pulled back with a leather thong, leaned back in his leather desk chair in his office at the Little Eagle Casino. His ceremonial headdress hung across a mahogany hat and coat rack. Smoke curled above the ashtray from a forgotten cigarette. He held his cell phone next to one ear and gazed at the ceiling. John, the cadets' flight instructor from San Luis Obispo, reported that FBI agents had searched The Guards.

Aquila was glad that he had moved his laboratory back to the reservation—just in time. California gull guano was fit only for growing mushrooms. He needed bat guano for his abracadabra catalyst and roburite from the Badlands Mine, a smokeless, flameless explosive using ammonium nitrate and di-nitrobenzene that he had learned about in a college mining course.

Aquila looked at his cell phone and turned it off. A tragic mistake: developing a cadet air force with Cessnas. He rested his elbows on the desk and held his head in his hands. Kedar Khazari: his best student and braver than most Indians, presumed dead. His Wartech explosives: gone. Kedar Bird-Caller—maybe he wasn't dead. Someone had told about The Guards.

That pesky interfering woodpecker Jerry's meddling, The Guards had to close. Aquila's best students spent the winter there. He enforced strict discipline. The students needed discipline—for after all, they *were* wild Indians.

Yes, Indians. The reservation schooling had been so poor when he was a boy that college took him two extra years. Socially, he had been an outcast: taunted about his eyes in elementary school, told he belonged on the reservation in college, not seated in restaurants in Rapid City. He didn't belong in either world.

His grandmother Buffalo Mother hadn't learned to read or write . . . Aquila had returned to the reservation when she needed him. He took care of her for the last three years of her life. Why had she let herself get so grossly fat? She should have lived to be a hundred like her mother and grandmother. Instead, she developed diabetes and had trouble walking. When Buffalo Mother had wanted to go to *Paha Sapa,* she was too big for him to carry. He couldn't take her into the rough terrain in the Badlands, not with her wheelchair. He couldn't let her see the four Great Chiefs from Washington carved into the rock in her holy place. Instead, he brought her to a priest and cared for her himself, until the last . . .

The clock struck ten. Aquila glanced at his grandfather clock, fine polished walnut, with the golden eagle that appeared every hour. A gift from the tribal council at the casino's grand opening, before Buffalo Mother died at age 88.

Aquila had opened the casino not long after he had learned that the Treaty of 1868 made the Sioux a sovereign nation. He had applied as Quill Rethcaw, V. A., because Quill was a good name for a casino manager. Chief Eagle Feather, Little Eagle Casino. No one else knew what it meant. All anagrams: Warchet, Wachter, Rethcaw. His private double joke: Rethcaw sounded like Big Horn Mountain in Sioux. And Warchet: a corruption of "War-Child," Story Teller's answer in broken English when asked about her baby's father. No Sioux had family names in the old days.

Wachter was special. He smiled slightly, thinking about the Red Baron, Captain Von Richthofen. He flew a red Fokker tri-plane in World War I and downed twenty-two British aircraft in one month. Captain Von Wächter, captain of the guard. When he called himself Wächter, he passed for white and rented an apartment in Rapid City—until the landlord found out he was an Indian.

Aquila glanced at the clock. Time to put on his headdress and make the rounds. The Little Eagle Casino brought gold to his tribe: fool's gold. The red man wasted his money on liquor and junk food. The real gold Indians needed: education. Yes, education. Those two redheaded pilots were teachers—they should understand. Instead, they brought the FBI to investigate The Guards. Too bad the FBI wouldn't do something useful, like investigating those murders in Rapid City.

On Wednesday morning, Mary lingered over a cup of breakfast coffee at her kitchen table and turned the pages of the local San Jose paper to news from other areas. As usual, Frank had buried himself in the business section. An article about Rapid City caught her eye.

"Rapid City murders. We're going there Friday." Mary read the story aloud to Frank: "Timothy Crow, age 32, and Allen Black Bear, age 30 . . . bodies found near East Boulevard Bridge. Last week, Wilbur White Wolf, age 42, and Lonnie Long Horn, age 26 . . . face down in Rapid Creek."

Frank dropped the paper onto the table. "Those sound like Indian names."

"Four murdered Indians, then. The rest of the article seems slanted. A spokesman for the American Indian Movement referred to Rapid City as *skinhead central.*"

"I've heard of that group, AIM. They staged a protest in Wounded Knee in 1973 and overran the place with two hundred armed men. Some of them were killed. At the time, the papers reported open tension between Indians and whites but in a short time the story dropped out of the news. Problems like that don't go away easily. Trouble right here, in Rapid City."

"That's *River City,* dear. From the musical, *The Music Man.*"

"AIM claimed discrimination against Indians. Painfully poor Indians live on those reservations."

"That's right," Mary said. "Our Indian reservations are an ugly little piece of history conveniently ignored. A third world living in the heartland of the richest country on earth."

On Wednesday evening, Jerry stared into space, cell phone held to his left ear. A cold cup of forgotten coffee left from dinner sat before him on the kitchen table. He couldn't sleep until he could take action. The major had to help him and he had to go to Rapid City—a hard sell.

"Little Eagle Casino is our last lead."

Major Blakely didn't reply. That meant *no*.

"No, I won't interfere with the FBI investigation—they don't do Indian reservations," Jerry said. And they won't work on this one anyway, he thought.

He kept his voice firm and strong. "Sally and I are going to Rapid City on Friday night, Frank and Mary as well. Discover more about Rethcaw . . . Wachter . . . Captain Fish Eyes, whoever he is. How he thinks—the only weapon left in our arsenal."

No answer from the major.

Jerry choked the phone with a white-knuckled fist. "We have to stop him."

"You're going into enemy territory. You'll be in over your head," replied Major Blakely's voice on Jerry's cell phone. "Do not, I repeat, do not go there."

"He'll be back. We have to understand him to combat him. Sally will come with me to the casino." Jerry used his calm, soothing voice to add a hook: "The only way for you to get a lead on his explosives."

"He knows what you look like." Major Blakely's voice roared, so loud that Jerry held the phone away from his ear. "He's dangerous."

Jerry kept his voice low and smooth. "I'll dye my hair and wear glasses."

Major Blakely made a guttural sound.

"Mary and Sally are excited about seeing Mount Rushmore. Betty will love it." Jerry exuded confidence. He wondered if Major Blakely was still on the line.

"We'll be safer if you come," Jerry continued. "Besides that, we need Betty's knowledge of Indian lore: She'll learn more at the museum at Crazy Horse. Frank made reservations for three couples at a motel in Rapid City and reserved a car. We'll meet you at the airport there, if you want to fly your Mooney." How could the major resist a chance to fly for fun?

After such a long silence that Jerry wondered if he had lost cell coverage, Major Blakely answered, "Do you sell used cars, too? I'll meet you in Rapid City."

30.

The buildings in Rapid City lined up like boxes on cleaning day in a giant's attic—all rectangular parallelepipeds, all subdued in color, even some flat roofs—along streets laid out on a rectangular grid. Frank watched the scenery while Jerry drove. Jerry couldn't get into trouble this time, not with the major along.

Inside the Buffalo House Restaurant, the tables were round. Frank sat between Mary and Betty and opposite Jerry, Sally, and Major Blakely. They all ordered buffalo steak, a specialty. So Captain Wachter was a Sioux Indian. Frank wondered if he ever ate buffalo. Probably not in Rapid City, not if it was "skinhead central" as Mary had said.

A waitress with long black braids and flashing brown eyes served Jerry a steak on a sizzling platter. "This is really buffalo?" Jerry's eyes traced the outline of her prominent breasts. "It's big enough."

Frank almost said, "It's bison," then thought better of it. Except for the way he eyed the waitress, Jerry seemed on his best behavior. Major Blakely, dressed in slacks and a turtleneck, sat as stiff and proper as though he wore Air Force dress blues.

"Just the best mid-western beef," the waitress said. She looked away from Jerry, and she didn't smile. "Buffalo-sized."

"And served by an Indian princess," he said.

The waitress fled towards the kitchen and glanced at Jerry over her shoulder.

While waiting for coffee and out of the blue, Frank said, "*Ku-an-shee*. That means grandmother in Sioux. I found eagle on the Internet—it sounds like wam-blee."

"*Tatanka* is buffalo, says so right here on the menu," Mary said, smiling.

"Local legends, that's what we need. Do you know any?" Frank asked Betty.

Betty's face lit up. She pointed out Wind Cave on the tourist map and lost herself in the telling. "The Sioux Indians have a creation story. Long ago, the Great Spirit *Skan* made men with bones from Stone, bodies from Earth, and souls from Wind and Thunder. When the gifts of Sun, Wisdom, Moon, and Revealer gave them life, they hurried up to the light through Wind Cave, but life was hard. The holy man *Tatanka* came to help them—as a great, shaggy beast, a buffalo. The spirits named them *Buffalo Nation*."

Buttering a second roll, Sally said, "That's a charming story."

Leaning towards Betty with one elbow on the table, Frank supported his chin on his hand. "Then the Black Hills are holy for the Sioux?"

"Yes, and that led to Indian wars, actually." Betty fingered a carved animal on her necklace. "The Sioux viewed the forces of nature as holy with balance among all things in the universe. Their cardinal virtues were wisdom, bravery, and fortitude."

Frank shifted in his chair and waved at a waiter. "Sounds like the Zen of the prairie. Early settlers here didn't treat the indigenous peoples very well, you know."

A frowning waiter holding an order pad said, "You need something?"

"We're still waiting for our coffee. Lost our waitress." *Rude waiter, terrible service,* Frank thought.

"She refuses to come back to this table. Somebody called her an Indian."

"Indian princess," Jerry said, smiling and pleased with himself.

The waiter didn't lose his frown. "She said you made her feel like a squaw with big tits. In the Deep South, would you call a black woman a Negro princess?"

Jerry's face flushed scarlet. "I had no idea. Tell her I'm sorry."

The mood at the dinner party dampened, as though ice water from the ceiling had cascaded over their table. Major Blakely smiled artificially, his grin as stiff as a swath cut from a Halloween pumpkin. Sally and Mary looked puzzled. Betty rested her forehead on her open palms. Frank felt the back of his neck flame with embarrassment.

"Last week, some hate murders happened right here in Rapid City," Mary said.

Jerry tried to restore the conversation. "Frank had it right: Settlers didn't treat the Indians well. Sounds like they still don't." Jerry had taught his history classes about Custer's Last Stand, Little Big Horn, and all that. "Basically, the United States Government took their gold, fenced them out of their holy places, and stuffed them into the worst land. We violated our own treaties. No wonder we had recent protests at Wounded Knee, near here, what? Thirty years ago?"

Major Blakely looked tired. "So we're the ones who are Indian givers."

"The Sioux had no royalty and no princesses," Betty said. "They see whites taking their images and sacred symbols without understanding as a form of mockery."

Frank came to life like a student wanting attention. "The treaty made them a sovereign nation. That's why Indians can have gambling casinos on the reservations. Quill Rethcaw probably pictures himself as the last warrior in the Indian Wars."

In a gruff voice, the major cut him off. "Okay, Quill Rethcaw, Indian chief, warrior, gambler, thief. So what's our schedule for tomorrow?"

"0700: reconnoiter. Fly over Mount Rushmore and past the Wind Cave and Hot Springs, and circle the Eagle Creek Reservation. Afterwards, we visit the Little Eagle Casino as tourists." Jerry held up his right hand, freshly out of its cast. "And I won't get into trouble. Honest Injun."

The major frowned and looked like he had indigestion. "He'll recognize you."

Back in his room, Jerry combed in a dark-colored *Hide the Gray* hair dye and shared the bottle with Frank. Frank's beard looked so bad in the mirror that he didn't want to leave the bathroom. He borrowed Jerry's razor and emerged sans beard, his naked white chin exposed.

Sally stifled a giggle. Mary stared with wide eyes, one hand over her mouth, and said, "It'll grow back, honey. Just slather on some of that Instant-Tan stuff."

"Tomorrow, we won't recognize either of you at breakfast," Sally said.

Flying helped Jerry to feel a place. In the early morning, he took off from Rapid City in a rented Cessna 172 with permission to fly low over the area. Jerry, Frank and Major Blakely crossed over Highway 16 westward to Keystone and circled the monument at Mount Rushmore before the summer swarm of tourists smothered it.

"Perfect light for pictures." Major Blakely snapped a shot out a side window. To communicate, he had to shout and lean forward from the back seat.

"We're a bumblebee, buzzing a presidential nose," Jerry said.

"See that white streak in Lincoln's forehead?" Frank pointed at the hill and tapped the right window with his finger. "Supposed to be a pegmatite dike, like Mother's mine."

"Rough country down there," Major Blakely yelled.

"Badlands National Park. The name says it all. Ground too rough to till the soil, or hunt, or graze cows." Jerry circled over a heavily forested area. Bison grazed in a mixed grass prairie. The parking lot at Wind Cave was already filling. "Bats must swarm out at night."

Jerry aimed the airplane toward Little Eagle Casino. He scouted the area for a private airstrip but he didn't see one. At the casino, the giant figure of an Indian chief with a bald eagle perched on his outstretched arm towered over a large parking lot, half full, even at this time of day.

"Captain Eagle Eyes never sleeps," Frank said.

"Fish Eyes suits him. Help me out: What are the major ingredients in explosives?"

"A giant mental leap, Fish Eyes to explosives. According to NOVA: saltpeter, sulfur, honey, and charcoal."

Leaning forward, Major Blakely yelled from the back seat, "Gunpowder, discovered by the Chinese. Good fireworks, not a powerful explosive."

"What's salt peter?" Jerry asked.

"Guano. Bird poop," Frank answered. "The captain had lots of it at The Guards."

"Bingo! We have to visit Wind Cave."

"Bingo—Bird poop?" The major studied the back of Jerry's head. "Indians and gambling get to everybody."

Jerry turned towards the back seat and yelled, "Bat guano from Wind Cave." Combined with brimstone from Hot Springs in the Badlands—everything Fish Eyes needed, except abracadabra.

Jerry held half a melted strawberry milkshake and stood in a small patch of shade in the tourist area beneath the four carved presidential heads. A shrine to democracy, carved into the granite heart of an Indian holy land. Jerry, in a pensive mood, wondered what Sitting Bull would make of Mount Rushmore. More to the point: Quill Rethcaw would feel angry.

After lunch, Jerry, Frank, the major and their three wives visited Wind Cave. Tours happened every twenty minutes. The stalagmites in Wind Cave, the place of creation of the Buffalo Nation in Betty's story last night, were broken and looted, the pieces taken by curiosity seekers years ago and replaced by gum wrappers and empty water bottles. Overrun by a gazillion tourists but only a few bats. *No bat guano.* His stomach roiled and a network of lines crossed his forehead. Had Jerry guessed wrong about that, too?

In the early evening, Jerry parked the rented Lincoln town car behind Little Eagle Casino at the far edge of the lot in the shadow of Chief-Perched-on-the-Roof, along with hordes of sunglass-bespectacled tourists dressed in shorts and loud T-shirts. Without his red hair, he'd blend into the environment like a speckled grouse hiding from an eagle. Jerry held the entrance door at the casino as the others trouped in. He reminded Major Blakely to ask if Chief Eagle Feather still appeared on Saturday nights. "He won't look at me twice, as long as he doesn't hear my voice."

"You got it. Say nothing. You and Frank do not talk."

Inside the casino, lights flashed, bells rang. A microphone blared out winners at Keno and announced a nightclub show. Row upon row of slot machines: triple-7, progressive jackpot, old-fashioned oranges and cherries. Loud noises. Loud T-shirts.

"This place would fit right in along the Strip in Las Vegas," Frank said. He had picked up a brochure, listing 900 slot machines among the attractions at the Little Eagle, with a note at the bottom that proceeds financed the tribal high school, none finer in South Dakota. Trying out the slots, Frank won a bucket of quarters; Jerry lost them.

Major Blakely watched everything nervously from a blackjack table. The Indian-princess dealer made twenty-one too many times, slick dealing. He couldn't catch her. He couldn't change her focus with conversation. He asked, "Does Chief Eagle Feather still show up on Saturday nights?"

She shrugged her shoulders and answered only, "Sometimes."

After they each emptied two rolls of coins into the slots, Sally and Betty watched the roulette wheel for an hour. An Indian maiden in a short deerskin dress sold them change. She hadn't seen Chief Eagle Feather "in a while."

At midnight, Chief Eagle Feather still hadn't made his casino appearance.

"Where's Mary?" Frank asked. "Has anybody seen her?"

Mary took a roundabout route to the women's restroom behind the room of slots and away from the loud music at Eagle Feather Casino. No one knew her here. She would do a little investigating on her own. She crept through dark hallways, feeling the mounting excitement of doing something naughty and secretive. If anyone asked, she would claim to be lost.

Mary heard a noise and stepped behind a watercooler, her heart pounding. She peered out, playing hide-and-seek with an imaginary Indian chief. The floor creaked. She jumped and ducked down. After a few seconds of silence, Mary moved into the deserted walkway and turned the corner. A few steps more: an office door, dimly lighted from within. On the translucent glass, she read Quill Rethcaw, Casino Administrator, painted in gold gilt.

She checked the knob: unlocked. She looked both ways, opened the door, and stepped inside, closing the door behind herself. Beside a hand-carved walnut grandfather clock, she saw an executive walnut desk, piled high with papers and a canvas banking-bag. Duplicate deposit slips, a receipt from the Homestake Mine for roburite—whatever that was. Mary stuffed a handful of small papers into a pocket in her tan shorts.

The clock stuck eleven. Mary's heart leaped into her throat. Run away. Hide. She ran to the door. Someone was coming. She ducked under the desk. What if he found her? She froze in place, afraid to breathe.

The door opened. Someone turned out the light and locked the door on his way out. Mary popped out from under the desk. Could she get out? She felt the doorknob in the dark and turned a button-lock. Freedom.

Mary ran in the direction of the women's restroom and knocked over a dust mop that clattered onto the floor. She ducked into safety in the restroom and peeped around the edge of the door. She forgot to close the office door—too late now. Someone tall, wearing a feather headdress, strode by. A door slammed.

Following the feathers, Mary tiptoed through the hall to the outer door, marked *emergency exit only* with a small neon sign. She pushed it outward and smelled cigarette smoke. She didn't see the smoker, only the glow of a cigarette in the dark. She stepped outside. The door slammed itself shut, locking her out.

Mary stood beside two dumpsters and beneath a floodlight illuminating the area around the service entrance to the casino. The tall person with the headdress emerged out of the shadows. Mary didn't know which way to run.

"What are you doing here?" He had a deep, stern voice.

Mary grabbed his buckskin sleeve and looked up at his face. "I locked myself out," she said. "I can't go back inside. Please, can you help me?"

He stared down at Mary.

Transfixed, Mary studied his eyes—wild eyes, like a coyote caught in a trap. Cold and metallic like polished silver. He didn't speak but his gaze softened.

"Are you Quill Rethcaw?" Mary asked. "The casino administrator?"

"Yes. With all these feathers, how did you know?"

"I saw your name on the office door. The casino brochure said you sponsor the local schools. I was wondering, how did you make them the best in South Dakota?"

"Bootstraps." His mouth relaxed and his face animated. His voice changed from gruff to proud. "Older students help the younger ones. Hired the best teachers, paid them more. Rewarded the best students with a school year in California."

"I'm from California," Mary said. Keep him talking. Find a way to leave. "Our schools are not the best."

"We have a private school." He ground his cigarette butt into the sand in an earthenware urn, painted with black and red geometric designs.

Mary didn't answer. This was the guy who sent his students on suicide missions. How could he seem so normal?

"I'm not greeting guests tonight," the big Indian said. "I'll take you to the front entrance."

She followed him into the dark parking lot. The evening was warm and muggy; she felt cold. Mary had goose bumps.

Quill Rethcaw unlocked a black pickup with a gun rack mounted behind the bench-style seat. He reached around Mary to hang his headdress on a jacket peg beneath a hunting rifle. Without uttering a word, he grabbed her around her waist and hoisted her onto the seat.

Mary smelled his cigarette and his after-shave. She gasped a silent scream.

He drove the black truck along the service road and turned through the front parking lot. Mary saw the front door to the casino, but he wasn't slowing down. "You can let me out right here," she said. "I can walk to the door from here."

"I want to show you something important. Tonight is the full moon."

"I have to go now—"

"Later." The black truck sped out to the parking lot. Where was he taking her? The cool air blowing through the open window lifted her sweaty hair and fed her fear. Did he want her scalp?

"You're a nurse," Quill said. "You will understand. My great-grandmother was Medicine Woman. I want you to see her holy place."

How did he know that she was a nurse? She didn't tell him. She sat quietly and watched the impenetrable black landscape whiz by. She had read about Medicine Woman in the computer files that Frank had pilfered from The Guards. She remembered the Arabian Nights and how Scheherazade had postponed her execution with a thousand and one stories. She would keep her scalp by making him tell about his grandmothers.

Quill Rethcaw told Mary how he had gathered herbs with Medicine Woman and learned to find his way in the forest at night, to feel the smoothness of an unseen path underfoot, to hear the movements of creatures, to follow warm air currents, to identify birds by sound alone. His stories calmed Mary, until Quill turned onto an unpaved road and stopped the truck at the top of a hill.

Mary felt tense enough to shatter into a thousand and one pieces.

The rising full moon came over the trees and illuminated the rough land in fierce beauty. Quill called for two minutes of silence for Medicine Woman there, overlooking Paha Sapa; the United States Government had stolen the holy place of his grandmothers. As a boy, he had sworn to take it back. He asked Mary to understand. Under the magic mood of the moment, Mary relaxed and felt compassion.

Afterwards, Mary walked through the front door of the Little Eagle Casino, her hair rumpled, her cheeks flushed. She felt disoriented, as if she had been abducted by aliens and released unharmed. She smiled as though she knew a secret too good to share.

"Where have you been?" Frank asked, furrows running across his forehead. He had white creases in the instant tan around his bloodshot eyes and a red mosquito-welt on his nose. "Geez, Mary, I was so worried. Thought we'd find you face down in the river."

"Crimeny. I just went outside." Mary jutted her jaw to the left.

"At two in the morning?" Frank's angry voice rose above the din of the machines.

A portly woman—poured into her shorts—turned from her stool by a machine and stepped over beside Mary. She stood with her hands on her hips and glared at Frank.

Mary shrugged.

"Come on, everyone's looking," Frank said. "Chief Eagle Feather didn't show."

Without a word, Mary followed Frank and the others to the car. Sally glanced back over her shoulder and stumbled. Betty waited to walk silently beside Mary.

On the return drive to Rapid City, the three wives sat in the back of the Lincoln town car. As the smallest one, Mary sat astride the hump in the floor. In a conspiratorial tone, she said, "Did I tell you what Frank found on the iMac at The Guards?"

"I expected something juicier than that," Sally said. "What were you doing until two in the morning?"

Ignoring Sally, Mary continued, "An authentic chapter for Betty's book on Indian lore, dedicated to Medicine Woman. You know, the book we were talking about doing."

"We can't steal Captain Wachter's work," Betty said.

"How about trading him for a few airplanes?" Sally asked.

"Computer files," Betty said. "That's what you talk about, when you disappear for hours and come back with your hair in disarray?"

"Windblown, it was windblown. Quill treated me like a lady. We talked about Medicine Woman and Indian medicines." Mary folded her arms and clenched her jaw.

In the front seat, the men rehashed the day. "I really, really wanted to see Chief Eagle Feather, see if the captain is hanging around that casino," Jerry said. "No Captain Wachter, no break-through clues." As usual, he was driving. As usual, he was wrong: *nutcase.* Would he ever live it down?

"Be glad he didn't see you," Frank said from Jerry's elbow.

"He was there, wearing all his feathers," Mary said in a matter-of-fact, *only-the-truth-ma'am* manner. "He gave me a ride in his pickup and showed me around. We talked about education and how he improved the schools."

"Why didn't you tell us?" Frank turned and his voice rose. He couldn't see Mary's face in the dark.

Mary glowered and her voice had an edge to it. "Major Blakely said not to talk at the casino."

"You didn't tell us you were leaving," Sally said.

"How'd you do that?" Jerry braked and pulled onto the shoulder. The car bumped to a stop, scraping through bushes. Jerry spun around in his seat. "You found Fish Eyes?"

"I ran into him while trying to find the ladies' room. Okay—I was snooping. I put some interesting papers from his office in my pocket. I told him I was lost."

"How'd you know who he was?" Jerry unsnapped his seatbelt and pulled himself up onto his knees to stare down across the seat into the dark.

"I asked him. He gave me a ride to the front door." Mary laughed. "You men: all those elaborate schemes. Next time just send in a woman to interview him."

"You could have been killed," Frank scolded. He unfastened his seatbelt and turned towards the rear to face Mary, who sat directly behind him.

"He liked me. I wasn't in danger and I can take care of myself."

"Exactly what did you say? All of it, now," Major Blakely said in a gruff voice. "The FBI is still investigating. You told him your name. What else?"

"Quill's passionate about education. He said California schools lack discipline."

"Oh, no. You told him your husband teaches school in California? He knows that was Frank or Jerry. He probably has your picture, too, from when he kept their wallets."

Mary chewed one thumbnail. "California has 33 million people. I only told him my first name."

"You say a lot for someone who isn't talking. Way too much." The major slapped the back of the seat. "Why did Frank and Jerry bother with the hair dye?"

"You called him Quill," Frank said. "Don't go out with him again."

"Don't cross over to the dark side," Jerry said.

Major Blakely leaned across Frank to direct his remarks to Jerry. "Quill Rethcaw is a local hero. He founded that casino and the proceeds finance local schools and who knows what else."

Mary patted the wad of small papers in her pocket. The men were discussing Quill as if she weren't there. The major said she talked too much, yet she was the only one who found any clues. She set her jaw and decided not to tell him anything.

"Rethcaw's safe on the reservation," the major continued. "No one will turn him in, especially now that we have alerted him."

Jerry answered, "Then we'll just have to lure him out of there."

31.

Less than an hour after returning home from Rapid City, Jerry called Ruben. "When can we pick up our special Cessna? I'm itching to fly it." Cell phone in hand, Jerry relaxed on the new leather couch. Sally, completely into Indian culture, had hung three of her watercolors of Kachina dolls and displayed a Navajo rug above the fireplace.

"You and Frank can bring the money on Friday. We'll celebrate with a hamburger at Wings." Ruben sounded ready to party. "You can fly it home right after the Fourth."

"Yes! July 5!" Jerry jumped up and waved in celebration and walked completely around the couch. "By the way, how are your book sales coming?"

"*¡Estupendo!* Half a dozen orders from each mechanic."

"Great. That Comanche, the one I did the seats for, did you sell it?"

"Got top dollar."

"Way to go, Ruben. Now that I have a working thumb again, I'll help you with another aircraft cabin."

Jerry wanted to keep a close eye on Auburn Airport. He was on his own with this, unless he found a clue significant enough to overcome his *nutcase* status. Too bad he couldn't ask Robina about tall strangers: She wasn't speaking to him. Fish Eyes would be back, circling Ruben's airplanes like a hawk hunting a rabbit.

On Tuesday, Jerry and Frank brought home their new bird and left it in transient parking at Palo Alto Airport overnight. The replacement Cessna 256PV, one of Ruben's reconstituted airplanes and even nicer than One-Eight-Echo, had a souped-up engine and long-range tanks. Jerry expected to lease a hangar right away. At the start of business on Wednesday, he dialed the manager of the Palo Alto Airport Leasing Authority.

"What do you mean, still no hangars available?" Jerry asked. "We've been on the waiting list for three years." Jerry punctuated *three years* by raising his voice and slapping the table. He needed that hangar, and he needed it now. He couldn't risk parking the white, orange, and gold plane outside at Palo Alto.

Jerry shifted his argument and sat straighter to bring an authoritarian tone to his voice. "Yesterday I brought home an airplane to replace Cessna 3318E, which, as you will recall, was stolen out of its tie-down space. When will you have something? I'm still parked over in transient."

"Sorry." He didn't sound sorry. "A rule is a rule."

Holding his temper, Jerry said, "I'm the one who implemented the pilot watch program. Can't you make an exception and bump me up on the list?"

"Nope. Can't will your hangar to your son or sell your place on the list."

Jerry threw his hat across the room and clenched and unclenched his jaw. Who was that rigid scumbag anyway? Yelling wouldn't accomplish anything. He and Frank would be flying it for a few days anyway. Next week, maybe he could find a hangar space at South County. He'd fly the pants off that machine while waiting for a space.

"Then move me to a different tie-down until I can do something," Jerry said before he hung up. Not to worry. He would romance Sally and enjoy the new Cessna.

Wednesday evening, Jerry took Sally out for dinner, telling her only that they were celebrating. His hair was uncharacteristically short, red at the scalp and dark at the tips—his barber had trimmed off most of the ugly dye from the visit to Little Eagle Casino. He looked smart in a maroon shirt and a tie. Sally wore a coral-colored summer dress. While they waited for glasses of wine in a candlelit booth at their favorite steak house, he handed her a bulging white envelope held together with a piece of cellophane tape. Grinning, he said, "Go ahead. Open it."

Sally, bursting with curiosity, shook the envelope and tore off the end. A set of aircraft keys fell onto the table along with a card picturing a dozen red roses. Jerry had written, "Come fly away with me."

She smiled at Jerry and palmed the keys. "How romantic."

"We'll fly to Paradise," Jerry said, leaning towards Sally, thinking he'd outdo Major Blakely on the romantic.

"Ooh-la-la, I'm ready." She patted his knee under the table.

Shortly after breakfast the next morning, Jerry and Sally left Palo Alto in the new Cessna 172. They climbed across Sunol Pass, the usual route towards all inland destinations. "I see we're going north," Sally said, pointing to the compass. "You still haven't told me where you're taking me."

"Yes, I did. Paradise," Jerry said. Sally looked pretty cute, wearing the headset—and smiling. "You asked me to take you there. I can't do a sunset at 25,000 feet, but I can do Paradise. It's near Chico at the north end of the Central Valley. We'll circle over it on our way to lunch in a special place."

Jerry showed her how to put in the frequency for a VOR—a navigational radio—and how to listen to the Morse code identifier, marked on the chart along the blue airway course lines. "I need you to dial in those numbers, there, to double-check my navigation."

"That's how Paul does it, too," Sally said.

"He doesn't have one of these." Jerry showed her the little airplane traveling along the course line on the small map and let her hold his handheld GPS.

On the horizon, he saw clouds ahead. "Some light rain coming up. If you feel uncomfortable, we'll go back." Jerry wondered just how comfortable Paul had made her feel on that Mooney ride in June.

Sally tightened her seat belt. "Just don't hit too many bumps."

About fifteen miles from Paradise, they flew through rain with broken cloud cover above. The sun cast their shadow onto a cloud below and surrounded them with a rainbow, a complete circle of brilliant color with the Cessna's shadow at the center. Fascinated, Sally studied the phenomenon under the right wing.

"We're about as close to Paradise as we can get, and a glory hole. Most pilots have never seen one." Jerry began a descent through a break in the clouds over Shasta Lake. With visibility more than ten miles, the lower part of Mount Shasta was visible on their right while the peak was shrouded by cloud.

"A glory hole over Paradise. You're even more romantic than Paul."

"Why do you call him Paul, when I still call him Major Blakely?" Jerry asked. Paul this, Paul that; he was sick of hearing about Paul.

Sally laughed. "I'll never tell."

On Wednesday night, Frank took Mary for dinner their favorite fish restaurant, a plain little place with good food, to celebrate bringing home the replacement airplane. After they clinked glasses of white Zinfandel, Mary said, "Major Blakely proposed to Betty while watching a sunset at Paradise. That's so-o-o romantic. Why haven't you taken me there?"

Frank brushed crumbs from a breadstick off his T-shirt. "I'm afraid I'm more a geek than a romantic. We can't go to 25,000 feet in a Cessna—14,000 feet tops. Paradise is an automated radio signal in the Los Angeles basin, an imaginary destination. It's close to LIMBO, another imaginary point on the chart, another strange name."

"You're no fun at all. Paradise sounds much more romantic than an imaginary point." Mary smoothed a bead of condensation down the side of her glass. "When will you show me the new plane?"

"I'll take you to Heavenly Valley this very weekend. We can ride the ski lifts for the view over Lake Tahoe."

"Heavenly Valley sounds almost as nice as Paradise." Mary reached over to touch Frank's hand. Even that Indian, Quill Rethcaw, was more romantic than her husband— moonrise over the Badlands. Then she pictured wild coyote eyes and a cold shiver ran down her spine.

"We can rent a car at Lake Tahoe Airport and drive to Emerald Bay, freeze our buns swimming in the lake while we cook our shoulders in the sun."

Mary held her wineglass to the light to enjoy its delicate pink color. "You make us sound like hot dogs, not exactly hot romance." Hot—like the small papers she had stolen in South Dakota. She had to tell somebody. "Uh, last week, at the casino—I didn't tell you—I snuck into Quill Rethcaw's office."

Frank's bushy eyebrows shot up.

Mary up-ended her purse over the table. Her lipstick and some coins rolled out, surrounding a wad of crumpled paper. Smoothing out a scrap, she said, "This is a receipt for roburite. That's an explosive used in mining. That casino takes in more in a day than a teacher earns in a year. And Quill told me he had sworn to take back the Indians' holy land, *Paha Sapa*."

"You could have been hurt." Frank put his hands over hers and leaned closer. "Oh, Mary, Mary," he said, caressing her with his eyes. "I don't know how to be romantic, but I love you with my very soul. Promise me you won't see Quill again."

Mary felt a rush of warmth, a breathless thrill. She smiled, for a moment a shy bookish girl on a date. "You are romantic after all. More romantic than Major Blakely."

Then a faraway look came into Mary's eyes. "Major Blakely scolded me as if I didn't have any common sense, but I was the only one to come home with any clues. Do you think we should give him the receipts from the casino?

On Thursday, Major Blakely reported to the ready room at Nellis AFB for flight duty. Mid-afternoon, headquarters reported a small plane approaching a prohibited area outside of Tonopah. In three minutes, he and his flight partner were airborne in F-16s and heading north from Nellis.

The major spotted a small four-place Piper inside of the prohibited area. With his partner close behind, he pulled alongside and rocked his wings. The off-course aircraft, too small to be a threat, needed to be escorted away from there. He transmitted across the sector and repeated on the emergency frequency: "Piper over Tonopah, you have entered prohibited air space. Turn away."

Standard interception procedure—until the small plane ignored his F-16. All pilots study rules of the airways, types of restricted airspace, and communication procedures required if military or law enforcement officials intercept an aircraft, similar to the situation when a highway patrolman pursues an automobile. Since 9/11, every time a pilot filed a flight plan, he reviewed intercept procedures. Even in peacetime, the penalty for non-compliance is to be shot down.

The major circled back closer to the aircraft and again rocked his wings. He made a slow turn to the left, indicating for the plane to follow him. "Piper over Tonopah. You have entered prohibited airspace. Follow me."

The small Piper flew deeper into the sensitive zone. Did not reply on the radio frequency for the sector. Did not waggle its wings. Did not turn left.

The major made a third pass. Was he a terrorist? "Piper over Tonopah, do you read me? Comply or be shot down." His F-16 swooped beneath the Piper and climbed vertically at full power, passing close by the aircraft's nose, a maneuver no pilot could ignore.

The small aircraft danced across the F-16's wake and continued its same straight-ahead flight path, like an arrow piercing the heart of the prohibited area. Did not reply on the emergency frequency. Did not reply with its transponder. Did not turn.

The pilots of the F-16s had no choice. One F-16 would give the formal order; the other would fire. Follow orders without question was the first tenet of boot camp. His partner was armed with missiles; the major would fire.

For a split second, Major Blakely wondered if the pilot was only a terrified kid, like Kedar. He radioed, one last time: "Piper over Tonopah. How do you read?"

No response.

The major returned to a position beside the wing of the Piper. He had no choice. He had followed intercept procedures as published in the Notices for Airmen. The Piper had not complied. His partner radioed, "Falcon One, Falcon One. Fire."

Major Blakely depressed a small button on the yoke. He didn't hear or feel the one-second burst of bullets, over-kill for such a small target. Falcon One hit the tail and the fuselage and the cockpit, a line of small puffs of smoke at contact.

The small Piper flew erratically and started a downward spiral, trailing white smoke, then a wider tail of black smoke. After one flash of flame, it exploded. From the major's cockpit, there was no sound. Smoke mushroomed. Small pieces rained onto the desert, cinder black rain.

His first kill—a civilian. He had never flown combat. He was a flight instructor who also guarded Hoover Dam. This could not have happened. *Aviate. Navigate. Communicate.* He concentrated on the job at hand.

Major Blakely felt cold sweat run down his upper lip under his oxygen mask. "My dear God . . . A civilian aircraft . . . I shot it down." He didn't know if he transmitted or if he only agonized with himself. He drew in a deep breath and controlled his breathing. His eyes followed the debris to the ground. The memory followed him for two days.

He needed to talk to another pilot, as a reality check. He called Jerry.

On Saturday, Jerry's day to stay home and mow the lawn, his cell phone rang while he balanced himself on a ladder trimming the apple tree away from the utility cables, just three rungs from the ground. He hopped down and tossed his cell phone into the air, then caught it again.

"Jerry, here. Oh, Major Blakely. Good to hear from you. I was just three rings from the ground, pruning a tree." Rungs, rings . . . Jerry was in a happy mood, just back from a short get-away with Sally.

"Are you free to talk for a while?" The major's voice was serious enough to report a death in the family. "Something so disturbing happened that I need a reality check from another pilot."

"That doesn't sound good. What happened?" Jerry sat down on the lawn and drew his knees up, supporting them with one arm.

"Well, it was bad." The major's low voice sounded flat. "I shot down a civilian aircraft, a four-place Piper, inside prohibited airspace. At the last moment, I saw Kedar, the pilot only a terrified kid."

Jerry's eyes widened in surprise and shock. "It was your duty. The Piper was in a prohibited airspace." He pictured the major, perfectly groomed, his summer uniform without a wrinkle. Jerry would like to wear that uniform but he wouldn't want the responsibility of shooting someone down.

"You're a private pilot—just fly recreationally. Tell me," Major Blakely asked somberly, "what you'd do, if you were intercepted by a F-16?"

"Sure. That's easy." Jerry relaxed: a more neutral subject. "Rock my wings, turn to follow him, communicate on the emergency radio frequency, squawk 7700 on the transponder. Pilots review intercept procedure every time they file a flight plan."

"If you saw a F-16 along your wing, you'd know what that meant?"

Jerry moved the cell phone to his other ear, as if changing ears would bring more cheerful news. "Sure. But I'm careful about where I fly."

"Now I feel a little better." He still sounded stressed out to Jerry. "After an explosion and fire like that, there's not much left. We don't know the pilot's identity."

For an instant, Jerry pictured Captain Fish Eyes, his gray hair ablaze, flaming like a candle. Could Jerry have done it—shot down a Piper? He didn't think so.

After a pause and speaking from his heart, Jerry said, "What an awful burden for you to carry, shooting down a civilian. I can't imagine how that would feel." Jerry wouldn't want that job or the gruesome responsibility of tagging dead bodies or the emotional task of notifying next of kin.

Jerry continued to think about the major's call. He finished mowing the lawn mechanically, as though he were on autopilot. How would they identify the pilot's charred remains?

32.

Aquila lingered over his favorite weekend breakfast at Wings Grill in Auburn served by Robina, the small blond waitress who called him Bill. He hadn't been there since he started moving out of his camp, The Guards. He had forgotten how beautiful she was. She wore a tight, rose-pink tank top that outlined her nipples, rosebuds ready to burst into bloom. He wanted to pluck one, to touch that nipple.

Robina. That meant *little robin*, he told her. When he called her Little Robin Rosebud, she gave him a smile that bathed him in California sunshine. That musical laugh, that voice. He smiled and daydreamed that she would ride with him to Rapid City. He wondered if she'd like South Dakota. He couldn't ask her: Women didn't usually like him. One look at his eyes, and she wouldn't like him either.

Aquila turned his chair to face Ruben's shop. He had had his eye on Cessna 256PV, one of Ruben's special Cessnas. He had taken pictures for his wallet, but several days ago, those two redheaded pilots flew away with it.

That *kan-ke-tan-ka* Jerry dyed his hair and dropped in at Little Eagle Casino. He even sent Mary. Aquila pictured Mary, petite and charming. She hadn't flinched when she looked at his eyes, and she understood about Medicine Woman, but she stole papers from his office. He wondered what she saw in that red-throated finch Frank. Without his red chin-feathers, he looked like a plucked chicken.

Jerry took the FBI to The Guards. Jerry followed him to Pahrump. Jerry followed him to South Dakota and snooped around at his casino. Then Jerry got himself a new airplane, the very one Aquila wanted. Not fair. Not fair at all.

Aquila addressed the back of the airplane's picture. He had a stamp in his pocket. There was a postal drop box on the corner.

Until the mail dropped onto the floor behind the front door, it was a normal lazy July day. Sally cleaned house on her day off from the art gallery while Jerry waxed the new Cessna at the airport. When she sorted the afternoon mail, Sally almost threw away a postcard picturing an airplane.

Usually, a card like that offered to buy Jerry's airplane—a name and a telephone number on the back—a generic ad. But this time, she recognized the Cessna they had taken to Paradise, with the typed message: *I want your airplane.*

When Sally showed the card to Jerry at supper, he slammed down his coffee cup and waved the card in the air. "Damn, damn, damn. It's him again, Captain Fish Eyes."

Jerry shot out of his chair and started a circular pacing pattern around Sally and the kitchen table. "He took that picture. He's watching everything we do."

After three circuits, Jerry's eyes had a wild look. He snorted and flared his nostrils, a bull ready to charge, lacking only the pawing of the turf with a hoof. "He's stalking my airplane. I have to guard the Cessna tonight."

Sally couldn't talk him out of it. Not on that day and not on the days following.

Later in the week, Frank dropped in for coffee. He followed Sally to the kitchen where a morose Jerry stared into space, leaning on his elbows over an empty cup. After a few sips in silence, Frank said, "Look, Old Buddy, it isn't necessary to sleep with that airplane every night. That's paranoid."

"So now I'm a nutcase?" Jerry didn't look up. His voice sounded flat.

"Borderline: just suffering from sleep deprivation."

"He's stalking the Cessna." Jerry fixed Frank with a woeful stare.

"Fish Eyes knows the FBI is after him. Why would he waste time watching you?"

"He wants our airplane. He sent me a picture of Six-Papa-Victor."

"He's probably not even around here, just wants to keep you on edge."

"Works, doesn't it?" Jerry rubbed bloodshot eyes.

"The FBI will find him before the end of summer vacation. In the meantime, take Sally somewhere on an overnight trip and keep the airplane away from Palo Alto," Frank suggested. "How about Sedona? The airport is on top of a mesa—almost like landing on an aircraft carrier. It's a romantic place with lots of Indian legends and souvenirs. Sally's into that big time now, isn't she?"

Jerry set his jaw, determined to stop Fish Eyes. "Maybe in August, after Sally's art show. I'll watch until then."

Frank frowned with concern. Jerry looked haggard. "You have to get more sleep."

"I'm fine," Jerry insisted.

Frank shrugged. He fished around in his pants pocket and opened a folded advertisement torn from *Pilot Magazine* depicting a stainless steel plate attached to a heavy-duty lock, a lock-guard for the airplane that covered the instrument panel and immobilized both yokes. "You won't have to guard the Cessna after next week. One of these will protect Six-Papa-Victor against anything short of an atomic attack."

Sally watched Jerry get thinner. He bought an air mattress for his van and spent every night at the airport until he looked like a raccoon, his eyes sunken and rimmed by dark circles. When she pleaded with him to sleep at home and get some rest, he said only, "Fish Eyes," or "Can't let him win." He had a complete fixation. Sally fumed.

Major Blakely had to help. Cell phone in hand, Sally settled in on the couch, her feet resting on one arm, her head on the other. "I really, really need your help. Could you finagle a pass for Jerry to park his airplane at Moffett, just until you catch the captain?"

"That's not so easy. What's the problem?"

Sally loved the strong sound of his voice. "Jerry insists upon guarding that airplane every night instead of sleeping, nightmares about Captain Fish Eyes. If the bags under his eyes get any deeper, he'll trip over them."

"Good Heavens. How long has this been going on?"

"Ever since Jerry got a strange card in the mail: 'I want your airplane,' typed under a picture of his new Cessna Six-Papa-Victor." Sally twisted a lock of hair between her thumb and her first finger. "He said Captain Wachter sent it."

"I see." The major paused.

"Somebody has to die before Jerry gets a hangar at Palo Alto. He'd rest easy if he could park it at Moffett."

The major coughed and said something about running late. He called Betty.

In a few seconds, Betty came on the line. "You saved me from the ironing. How're you doing?"

"Sort of fine. Uh, I finished several watercolors of your Katchinas." Sally had not expected to visit with Betty.

"You called just to tell me that?" Betty's laugh was low and hearty.

"Jerry flew me to Paradise, . . . and I got pregnant there." Sally felt like singing. She hadn't planned to tell her, until she remembered where Paul had proposed to Betty.

"Pregnant at Paradise—you joined the mile-high club?"

"No," Sally giggled. "But I saw a circular rainbow, a glory hole." She had been pregnant before the trip with Jerry, but Paradise made a better story.

"Have you told Jerry?"

"Actually . . . no, not yet." Sally's face fell. "He won't come home from the airport. He's babysitting with his Cessna, afraid Captain Wachter's going to steal it."

After Sally hung up, she sat with her head in her hands and listened to something mindless on TV. Jerry worried every day about Fish Eyes stalking his airplane, worried so much about tomorrow that he forgot to enjoy today. Captain Wachter wouldn't be back. How could she make Jerry forget about Fish Eyes?

On a warm July night with a full moon, Aquila slipped through the cut fence near his former office at his encampment at The Guards' Academy. He shoveled a group of chanterelles growing under an oak tree into a large box, careful to include a section of lacy white mycelium filaments attached to decaying wood. He was moving his prize mushrooms, a few at a time, to the fungi cloning and propagation laboratory he had prepared on the reservation.

How zany, stealing his own mushrooms. Aquila smuggled them out at night to avoid the arrest warrant that John had warned him about. Those irritating, interfering redheaded pilots: That woodpecker Jerry, that pesky *kan-ke-tan-ka*.

He paused to admire a particularly fine tree mushroom bathed in subtle bands of gray by the moonlight and faintly luminescent—yellow, orange and brown in daylight and difficult to propagate. His great-grandmother Medicine Woman would have loved it. He thought about the times they had walked together, gathering mushrooms and herbs.

Aquila pictured Medicine Woman wrapped in her buffalo robe, her white hair proudly braided. On the day she had died, he knelt by her side in the *tipi*. She wanted to go to Wind Cave, the holy place in *Paha Sapa* where *Tokahe* had led the Buffalo Nation up to the surface of the earth. "Ak-wee-la," she said, "Stay out of Wounded Knee."

Aquila had thought she confused the massacre of 1890, the last major battle between the Sioux and the United States, with the current conflicts. He didn't tell her that, using sacred bat guano and powdered *ka-pop-a-ta-tan-ka* mushroom, he made such a powerful explosive that a sample the size of three buffalo nickels blasted a hole big enough for a white man's burial. He hadn't used it at Wounded Knee.

Aquila had taken Medicine Woman to *Paha Sapa* in his pickup. While he drove and held back tears, Buffalo Mother had silently cradled her mother in her lap. He felt a deep anger at the unfairness. His grandmothers' stories were true: the United States Government had stolen the Black Hills and the gold from the Great Sioux Nation. And worse: Indians suffered humiliation—even murder—if they lived off the reservation. His college friend Fred Deepwater had died in armed conflict at Wounded Knee.

He had sworn revenge . . .

Aquila kicked a tree root.

He stumbled in the dark and spilled a box of dirt. Silently, Aquila brushed himself off and reset the cut fence. Leaving The Guards was only a minor setback.

33.

Early in July in his afternoon mail, Frank found a note from Kedar with an essay on a second sheet of paper:

Mother and I are fine, except that I'm stuck on geometry. I can figure out all the problems, but I don't understand proofs *at all*. It's so easy that there's nothing to say but they say it anyway. Can you come and help me? Mother said she'd bake the bread you liked and please bring Mrs. Peterson. You can stay in our crystal hotel. (Ha, ha.) Please come. Mother said I have to write essays. Here's one:

Mother's Accidental Mine

Mother found her mine by accident, an accident that blew a hole in the hill and made a black crater beneath a white jagged pegmatite dike. Her pegmatite dike is like a cave filled with red and green sparkling crystals, like walking inside of a geode; the Indians called them *thunder eggs*. Technically, a pegmatite dike is formed by a magma intrusion which cools slowly, forming huge crystals and sometimes gold. That means that magma oozed into fissures in granite, about a million years ago. Mother should call her mine the Accidental, but she calls it the Argonaut because that's what she always has called it. —The End.

"It's hard to say no, isn't it?" Frank handed the letter to Mary with the rest of the mail. "Want to have an adventure this weekend?"

"Why not? You've been itching to fly that airplane somewhere," Mary said. "Besides that, you can't resist a chance to talk geometry. I'll go for the scenery."

Early on the next Saturday morning, Frank and Mary took Six-Papa-Victor away from Palo Alto, away from any stalking activity. Jerry still guarded the Cessna every night, even though the FBI was pursuing Captain Wachter a.k.a. Fish Eyes. Frank was content to let the FBI do its job, and he had promised Kedar tutoring with geometry. It was still early, early enough to reach the Argonaut Mine without melting in the heat.

At Daggett-Barstow Airport, Mary dashed for the ladies' room while Frank secured the aircraft. Kedar sprinted towards Frank and almost knocked him over with his enthusiastic greeting. "Your hair looks funny, Mr. Peterson. It's red at the roots and brown on the ends. Where's your beard?"

Frank clapped the boy's shoulder and smiled. "I'll tell you a long story about a short beard later tonight."

On the way to the parking area, Mother said she knew a shortcut. Kedar drove the pickup over the roughest terrain since the road to The Guards, Mother by the passenger door, Frank in the middle, Mary stacked on his lap. After bumping and lurching the truck over the non-road for half an hour, Kedar leaned across Mary and said, "Snails."

"*Nein, nein. Schnell*-truck." Mother and Kedar howled with laughter, a secret joke of some sort. *Schnell*-truck dodged rocks and rode the edge of ragged ruts, bouncing Mary and Frank back and forth in the desert heat. In a bit longer than Mother's "no time," Kedar stopped the truck with a bump and a cloud of dust. Mary was eager to see what Frank had described, the habitation carved deep into the hill with mining equipment.

Without natural light, Mary found Mother's home dark and claustrophobic, even though crystals captured yellow incandescent light across the walls and ceiling like flecks of golden butter in buttermilk, small irregular crystals of quartz in natural granite scooped out by mining equipment. Mary wondered how Mother kept it dusted.

Mary followed Kedar through the narrow doorway into the living room to work on writing assignments. He sat quietly, his eyes dancing, long enough for Mary to read the first two pages in his spiral notebook. Then he started to fidget and hopped up.

"Thank you for the book," he said. "How did you know it was my birthday?"

"Your birthday? Is it today?" Puzzled, Mary frowned, but her eyes smiled.

"No. I really have three birthdays— June 15 like real, February 23 like Mother wrote in the Bible, and April 15 like my driver's license."

"Be glad you weren't born February 29."

"That would be like almost never." His dark expressive eyes gazed at Mary.

She answered with a hearty laugh. Mother must have adopted him at first sight.

"Do you like my essays? Mother says I have to write them."

"Your compositions are unusual and your grammar isn't bad," Mary said. "Just keep writing. I'll comment and send them back—we can be pen pals."

"Okay. I'm ahead of Mother. She didn't go to high school."

"A lot of women her age didn't finish high school."

"Did you go to college?"

"Yes. I'm a registered nurse."

"Could Mother go to college with me?" Kedar asked. "Could she be a nurse?"

Mary stopped reading and smiled. "Why not? I majored in nursing because I'm interested in medicine."

Kedar leaned over to pull her up with one hand. "Want to see my room?"

At the doorway, he switched on a pole lamp. His small space held a twin bed, its blanket tucked taut and military, and a student desk with a lamp and bookshelf. A rolled-up prayer rug leaned in a corner. No posters, no radio, no television. The light reflected red and green patterns from a large crystal onto a white dresser scarf beside a small gold biplane ornament, the decoration Mary had wrapped with the book last month.

Kedar, shy and hesitant, held a small green crystal up to the light. "Mrs. Peterson, this is for you, a tourmaline crystal from our mine. It's green, like your eyes."

"As perfect as an emerald. I'll cherish it." Mary twisted the stone between her fingers, admiring it. She wondered how such a charming young man could have flown a suicide mission, and how a dedicated teacher like Quill had allowed it.

Later and after dinner, Kedar served Mary's dessert first—strawberry shortcake. Mother followed him and scooped ice cream onto each plate. When everyone settled at the table, Frank started the story about how he lost his beard.

"The FBI is still working on the case. No one knows the whereabouts of the captain. We tracked him to South Dakota. I dyed my beard to disguise myself, but it looked so awful that I shaved it off."

Kedar didn't listen at first. He liked the way Mrs. Peterson laughed with her eyes, her green eyes, like the crystals. He liked her lilting voice and the way she looked right at him when she spoke. He wondered if she was an angel in disguise.

"His name is Wachter—"

"Not Whack-ter," Kedar said. "That isn't right. It sounded like Phone-Vector or something. I never knew exactly."

"Von Wachter—that must be it. Some German last names use von: means of or from . . . Captain of The Guards. The German *v* sounds like an English *f*, *w* like a *v*, . . . might need an umlaut . . ."

Kedar's eyes widened.

Mary shook her head.

"*Ja, Ja.*" Mother smiled and nodded, her white braid bobbing up and down.

"Back to South Dakota . . . We went there to visit his gambling casino, a huge building with a statue on the roof—an Indian chief holding an eagle."

"Is Captain Vector an Infidel?" Kedar sat forward and puckered his forehead between his eyebrows. The captain owned a gambling casino. He remembered flying in One-Bravo-Bravo. Major Blakely wasn't an Infidel: he didn't gamble and he knew about the lightning from God.

"Now how would I know that?" Frank asked.

"Then would I fight the captain in a holy war?"

"He is fighting a holy war," Mary said. "Mount Rushmore National Monument is right in the middle of the Black Hills, a holy place for the Sioux Indians. The United States Government took their lands away."

"He can't be an Indian. His eyes weren't right," Kedar said. The captain wasn't fighting a holy war. He was an Infidel.

"He's only part Indian," Mary said.

Kedar leapt out of his chair, his face like a thunder-cloud. "He said I was a soldier in a holy war."

"You were brave and you followed orders and you could have died. You must feel sad, angry, betrayed. Write to me about it, Kedar, and heal the bruises on your soul. I won't let anyone else read it, not even Mr. Peterson."

Kedar didn't answer. His frown softened. He wanted her to hold him. He wanted to touch her dark brown hair.

Mary asked, "Tomorrow, can you take me to see a desert sunrise?"

All that night, Kedar didn't sleep. She said he was brave and she liked his essays. Her voice was beautiful. He liked the way that she looked right at him when she spoke. She liked the green crystal, the one like her eyes. He wondered if she knew him well enough to give him a hug before she left tomorrow.

Up before dawn, Kedar made a cup of coffee for Mrs. Peterson. He noticed her low cut shoes; he would be careful where he took her. He bent over in the entry porch and slapped his sturdy boots together upside down.

"Always shake out your boots—there might be a scorpion."

Mary's eyes widened. "Have you had scorpions in your shoes?"

"No. It works, doesn't it?" Kedar said, his tone serious, his eyes twinkling.

In a few minutes, the fireball rose over the horizon, red glare silhouetting jagged peaks. Mary shaded her eyes with one hand. "I love sunrises and sunsets. I'd like to collect them and play them back on drizzly foggy days."

Kedar pictured an oversized projector painting misty red and orange patterns onto the sky. He didn't think it would work.

After a pause, Mary asked, "You are going to write more for me, aren't you?"

"Every day," he said. Twice a day, he thought.

"Then I'll make an assignment. I want you to write an essay—arguments for and against, like a proof in geometry. Examine your feelings, too. Your topic: Holy War is an Oxymoron. Do you know what an *oxymoron* is?"

"A stupid person?"

"No, but that's a good guess. An oxymoron is a self-contradictory statement, like *hot ice*. Killing people isn't holy. I've heard veterans say that war is hell."

"Then war sucks but oxymoron is politer." Holy wars were holy but war was hell. A soldier in a holy war that was an Indian's holy war so he wasn't really a soldier in a holy war: the situation itself was an oxymoron. That was what he would write.

Mary laughed. "You could say that."

Kedar didn't answer.

When they returned to the cabin, Kedar burst through the door. "Good morning, Mr. Peterson. Do you know what an oxymoron is?"

"Let me see. A one-eyed mule belonging to Oxylus in Greek mythology."

"No." Kedar shrieked with laughter. "It's not a mule and it's not a stupid person."

"Maybe it's a hungry person," Mother said. She set a platter of biscuits on the table next to a bowl of fresh fruit. "It's a pity you have to leave so early."

Afterwards Kedar drove and bounced the truck to Daggett. He sang duets with Mary for an hour, popular songs from the radio, but Frank declined, saying that he sang like a frog but tapping the beat on the door beneath the open window. At the airport, Kedar helped Frank to preflight and waved from the truck until they were out of sight.

On the way home from Daggett, Frank said to Mary, "Now we know why no one at The Guards had heard of Captain Wacher: his name sounds like *vector*. Should we share this information with Major Blakely?"

"Why bother? He never used what I found out for him in South Dakota. Just let the FBI take care of it."

"Do you think Wachter will try something again with our Cessna?"

"Of course not. He knows the FBI wants him, and Quill's an intelligent man."

On Saturday somewhere along the 101, Aquila thought about Auburn tomorrow and Robina with her golden-fleece curls. He pictured her in the patio at Wings. She would bend over to serve his coffee, her nipples erect beneath her rose-pink tank top. He wanted to put his hand against that soft fluffy hair and draw his Little Robin Rosebud to him, kiss her, hold her soft body against him. He heard her musical voice, *Bill, my Bill,* and she smiled her special smile. He reached under her shirt and cupped her breast in one hand to fondle the nipple. Little Robin Rosebud, come to South Dakota—

Danger Flammable Liquid

The tanker stopped right in front of him—the one carrying fuel. Aquila stomped the brakes and held them with full strength. His rented truck skidded along the pavement and its bumper tapped the tanker. His sunglasses fell off. His heart pounded. His hands shook.

Aquila slowed the truck and fell back into his lane. Under control again, he bent to pick up his sunglasses and pictured Robina looking at his eyes with revulsion. When he was a boy he had practiced before the mirror, puffing himself up and making his eyes widen and bulge out, until his tormentors at school were too afraid to tease him. *Ghost Eyes,* they had called him. How he had hated that. Captain Von Wächter never gave his students the full eye treatment. Any jokes about his eyes, they ran laps and did push-ups.

Late that afternoon Aquila parked the rented truck behind Ryan's Place in Los Banos. He'd heard Ruben say their pie was *numero uno.* That would be his dinner tonight. Tomorrow he'd have his favorite Sunday breakfast at Wings in Auburn and see Little Robin Rosebud once more on his way eastward on Interstate 80. He'd stay on I-80 until Cheyenne, then head north to Rapid City.

34.

A low mist, smelling fish-like and earthy, hung over the brackish water in the sloughs in the San Joaquin Delta. The best fishing was in the last two hours of a receding tide. Frank killed the outboard motor in the small boat, and Jerry rowed them through some reeds. Waterfowl called one another: "Kee-yah, Kee-yah," kibitzing and circling while Frank set out borrowed rods and tackle. He hoped that fishing would take Jerry's mind away from worry about the Cessna. He handed Jerry a rod with a baited hook and said, "You're sure to catch a big bass."

"I haven't been fishing in years and years." Jerry sounded enthusiastic for the first time in weeks. The deep dark pockets under his eyes bore silent testimony to his chronic lack of sleep.

"You can work off some aggression cleaning it. Just pretend you're scaling Captain Fish Eyes."

"Sure, sure." Jerry, who hadn't felt any action on his rod, decided to move his line. Something heavy held it down, maybe a snag.

"Reel it up. Either an old tire, or a catfish."

"Whoa! What *is* that thing?" Jerry looked at a bulging head with feelers around the mouth. "That's one ugly puss."

"They're good eating, it you know how to cook it."

"I'll let him go," said Jerry, grabbing the fish with bare hands.

"Ouch! What the heck!" Jerry put a bleeding finger into his mouth. The fish flopped around in the boat.

"Out you go," said Frank, pulling the hook out with a forceps and pitching the fish overboard. "They have a spiny fin that sticks you." Frank handed Jerry a medicated wipe for his injured finger.

"I read about catfish last night," Frank said. "A mean one in Brazil, called a *candiru*—a cool candidate for Captain Fish Eyes' collection of cruel critters. A swimming parasitic finishing nail: two inches long, slim with sharp teeth, bloodsuckers. They slip behind the gill cover on larger fish, set their spines and bite. Swimmers dread them: they enter the urethra. Terrible pain, when they set their spines."

"Whoa!" Jerry squinted. "Just thinking about that gives me terrible pain."

When Jerry caught a large small-mouth bass, Frank dropped it into the boat.

"My grandfather used to do that, take it off the hook for me," Jerry said. "I caught a wall-eyed pike once. They're spiny, lots of teeth. Those eyes rival the captain's."

That evening, with a pilot he trusted on duty at the airport and a new lock on Six-Papa-Victor, Jerry decided to sleep in his own bed. He tossed and turned for hours, then dreamed he was fishing. He caught a catfish with big eyes that kept growing. It flopped and jumped in the boat and Jerry backed away, falling out into the water. In the moonlight he saw small slivers of flashing light, all around him.

Then the pain began: real pain, in his bladder or his abdomen or his flank. Jerry needed help. Sally took him to the hospital emergency room.

No flying today, not with Jerry in the hospital. Frank carried a single pink rose in a disposable vase and hurried down the hall at Kaiser Permanente to Room 401.

From the door, Frank noticed how pale and skinny his friend looked, lying there against a white sheet on a hospital bed. "Hey, Jerry. Hear you have a cute nurse."

Frank still held the rose. If he put it on Jerry's chest, he'd look like a corpse. Frank shivered and asked, "What happened? Sally said something about kidney stones."

"That's right. I was full of gravel, now it's sand. You know those candiru dudes, the swimming finishing nails you told me about yesterday? I dreamed that I was surrounded by them, just before the pain woke me up."

"Good heavens, man. Your imagination has run amok."

"Before that, Captain Fish Eyes on the hook, with teeth you wouldn't believe."

"Should have left him on the hook, dropped him over the side—gone for good."

Then Sally came into the room. Jerry asked her for an aspirin, or two, or three.

"You get two every four hours and that's all. Did you know that aspirin is an Indian medicine?" Sally asked. "They used to chew willow bark—Mary told me."

"You're really into that Indian stuff, aren't you?" Jerry said. "How about two aspirin and all the willow bark I can chew?"

"Sounds like you have termites now," Frank said. "Get some sleep, pal. I'll be back tomorrow." Frank knew Jerry needed to rest, both physically and mentally. Two nights away from guarding the airplane wouldn't do much for his sleep deficit. The trip to the Delta hadn't helped him with his chronic worry-habit. Instead, Jerry's nightmares had shifted from Fish Eyes and a stolen Cessna to monster fish. Frank had one other idea, a gift he would buy for Jerry.

The next morning, Jerry went home from the hospital. When Frank telephoned to check up on him, Sally answered the phone. "Jerry still isn't sleeping."

"More insomnia?"

"Last night Jerry dreamed that a huge wall-eyed pike kept growing as it swam after him. Mouth open, all those sharp teeth, bigger all the time. He tried to get away, kicked, kicked, and kicked harder. Then he kicked me. Hard. Those nightmares have to stop."

"Hey, I'll take him to lunch, get him out of your hair," Frank said.

An hour later when Frank picked him up to go to lunch, Jerry looked stronger, except for serious dark circles under his eyes. At the restaurant, Frank treated him to a turkey sandwich, fresh roasted turkey on a French roll. When they were down to iced tea, Frank said, "Look at you. You're skinny, not sleeping, a candidate for a shrink. You kicked Sally last night. She's hopping mad."

Jerry's eyes widened and he paused before answering.

"It's those dreams." Jerry frowned and added, "I know what you're going to say. I don't go for any of that psychotherapy junk."

"I was hoping you'd say that."

Frank pulled out a bag he had carried with him. "I found this book for you, *Control Your Dreams, Dream Your Control*. You imagine situations—the more bizarre the better—where you win against Captain Fish Eyes, or whatever is out of control in your life. It helps you to regain your equilibrium."

"Sounds heavy and stupid and boring." Jerry grimaced and crossed his arms.

"No, no. It's a plan of action. You confront your devils. For example, something awful chases you. You can't escape. You wake up, your heart pounding. Force yourself back into the dream: turn around and punch him one, he falls down dead. Or, he's carrying an ax, you grab it, let the momentum swing it around, cut off his head. You have to steal the ball and run with it."

"Well, I guess I'll at least read it."

Jerry showed no enthusiasm. Frank hoped he'd read the first chapter before he threw the book into the dumpster.

"It does make some sense," Jerry said. "My grandfather—he coached me when I played football in high school—always told me to steal the ball from the opposing team."

"Exactly right." Frank wondered if Jerry would channel his overactive imagination into dream control. He'd ask him about it next week, when Jerry changed the oil.

"Like opening a Christmas present," Jerry said. He removed the aircraft's cowling, like lifting the hood on a car, and prepared to drain the oil from Six-Papa-Victor's crankcase. Mineral oil facilitated the initial wearing in of new cylinders. The shiny new engine had flown its first twenty-five hours and needed to use the usual 15/50 Aero-Shell.

"More like putting a diaper on a baby." Frank arranged a plastic drop cloth under the engine to keep the tie-down space clean and wrapped a plastic trash bag around the nose wheel tire and its new orange fairing.

Jerry opened the drain and collected the mineral oil in a plastic tub. Using a funnel, he poured it into empty quart oil containers for disposal with other hazardous waste. "I hope somebody recycles this stuff."

Frank wiped the oil out of the tub with paper towels and started filling a trash bag. When he policed their tie-down area, he found an empty Starbucks coffee cup and a handful of sugar papers. "Somebody likes sweet coffee, and he's messy, too."

Jerry pointed out an area on the taxiway near the next parked airplane where someone had emptied an ashtray. He swept the mess into a dustpan and sealed the butts into the trash bag along with the coffee cups. "They smoke, too. I hate that stink."

"Who would be careless enough to light up surrounded by gas fumes?" Frank remembered how Jerry had dumped the Captain's ashtray down the toilet at The Guards. He tried to picture the smoker blown into small pieces, fish food raining down over the bay, as recommended in Jerry's controlled daydreams book; he hadn't the imagination for it. Frank said only, "He'd light up the whole place."

"You have to be addlepated to smoke anyway."

Frank knew that Jerry hated cigarettes in any form: ashes, smoke—and Captain Fish Eyes, too—he left butts in Foxy Lady's ashtray. Jerry hadn't smiled about lighting up the whole place. In fact, he hadn't smiled lately. Frank asked, "Would you like to fly Six-Papa-Victor? I could go to Stockton later."

"No, go ahead. Call me for a ride home in two or three hours." Jerry stood by the side of the runway until Frank took off. Pilots always flew two or three traffic patterns over the airport to check everything after maintenance or after an oil change.

After his second landing, Frank gave a thumbs-up when he taxied past Jerry, now seated on the instructor's bench. Jerry waved and walked towards the parking lot.

Frank waited, propeller turning, for departure clearance to Stockton for his Friday errand. Ruben's perfectly balanced control surfaces made Six-Papa-Victor a joy to fly. Certainly the nicest Cessna Frank had ever flown, and the first time he had broken in a new aircraft engine.

Frank advanced the throttle when he heard, "Six-Papa-Victor. Cleared for takeoff. Hold runway heading until the Dumbarton Bridge." He imagined Six-Papa-Victor as eager to fly as he was.

Airborne above the bay and near the salt evaporation ponds, Frank expected the tower to clear him to call departure control. Instead, he heard, "Cessna Six-Papa-Victor, immediate right turn. Return for landing. Cleared to land either runway."

Must be another Cessna out here, a similar call number. Frank didn't respond.

"Six-Papa-Victor, if you hear me, return Palo Alto. Cleared to land. Either runway. Six-Papa-Victor, how do you read?"

Frank began a right turn and keyed the mike. "Six-Papa-Victor, returning Palo Alto. What's the problem?"

"You're filling the sky with black smoke."

At first, the gauges seemed normal. The engine backfired, almost as if Six-Papa-Victor heard *black smoke*.

The Cessna shuddered and shook. In seconds, the temperature gauge shot up. Frank yelled into the radio, "May Day! May Day!"

Frank hoped he would make the runway. Was it on fire? Should he shut down or let the engine continue with partial power? Some power was better than no power. San Francisco Bay looked dirty gray—polluted and frigid—a hostile environment. If he ditched, the Cessna would flip over and sink wheels up.

The tower radioed other aircraft in the area and sent them to circle over Moffett or over the KGO radio tower, clearing everyone away from the runway.

What was wrong with Six-Papa-Victor? Its new engine had flown so smoothly. He hadn't practiced emergencies lately. Best glide, trim for best glide.

Frank slowed the aircraft and slowed the descent. The engine burped and growled. The shaking was the worst. Back fire. Pop-pop-pop. Six-Papa-Victor jerked.

Frank leaned the mixture. Louder pop, bigger bump.

Gentle turns. Make a close-in base swoop. A sharp turn would make him lose altitude. He couldn't turn smoothly with jerks and bumps. How far was the runway?

No time to think. Bump, hop, hopscotch forward: too low. Could he make it?

The engine seized just as Frank turned to line up with the runway. Quiet. No jerking. Wrong way, wrong wind. *Just do it.* Dead-stick landing. Land on those numbers. He shut out every thought, except the picture of a perfect landing.

Fuel: off. Radios: off. What else? What else?

Stay alive.

Frank's medulla took over.

Somehow, Frank was down safely. Stopped. Fire engine. Siren. He stepped out of the cabin. His knees buckled. He grabbed a strut.

"What happened? What the devil?"

"Clear the area, sir. Can you make it? That way, sir." A fireman pointed away from the Cessna.

Frank left the runway under his own power. The airplane had to be towed.

Frank still clutched the aircraft keys, suspended on a ring with Jerry's Lucky Day Locksmith medallion. *Damned lucky.* What made a new engine freeze?

"Sugar? Sugar? What the Hell?" Jerry was in shock. He held his cell phone at arm's length as though it were a cobra ready to strike. The flowers on the wallpaper in his kitchen seemed to dance, swaying in an unnatural breeze. He turned to Frank in disbelief. "Don, from ZP Maintenance."

Frank suspended his coffee cup in mid-air, as though frozen in place.

Jerry punched the speaker button on his phone. Don reported that Six-Papa-Victor's new engine needed replacing. He'd never seen anything like this, sugar in the gas tank. That happened to some unlucky pilot at Reid-Hillview Airport ten years ago.

"We'll be right down there." Jerry snapped the cell phone shut.

"Good Lord. The Starbucks cups," Frank said, his face contorted in horror. "Somebody deliberately put sugar in the tanks."

Jerry turned red and his eyes bulged. "It was Fish Eyes! He almost killed my best friend. A new engine will cost plenty. He'll pay. It'll cost him." Jerry began one of his circular pacing patterns and pictured Captain Wachter . . . eight feet tall, arms extended over his head, a movie monster. Jerry twirled the rope around his head and threw a lasso over the monstrous captain. He towed him to the windsock standard and strung him up by the feet—coins and money raining down from his pockets, Captain Fish Eyes begging for mercy . . .

Frank watched Jerry circumambulate with arms extended. "Dream control?"

Jerry nodded and acted out wiping the sheepish grin off his face.

287

"Works, doesn't it?" Frank jumped to his feet and put their cups in Sally's dishwasher. "Let's get on the road. My flight bag and sunglasses are still on Six-Papa-Victor's backseat."

A little later, Frank parked his car in front of ZP Maintenance at Palo Alto Airport. Six-Papa-Victor, beautiful as ever, sat just inside the door. Frank wondered how he could have ruined its engine. Jerry put one hand on Six-Papa-Victor's cowling as if comforting a sick friend. Frank had butterflies in his stomach, remembering his emergency landing that morning.

"Such a pretty little airplane." Don stopped work on the Bonanza just behind the immobilized Cessna and set down his wrench. He wiped oil off his hands and patted Six-Papa-Victor's propeller. "Not a scratch on her, even with that emergency landing. Frank should've made a propeller strike. Then the engine work would be covered by insurance. Want me to replace the propeller with this curled up one, temporary-like?"

Speechless, Frank turned to Jerry and shook his head.

Jerry weighed Don's offer. After a pause, he answered, "No thanks, Don. It's really tempting—we don't have that kind of money—but we have to sleep nights."

A few minutes later, Frank opened the Cessna's back door to retrieve his flight bag. Jerry grabbed the tow bar to take home, because, he said, it was really irritating to rent a plane with no tow bar. Then Jerry ordered fuel.

"Come on, Frank," Jerry said, already in motion and walking to the empty tie-down. "Maybe the fuel jockey saw something."

The fuel truck didn't slow until Jerry waved it down with the tow bar.

"You called for fuel, but I don't see any airplane," said the fuel driver, a college student with long brushy hair under a backward facing baseball cap. He looked at the two redheaded dudes with a flight bag and a tow bar. "Must be some mistake."

"We don't need fuel, just the fuel truck driver who was on yesterday," Jerry said, leaning on the tow bar. "Somebody tampered with the fuel in our airplane—a white Cessna with orange and gold trim—right here. Did you see anyone fooling around?"

The driver remembered someone checking the fuel in one wing, a pilot he hadn't met, but he didn't know everybody who flew out of Palo Alto. The man he had seen was tall and gray-haired and had a slight limp. "His limp didn't slow him down when he jumped up on the strut to take off the fuel cap. But it was peculiar. I had never seen a pilot preflight with a lighted cigarette hanging out of his mouth—lucky it didn't explode. He had a Starbucks coffee cup in one hand, still held it when he climbed up on the strut."

"*Bingo.* Captain Wachter is a smoker. I told you he did it. Right now, I want to hit him in the head with a tow bar." Jerry raised the tow bar above his head as though an eight-foot tall captain laughed at him, staring with those evil eyes. He imagined Captain Fish Eyes, a lighted cigarette drooping out of his mouth, lifted into the air by exploding fuel, one eyeball blown out of its socket. Fish Eyes fell back into the flames, an oversized chestnut roasting on an open fire, the eyeball blown over the fence to the golf course, hit by a golfer into the cup. Just one eyeball, staring up out of the cup . . .

"What are you doing, waving that tow bar?" asked the fuel jockey.

Gazing skyward, Frank said, "Maybe he'll blow himself up while refueling."

The driver's eyes widened and his mouth opened as if he feared mad-cow or Alzheimer's or worse. "What gives with you guys? Who is the captain person?"

As though coming out of a trance, Jerry slowly lowered the tow bar and turned towards the bushy-headed fuel truck driver. "Thanks for your help. That person you saw, with the Starbucks coffee, we think he put sugar into our tanks."

Just one eyeball: staring out of the cup. Jerry arced the tow bar and followed through, a perfect stroke. Take that, Fish Eyes.

On Saturday morning Aquila took up residence at his favorite table at Wings Grill at Auburn. The windsock floated in a gentle breeze. A Piper Cub swooped in for a touch and go. Little Robin Rosebud brought his coffee and she seemed glad to see him. He leaned back, enjoying simple pleasures. He liked it here. The only thing better would be if Little Robin would fly away with Little Eagle.

When he turned to face Ruben's maintenance shop, he saw another Cessna for sale, a snow-white beauty with long-range tanks and a built-in GPS. Aquila thought he could fly the white Cessna through Tonopah, because they wouldn't expect it—the airway less traveled. At Tonopah, he would have to get fuel in daylight on a weekday, no self-service there. He'd change tail numbers first. He'd fly through Rock Springs to Rapid City—beautiful this time of year—and fly early in the mornings to avoid thunderstorms.

Aquila didn't ask Robina about South Dakota when she came out to the U-Haul to admire his 19-kilogram coconut. No, he didn't know how that double coconut palm had traveled to The Guards. Next time, he'd show her his monster mushroom.

The next time he came to Auburn, he thought he'd wear colored contact lenses. Blue would be nice. Then he'd risk it: take off the sunglasses. Would she still like him?

Aquila would return soon.

35.

Jerry's cell phone grew out of his belt as though attached by an umbilical cord. He usually answered on the first ring, but this time, nursing a headache while watching a *Star Trek* rerun, he waited until the fourth ring. His caller ID showed Major Blakely.

The major sounded stiff, as if his teeth were clenched. "We have a body at the morgue here at Nellis that we can't identify. I thought you might have an idea."

"A body! What do you mean?" Jerry sensed that the major needed more than an idea. "Why do you think I could help?"

Major Blakely continued without answering Jerry's question. "This morning, a stolen Cessna 172 crashed and burned. The pilot was decapitated, his body charred. The only part left, really, is half of his face with one eyeball."

"How gruesome!" Jerry pictured those awful eyes, the captain staring and laughing . . . one eyeball staring out of a golf cup, a driver in Jerry's hand . . . Fish Eyes got what he deserved. "One eye?"

"That's why we can't identify him." The major's voice, unusually flat, sounded matter of fact. "The aircraft flew into terrain, broke apart, and burned."

Shocked, Jerry said, "At least you didn't have to shoot him down," the first words that came into his head. He hesitated, remembering the major's anguish last month.

"A stolen Cessna 172, you say?" Jerry paused and stared at the ceiling, as if for inspiration. "*Bingo!* That just might work. Say listen—let me call you back in ten minutes."

Jerry tossed his cell phone into the air, caught it with one hand, and hit auto-dial for Frank's home number. Mary

291

was a cancer nurse; she had to know. "Mary, is that you? I need to ask you a question."

"Are you okay? This is Jerry, isn't it? You're so excited, I can't understand you."

"It's a matter of life and death." Jerry started pacing. "What a dead person's eyes look like."

Mary shifted the telephone to her other ear. "Are you on something?"

"No, onto something, and I have to hurry. Mary, it's terribly important. Can you recognize a dead person's eyes if he's been dead a day? Can you still tell the color?"

Mary muffled the phone with one hand and called Frank, but Frank didn't hear her. "It's not hard to recognize the eyes because they're usually right there, in the dead person's head, and they're the same color they've always been." After a pause, she added, "We always close them right after death."

"Okay, then, why do you close them?" Jerry's voice got louder. "Would they be the same color the next day if you opened the lids?"

"We close them to make it appear that the person is peacefully sleeping," Mary said. She paraphrased a chapter on death in a medical book. "At first, the eyes are stock still, with dilated pupils. If the doctor checks the back of the eye, he sees boxcar-like sausage-links of dark clots in the tiny blood vessels in the retina. Later, a haziness appears, like a film drying over the surface of the eye, and the light pathway through the cornea, lens, and vitreous humor clouds over."

"You sound just like Frank, like a medical textbook." How could anyone make sense out of clouds in vitreous humor?

"It says right here . . . something about the overall stillness, waxy appearance, coldness that seems colder than the ambient temperature . . . cloudiness of the eyes . . . instantly recognizable as death to the most inexperienced observer." Mary paused. "A dead person just looks, . . . well, *dead*."

Jerry sighed. The captain's eyes in life had seemed colder than the ambient temperature. He tried again. "What I really need to know, can you tell the color of a dead person's eyes if he's been dead a day, if you lift the lids?"

Mary voice had an edge. "Probably. It might be helpful to shine a pocket flashlight onto the anterior chamber. The cornea clouds over, the cornea covers the pupil and the iris, but the color of the irises should still be there."

"Now we're getting somewhere: a flashlight."

Mary clipped her words and her voice sounded cold. "Look, I am not going to ask why you want to know about a dead person's eyes. I am calling Frank."

Jerry heard her yelling, "Frank! It's Jerry, asking about dead people's eyeballs." After a few seconds, Frank said, "What's this about dead eyeballs? We don't need any."

"We're going to see one. Grab your toothbrush and some clean underwear. I'll pick you up in fifteen minutes. We have to catch the last Southwest flight to Las Vegas."

"Now, wait a minute. What preposterous plan are you plotting now?"

Jerry's voice rushed on. "Major Blakely has a body, or parts of one. I have to explain on the way or we'll miss the flight."

"You're on your own. I'm not going."

"Just one eyeball—it might be Fish Eyes. I need you there as back-up."

Frank paused and sighed, audible through Jerry's receiver. "All right. Sounds insanely interesting: key word, *insane*. Why don't I have a simple word like *no* in my vocabulary?"

Jerry picked out some clean underwear and ran back and forth checking flights on his computer. He dug the small flashlight out of his flight bag before he called Major Blakely. "I can identify Captain Wachter with just one eyeball. We'll grab the last Southwest Airlines flight out of San Jose. Can you meet us at McCarran-Las Vegas?"

Twelve minutes later, Jerry rang Frank's bell.

Mary opened the door. "This is your most outrageous idea yet. I don't know why Frank agreed to go. What about your car?"

Jerry hadn't planned for parking, always a nightmare at San Jose. He hadn't left a note for Sally, either.

"I'll take you but don't expect a ride home when you miss the last flight." Mary wondered why Major Blakely hadn't asked *her* to identify the eye. She had seen Quill's eyes under more objective circumstances than Jerry had. She was the only one to bring back clues from the Little Eagle Casino. The major didn't give her credit for half a brain.

After what seemed like a week, Frank and Jerry arrived at the front of the line at the Southwest ticket counter in San Jose. The last call for boarding sign flashed, red neon, on and off. They handed credit cards and picture IDs to a trim little blonde wearing a royal blue and gold shirt and tan slacks. She turned friendly blue eyes towards Jerry. "You might not make it through security in time. There isn't any refund. Do you still want to do it?"

"It's a matter of life or death," Jerry said. "We have to go, even if we have to hold onto the tail."

The ticket agent gave them boarding passes and closed her window.

Frank hurried towards a security line snaking out the door. "Hurry. We'll never make it," he called over his shoulder.

Jerry turned back and grabbed the ticket agent's arm. Something he said made her blush. Jerry beckoned to Frank, and she led them through the mysterious closed areas behind the counters, directly to screening at the front of the line.

"Through Gate 10, sir." She saluted Jerry and winked before she scurried away.

Frank and Jerry sprinted through the walkways. "She must have liked your looks," Frank said to the back of Jerry's head. "You have better luck with ticket agents than with waitresses."

The waiting room was empty, the door closing.

"Wait," Jerry yelled. "We have tickets on that flight."

The almost closed door sprang open. A young man with a fistful of boarding passes grabbed theirs and pushed Jerry towards the door. "Run, fellows, run for it."

Frank stumbled and scrambled to make it up the ramp. Two seats left, in the far back. Out of breath, Frank shoved his carry-on under the seat, slid into the window seat, and watched Jerry stuff his bag into an overflowing overhead bin. Frank buckled up and listened to the safety briefing.

When the jet leveled off for cruise, Jerry told Frank about identifying Captain Wachter's remains from an eyeball and fished a flashlight out of his pocket. "Mary told me what to look for."

"Oh, she did, huh? Give me that thing," Frank said. "Take off the red lens and pull off your jacket. I want to show you something."

Following Frank's directions, Jerry wrapped his jacket over both of their heads and held his hand over the flashlight; his fingers glowed red about the edges. "What is this—Boy Scouts 101?"

"No. If you were dead, your fingers wouldn't be translucent."

Jerry laughed from under the jacket. "Good. I'm not dead yet."

"Count yourself lucky, with all the dumb things you get me to do. Is this what you're going to do with the eyeball?"

Before answering, Jerry pulled off the jacket to take a soft drink from the wary flight attendant. Then he said, "I don't exactly know."

"Well, you'd better think of something fast," Frank said. "We're almost there."

At Las Vegas Major Blakely, who didn't need to pass through security screening, met Jerry and Frank at the arrival gate and drove them in a golf-cart jitney to the general aviation terminal. Within ten minutes, they were airborne in Mooney One-Bravo-Bravo, and twenty minutes later, on the ground at Nellis Air Force Base where a Jeep waited to whisk them to the morgue or whatever the military called their death receptacle. Frank didn't want to go there.

Inside a bleak gray building, Major Blakely began their briefing while they waited for the military equivalent of a coroner to meet them at the morgue. "You have to steel yourselves before viewing the body, completely charred. Clothing and skin have melted together, on the parts still together, that is. His head cooked on the exposed side."

Jerry, always ready for action, swung one foot under the table and leaned forward eagerly. "We're tough. We can handle it. I'll tell you if it's Fish Eyes or not."

"What happened to cause the charred body?" asked Frank. His stomach didn't know if it could handle it. Did he really want to know? How could anyone identify half a head, half a cooked head?

The major turned to face Frank. "This morning, my wingman and I were on call when a small Cessna invaded prohibited airspace. At first, we expected to escort him out, but this wasn't a normal case of a pilot off course. He was inside a special surveillance area, flying low towards something top secret. He ignored our F-16s."

"What did you do then?" asked Frank. "Warn him? Shoot him down?"

"It happened fast and close to the ground. We had to climb fast to avoid collision with terrain. He flew right into the rocks."

Frank grimaced. "Sounds like he was on autopilot."

"You did what you had to do." Jerry paled and bit his lip. "So, it burned, then?"

The major looked pained, drained. "The aircraft was completely destroyed, a fire so hot that they waited three hours for it to cool enough to go in. Now here's the grisly part. The head had rolled behind a boulder."

Frank swallowed hard and turned away. A Franken-stein-monster head rolled through his imagination. Almost midnight, the hour of witches and ghosts: he'd have nightmares for a week. No one could identify a body from *an eyeball.*

The waiting increased Frank's anxiety, waiting by the morgue at Nellis Air Force Base, waiting by an unmarked locked door. Footsteps echoed down the hall, and someone dressed in khaki-colored hospital scrubs rounded the corner. His gray eyes squinted as though they had seen too much sun.

Major Blakely snapped to his feet. Seeing him stand up, Frank did the same. The major saluted. "Colonel Phillips, these are our civilian witnesses, Jerry Christensen and Frank Peterson. I warned them about the condition of the body."

Colonel Phillips ushered them through the door to the morgue, a single room with a cement floor and a bank of fluorescent lights across the center of the ceiling. Something lay under a white sheet atop a stainless steel table on rollers. Frank smelled a faint burnt odor—steak left on the grill way too long. Frank choked down his nausea, while Jerry tried to hold his in by covering his nose and clenching his teeth. Colonel Phillips gave everyone a mask before he pulled back the sheet, but it didn't mask the odor.

The sight of the body, like an overcooked Hawaiian luau pig, didn't bother Frank as much as the stench. There were no hands, no fingerprints. The head had no hair on the burnt side, fragments of flesh clinging to charred bone, the skull painted black and yellow-brown. How could anyone identify that? It could just as well be a pig.

Colonel Phillips touched the body with one white fingertip through latex gloves. "Are you ready for me to turn over the skull?"

When the colonel lifted the burned-out cranium, Frank thought of the head twisting completely around in *The Exorcist.* The eyelid closed, the skull's remaining skin severely sunburned with deep and dirty lacerations. No blood. He had pictured blood dripping down beneath a staring, oozing eyeball. After all the other horror, this side looked more normal. But it didn't smell any better.

Frank stared at the half-head with the sunburn. He noticed a wisp of gray hair. If someone had washed off the blood, why hadn't he cleaned the dirt out of the lacerations? Mary had said that dead bodies didn't bleed, after a certain period of time—he didn't remember how long—but they could defecate. For now, all he smelled was burnt flesh. It could be worse. His brain wanted to shut down from the moment the skull was turned.

Jerry watched the colonel turn the skull sunny-side up, the eyeball like a staring egg-yolk. He felt as dizzy as though the colonel had turned him rather than the skull, spinning him around. He concentrated on not throwing up. As a joke, Ruben had once suggested barbecuing Captain Fish Eyes. Jerry swallowed back vomit.

How could he identify a burnt out skull, left over from Halloween? But he had to. Jerry cleared his throat.

"All that's left is one eye. I have to look. This could be Captain Wachter."

Colonel Phillips selected a scalpel and leaned over the steel work surface. "I have to cut the eyelid and peel it back, slowly and carefully. Let's hope the eyelid hasn't adhered to the surface of the eyeball."

When he stepped back from the table, a single eye stared out from the half-head. The head had no hair. The eyeball had no lid.

A chill ran down Frank's back, a millipede with frozen metal feet. He broke eye contact and concentrated on his shoelaces.

The eye glared at Jerry at the same time that it seemed to stare directly at Frank, like a portrait from a horror movie, the eyes following the hero walking down the hall. A game of chicken: who would be first to blink. Jerry stared unblinkingly, mirroring the cold eyeball, a contest of wills.

Jerry cleared his throat. "All that's left is one eye. I have to look. To see if this could be Captain Wachter."

No one spoke. The eye had a gray iris or maybe pale blue or maybe a trick of the fluorescent lights, as cold in death as it had been in life. It could be Captain Wachter, but Mary said that corpses had such a cold stare that the eyelids were always closed for viewing at funerals. Some primitive tribes sewed them shut. In fact, they used to cover the eyelids with a silver coin before holding a wake. *Awake*—now, that would be *horror*. Frank scared himself with the thought.

"I'll use the flashlight. I want to be sure," Jerry said. He pulled out his tiny pocket light and twisted it to remove the lens. After a pause, he checked the alignment of the batteries and reset the lens. He held it above his head and stared at the bank of ceiling fluorescents as though they might illuminate his thinking. With a flourish, he turned its beam onto the eye. The iris shimmered like a living thing when it reflected the light, as evil in death as in life.

Jerry shuddered. "That's him, all right. I would recognize that eye anywhere. It follows me in my nightmares."

"How do you know, for sure?" asked Frank. "That iris has a blue tinge."

"Oh, it's gray, all right. Glare from the fluorescent lights. Mary said to shine a penlight onto the anterior chamber."

Major Blakely, silent until now, asked, "What's an anterior chamber?"

"It's the part that looks all cloudy, under that blue iris," Frank said.

Jerry again turned the flashlight onto the eyeball, which returned such a frigid, unyielding stare that he was sure he recognized the captain's evil eye. This time the captain wasn't laughing. Jerry wasn't, either. He had let himself hate Captain Fish Eyes. He had hoped for his death over and over and in the most uncomfortable ways imaginable. But now, he felt only compassion.

Illuminated by flashlight, the eyeball with no lid in the charred skull regarded Frank with an icy stare, rigid and frigid but compelling. Had it been Captain Wachter's? Those eyes: ordering the sledgehammer to crush Jerry's thumb, focusing on Frank next to the colony of bullet ants. Frank couldn't look away. Kedar's story, how to ward off the evil eye. Superstition or not, Frank held his hand—palm outward—between his face and the eyeball and repeated: *The Lord is my Shepherd, I shall not want. He maketh me to lie down in green pastures . . . Yea, though I walk through the valley of the shadow of death, I will fear no evil . . .*

Jerry backed up a few steps and put his hands on his hips. "This eyeball belonged to Captain Wachter, or whatever he called himself, the person who stole Cessna 3318E. I'll remember those evil eyes as long as I live."

"I hope you're right," Frank said. "Dead eyes always seem to stare."

"Let's give him a moment of silence." Jerry made the sign of the cross over his heart and bowed his head.

36.

"Big Mamas, Jerry." Mammato-cumulus clouds, pendulous bubbles glowing rose pink and rimmed with gold light, hung over the southern horizon like breasts caressed by the rising sun. Frank, holding a fresh cup of coffee, leaned on the railing on Major Paul Blakely's patio and gazed at the harbingers of wicked weather. He expected Jerry to comment, something crude and outrageous and off the wall, like *a tub full of titties*.

Jerry studied his empty coffee cup.

"Those clouds are cumulus serious," Major Blakely said, but no one laughed. He moved his chair to make room for Betty, who refilled everyone's mug. They all needed a second cup of coffee. No one had had sweet dreams.

"Well, now that it's over, how do you feel?" asked Betty. She was dressed all in white, except for a striking turquoise and silver necklace.

"Relieved, anxious, sad, you name it," Jerry said. "I want to get back to my regular life, now that the captain won't be looking for my airplane." He shuddered and added, "Frank was right. They were eagle eyes, not fish eyes."

"Just thinking about that single gruesome eye," Frank said, "I still feel its cold glare. But, he wasn't one hundred percent bad. Captain Wachter brought money to his tribe and gave them a decent high school."

"What about the suicide mission and the explosives?" Major Blakely asked.

Frank frowned and said, "He died with his secret recipe." For explosives powerful enough to blow up Hoover Dam . . .

Jerry studied his thumb. His lime-green arm cast was history. "Captain Eagle Eyes is finished . . . gone."

His coffee forgotten, Jerry stood in front of his chair and faced the others seated at the table. "To tell the truth, Betty, this is real personal. Last night I had another nightmare. That single awful eyeball stared out at me from a burnt and blackened skull. I forced myself to think of the eyeball and meet its stare. It caught fire and burned with steam shooting out and shriveled to nothing. The captain finally has peace, and so do I."

"Aha. You used the dream control book," Frank said, a pleased smile on his face.

Major Blakely straightened the collar on his crisp suntans and stirred hazelnut creamer into his coffee. "I'm glad it's over, too," he said. Under his breath, he added, "And glad to be done with the whole half-assed affair. Dream control, what poppycock."

The major looked up from his coffee. "By the way, I didn't tell you." His voice was quiet and calm as though he were passing butter for their toast. "It was Ruben's airplane that crashed and burned."

"No kidding?" Frank's eyes did a little dance behind his glasses, and he swallowed hard. "Is this ever going to end? Ruben will be upset, really upset."

Jerry face paled. He sat down so hard that he sloshed everyone's coffee. "No-o-o! It's *my fault* . . . chasing Captain Wachter at any cost. You tell Ruben—I just can't."

"I think Wachter-Rethcaw was taking an airplane home with him and wanted to stop at Tonopah for fuel," the major said. "He thought we couldn't track him on radar if he flew low enough. At least, my conscience is clear. I didn't shoot him down."

"If there was nothing left, how did you know it belonged to Ruben?" Frank asked.

"Ruben reported it missing that very morning, a white Cessna 172. I didn't tell you before you identified the body, because people see what they expect to see."

Frank's eyes shot a question at Jerry. Before either man could comment, Betty leaned over the table and said, "I'm glad this was over before one of you developed high

302

blood pressure. You've seen my white wolf Kachina. There's an Indian legend about the battle between two wolves we carry inside. One is evil. It feeds on anger, hatred, lies, guilt, greed, and jealousy. The other is good. It feeds on love, peace, hope, kindness, truth, understanding, and faith. The wolf who wins is the one you feed."

No one spoke for several minutes.

Betty picked up two empty mugs and the creamer. "You need to work this out of your systems. Paul, take them home in One-Bravo-Bravo, before it gets any later. Don't let the wrong wolf win."

On the way to the airport, Frank said to Jerry, "It's hard to believe he's gone, even if I saw it myself. What do you think Ruben will say when you tell him?"

"No, no," Jerry said. "The major has to tell him. Ruben will go into orbit."

Frank adjusted his oxygen mask—his first time high enough to need one. No different from normal air, except in effect. Major Blakely flew high and north from Las Vegas, away from thunderstorm country and the menacing clouds. Both Ruben and Kedar needed to know, but the more direct route Las Vegas-Kelso-Auburn wouldn't work, not with cumulonimbus clouds hovering in the Kelso direction. Frank hoped that the major's fast airplane would keep today's tight schedule.

One-Bravo-Bravo swooped down towards the short runway at Auburn, like an eagle with wings sleeked back zeroing in prey. Jerry's boyhood game, swooping like an eagle . . . Frank thought about the dead captain, the last Sioux warrior: Aquila-the-eagle would swoop no more.

Major Blakely landed his Mooney in time to take Ruben to breakfast, but Ruben didn't run out to greet them. Jerry, in the right passenger seat, hopped out. Frank half-rose to step through the aircraft's single door and went to find Ruben while Jerry and the major clipped the chains to anchor it to the ground.

303

Next door to Ruben's shop at Wings Restaurant, Frank sat at a patio table next to Ruben and across from Jerry. Before Major Blakely broke the news about Ruben's stolen airplane, Jerry asked the blond waitress Robina, the one he usually flirted with, if she had seen a tall pilot with gray hair and a slight limp hanging around. Frank wondered why Jerry hadn't asked her about the captain before this.

"Oh, you must mean Bill," she said. "He's been a regular here since April. He calls me Little Robin Rosebud. He's some gardener, raises exotic mushrooms. He always hides behind a pair of sunglasses. Just when I think he might ask me out, he runs away."

"Come on to him next time. Encourage him," Frank said. No need to tell her that Bill was dead in a plane crash—an airplane he had stolen. *Robina*: that meant little robin. So that's the bird the captain was watching at Auburn. That hot pink tank top, profiling her nipples. Nipples like the mammato-cumulus clouds this morning.

Major Blakely, silent so far, stirred the cream in his coffee and studied Ruben's face. He cleared his throat and said, "The white Cessna, the one you reported missing: the insurance company just bought it."

Ruben accepted the news without the emotional storm Frank expected. He merely shook his head and said, "*Ay caramba*. Okay, tell me the rest. Who was flying it?"

Jerry leaned forward. "Are you ready for this? Captain Wachter. Except this time, he crashed and burned."

"Him again, *loco y tonto*." Ruben glowered at Jerry. "If the insurance company pays, I guess it's the same as selling it, but I wanted somebody to love it."

Ruben swirled the coffee in his half-empty cup and frowned. "Tell me more about the crash and burn part."

"It was on my watch," Major Blakely said. "A white Cessna entered a Prohibited Area. When I flew the F-16 by his left wing to escort him out of there, he smacked the hill and burned. Jerry identified him by his distinctive eyes. Or eye, actually, in a charred skull."

"*Ay chihuahua.* Don't tell me any more." Ruben pushed away his coffee. "It takes away my appetite. But, then, how did you identify my Cessna—with nothing left?"

The major scooted his chair back and looked at the floor. "How many white Cessna 172s are stolen on the same day in the same area? We had your report, and the time frame was right. No other Cessna 172s were reported missing."

Frank wondered if the major or his wingman had read the tail number in their fly-by. Circumstantial: like the painted *eight* at One-Eight-Echo's crash site. Like the gray iris that could be blue. Frank made a mental shrug; he was eager for Kedar and Mother to hear the news. Everyone could relax—with Captain Wachter out of the picture.

In less than fifteen minutes, Major Blakely, Jerry, and Frank were underway in the Mooney. Next stop: Barstow-Daggett Airport in the Mojave Desert.

The intense sun bleached the sky white over the Mojave Desert at midday, too hot for conversation on the rough road to Mother's mine and cabin. Jerry drove because he knew the way. The major, perched on the seat in front of Frank, hung onto the edge of the open door with his right hand and scrunched a straw hat against his head with his left.

Frank bounced in the back of the rented Jeep and fanned himself with a wide-brimmed *Gateway to the Mojave* hat from the pilot supply and souvenir shop. The jeep's engine lulled him at the same time that its progress over rocks and potholes jarred him awake, a curious mix of noise and heat and rocking. The area began to look familiar. "I hope today's news will relieve Kedar's anxiety," Frank said. "We're almost there."

Jerry turned off near a familiar pile of rocks and parked the Jeep close to Mother's dusty green truck. Jerry's face was red, and his T-shirt showed wet stains around the armpits. The major looked comfortable and his summer uniform was unwrinkled. Frank wondered if the man ever perspired.

"No trespassing." Mother seemed to materialize out of the shimmering heat. She towered over them from the top of the hill and pointed her shotgun in their direction. "Just back up, right on out of here."

"It's Mr. Peterson." Kedar ran down the hill from a position behind Mother.

"*Hereinkommen.*" Mother's voice was not cordial.

Mother lowered the gun and pointed its muzzle toward the entry porch. Jerry and Frank left their hats in the Jeep and waved at Mother. Major Blakely exchanged his Mojave Desert straw hat for his usual Air Force issue.

Kedar led the three unexpected visitors into the cool crystal cabin. Within three minutes, they sat relaxing around the kitchen table with tall glasses, each filled with ice and one thin slice of lemon. Mother exchanged the shotgun for a pitcher and poured lemonade as though nothing was out of the ordinary. That shotgun had peppered the hillside the first time Frank had met her. Mother always served lemonade. An artesian well, lemonade bubbling over a football-sized lemon . . . Frank's imagination was improving.

Major Blakely smoothed his uniform and stepped to the middle of the room. He cleared his throat, held his hat at his waist, and waited for full attention.

"I am here on official business, to notify you of the death of Captain Wachter."

Mother banged the lemonade pitcher onto the table and put her hands on her hips. "Why are you telling me about him?" Her voice rose. "Nobody told me about Robert who died serving his country. That captain wanted to blow it up. Hoover Dam, kaputt."

The major twisted his Air Force hat between his hands and shifted his weight from one foot to the other. "But no one knew where you lived."

"Well, they certainly do now," she said, ice in her voice. "You promised no one would know where my mine is."

The major, still standing, turned his hat over and over. Frank had never seen Major Blakely so flustered or Mother so upset.

After an uncomfortable silence, Major Blakely said, "Kedar needed to know."

"You could have sent a letter, but I guess we'll have to hear the whole story, now that you're here." Her voice had softened.

The major sank into a chair. He planted his lop-sided hat on the table next to his untouched lemonade and let Jerry tell them that Captain Wachter had crashed and burned in yet another stolen Cessna.

Kedar sat somber and silent. Rivulets of condensation ran down the sides of his glass like tears. He swallowed hard. His voice, when it came, sounded hoarse and hushed. "He gave me a scholarship to The Guards, and he let me learn to fly."

Frank raised one bushy eyebrow in puzzlement. "He sent you on a suicide mission. I thought you'd be relieved to hear the news."

"It's wrong to speak evil of the dead, Mr. Peterson." Kedar hunched over his lemonade. "We have to show respect. The Koran tells us to wish him peace."

"But you were afraid he'd kill you."

Kedar focused on Frank, then shifted his gaze down and traced the loop of his shoelace with his eyes. "Did you know that chickens chew their food with rocks because they don't have teeth?"

Puzzled, Frank waited for Kedar to continue.

"The science class barbecued some chickens and made soap from ashes and fat. The captain put one hand over the chicken's eyes and head, and grabbed its neck with his other hand, like this." Kedar held out both fists and made a quick twisting motion.

"Farmers used to wring chickens' necks in the old days," Frank said.

Kedar changed the topic from gizzards to flint-stones. "I couldn't start my fire with sparks from a flint-stone so he

307

let me use his cigarette lighter." He looked down and bit his lip. His voice quavered. "The captain said I could be silent the longest."

In a quiet voice, Frank asked, "Then what made you think he'd kill you?"

Kedar gave Frank a woeful stare. "He told us, if we failed our missions, he'd wring our necks."

No one spoke. After a pause, Frank said, "That's a common cliché. That means a lot of people say that, even those who only know chicken in a plastic package. Do you think he meant it?"

Kedar drew a circle on the floor with the toe of one house slipper and spoke so softly that Frank strained to hear his words. "The captain could identify a bird with a single glance, by the way it flew, its shape, and its call. I could copy the sound the first time I ever heard it. He called me Bird Caller."

Frank heard the anguish in the young voice: Kedar had loved his teacher. "Of course he liked you. You were his best student. I can tell."

Mother grasped the boy's hands. "The captain's explosives blew you to Kelso."

Kedar gazed at something above Frank's head as though his mind had traveled to outer space. As though uttering an epiphany, he said, "Not lightning from God."

Frank couldn't make sense of it.

Only Mother seemed to understand. "Let's keep our good memories, and let the desert heal the bruises on our souls."

The major frowned and worked his jaw and crumpled his hat. "I never thought about souls in that way."

Jerry's eyes focused on something far away.

Frank recognized one of his wife Mary's sayings, about bruised souls.

Jumping to his feet and compressing his hat between his hands, Major Blakely said, "We really need to start back. Thank you for the lemonade."

"Are you sure you can get out of here before dark?" Mother asked, as a formality.

Frank didn't answer. Mother didn't mention staying overnight. The major's warped hat would never be the same.

"No problem, not with three of us and a handheld GPS." The major glanced down the hall, towards the exit.

"We're fine. We can visit again when this all settles down," Jerry said.

"Will you come back, and bring Mrs. Peterson?" Kedar asked Frank.

"In a few months. School starts on Monday, and we won't have our airplane for a while. Replacing the engine because we took on some contaminated fuel." No sense mentioning the sugar put in by the captain.

"You don't have an airplane, again?"

"Just a little bad fuel ruins an engine. You know how you always check the fuel before you fly," Jerry said, shifting from one foot to the other.

"That captain-person had something to do with it." Mother frowned.

"We thought that, too. No way to prove it," Jerry said.

Mother turned to face Major Blakely. "It was kind of you to come all the way out here to give us the news in person. Now I won't worry when Kedar goes to college."

"Kedar is making excellent progress," Frank said. He noticed that she called the boy Kedar, not Robert. "He finished geometry over the summer. I'm proud of him."

Kedar smiled at Mother. "What I really want to do," he said, "is to fly F-16s. But I want my mother to go to college with me so she won't be alone out here."

Frank picked up on Kedar's "my mother," a subtle change in the boy's attitude, and noticed that he still wanted to fly F-16s.

"Well, then, the first step is to finish high school." Major Blakely spoke in a gruff voice and raced towards the door like he had heard a starter's pistol.

Frank and Jerry waved goodbye to Kedar from the Jeep. The major sat in back, facing forward, definitely unfriendly for some reason. Down the non-road a mile or so, Frank turned to Jerry and asked, "What do you think Mary will say when you tell her how you identified that corpse?"

Since last summer, Mary had become fascinated with all things Indian. Frank wondered how she would take the news of Captain Wachter's death.

The setting sun painted red mares' tails across the western sky before Major Blakely took off from Daggett-Barstow en route San Jose with Jerry and Frank. The intense heat would have kept a Cessna on the ground but didn't seem to affect the turbo-charged Mooney, except for turbulence near the ground. Airborne, the temperature became more comfortable in the aircraft cabin. Frank dozed in the right seat.

Jerry had the back seat to himself. His intense experience with the charred body made him introspective, made him think about what really was important in his life. He wanted to hold Sally. He could have lost her by neglect, always off somewhere flying. Mother had struck a chord with him with 'Bruises on your soul.' He wondered how long his would take to heal. He'd never tell Sally about dinner with Robina. He would tell her that he had allowed himself to hate Fish Eyes and almost let the wrong wolf win. Jerry couldn't hate a dead man, the captain of the opposing team.

Jerry forced himself to sit straight and helped Major Blakely scan the sky for traffic. The iron-man major said he wasn't tired; Jerry didn't believe him.

Less than two hours later, Sally and Mary met their husbands at the Jet Center at San Jose. Major Blakely joined them while his Mooney was being refueled.

"Thanks for bringing the guys home, Paul," Sally said, looking at the handsome major over her shoulder while hugging Jerry. "Can you come with us for dinner?"

"No, thanks. I'll fly home in a few minutes and take a sandwich with me." The major shifted from one foot to the other, his habit when he felt uncomfortable. "I need to fly high over the Sierras alone with my thoughts."

"No, you can't do that, not mountains at night," Mary said, expressing her concern even though Major Blakely was not one of her favorite persons. Last June, the major had made her feel as though she didn't exist when she had given him the only clues anyone had unearthed from the Little Eagle Casino. She took the major's arm. "Have dinner with us and fly home tomorrow. I won't take no for an answer."

Next door at The Aero-Squadron Restaurant, model airplanes revolved above their heads and a searchlight periodically lit a First World War diorama. Jerry waited until the waiter brought the wine. "I know you are bursting with curiosity. So, just out with it. We identified a charred body in the morgue at Nellis AFB. It was Captain Wachter."

Mary suspended her wine glass mid-air, halfway to her mouth, and bit her lip to keep it from trembling. Frank leaned back and watched Mary. Major Blakely sat quietly.

Sally leaned forward, her elbows on the table, her chin resting on steepled fingers. "I thought you'd say that. Now I can get a kitten." Her voice, bright at first, turned serious. "He killed my cat."

"I'm so relieved that you two have finished your search. I thought one of you would die out there, dueling with a madman." Mary brushed away seeds from a crumbled breadstick and picked a seed off her sweater as carefully as she chose her words. "I feel sad and a sense of loss. He was a good man, despite doing bad things. Secretly, I had wanted to write to him about his research on Indian medicine. Now we will never know what he discovered."

Sally twisted her napkin and turned toward Jerry. "The captain did some awful things, but he wasn't evil—just amoral, like an eagle swooping down on a meal. I'm glad you weren't the meal. You had such total Fish Eyes fixation that I didn't tell you . . . honey, I got pregnant at Paradise!"

"A baby! Oh, Sally!" Jerry hugged Sally with delight and upset his wineglass.

"Let me get that." Mary sopped up red wine with her white napkin. Sally, like Mary, was thirty-two; they had discussed their ticking biological clocks.

"Actually, twins," Sally said. "That's my karma."

Mary, still listening to Sally, slid back next to her husband and squeezed his hand under the table. "I hope you'll tell Frank *exactly* where this Paradise place is." She smiled at Frank mischievously and added, "I have plans for him."

Frank stared at the floor, his face flushed beyond the pink caused by wine.

"Ask Major Blakely. He proposed to Betty at Paradise while watching a sunset. He tried to kiss her but the oxygen hoses got all tangled up, like kissing wearing braces."

Everyone except Sally laughed. Jerry wiped tears out of his eyes and blew his nose. The major dabbed a drop of wine off his lips and rearranged his napkin.

Frank said he had tangled the air hoses a few times himself—not kissing, just clumsy. "You know what I learned from this? Jerry's right about half the time. Mathematically speaking, one way to be right, out of two possible outcomes."

"Are you talking wisdom or wine?" Sally asked.

"Loose nips sink ships," Jerry said unexpectedly.

Frank choked on his wine.

Jerry leaned towards Sally and whispered something.

"You're positively crude." Sally stifled a giggle behind her hand.

"That reminds me," Jerry said, almost knocking over Sally's water glass. "Why is it that you call him *Paul* while the rest of us still call him Major Blakely?"

"I do believe you're jealous."

The major raised his eyebrows in surprise. "Seriously, all of you should call me Paul. Now that we're not involved in an investigation."

"Hear, hear! I'll drink to that," Jerry said, raising his wineglass.

"Hear, hear," they chorused. "For he's a jolly good fellow—"

"Maybe I should take Betty back to Paradise myself," Paul said.

After a jovial pause, in a more serious tone, Mary said, "Now that this is over, I want to use Chief Eagle Feather's manuscript on Indian medicines. His writing is careful and sensitive. His dedication to Medicine Woman made me cry." That male chauvinist Paul had never credited Quill for doing any good and had never thanked her for the information she had acquired from the casino. She added, "We'll never know what he learned about mushrooms."

"Or how he made explosives," Paul said.

Jerry grimaced and slumped in his seat. The major cared only about the explosives, nothing about the man, nothing about the boy. Not one word about stolen airplanes or the Cessna with sugar in the tanks. Mary had forgiven the captain, and the whole affair was already out of her mind, except for the mushrooms. Last night, lord, was it only last night? The eyeball with its unyielding stare . . . people see what they expect to see . . . Paul wanted the case closed and Jerry wanted it finished. He had seen one slightly broiled eyeball. Jerry shivered. He hoped it had belonged to Captain Wachter. He asked Mary, "Do you remember telling me about a dead person's eyeballs?"

The conversations stopped. Everyone turned towards Jerry.

"That's how I identified him. Just one eyeball, staring, glaring, out of a blackened, charred skull, like meat left too long on the barbecue."

"From only one eyeball?" Mary asked.

"That's what closed the case," Paul Blakely said.

"Like you said, about a dead man's eyes." Jerry's stomach churned. A funny feeling, beyond wine, beyond remembered gore. Could he have been wrong?

"Are you wondering if you were right?" Mary asked.

Paul frowned. "Jerry and Frank signed statements identifying Wachter."

"It was him," Jerry said.

Mary examined the last sip of red wine in her glass and held it to the light. "Don't you see? It doesn't matter. Quill won't be back."

37.

Aquila parked a rented U-Haul van carrying his last load of mushrooms behind Wings Grill at Auburn Airport. He couldn't leave his two most unusual specimens at The Guards. Auburn was dangerous, but he had to see Robina, just one more time.

His digital watch showed September 11. The tragedy of 9/11 had given him the idea for the cadet air force and the Muslim mercenaries—they agreed to be his soldiers in exchange for learning to fly. Revenge for *Paha Sapa* wasn't Kedar's war; he did it for his captain. Cadet Kedar Khazari had been braver than most Indians.

Kedar's dark expressive eyes regarded Aquila through the window of his imagination, trusting, eager to please. He realized that the boy had loved his teacher. As Captain Von Wächter, Aquila had betrayed him. He despised himself.

Aquila wished he could live that all over again. No Muslim orphans. No senseless war impossible to win. No soldier sacrificed for nothing. Kedar Bird-Caller, the only one since Medicine Woman with enough patience to observe wildlife. Kedar must be dead, and for what? Aquila's blind and foolish revenge: an evil tragedy of his making. He wanted to forget, become Quill Rethcaw again. But for now, he needed a cup of coffee.

The customer that Robina called Bill took his favorite seat in the patio of Wings Grill and held a menu without reading it. The morning sun warmed his skin: another fine California day.

She brought his coffee before he ordered. "Hello, stranger. I missed you around here. What'll you have?" She smiled.

315

His heart skipped a beat. She missed him. He took off his sunglasses and set them on the table. Would she still like him? He looked at her through his new blue contacts.

"Hey, Good Looking . . ." She reached over and gently removed his baseball cap. "I wondered who was hiding behind those shades."

She regarded him for a long moment. "You have an aquiline nose—regal, like the eagle, my favorite bird. When I get reincarnated, I want to come back as an eagle."

"Me, too," he said. People never noticed his nose. No one looked past his eyes. She liked eagles. "My mother called me *Aquila*. Like the Constellation."

"Aquila the Eagle. Cool. Way cooler than Bill." Robina leaned across the table, close to him. "So, where've you been?"

"Just around, I guess." His heart raced.

Robina pulled a chair next to him and sat down. "Those two red-headed pilots, you know, Ruben's friends? They asked about you, couple weeks ago. They were so somber that I thought you weren't coming back . . . like, *ever*." Robina touched his arm. "Then the one with the red beard told me to come on to you, said you'd ask me out. So, will you?"

Aquila's neck flushed red. "Want to see my mushrooms?" With all the things he wanted to say, that was all that came out. He was not good with women.

Robina smiled again. "Of course I want to see your mushrooms."

"What about the other guy—Jerry?" Asking about him—was it a trap?

"He was quiet, not like Jerry at all. He looked positively glum. No crude remarks about my body parts—he does that when he thinks my ears are out of range."

"Some guys are like that." Aquila relaxed. That woodpecker. He probably said that Robina had big boobs.

Robina stood up and pushed the chair back. "I have a break soon, after I bring your breakfast. I know what you like."

"Thanks." What he liked was Robina.

When she returned with pancakes and eggs, she told him the insurance company paid Ruben for his airplane, the one somebody stole last month. No, not the one with the red tail: the white one. Ruben got his price, but he had wanted someone to love it.

"So what happened to the white one?" He knew it was in a warehouse on the reservation, with new blue markings. No problem there; he did love it. Why didn't Jerry follow the white Cessna and try to track him down?

"It crashed and burned," she said. "I heard them talking. They said the pilot flying it—some captain guy—died."

"That's too bad." His eyes opened wide with surprise. Captain Von Wächter, *dead*. His chance, start over. He felt clean, elated, as if he had been reborn. Everyone, even Aquila, had wanted the captain dead.

How did they mistake him for the pilot who died? Jerry would have known that Captain Von Wächter flew away in Ruben's plane. How did they mistake the airplane? Maybe a fierce fire . . . He toyed with his food but finished the coffee.

On her break, Robina followed him to the U-Haul. Behind the double back doors, pieces of decayed logs filled several boxes, some topped with white spherical fungi, others with large pink ruffled specimens.

"Puffballs are edible," he said, handing her a mushroom as large as a soccer ball.

"Do I have to eat it all?" Robina held it up and examined it, firm and creamy white and lighter weight than a cantaloupe. "I could make a whole platter full of pancake-size slices, but aren't most wild mushrooms poisonous? And what are those things, the ones like big pink ears?"

"Ear mushrooms, not edible."

"Oh, the Dumbos. Ears like a flying elephant, you're dumb if you eat one."

He laughed in spite of himself. He felt relaxed enough to ask the big question. He could talk to her about anything, about everything.

"They're beautiful," she said. "Why are they riding in a U-Haul?"

He looked down on her blond curls. He didn't hear her question. "Robina, come with me to South Dakota. That's where I'm going." There. He got it out.

"On a first date? Are you serious?" She laughed, the laugh he loved.

He blushed and nodded. "The casino needs another waitress. I'll pay you twice whatever you make at Wings." His ears were hot. His heart pounded.

"That's all you want—a waitress?" Her face fell.

She wasn't smiling. He'd lost her! What had he done wrong?

"So . . ." Robina stamped one foot and cocked her head to one side. "Do you want Little Robin Rosebud to fly away with you, or do you want to hire the best waitress in California to work in a casino?"

"Yes."

"Well . . . which is it?"

"Little Eagle wants to fly away with Robin Rosebud," he said in a small voice, too small for the most important words he had ever spoken. He had need in his eyes.

Robina looked up at him, hands on her hips, and gave a tentative smile. "Before the guy runs away with the girl he's supposed to kiss her."

He bent down, and she stood on her toes. Their lips brushed. *Ka-pop-a-ta-tan-ka*: fireworks in his head. She wrapped her arms around him and he heard her musical laugh.

Robina smoothed his hair and touched his cheek. "Did you think I'd say no after all that work to get you to ask me out?"

Aquila lifted her down and stood gawking like a star-struck kid. He knew she'd do it, go to South Dakota with him.

Robina smiled up at him. "I've always wanted to see the Great Salt Lake. I hear they have seabirds, eight hundred miles from the ocean, California gulls and white pelicans. The gulls breed there, and their appearance changes from juvenile to adult. The bird guide shows seven different pictures of California gulls."

"You can identify them by their calls. I'll show you."

38.

Ruben's stolen white Cessna, Jerry's identification of Captain Wachter, a closed FBI case for more than a week. Major Blakely was cleaning up paperwork at his desk at Nellis Air Force Base. He expected to file Colonel Phillips' DNA report routinely and be done with it, until he read it.

It had to be a mistake. What the heck? Colonel Phillips had submitted fluids from the eyeball and a sample of hair for testing with his coroner's report—strictly routine, with no DNA available from the captain to match. The major had expected nothing; he thought DNA deteriorated above 500 degrees Fahrenheit. He checked the routing numbers. Everything seemed correct, except for the conclusion: Captain Wachter's eyeball matched the DNA of an Icelandic female.

Paul had a sinking feeling in the pit of his stomach. He hadn't followed procedure, filing the report before all the evidence was in. He had wanted the whole thing finished. *That eyeball again.* How could it belong to anyone else? Jerry had been so positive; he said he'd never forget that eye as long as he lived and signed the statement identifying Captain Wachter. He thought he'd finished with that quixotic case and with Jerry's audacious schemes; he couldn't handle another of Jerry's *bingo* moments. The major stuffed the DNA report into his briefcase to be dealt with later.

Under the rest of the day's mail, his in-box held a new report: another Cessna, missing within the same time frame. Pilot: Hildur Sigmundsdottir. Age 77. Reported by son, Bruni Haraldsson. Special note: Aircraft scheduled for painting in Tonopah. Did not arrive. No flight plan filed. Report filed 29 August but date of flight not known. He could pursue this one. He picked up the phone and dialed Bruni's number.

"Major Blakely, Nellis Air Force Base. I'm investigating your report of a missing Cessna, and I need more information. The pilot: Hildur Sigmundsdottir. Can you describe him for me?"

"That's my mother," Bruni answered. "If she were male, her name would be Sigmundsson. That's the Icelandic custom. She was too old to fly, but you couldn't tell her that. She was named for a Valkyrie and she thought she was one. After Dad died, she would fly around on autopilot and sing eight-bar snatches of Viking songs."

"I see, a woman who loved to fly. What about the paint job she scheduled?"

"Somebody in Tonapah gave her a cheap price on painting the old Cessna 172, so she stripped off the paint herself and sprayed it with white primer at an auto body shop. She took all the leftover solvents with her—the guy was going to buy them. Had a bunch of loose tools in back, too. Except she never got there. She told him she'd bring it in Thursday or Friday. He called here Monday when she didn't show up. I reported her missing Tuesday after I found her and the airplane both gone."

"H-m-m-m . . . a strong-willed woman." Female. Icelandic. Loose tools in the back: the severed head. "Can you tell me what she looked like?"

"Tall—would you believe six feet? She had gray hair and blue eyes."

"Please describe her eyes," Major Blakely said, beginning to tap his pencil rhythmically.

"Pale blue, so pale they're almost like silver plate."

"And what was the tail-number?" The major's heart pounded in rhythm with the pencil, still drumming on the desk, almost with a will of its own.

Bruni told him the numbers and reminded him they were stripped off with the paint. "It was dull white, no colors."

"So, she flew on autopilot in an enclosed space, breathing in solvents." She was unconscious. The unusually intense fire . . . The major's heart, and the pencil, beat faster.

"You got it."

"What about the insurance company? Have you reported it?" *Does anyone know about this?* He held the pencil mid-air, and his heart skipped a beat.

"She didn't believe in insurance."

"I'm out of questions for now. When I go through the unsolved accident reports for that area, I'll call you if I find a match." *It's a match. How can it not be?* After a pause, he added, "Or, if I have another question. Thanks for your help."

Major Blakely hung up and sat with his elbows on his desk, supporting his chin with his hands. He thought back to Thursday 25 August. What had he seen? The aircraft was a white Cessna, like Ruben's, but dull white paint, no tail numbers. The pilot was tall, gray-haired, leaning forward. *People see what they expect to see . . .* He had seen Captain Wachter . . . and Ruben's Cessna after a fast pass from a can of spray paint. The aircraft had remained on course. The pilot had not responded to his interception passes. The pilot could have already been unconscious or dead, slumped over the yoke, the airplane on autopilot.

"Good Lord!" Major Blakely jumped to his feet and pounded the desk with one fist. "Captain Wachter got away with Ruben's plane. The whole investigation: wrong. I screwed up the whole thing!"

His mind raced. The investigation was compromised, totally goofed up. He was responsible. And Colonel Phillips, the coroner at Nellis, he'd signed the report and requested DNA analysis. The preliminary investigation had the wrong conclusion. Major Blakely, and his whole group of pilots, under the gun. He wouldn't have to worry about promotion, and neither would the coroner. He couldn't put everybody through the wringer. He was damned incompetent. That damning DNA report: could it be wrong?

The FBI had a closed file. The captain should be brought to justice, but the FBI hadn't dragged him off that reservation in what, two months? If they caught Wachter, he'd never reveal his secrets. The FBI's investigation had been lukewarm at best.

Major Blakely pulled the DNA report out of his brief case and sank back into his desk chair. He leaned back, hands behind his head. What would Betty say if he asked her what to do with the report? He chuckled to himself, picturing Betty snatching the report and gleefully shredding it. He couldn't tell Betty: she'd tell Mary and Sally and the whole thing would unravel. Misfile it. That went nowhere. Start a new file, for Hildur. That made more sense.

What about the other people involved? Ruben would have to return the insurance check for the white airplane; he had just picked up Foxy Lady—what about that case? Jerry would worry about his airplane, back to the flight line only last week; he'd be mortified by his misidentification and start hunting Fish Eyes again. And Frank had signed the statement identifying the body from one eyeball, right under Jerry's signature. Could he put them through reopening the case?

There was only one way out. No one needed to hear about a female Icelandic Captain Wachter. The major reached down and ran the report through the shredder.

Hildur. The skull and eye belonged to Hildur, the Valkyrie. Major Blakely called Bruni Haraldsson. It was the right thing to do; he wouldn't need the report for that.

"Mr. Haraldsson, I have a matching accident report. On Thursday 25 August, a white Cessna 172 flew into a prohibited part of our Military Operations Area. It was flying low and did not deviate when an F-16 attempted interception. It flew into a box canyon, hit a wingtip, and spun in. It burned with unusual heat. We found some charred remains of the pilot, impossible to identify by visual recognition. I'm sorry to deliver this sad news, and I'm sorry that you lost your mother."

323

After a pause and in a subdued voice, Bruni said, "I knew that would happen. I knew it when I reported her missing. Mom was too old to fly, too old to drive, too. She kept backing into things."

In a voice he hoped was comforting, Major Blakely said, "Yes, I know. Older people hate to give up their freedom. That doesn't make it easier, losing your mother. I am truly sorry."

"Hey, now, she died doing what she loved." Bruni's voice sounded strong, independent, in control. "She could have given up her car, but it would have killed her to stop flying. She liked to do everything herself, even stripping paint off an airplane. She wanted to be cremated and her ashes sprinkled over the desert. Even managed to do that by herself. She left me with a beautiful picture . . . flying her old Cessna to Valhalla."

The major's throat tightened, touched by the love in Bruni's voice—the bereaved, comforting the bearer of sad tidings. He managed to say, "And you've left me with a beautiful picture. Take care, and good luck."

Major Blakely leaned back in his desk chair. In his head, he saw a young tall blond Hildur standing on one wing, holding her sword and shield, singing a Wagnerian aria. She'd sing a Viking song in Old Norse, but Wagner would have to do. The Cessna ghost floated down a dark river, towards a celestial light show, a green and yellow flickering aurora borealis curtain . . .

The desk chair started to roll and tip, smacking the major's knees against the desk before he caught himself. He was surprised by what he had learned from Jerry's dream control wanderings. His imagination had painted such a strong scene that he wanted to share it with Betty. No, not a good idea; he couldn't tell Betty because he'd tell *all* of it.

Jerry had had a leftover alligator when he brought Foxy Lady to Nellis. Now the major had a leftover skull, frozen at the morgue, the single eye staring. How would he get rid of the skull with the frozen stare?

39.

Six weeks in the shop, almost to the day. No one would stalk the airplane this time. Jerry felt like he had his life back. In a jubilant mood, he waited for take off clearance at Palo Alto Airport in Cessna Six-Papa-Victor, its first flight with the replacement engine, his turn to take it up after maintenance. He sang a snatch of a tune: *Off we go, into the wild blue yonder . . .*

Frank, in the co-pilot's seat, fiddled with the radio and double-checked his seat belt. He wiped his damp palms on his jeans. Last time he flew Six-Papa-Victor he hadn't made it over the bay—engine failure from sugar in the gas-tank—Captain Wachter must have done it, but it didn't matter anymore, now that he was dead. Frank shivered and said, "I almost wish we had parachutes."

The radio boomed, "Cessna Six-Papa-Victor, cleared for take off."

Jerry taxied onto Palo Alto's runway, close to the wildlife refuge, then pushed the throttle full-in. Six-Papa-Victor raced across the pavement and lifted into the air. At 1000 feet, Jerry turned right across the bay.

Frank's heart hammered and he swallowed hard. He almost forgot to breathe. He relaxed when Jerry turned north at 7500 feet.

"A valley tour today," Jerry said. "The new engine needs two hours at cruise power. We'll drop down into Auburn for lunch. You can fly us home."

Frank didn't answer. He felt apprehensive about the trip home; he had to get back on the horse, so to speak, to regain his confidence. He watched traffic on Interstate 5 and water-ski trails on the Sacramento River below. He entertained himself by locating unfamiliar airports—Lodi, no parachuting today; Nut Tree, restaurant still closed—until he saw the eyebrow landmark that located Auburn and felt the Cessna drop down over the canyon.

Jerry touched down with one squeak of the stall horn, a textbook-perfect landing. He parked the aircraft in front of Gold Country Aviation as usual, but Ruben didn't come out to meet them.

Frank saw Ruben through the open hangar door. Jerry called out, "Hey, Rube, I'm buying today. Can we take you to lunch?"

"Well, if you're buying. I'm right in the middle of something." Ruben sounded grumpy and he lacked his usual smile. He hung up his coveralls and walked next door to Wings' Grill in step with Frank.

Uncharacteristically, Jerry lagged behind.

"What's the matter—Wings' hamburger slipped to Number 2?" Frank asked.

"No, still *numero uno,* but every time I see you guys I think about stolen airplanes and fried skulls, and I lose my appetite."

"All right," Frank said. "We won't order barbecue."

Jerry held the door at the restaurant. "I'm sorry, Ruben, I really am."

A waitress Frank hadn't met brought glasses of water and menus to their table. She shook her chestnut brown ponytail at Jerry and leaned on the table. She wore a tight red sweater, flaunting breasts as full as Robina's. Reading her name badge, Frank said, "Say, you're new, and you're Alaine?"

She nodded her head and swished her hair up and down, catching the light.

"Did you know Alaine means beautiful in Gaelic?' Frank asked.

She smiled at Frank and turned to lift a glass coffee pot off the hotplate beside their table. "How about coffee to start?"

Jerry ordered a hamburger with his cup of coffee. No flirting, Frank noticed. No funny stories. Ruben ordered a hamburger after all.

"Make that a hamburger for me, too, and extra fries," Frank said. "Is Robina off today?"

"She up and quit, while back. Went running off to Utah with that boyfriend of hers. Looking for gulls she said, of all things. Like Auburn birds weren't good enough."

"When was that?" Frank asked. The boyfriend couldn't be the one Robina called Bill; Captain Wachter was dead. Jerry and Ruben seemed unconcerned.

Alaine shrugged, put her order pad in the front pocket of her apron, and stepped to the next table.

Jerry made no rude references to Alaine's prominent mammaries—'jiggling jugs' he used to say when Robina didn't wear a bra, and Ruben would add 'loose nips sink ships.' Frank was glad that they were less sophomoric today.

"That does sound a bit strange, Robina going to Utah so suddenly." Frank wiped rivulets of water off his glass with his index finger. Discussing Robina would bring everything up again, but he couldn't leave it alone.

"Why would anyone go so far to look at gulls?"

"*Quien sabe . . .*"

"The lone stranger rides again." Jerry interrupted Ruben and they both laughed.

Almost back to normal, Frank thought, like before Captain Fish Eyes came into their lives.

Later that night or early the next morning, Jerry awakened in a cold sweat. His recurring nightmare: the eyeball stared from its socket in a charred skull. Except this time, it winked. Did he misidentify Captain Wachter's body? Mary had said all dead eyes stared like that, but Frank thought the eye was blue, not gray. No—he couldn't have mistaken that eye.

Why did Robina go to the Great Salt Lake to see gulls? Something didn't fit. Interstate 80 passed Auburn,

Reno, Salt Lake City, on the way to Wyoming and South Dakota . . . Rapid City. No—he would have known that terrible eye anywhere. What if he had been wrong?

Bingo! She's with Fish Eyes!

Jerry slipped out of bed without waking Sally. In the dark living room, he dialed Frank's number. "Hey there. We have to check out Rapid City, find out who puts on the headdress when Chief Eagle Feather walks through that Indian casino."

"Come on, Jerry. It's the middle of the night. Why are you waking me up?"

"I have to go to Rapid City, see for myself what's happening at the captain's casino. I'm going to take a week off, settle this thing for good. Will you come with me?"

"I'm afraid not, Old Buddy. Nobody's pants are too short this time. And the captain's dead, remember?"

"But why did Robina go bird watching so far away? Captain Fish Eyes was a bird watcher. She quit her job—just up and left."

"What part of *no* don't you understand? No. No. No." The dial tone buzzed in Jerry's ear.

"You promised you wouldn't chase Fish Eyes anymore." Sally stood naked after her morning shower, her arms crossed above her rounded belly, the twins pouching out. She had been pregnant before Paradise, but Paradise made a better story.

"Besides, you said he was dead." Sally's hazel eyes flashed ice.

"You're beautiful when you're angry." Jerry sat on the edge of the bed and patted the mattress. "Come here, lovely."

Sally stamped one bare foot. "Why are you going back to South Dakota?"

"I may have misidentified that grisly eyeball. The Cessna that crashed and burned could not be positively identified. I have to find out and maybe get rid of the nightmares."

"So you're going alone because Frank has more sense."

"Something like that. I want to trace Ruben's Cessna and to find out if Quill Rethcaw still makes a Saturday night appearance at Little Eagle Casino. I'll lay this to rest, once and for all."

"I don't want you to go. But you will. So I'm coming along."

"No, Sally. It's too dangerous."

"I can't stay here, worrying about you. I'm going with you to Rapid City. End of discussion."

40.

Just at noon, Jerry and Sally's United Airlines flight arrived in Rapid City, the best place for aircraft repairs in western South Dakota according to the airport guide. Ruben's Cessna might still be flying—if that Indian were still alive—and its most likely service center would be Rapid City, the only suitable place within a hundred miles of the reservation and the Little Eagle Casino. Ruben, however, hadn't helped. As far as Ruben was concerned, the case closed on the day the insurance company paid for his destroyed white Cessna. But was the case really closed? Was Fish Eyes alive? Jerry had to know.

After lunch in the airport terminal, Jerry planned to track Ruben's missing airplane by visiting mechanics across the field. He had the tail number, the GPS serial number, and the hours on the Hobbs meter—like the odometer on a car. Not a lot to go on, if the registration had been altered. The first place to check was in the building that adjoined the restaurant.

Jerry held the door for Sally at Western Dakota Air Center. A Nordic-looking man chatted on the telephone across the counter; his badge read *George*. Jerry waited for George to hang up the phone and turn towards the counter. "I need an oil change and a new battery for my Cessna, and I'd like to speak to the owner, please."

"Speaking." George leaned towards Jerry and smiled.

"Uh, I'm traveling, and the log books aren't in the aircraft. Can you give me a stick-in repair label?" Ideally, the aircraft logs reside in the airplane, but as a practical manner, many pilots keep them in a safer place.

"Not a problem. How about tomorrow morning?"

Jerry shot Sally a what-do-you-think look. She nodded. He leaned across the counter and said in a low voice, "No, that's not really it. I have to trust you. I'm looking for a missing Cessna. When last seen, it was white. The tail number probably was altered. Have you worked on any Cessna 172s in the last two months—with no log books?"

George's smile turned into a frown. "Why are you asking?"

"It belonged to his friend, and it was stolen," Sally said. "Please help us."

George's smile returned. "That's different, then. If you can come back in a couple of hours, I'll pull all the files for Cessna 172s. I hate aircraft thieves."

"Thanks. I'll be back."

Sally followed Jerry across the tarmac to visit the other airport businesses. At the second maintenance hangar, a dark skinned fellow named Willie White Hawk came out from under a low-winged aircraft. Sally shook her head *no*.

"Do you know if any hangars are available?" Jerry asked.

"No, not unless you have a gold-plated twin or a Lear jet." White Hawk spoke as if he had gravel in his mouth.

"Thanks." Jerry stepped outside to consult Sally and the list he had made from the airport directory, still nothing to go on.

"He looked like an Indian. Be careful," Sally whispered.

"One more place to check at this airport, Eagle Aviation." Jerry pointed out a building about the length of a football field away from where they stood.

"The name is good," Sally said, walking past an open hangar door.

"Oops. The sign in the window says they specialize in jets." Jerry asked at Eagle Aviation anyway. The mechanics hadn't worked on a Cessna 172 since last winter.

"Good job, Super Sleuth," Sally said, following Jerry away from the Rapid City business last on his list.

"Well, what do you think—let George do it?"

"Sounds good to me." Sally returned Jerry's list to her purse.

After a soda from the vending machine, Jerry and Sally returned to Western Dakota Air. George pulled up the repair tags for Cessna 172s for August and September. The computer sorted the list by tail numbers. Not useful without the right number.

"Do you remember any especially nice Cessnas?" Jerry asked. "Snow white, new white leather interior, everything rebuilt to better-than-new."

"Only one real nice one, but not snow white." George aided his memory by glancing at the ceiling. "It was white with a vibrant blue tail, and the paint on the wing tips was scalloped to look like feathers. The tail number ended in LE, and he called it Little Eagle. A tall guy, well over six feet."

Jerry read the repair order on the screen. A tall man who named a pristine white Cessna *Little Eagle*. As though he had just struck gold, he said, "*Bingo!*"

George lifted his eyebrows in a silent question.

"Mineral oil. Must have a new engine."

"Told you it was nice."

"Gosh, thanks. I really appreciate it." Jerry exchanged looks with Sally. His face radiated excitement.

George closed the file and turned away from the computer. "That's okay. The only good airplane thief is a dead airplane thief."

Jerry waved goodbye. That had to be Ruben's plane. It couldn't be . . . how'd it get here . . . Fish Eyes must be alive. No, he couldn't be . . .

Outside the shop and walking towards the rental car, he asked Sally, "Well, what do you think? *Little Eagle,* that's the one for sure. No other mechanics available for miles around here."

"George's tip sounded right, but don't jump to conclusions." Seated in the rental car, Sally opened the map and tapped the nearest airstrip with her index finger. Jerry had marked all the known airports in the area, all unattended landing strips, some with self-service fuel, none with repair facilities.

"Keep checking every possible place," Sally said. "Just don't pick anybody who knows Fish Eyes."

The late afternoon Saturday sun threw shadows of trees across the South Dakota highway, black shadows against the faded gray asphalt. "It'll be okay, I'll just look," Jerry told Sally while driving from Rapid City towards Eagle Creek and the Indian reservation. "I have to know if Captain Fish Eyes still appears as an Indian chief on Saturday nights at that casino."

"Maybe somebody else is dressing up —if he's dead."

"Then I'll know he's really dead, and I can rest in peace."

"Remember—he's the one who's supposed to rest in peace."

"We'll soon find out. There he is." Jerry pointed and turned onto Casino Drive.

The over-sized figure of an Indian chief with an eagle perched on his out-stretched arm still beckoned from the roof of Little Eagle Casino. The eagle's long shadow covered the hood of their rental car when Jerry parked.

Inside the casino, the cigarette stench almost made Jerry gag. He checked their outerwear at the cloakroom. Sally found an old-fashioned pull-down-the-arm slot machine and laughed when a bucket of quarters rained out onto the floor amid bells and flashing lights, a major jackpot.

Jerry tried to look busy at the next one-armed bandit. Anxiety gnawed at his gut.

Sally saw him first—Chief Eagle Feather—dressed in a buckskin jacket and trousers, walking over to greet the winner. He wore a full feather headdress and red paint zigzags on his cheeks.

"Is that Captain Fish Eyes?" Sally asked in an excited whisper.

Jerry nodded, his eyes riveted on the Indian's face. His stomach felt punched, flattened, as though he had just belly-flopped from a high diving board. It's him—Oh-my-god—he's still alive. Jerry forced himself to look away. Two older women eyed Sally's pile of coins.

He turned to Sally. He had never seen such a look on her face—anger, rage, directed at Fish Eyes. She was his rock; she always calmed him and kept him out of trouble. He reached to restrain her.

Before he could stop her, Sally darted away and stopped right in front of the Indian. She poked his chest with her forefinger and bellowed, "You killed Samantha!"

The Indian stepped back, poker-faced, as still as if he were carved from wood.

A crowd started to gather: a bald man as wide as he was tall, a pseudo-cowboy in expensive boots and new jeans, noisy people whispering and staring.

Sally took another step forward and poked him again. Her voice rose. "Why did you kill my cat?"

"Ma'am, I have never seen you before. How could I kill your cat?" His voice was low and calm and soothing. A knot of customers drew nearer and gawked at the loud pregnant woman accosting the casino icon.

The color left Jerry's face. He rushed to Sally's side.

"You almost killed my husband!" Sally screamed, her face beet-red. She smacked the big man's chest with both her fists. The casino was suddenly silent. Everyone turned to stare at Sally and Chief Eagle Feather.

"What's the problem here?" The quiet voice belonged to a small woman in elegant crème-colored slacks and a gold thread blouse. The top of her blond head didn't reach Sally's shoulder. She grabbed Sally's fists.

"He killed my cat," Sally sobbed.

"Quill, you wouldn't kill a cat, would you?"

Jerry recognized Robina. He tugged at Sally's arm. "Let's get out of here."

"That was between two chiefs and none of your affair." Aquila stood regally in his headdress crown, his chin thrust forward. He faced Robina. He crossed his arms in front of himself and scowled, his strange eyes intense and hard.

"Not a cat. Not killing a cat." Robina grabbed one buckskin sleeve, her voice low but hard. "What about it, Aquila?"

Even the feathers in his headdress sagged. His face grim, he deflated like a balloon with a slow leak. The Indian chief didn't answer.

Sally, encouraged that Robina didn't approve of killing cats, added, "And he tried to kill my husband."

"You mean Jerry? I'd like to kill him myself." Sparks flew out of Robina's narrowed eyes. Her words hissed and boiled out like steam from a volcano. "He never said he was married. He was all over me. Thought I was easy. And he always joked about my big boobs."

Sally's eyes radiated fury. She turned to her husband and slammed his shoulder. "Jerry, what about it?"

Jerry stood, his mouth wide open. His face reddened. How could he tell her?

"I should have scalped somebody," the big Indian said in a deep voice, feet wide apart, hands on his hips. Three hefty stone-faced men backed him up.

"Cat killer!" Jerry yelled. He balled his fist and punched Aquila in the solar plexus. *Hard.* With a surprised look of pain, the tall Indian bent forward. Jerry's left fist hit the big man's jaw and knocked him to the floor. Jerry wanted to do that for months.

"Take that, Fish Eyes." Oh-my-god—blue eyes: not silver-reptilian. No, they were the same eyes. His twin? Blue contacts?

Two casino security guards pinned Jerry's arms, one on each side. "You're gonna spend the night in jail. Assault and battery."

Aquila, the breath knocked out of him, stood up and rubbed his chin. He picked up loose feathers from the floor and readjusted his headdress. He spat out his words: "I'll sue your feathers off, you woodpecker."

335

The crowd pressed closer, enjoying the show. Jerry couldn't think. How would he explain Robina to Sally?

Robina stamped one foot and crossed her arms. "Quill, this is bad for business."

Aquila snarled at Jerry with hungry-bear eyes, otherwise ordinary eyes, as though Robina had shorn his wild looks.

Robina pointed at the security guards. "Let him go. Escort him to the door. Just get him out of here." To the crowd, she announced, "A round of drinks on the house."

The burly bouncers, one at each elbow, fast-marched Jerry to the door and pushed him out. He stumbled and fell to one knee.

Sally didn't help him up. She started to shiver. "I'll get our coats," she said, turning back towards warmth. She had taken only a few steps when Jerry's jacket and her poncho sailed out of the Casino's front door.

Back at the car, Sally crossed her arms and scowled at Jerry. "I'm not getting in until you tell me what gives with you and Robina."

Jerry, sitting in the driver's seat, squirmed with discomfort. "It wasn't as bad as she made out."

"Bologna. Why'd she say that then? Jokes about boobs, sounds like an eighth-grader, not his teacher. That's the least of it. Playboy!" Sally threw her purse at Jerry, the only handy ammunition. Through tight lips, she said, "So, what else?"

He ducked and covered his head with his arms. "I won't lie to you."

Jerry took a deep breath. He had hoped he would never have to tell her about Robina. His words spurted out, one on top of the other. "The night I slept at Auburn before I followed Fish Eyes to Pahrump I took her out to dinner and I had too much wine and I shouldn't have and I won't ever do it again and I'm sorry."

"So, you leave me home alone weekend after weekend and fly that damned airplane so you can be with some hussy? Bad enough an airplane—I won't stand for another woman." Too mad to cry, Sally wrapped the poncho around her shoulders.

"Sally, I'm sorry."

She slammed the fender with a fist. "What about the he-was-all-over-me part?"

"I tried to kiss her goodnight."

"How dare you, and then what? How dare you, you womanizer. You married me in the Catholic Church until death do us part. How dare you, kissing a harlot."

"Sally, I am sorry and I feel ashamed. But with that cast on my arm, I was hardly all over her. I've learned my lesson. No flirting, no sexy jokes, no kissing other women. Never again."

"And you'll keep that promise, or I'll leave." Sally climbed into the car. She tucked the poncho tightly around herself and fastened the seatbelt. "So, that's all? You're sure that's all?"

"Honest Injun."

"That's just the trouble. Don't go around them again, either of them."

"Okay. I have an idea to wind all this up. No, don't say it. Don't worry—I won't go to South Dakota again." Jerry hoped he could keep that promise, both promises. He had to, if he wanted to keep Sally. He had found Ruben's Cessna and Captain Fish Eyes. He thought he knew how to lure the Indian and the airplane off the reservation.

41.

"A mechanic can refuse to release an aircraft with a stolen GPS," Jerry told Sally aboard the United Airlines flight returning to San Jose. "George said he'd check the GPS serial number if the Cessna with the blue tail comes back to Rapid City for maintenance. Undoubtedly, the federal authorities will find altered registration papers. With a name like Little Eagle, that has to belong to Chief Eagle Feather or Captain Wachter or whatever he calls himself now."

"So, that's your plan?"

"All I have so far. To be truthful, I tend to make it up as I go along." Jerry hoped that Fish Eyes would need a mechanic for at least an oil change.

"Just run it by me, all of it. Promise?"

"Promise. Honest Injun."

"That's what got you into trouble in the first place. You don't have to worry about him coming to California. Robina wouldn't stand for it." Sally opened her sketchbook and settled in for a drawing session.

"You were wonderful, pushing Fish Eyes around like that. I wouldn't want to be on your bad side," Jerry said. And that's exactly where he still was, but she'd get over it.

"Just don't pull any more Robinas out of your hat. I mean it." A hard tone came into her voice. "I'll leave you if you ever do that again."

"*Touché.*" Jerry was glad that Sally wasn't breathing fire today. "It felt so good to punch him out, to actually knock down Old Fish Eyes. I wanted to do that for months."

"You forgot to mention stolen airplanes. I wonder what Robina would have said. She keeps him on a short leash, and it only took her two months." Sally started a sketch of Chief Eagle Feather, his regal bearing, his aquiline nose, and his painted cheeks.

"Love has tamed him," Jerry said, thinking that Sally had put *him* on a short leash.

"They deserve each other."

"We can't let Captain Fish Eyes get away with it, but the FBI file is closed—who would believe he is still alive?" Jerry glanced at Sally's sketch; she wasn't listening.

He couldn't tell Major Paul Blakely—open up the whole mess again—until he actually caught Captain Wachter, off the reservation. How the heck would he do that?

At home again after the trip to Rapid City, Jerry leaned back in his leather recliner, watching *Jeopardy* on television. "Frank should get on that show."

Sally nodded, her mind elsewhere. She had crocheted halfway across a white and yellow crib afghan.

"Do you remember what George said about Little Eagle's paint job?" Jerry asked. "Could you do that with *Photoshop*— white Cessna, blue tail, blue scallops on the wingtips like eagle feathers?"

"I'd need a picture to start with." Sally dropped the crochet hook. Jerry's sudden change of topic set off an alarm in her head. "What are you cooking up?"

"One—it's a nifty paint scheme. Two—I could ask people to look for it."

"What people? Not Indians. Not anyone who knows the captain." Sally frowned and put away the yarn.

"I'll run it all by you after I get a picture of a Cessna." Jerry put his feet up on the coffee table and opened his cell phone.

"Hey, mister. Feet off the furniture," Sally said. Now that Jerry was home every weekend, he should help with cleaning, maybe dishes, too. And he never put away his shoes, either. Only two months—that's all it took for Robina to tame Quill.

"Okay, Okay. Hey, Ruben. Haven't seen you in a while."

He hadn't talked to Ruben in what, a month? Ruben, Auburn, Robina . . . He won't get away with that again— ever. Sally felt anger rising, a new and interesting emotion; she always had kept her temper in check. Hotheaded, that was what it felt like.

"And I haven't lost any airplanes in a while," Ruben said in a cold voice.

"*Touché.* And here I am, asking a favor again." Jerry sat forward in his chair and ran his fingers through his hair. "Not an airplane, just a picture of one. A friend of mine wants to sell his Cessna."

Liar, Sally thought. Jerry had an irritating habit, leaving the speaker on, the volume cranked up. He called everybody else with that cell phone—it practically grew out of his arm. He never bothered to call her when he was late.

"I don't need one." Ruben was short and to the point.

"No, no." Jerry's voice rose and Sally turned to watch him. "You made a terrific spec sheet to sell your *Snow Goose.* If you still have it in your computer, could you e-mail me a copy?"

"Why do you want that? It crashed and burned— remember?"

"It's a great example of a spec sheet for an aircraft sale." Jerry's salesman-voice again. "Sally has an idea for a unique Cessna paint scheme. She needs a picture of a plain white one to start with."

Blame it on Sally, now . . .

"You're still *loco,*" Ruben said. He sounded annoyed.

"And you're still the best mechanic in Northern California," Jerry said.

"Here we go again, you buttering me up. Whatever it is, I won't do it. *Nada.*"

Sally reached out and grabbed the phone. "Give me that thing." Her voice sweetened. "Hi, Ruben. Say, I need the biggest favor from you. I want to design a paint scheme but I need a photo of a Cessna 172 to use with *Photoshop.* If you'd send me one, I'd love you for it."

"Well . . . since *you* want it, I'll send you the picture of my dead airplane."

"Ruben, you're a dear. Tell Carmencita hello—I haven't seen her in ages."

Sally spent the next evening on the computer touching up the picture of Ruben's white Cessna. At first, she couldn't coordinate the pen tool; she needed to superimpose an outline onto the wing. She took a break to study eagles in flight on the Internet: the wingtip feathers spread out like fingers on an open hand. Fingers, blue fingers—that was it. She printed an 8 by 10 glossy to show to Jerry. "Well, what do you think?"

"That's gorgeous. If that isn't Little Eagle's paint job, it should be. I'll e-mail it to George and ask him if it looks like Little Eagle. I want to send a *I-want-your airplane* postcard to Captain Fish Eyes—oops, I mean Chief Eagle Feather."

"I love it," Sally said. "Won't that send him back on the warpath?" They called one another names like two small boys throwing rocks: *Fish Eyes, Woodpecker.* Jerry had a sharp nose and an unruly red topknot, yes, like a woodpecker.

"Who cares? I haven't had a nightmare since I slugged Old Fish Eyes."

"Remember—you're not going back to South Dakota." The eyes: Jerry always exaggerated, *Fish Eyes.* Quill's eyes were overrated: strange, but not that remarkable. "And you tell me the plan—all of it."

After lunch at Auburn Airport on the following Sunday, Sally watched Jerry open a manila folder and spread several 8 x 10 photos—her computer work—across an inside table at Wings. He wiped some spilled catsup off the folder with a crumpled napkin. Ruben tapped his fingers on the arms of a white plastic chair. Sally smelled stale grease and she hadn't eaten the fried egg with its crispy-curled edges; Wings was overrated. She sat back from the edge of the table, the twins-to-be making her bulky.

"The Snow Goose with blue make-up." Ruben directed his gaze to Sally. "*Muy bueno*. I didn't know you were into airplane paint design."

"You can have them," Sally said. "I had fun doing it. I can give you the specs to make a template, too. I can design custom paint jobs for you to use on your restored aircraft, and advertising brochures for you, too. How about a cover for your book?"

"You can make a design from my rough ideas?"

"Sure." Sally wouldn't ever let Jerry come to Auburn, *alone*, again.

Ruben pulled a small white envelope out of his pocket. "By the way, Carmencita said you're invited."

Sally opened an invitation to a baby shower. "How wonderful. So you and Carmencita are expecting, too."

"Jerry didn't tell me about that," Ruben said. "I wondered if you had swallowed a pumpkin seed."

"Two of them—*dos niños*." Sally's abdomen chose that moment to bounce as though the twins were practicing for a soccer match. She eyed the door to the ladies' restroom; she had an urgent urge to pee. "I haven't seen Carmencita since that barbecue outside your hangar. Tell her I'm delighted and I'll come."

Sally slipped away from the table when Ruben and Jerry started talking aircraft engines. Alaine, their waitress of the day, was washing her hands in the ladies' room. "So you're Robina's replacement," Sally said. "Do you ever hear from her?"

"Oh, sure. She's been my friend for years." Alaine dried her hands on a towel.

"I never learned her last name."

"Kyrosopoulos. Isn't that a mouthful? She said just call her Robina Kay."

Sally gazed into the mirror and refreshed her lipstick. She could think of lots of things to call Robina. "Did you know that Ruben's wife is pregnant, a baby next spring?"

"Looks like you are, too. Carmencita is having a baby shower next month."

"I was invited, too. Our husbands are friends," Sally said. Good: she's going to the party. "Would Robina like to come?"

"Robina liked Carmencita." Alaine's face lit up.

"Here. Let's send Robina my invitation. Just write her address. I have a stamp in my wallet. Let her know that everyone at Auburn misses her."

"Do you think she'll come, all that way?" Alaine asked.

"I hope so." Those men—they just didn't know how to do it. Sally had a plan of her own to apprehend Fish Eyes.

Later that evening, Jerry read his e-mail. George in Rapid City wrote: How'd you do it, copy Little Eagle without seeing it? Maybe Sally could sketch some other custom paint schemes for me.

Jerry hit the reply button: When do you advertise your services to get airplanes ready for winter? Here in California, we fly all winter, never worry about extreme cold. How do you get an airplane ready for that?

George's answer came in two hours: That's a good idea, a winterization special. Can Sally design a brochure?

George explained that an airplane engine can't be started without damage at a temperature of twenty below, and often the battery goes dead. For winter flying, he recommended installation of a Tannis heater and keeping the aircraft in a heated hangar, or replacing the engine oil with mineral oil for winter storage.

The next evening, Jerry sent George a brochure designed by Sally and requested a flyer to be sent to *occupant* at Robina's address.

Jerry wanted to get this over with quickly. However it worked out, the Indian had to come off the reservation sometime to have the Cessna serviced, and George's shop in Rapid City was the only suitable place within a hundred miles.

Would Captain Fish Eyes rise to the surface and swallow the lure?

42.

Aquila unlocked the barn doors and swung them open. Little Eagle: his beautiful white Cessna. He had added blue paint on her tail and scalloped the wing tips in blue—an eagle's wing feathers opened out like fingers. He pulled her out into the sunlight on the cool October afternoon. He ground out his cigarette before he drained a fuel sample from the left tank. "You have to be careful with sparks—avgas is volatile. Would you like to check the right tank?" he asked Robina.

"Oh, could I? I want to learn everything about this." Robina climbed onto the second step of the ladder to reach the testing nipple. Her new jeans showed off her trim little butt when she reached out. Afterwards, she watched his every move, as though he were a bowerbird building a maypole to attract a mate.

Using a winch, Aquila loaded the aircraft onto the trailer bed flagged *extra wide load*. His helpers climbed into the truck cab, and Aquila hoisted Robina onto his lap for the half-mile ride to the road. Robina snuggled tight against him, riding out the bumps between the barn and the highway.

Some distance down the highway, Aquila's helpers unloaded flashing road construction signs. The one who wore an orange vest stayed there with a stop sign. The driver reversed the truck and, half a mile back, parked in the middle of the road. Aquila and the driver rolled the Cessna onto the seldom-used paved road while Robina watched from the truck. Her smile made him want to strut.

After the aircraft was positioned, Aquila lifted Robina down from the high truck seat and gave her an extra hug while he held her. He loved her more than life itself. "I brought cushions for you, so you can see out over the nose." He stacked her atop two cushions in the co-pilot's seat and fastened her seatbelt. Before he started the engine, Aquila said, "I want to show you something important, *Paha Sapa,* my grandmothers' holy place."

"Is that nearby? I'm dying of curiosity, after all you've told me."

"I'll show you, my love." Aquila knew they couldn't converse over the engine noise. He wanted her to understand everything about him, especially about his great-grandmother Medicine Woman. Robina made him feel important, worthy, loved. He roared down the make-do runway and took off over the trees. "Fly away with Little Eagle, my Little Robin Rosebud."

As the land fell away, Robina laughed, the musical laugh that he loved. Aquila felt as though he were an eagle, soaring and swooping, his mate at his side. Over the Badlands, over the presidents carved from granite at Mount Rushmore where tourists scuttled about, over vast parking lots that paved the prairie, over Wind Cave where the Buffalo Nation had arisen from the earth, over the battlefield where the Sioux had conquered Custer. He wanted her to see the primitive beauty of *Paha Sapa,* the land stolen from the Sioux by the white man.

When Aquila landed for fuel at Hot Springs Airport, small like Auburn but without a restaurant, he showed Robina how to program the pump and how to check for impurities. He filled four five-gallon gas cans with extra aviation fuel and treated Robina to a cold soda from the machine for the return flight to the reservation.

As the afternoon shadows lengthened, Aquila sighted his improvised runway, invisible amongst the trees, and landed back on his quiet road within the reservation. Robina turned to him and said, "That's absolutely obscene, George Washington's huge head, right in the heart of *Paha Sapa.* Why did the government do that to your people, steal their holy place?"

"It wasn't right. When I was a boy, I swore I'd take it back, give the land and the gold back to my grandmothers."

"Oh, my, what a loving little boy you were."

"Do you really think so?" The way she looked at him, love in her eyes . . . His mother Dancing Dove hadn't loved him—she never came back—he had thought it was his fault. Robina's eyes bathed him with love. He felt cleansed.

"I think you are wonderful. And I wish I had known your grandmother. You thrill me with her stories when you talk to me, lying there in the dark."

Eyes, eyes, he saw eyes . . . His great-grandmother Medicine Woman had loved him. Story Teller had loved him—she'd born Medicine Woman in the Winter of Cold and Hunger when she was only thirteen. He needed to go to Paha Sapa, to climb the hills, to reach his arms up to the sky.

Robina tugged his arm. "Quill, are you okay? Quill?"

He swept her into his arms. Aquila felt flustered and warm and ten feet tall, all at the same time. He mussed Robina's hair and sent her to the warm house. He needed to stay out a few minutes longer, to clean bugs off the leading edges of Little Eagle's wings and to polish with a spray wax . . . and to think. Aquila wanted no secrets between them. He didn't want Robina ever to leave him. He had known fear— only one time—when Jerry had confronted him at the casino, but Chief Woodpecker had not told Robina about the stolen Cessna. Before Aquila told her, he wanted Robina to know that what the white man called crimes the red man would understand as necessary in the battle against injustice. Stealing a Cessna was no different than borrowing a horse.

What Aquila wouldn't tell her, couldn't ever tell her, still haunted him: Kedar's expressive, trusting eyes—trusting even when sent on a mission that the boy must have known was suicide. Those eyes—the boy had loved his teacher. Aquila's Caucasian *persona* reminded him of his sins; Captain von Wächter was dead, but his memories of that time lived on, damning Aquila. He should have met Robina years ago. Aquila wished that he had never tried to send a cadet air force on an impossible mission, to slay a dragon with a cap pistol.

Aquila lowered the barn door, its hinges complaining more than usual, and went inside for supper.

A few days later on another crisp autumn day, Aquila opened the barn to admire his white Cessna. The squealing hinges grated on his nerves; he climbed on a ladder to oil them. He couldn't have asked the tribal council for an aircraft for his personal use—it wouldn't be right—even though they would grant him anything. He stepped over close to the airplane—Ruben said he wanted someone to love it; Aquila certainly did. Ruben probably had rebuilt another Cessna by now with the insurance money. Aquila had never cared about cars or boats or motorcycles except for transportation. Now he enjoyed walking around his bird and polishing her paint, whether or not he flew her.

Little Eagle belonged in the air. He would offer one of his eager helpers a short ride; maybe Fred Blackbird would take him to the road. He hadn't filled the fuel tanks after his last flight. He needed to ready the aircraft before he bored holes in the sky.

Aquila dragged the metal ladder into position in front of the left wing tank. Even at six foot eight, he couldn't reach the fuel cap without it. He snuffed out a good Cuban cigar smuggled to him by a casino customer and left it in an ashtray to enjoy later. Then he zipped his nylon jacket, uncapped a five-gallon can of aviation fuel, and climbed two steps up the ladder to pour gas into the tank. Unseen, the fuel fumes from the open tank wrapped around his arm and circled outward and caught a spark from his nylon jacket.

The explosion knocked Aquila off the ladder and splashed his face with burning liquid. He screamed and slapped at his face. *His eyes. Burning.* The blue contacts melted in the intense heat. He fell into a puddle of flaming fuel and rolled back and forth to smother the fire covering his body. Licked by a tongue of fire, his nylon jacket shrunk into crisp bits and melded with his arms.

Aquila didn't see Little Eagle catch fire. He heard the fuel tanks explode. He didn't hear Robina screaming.

43.

Ready to party at Ruben's house and clutching her sketchbook, Sally watched Jerry tie down the Cessna at Auburn Airport. Jerry's friend Ruben Estrada would meet them in a few minutes to take them to the baby shower. Sally wouldn't know anyone there—unless Robina actually came. The last time that she had seen Robina, Sally had called Quill a cat-killer. Robina wouldn't dare comment on the situation, not with all her friends around. Sally would discover Robina's flight schedule and Quill would pick her up in Rapid City—*Voilà.* The FBI would catch him for sure.

Later at the party, Jerry and Ruben and the other husbands had beer and chips 'n' dips in the garage; the ladies devoured cupcakes and took turns pinning a diaper on a stuffed monkey for best time. Such a frivolous game—no one used diaper pins these days. Sally looked around the circle of pregnant women to see if she recognized anyone. Ruben's wife Carmencita, due after Sally, had the Madonna glow. So did the others, all except Alaine, the new waitress at Wings Grill; she seemed to be the only one not pregnant. Sally had not noticed any difference in her own face; her only change with pregnancy was her expanding waistline.

"Is everyone here?" Sally asked the woman on her right. She didn't see Robina, but she couldn't very well ask if she was coming—since Sally had slipped Robina an invitation without telling the hostess.

The woman shrugged and smiled.

Sally couldn't remember everyone's name. She didn't want to unscramble puzzle words for prizes. Sally was more interested in studying the group of healthy young women. What characterized the face of a pregnant woman, something about her eyes? Could she capture it? Sally lost herself in making quick portrait sketches.

After a while, it was time for Carmencita to pull the paper off the packages. Alaine handed her a small box and said, "Here, open this first. Robina couldn't come."

Sally snapped to attention.

Carmencita ripped open the package, dropping bunny-rabbit paper and ribbons and white tissue on the floor alongside her chair. She held up a tiny pair of buckskin moccasins for everyone to see and said, "There's a note: *Thank you for inviting me. It was too far to come this time. All my love and kiss the baby for me, Robina.*"

Sally was disappointed that Robina didn't come, Sally's small bid to help Jerry lure Fish Eyes off the reservation. Chief Eagle Feather a.k.a. Captain Wachter would have taken Robina to Rapid City to catch a flight—open game for the sheriff or the FBI or somebody. Oh, well, that didn't work. Darn! Maybe she would send Robina a little note, tell her that Little Eagle was a stolen airplane. That would start a fire—the way that Robina pushed Quill around. And it only took her two months to train him.

After Carmencita had opened all the gifts, Alaine sat down beside Sally and pressed a note into her hand. "Read this later—you should know. This is very personal."

A few minutes later, consumed by curiosity, Sally ducked into Carmencita's bathroom and opened the note—a letter to Alaine from Robina:

> It was so good of you to invite me to Carmencita's shower. That meant a lot to me. I miss you and my friends at Auburn, especially now. This is very bad time for me. I can't leave Quill—he needs me.
>
> Oh, Alaine—it was so terrible. Somehow Quill's airplane caught fire and he has burns over most of his body. He's blind—they're going to give him glass eyes to make him look

350

more normal. He's in the burn unit here in Rapid City.

Burned and blind—how awful. Sally stared at a poster depicting a leaping dolphin. Quill will never see a dolphin or anything else. Sally's throat constricted. That was absolutely awful, even if Quill was Jerry's archenemy, Fish Eyes.

I do have to tell you about the one miracle. Quill's face was badly burned. He told me about his great-grandmother's recipe for burns—she was a medicine woman. I powdered a special mushroom and mixed it with fat. I helped him rub it on his face—that was hard because it hurt him. The miracle, oh the miracle—his face is healing quickly and the doctor says he doesn't know why but there will be very little scarring. (I didn't tell him about the mushrooms: there aren't any more of them.)

At first Quill grumbled when I told him I used lard instead of buffalo fat because I couldn't find any. Then he said I was a brilliant woman, and beautiful, too, and he told me that he wished he could see my face. I cried, and I am crying as I write this letter. Now you see why I can't leave for a party.

Sally burst into tears before she read the final sentence: *Please come to visit if you get the chance. Love from Robina.*

Poor Robina. Sally covered her face with her hands and sobbed. What a tragedy. How would it be if Jerry were blind, how would she feel? It wasn't Robina's fault that the men had a feud; it wasn't her fault that she had big boobs; it wasn't her fault that Jerry had kissed her. That *woodpecker*, that's what Quill had called Jerry, that woodpecker.

351

After a bit, Sally dried her tears. She felt sorry for her harsh thoughts towards Robina and sorry for Quill. She was no longer in the mood to party, but she had to return to the baby shower before someone knocked the door down to get to the toilet.

An hour later, Ruben dropped Sally and Jerry at the Stardust Motel. In a pensive mood, Sally listened to them joke, something about eight hours from bottle to throttle. She hoped she could tell Jerry about Robina's note without crying.

Sally waited until Jerry was ready to settle in for the night. She sat on the edge of the bed in their motel room near Auburn Airport, holding Alaine's letter from Robina and reading aloud. "It's just too sad. Fish Eyes let you go. Now you have to let him go."

"No way. He can't just get away with it—he broke the law."

"You have to let him go. Even if you did kiss Robina."

Jerry's face reddened. "Now wait a minute—I thought we had a truce. What about killing your cat?"

"Indians did things like that—scalped settlers, set houses afire, stole horses."

"Not any more they don't. What about blowing up things?"

"You already punched him out in front of the whole casino."

"Stealing airplanes, stealing *my* Cessna?"

"Tell me how a blind man is going to steal airplanes," Sally said. "He's living with his punishment, a life sentence."

Jerry started pacing, his arms crossed against his chest. "He's in Rapid City, off the reservation. The FBI could nab him."

"It's a closed file, and where's your proof? Ruben's stolen airplane turned to ashes. With those burns, Quill won't even have the same finger prints." Sally folded the letter and put it into her purse.

"How do you know that?" Jerry stopped pacing and looked puzzled.

"Well—what would you do instinctively, if your face was on fire?" Sally waved away invisible flames.

"My God! And he's blind—that is terrible." Jerry perched on the edge of a chair, one knee up, and stared out the dark window.

"You have to tell them. Frank, Ruben and Paul." Sally crossed her arms across her chest—two can play that game. Jerry had to tell them.

"They will be really, really upset, that I didn't tell them that Wachter was alive before this. I was such a fool. At least, the FBI can wrap it up."

"No, Jerry. Not the FBI, not when he's in a burn unit, for heaven's sake. That's like kicking him when he's down."

"It was Paul's investigation. I have to tell him."

"Just tell the others about the fire and let it be. Fish Eyes won't ever steal another Cessna—he can't even see one. Quill and Robina have suffered enough."

"In that case . . ."

Sally knew she had won. She turned out the light and nestled under a down comforter. Jerry would see his buddies next week at her shower at Mary's house. When they were all together, Jerry could tell them that Quill wasn't dead.

On the following Saturday night, Jerry reached through a cluster of white ribbons that anchored pink and blue balloons to a heavy flowerpot and rang Frank and Mary's doorbell. Sally, guest of honor at Mary's party, bent over to admire a sign staked into a bed of star jasmine: *Caution Storks Landing.* Jerry heard talking and laughter. He expected to see everyone there who knew about the stolen Cessna: Frank, Paul, and Ruben, and he had dreaded the meeting for a week. How would he tell them that Fish Eyes was resurrected from the dead only to blow up Ruben's stolen Cessna and to be blinded in the fire?

Sally grabbed his hand. "Come on. Mary said she would leave the door unlocked."

"Come in, come in—you're the last ones here," Mary called out from somewhere towards the back of the condominium.

Jerry ushered Sally into the living room, passing a table set with Mary's finest porcelain cups and silver service. A floral centerpiece reigned beside a sheet cake decorated with two storks, each carrying a baby. He smelled the carnations and recognized Betty Blakely, Carmencita Estrada, Mary's cousin, and several clients from Sally's art gallery, a more sophisticated group than at last week's party. Jerry felt awkward and stood on one foot and then the other.

Mary, her cheeks pink, her eyes sparkling, hugged Sally. She wore a red sweater that matched the carnations. "Here comes Frank," she said. "The men are banished to the garage for the evening."

Jerry followed Frank to the garage, a small space that Frank had put in order with labeled storage boxes on neat shelves and on an overhead rack. Ruben and Paul, holding German beer steins and eating hot fresh pretzels with mustard, sat on stools next to Frank's workbench.

"We're having a beer-tasting," Frank said. Would you like *Amstel* dark or *Karlsburg* amber?"

"I'll try the amber." Jerry pulled over a stool.

Frank handed Jerry a stein. "We're celebrating, but without cigars. Mary's pregnant, too."

"*¡Viva cerveza!*" Ruben lifted his stein and grinned.

Paul smiled and saluted.

"I'll drink to that. Hear, Hear." Jerry swung his stein, sloshing suds onto the workbench. After a sip of beer, he started off, "Last week Sally and I went to a baby shower for Carmencita—"

"It's contagious. You're next, Paul," Ruben said, clapping him on the shoulder.

"Last week at Carmencita's shower—"

354

"Ruben served good Mexican beer," Frank said, finishing Jerry's sentence.

Paul waved his stein toward Frank. "Let's have another baby shower next week."

"Seriously, guys, I'm trying to tell you something. You know Alaine at Wings Restaurant? Well, she had a letter from Robina—you know, the waitress who went bird watching? Well, she went to South Dakota with Captain Wachter."

"Not him again." Ruben slouched on the stool and drew circles through the beaded moisture on his stein. "He's dead and gone."

"No, you don't say." Paul frowned and sat forward. He cleared his throat and asked, "When was that?"

"When last heard from, the captain left his skull with Paul." Frank's joke fell flat.

"Really," Jerry continued. "Robina left in September. That wasn't Ruben's Cessna that crashed and burned. But it burned last month, and Captain Wachter with it."

After a few seconds of shocked silence, Ruben said, "A delayed reaction crash and burn. So that's why you wanted the picture of Snow Goose."

"That skull doesn't belong to Captain Wachter." Paul's mouth was tight, and he filtered his words through clenched teeth.

"Of course not. He's still wearing it," Frank said. No one laughed.

"I misidentified that eyeball and I messed up your investigation . . . and I'm sorry," Jerry said in a small voice.

"You compromised everything, and you're just *sorry*?" Paul's voice had an edge. He worked his jaw muscles and clutched his stein with white knuckles.

"I was such a fool," Jerry said. Major Paul Blakely's investigation: screwed up. Ruben Estrada's painstakingly restored Cessna: stolen. Frank could have died: sugar in the tanks. Jerry, with his featherheaded schemes, had let down his friends. He looked down at his shoes.

355

Paul slid off his stool and stood leaning against the workbench. "The DNA report assigned the skull to an Icelandic female," he said without emphasis or inflection.

Jerry stared at Paul in disbelief.

Ruben's mouth fell open.

Frank, however, said in a conversational tone, "Iceland has a complete DNA analysis of its entire population."

Jerry thought Frank would report every detail, but he said nothing else.

"What did the FBI agents think of that?" Jerry said, starting a pacing pattern.

"We're in this together—I shredded the report," Paul said. "It was the wrong thing to do. I didn't want to tell the colonel and open everything up again. The skull is still in the colonel's freezer."

"Why didn't you tell us?" Jerry asked.

"I guess I hoped the problem would just go away." For a long moment, Paul was the one staring at his shoe. The cords in the back of his neck knotted and danced.

"Whose airplane died then?" Ruben asked.

Paul gazed at Ruben, Paul's face as tight as the aluminum skin on an airplane's wing. "The pilot was 77 years old, overdue to deliver her Cessna 172 for painting in Tonopah. Her son said she flew with open containers of solvents. She probably passed out from the fumes while using the autopilot."

"When did you find out?" Frank asked.

"About 15 September. On my conscience ever since." Paul looked from Frank to Jerry. "I haven't known what to do."

"Sally wants me to let him go," Jerry said. "She cried over a letter from Robina—Quill is blind and badly burned. Sally said it's like kicking a man when he's down."

"Just let him go?" Frank's eyes opened wide. "The FBI could catch him if he's off the reservation."

"Okay, suppose they take him in. My Cessna really burned this time. Do I have to give the insurance money back?" Ruben frowned and furrowed his brows.

"What about proof? With extensive burns, his fingerprints may not be the same. Will my pictures from Pahrump be enough?" Jerry asked.

"He won't be back," Ruben said, relaxing and taking a sip of beer. "That's enough for me."

"Mary says burns are extremely painful. Months to recover," Frank said. "A punishment worse than prison time. Blind—that's a life sentence."

"What will you do with the skull?" Ruben asked. "You could send it for cremation with an unclaimed body."

"My God," Paul gasped. "I couldn't do that. Those are human remains."

"This calls for more beer." Frank refilled the steins.

"It's not that simple. The skull is locked in the evidence freezer in Colonel Phillip's morgue." Paul face contorted in agony. He finished in a quiet and serious tone. "I could be court-martialed for tampering."

"If you unplug the freezer long enough, the meat will spoil," Ruben said.

"What happens if there's no action for, say, a couple years? Won't they clean out the evidence drawer?" Jerry wanted to come up with a solution, anything to ease Paul's discomfort, anything to resolve the situation.

"That isn't right. Captain Wachter can't get away with it," Paul said.

"Then here's what we do. I tell Colonel Phillips that I misidentified the body, uh, the skull. Then you tell the colonel that you have identified the skull." It felt good to put all the cards on the table. Pride be damned. Jerry knew he was right this time.

"All of this, we tell the colonel about misconduct during my investigation, and the Captain walks away? It's still my head that rolls."

"No. You take credit for solving the case. The FBI would never have solved it—you know that. I was the one who misidentified the skull. I'll take the blame."

"We still have to produce Captain Wachter and lock him away for trial."

"Tell Colonel Phillips that you have located Captain Wachter, outside the reservation. Sally knows where he is. Then send in the FBI. You end up a hero."

Jerry left his friends in an excited buzz of conversation. He needed a walk outside in the cold air. Jerry had promised Sally he wouldn't tell Paul Blakely, but he had to back him up. Now Sally would have to tell Paul where to find Quill. She wouldn't be happy.

Jerry thought about Betty Blakely's Indian tale about the two wolves we carry inside, one filled with love, the other hatred. He had almost let the wrong wolf win: he had been consumed with hatred while he chased Captain Fish Eyes. Now he felt only compassion for the Indian. He would try to explain that to Sally—after she calmed down.

All these months, he had wanted to catch the captain, make him pay for stealing his airplane, punish him. This chasing one another had to stop. A bittersweet ending to his search: he wished that the captain could escape. It would never happen, not in real life.

44.

Home from school later than usual, Frank squeezed out of his car parked next to Mary's in their tiny so-called two-car garage. He opened the door into the hall and plopped his briefcase—heavy with a three-inch stack of quizzes to grade—onto the tiles in the entry. He took off his shoes and called out, "Hello. I'm home."

Mary didn't answer, and he didn't smell dinner cooking. In the kitchen, Frank found a peculiar note under the penguin magnet on the refrigerator door: "I have been called away on an urgent errand. There's a casserole in the refrigerator, and you can shake out some salad from the bag. Don't worry, Honey. I should be home by Friday."

How could he *not* worry? Mary had never done anything like that, leaving for an unscheduled week. Expecting an easy answer, Frank called Sally.

"So Mary's gone," Sally said. "I haven't seen her since the baby shower on Saturday night."

"Well, do you know where she is?"

"You said she left a note. Don't worry—she said she'd be back Friday."

Frank replaced the receiver. *Don't worry* . . . sure. He checked Mary's car, parked in the garage, one more time: no clues. He couldn't imagine what would qualify as an urgent errand. Where was Mary?

Mary couldn't see beyond the skeleton of a tree in the semidarkness beneath a streetlight, a bare tree shrouded in a cocoon of light, like moonlight over the Badlands. She felt the same thrill of adventure and danger that she had felt last summer at the Little Eagle Casino, when she had met Quill

359

Rethcaw, also known as Captain von Wächter from Kedar's tip last July, another piece of information that Major Blakely had ignored.

It had been too dangerous to tell anyone, even Frank, about her errand—an errand of mercy. Only Sally knew. Sally had told her that Jerry had revealed Quill's location to Major Paul Blakely. Technically, not true: Jerry had told the major that Sally knew and that forced her to tell. Sally was so mad when she telephoned yesterday that Mary felt sparks over the wire. Hardly fair—that meant the FBI would hunt down a blind man, while he recovered from burns.

Mary wanted to see those burns. Sally said that Quill's mushroom ointment had healed his face with no scarring, a discovery too important to waste.

An arrow pointed to visitor parking.

The atrium at Regional Hospital in Rapid City was green with potted plants under a focal-point skylight, lighted artificially on dark winter evenings. Just as at her home-hospital in Palo Alto, candy-striper volunteers staffed the information desk.

Mary asked for Quill Rethcaw, then for Captain Wachter.

The smiling volunteer said, "Not here. They may have been discharged."

"Try V, V-O-N Wachter. The name is German, starts with a *von*."

"Not one V-name on the roster."

Mary leaned across the desk. "I'm a nurse, visiting here from California. Your burn unit is outstanding. I'd like to talk to someone about it, and maybe visit the facility." Mary thought she'd see for herself; Quill had to be here.

The volunteer called someone and directed Mary to the elevator. No one used it that time of day. On the sixth floor, Mary smelled antiseptic, a smell that she had never liked, despite her years as a nurse. A security camera flashed intermittently: entrance by invitation only. A short time after she pushed the call button, someone buzzed her in.

No one was at the nurse's station. Mary chose the hall to the right. At the far end, the room with the closed door had a chart for A. Warchet. His childhood name: Aquila Warchet—Mary had heard it once, last summer in Major Blakely's kitchen. The nurses should change shift soon. Mary slipped into a convenient women's restroom—only two stalls, staff only. As a stranger, she shouldn't be seen. Mary hid out in a stall.

Mary settled in for a long wait, plenty of time to reconsider everything. She pulled out her latest letter from Kedar. His brain was growing even faster than his body—he would take the high school equivalency exam before the year was up. He had sent the usual packet of essays for her review; she had left them at the hotel. Mary had not and would not tell Kedar that Captain Wachter was alive.

Someone opened the door and slammed it. Mary lifted her feet and left the door locked and tried not to breathe. She didn't relax until the other toilet flushed and whoever washed her hands and walked back into the hall.

Still a while before she could leave . . . She made herself more comfortable. Her thoughts shifted to Aquila. Such a fanatical teacher—he must wonder what happened to Kedar, surely his best pupil. How could he have sent the boy on a suicide mission? Mary hoped that guilt gnawed Quill's soul. She would never let him know that Kedar was alive and well. Uncertainty and guilt would be Aquila's life sentence—along with blindness.

Mary heard female voices in the hall, nurses leaving for the night. A nurse came into the next stall. Mary tucked her feet up. A second nurse banged on the door to Mary's stall. "Hurry up in there."

"Just a minute," Mary called out. "I have a female emergency."

She asked the first nurse, "Who's in there?"

Mary heard the answer: "Who cares? I need to get home." Through the space between the door and the frame, Mary saw that they wore green scrubs. She'd have to get some.

A male nurse had checked in. He would make a fast check of every room before he settled in by the telephone. She'd wait here until he finished his patient inventory. Was it taking the law into her own hands, to postpone Quill's arrest? Frank would back her up, whether or not he agreed with her. Would Jerry understand? She wondered if Robina knew about the stolen aircraft or the holy war suicide mission. No matter: Mary would do what she would do.

At midnight, Mary emerged from her cocoon. She saw no one outside the door. She crept down the hall to the nurses' locker room. No scrubs: she didn't see any clean ones. She borrowed a recently rinsed nylon uniform that hung from a hangar over the sink. A white uniform was better than jeans; she could say she was a private nurse. She left her jeans and sweater and coat in a locker; she had to wear her black knee-high boots. The soggy synthetic fiber felt cold against the skin on her stomach and dampened her nipples through her bra. She checked the mirror—they didn't show through. The waistline on the white dress hung on her hips and the hem fell below mid-calf. She hoped no one would notice her strange attire.

Mary stood with the door open half an inch until the male nurse on duty turned away from the hall to answer the phone. Her chance: hurry. She couldn't run and tiptoe at the same time. She tiptoed to Quill's room. She glanced behind her—no one in the hall.

Mary opened the closed door labeled *A. Warchet: Isolation.* A blazing white light illuminated his room and the hall, as though brightness would allow a blind man to see. The room was as cold as the South Dakota winter evening outside. Her breath came in little spasms and her heart beat loud enough to hear it in California. She closed the door.

At the sound of the door closing, the patient turned his head towards Mary, facing her as though he could see her perfectly well. He made no sound. Mary had expected him to resemble an Egyptian mummy, but white gauze bandages covered only his eyes. His arms lay on top of a white sheet, the white bedclothes tucked tightly around him. Only his lower face and his arms were exposed.

Mary recognized his nose. His face had skin like that of a new baby: pink, smooth, and unblemished. Robina's letter had called it a miracle, burns like those without scarring. Medicine Woman's mushrooms, knowledge too precious to waste. Quill's intense non-look raised the small hairs on Mary's arms like hackles on a rooster.

"Quill, it's me, Mary. S-h-h-h—don't make a sound." She touched the hand with the new skin, perfect and smooth. He smelled of medication.

Quill squeezed her hand and held it. His mouth relaxed into a slight smile.

Mary leaned over the bed and whispered, "The FBI knows you're here. Tell Robina to meet me in the lobby tomorrow and give her this note."

Quill squeezed her hand twice and held it, the grip of a drowning man, a silent squeeze of understanding.

"We'll get you out of here. It's for Medicine Woman, for what she taught you about mushrooms. I have to leave before someone catches me." Afraid the nurse would find her, she unclasped Quill's hands and dropped them next to him on the bed.

Mary opened the door a crack, bathing the hall with a wide beam of bright light. She had debated turning it off, but someone might notice the change. All clear. Mary, brightly illuminated from behind, stepped into the dark hall.

"Who are you? That room has restricted access. Where are your scrubs?" The authoritarian voice belonged to a male nurse who could have been a fullback on a professional football team. He blocked the hall between Mary and the women's restroom.

"I am Mary Peterson." She stamped one foot, forgetting about her boots for a moment. She hoped he wouldn't notice her footwear or the still dripping dress. "Who, may I ask, are you?"

"I'm in charge here at night." He moved back two steps. "How did you get in here?"

"Well, Mr. In-Charge, I am a friend of the Warchet family, and they hired me to be a private nurse for Aquila. I got here the same way you did, buzzed right through that door there."

"Well, in that case—"

"If you will excuse me, I have to change into my civvies and go to a hotel for the rest of the night." Mary thought she deserved an Oscar. She wanted to tell Sally.

"Well, in that case." That seemed to be the only line he knew. The male nurse returned to his station. "I'll buzz you out when you're ready."

Mary retired to the women's locker room. She changed into her own clothing and packed the nurse's uniform into a bag. She would shorten it tonight. Tomorrow, if she told a good enough story, she and Robina could arrange Quill's discharge AMA—against medical advice. Robina could take it from there.

On Wednesday afternoon, FBI agents Dale and Allen climbed out of their car in the parking lot of the Regional Hospital in Rapid City. Allen slammed the door. "Here goes nothing," he said. "None of the information from that nutcase Christensen panned out before, when we investigated Wachter's headquarters in California."

"True. But Wachter is here, and we have a warrant. We can finish it up this time." Agent Dale stepped through the main entrance and slapped his identification onto the information counter. "FBI."

The volunteer manning the desk asked, "How may I help you, sir?" She wore a pink and white striped apron over a pink dress. Her blue eyes registered surprise.

"We're looking for a patient named Wachter, or Warchet, or Rethcaw," Dale said in a gruff voice. "He uses several names."

The harried volunteer gazed wide-eyed at Dale, then at Allen. She flipped through the vertical file. Her eyes darted back and forth without connecting to a name. She scanned the computer listing and reported, "No one here by any of those names, sir."

"Then send us on to your burn unit."

"I'm not supposed to do that."

Agent Dale leaned across the counter, close to her face, and snarled, "We need to talk to someone in charge."

"Yes sir." She called the burn unit and sent them to the sixth floor.

In the elevator, Agent Allen said, "He's not here. It's another wild goose chase. We'll take heat for this."

"No way. Someone is hiding something." Dale still held his badge at the ready.

The elevator stopped on the third floor. An orderly pushed a cart through the door, large enough to require three rearrangements before he could close the door. Dale and Allen each crowded into a corner until the fifth floor.

The orderly pulled the cart out of the way, replaced by three nurses who wanted to go down. After a minor button-punching dispute, the door opened on six.

The head nurse Martha Whitewater—a soft-spoken grandmotherly woman—met them at the elevator and waved Dale's badge away. "That does no good here. Mr. Warchet discharged himself."

"He just walked out of here?" Agent Dale asked, his tone loud and aggressive. "Don't you control patient discharges?"

"It's not like being in jail, and this is my burn unit." Nurse Martha answered him louder with her hands planted on her hips. "A patient can leave if he absolves the hospital of responsibility by signing a release form. He said he had a private nurse."

"That's not good enough. We have to look around."

"You can't do that, and I don't care who you are. The rooms are sterile areas and you do not pass this point without scrubbing down."

"Well, then, show us how. We have to know if the fugitive is here," Dale said. He followed Nurse Martha.

Agent Allen elected to stay by the elevator.

"You change into sterile apparel, right here." Nurse Martha handed Agent Dale green scrubs in the largest size available and stood next to him in the men's staff room.

"Aren't you going to give me some privacy?"

"Sorry. I cannot let you wander around spreading bacteria. Get changed or I'll escort you out of here."

Dale changed. He guessed it wasn't any worse than dressing around his mother. He had to roll up the pants and cinch the waist. He felt uncomfortable, not in control.

"Follow me. We don't take any bandages off. You do not touch anything. I will show you the chart at the end of each bed."

In the first room, bandages covered most of the body of a sixty-year-old woman. In the second room, the patient was male but eight years old. Guided by Nurse Martha, Dale determined that Wachter was gone, not hidden somewhere, by a physical check of every room on the sixth floor.

Aquila rode in a wheelchair down to the pharmacy on the first floor at Rapid City Regional Hospital to pick up his medications. Robina carried Quill's suitcase; she had settled his account earlier. Mary planned to meet them in a few minutes to drive them home in her rented car.

Mary had stayed on the sixth floor—the burn unit—for a last minute consultation on Quill's after-hospital care. She was ready to leave when she overheard Nurse Martha tell some unpleasant male person that it was *her* burn unit and no one entered without changing into sterile apparel. Someone looking for a fugitive who had a private nurse: someone looking for Quill. The FBI: here.

Mary ducked into the women's locker room and waited for developments. She listened to Nurse Martha making a male agent change into scrubs; he followed the nurse into the rooms down the hall and to the right.

Mary came out of hiding and walked to the elevator. A man dressed in a suit leaned against the wall. Mary stood next to him and pushed the call button. FBI agents always had partners, didn't they? She tried not to show an interest. When Mary got into the elevator, the unknown man stayed on the sixth floor.

Mary met Quill and Robina in the pharmacy. She grabbed Robina's arm and whispered in her ear: "We have to hurry. The FBI is on my heels. They're on the sixth floor."

Mary rushed out to her car. When she pulled into patient loading, an orderly helped Quill spread out on the back seat. Quill moved slowly: too much time in bed.

Mary turned down the main road in the direction of the reservation. She heard a freight train's whistle and saw it coming, a long, slow train. Exceeding the speed limit, she crossed the tracks just before the gate dropped down.

After the nonproductive visit to the burn unit at the regional hospital, Agents Allen and Dale pulled out of the parking lot on the way back to their hotel in Rapid City.

"What a wasted day," Agent Allen said, turning onto the main road into town. "What can you expect, sent here by that same crackpot Christensen. We didn't find a shred of evidence at The Guards either."

"Amazing timing," Agent Dale agreed. "He was here this morning. Someone tipped off Wachter this time but we'll get him in the end."

"That's right. The FBI always gets its man."

"That's the Mounties, wise guy. This case isn't the most important one we're working. No proof of terrorism, only some kid's harebrained story. Nobody would attack Hoover Dam with a Cessna," Dale said. "That's like picking off a tank with a peashooter."

Allen stopped behind a flashing red light at a railroad crossing just as the gate dropped down. "Here's your amazing timing. That train's so long I can't see the other end. Must have ninety-eight cars."

"I can walk faster than that train's rolling," Dale said. Boxcars marked with obscene graffiti crept by, followed by flat cars loaded with shipping containers. He tapped the dashboard with impatient fingers and asked, "What about the explosives? Didn't Wachter's file say he made them?"

"Didn't find any, did we? He won't be making them now, not with those burns. He won't steal airplanes either."

"Yeah. Heard he's blind," Dale said. "That's got to be tough, even if he's just an asshole perp."

"All we've got is proof he stole that Cessna in Pahrump," Allen said.

"What about the bullet holes in the tail?"

"Twenty-two caliber. How many 22s are there in Nevada and Arizona?"

"The captain's school had 22s," Dale said.

"Not illegal. Christensen told Matthews the students were shooting paint."

"I have to admit this case has entertainment value."

The train stopped with a stock car almost against their front bumper. "Stinks, doesn't it? Still can't see the caboose," Allen said. "If someone catches Wachter off the reservation, we can run him in for stealing one Cessna, and that's about it."

"This case is like that red light—stopped, interrupted. Red like blood and battle and Indian war-paint."

"We can get Wachter for that Cessna, but it's not like he hijacked a jumbo jet. Light trainer airplane, worth less than a Porsche."

The train started to move. Agent Dale could see the last car. "It's the principle of the thing," he said. "We'll put this case on the back burner, get him in the end."

Right on schedule, on Friday morning Mary boarded the United Airlines flight from Rapid City to San Jose. Would Frank and Jerry forgive her for meddling with Major Blakely's case? Frank would. Jerry—that was another matter. She had helped Quill to evade the FBI. That made her some kind of an accomplice.

When Mary first met her at the hospital, Robina had known about one stolen Cessna—Little Eagle—but not about the two others and not that the FBI wanted Quill. Robina had been shocked.

Mary purposely had not mentioned Kedar and the suicide mission. She sensed that Quill felt deep guilt for what he had done. Not knowing what happened to the boy or when the truth would come out made a double torture, especially since he wouldn't want Robina to find out. He deserved to suffer.

Mary had helped Robina hire a nurse for Quill; he wouldn't need one for long. Quill would adjust quickly to blindness. He said he would be able to walk in the forest by listening, just as he had with Medicine Woman years ago. Mary had Quill's research files on mushrooms tucked away on a flash-drive in her purse, but she doubted that his cure for burns could be duplicated.

Mary shifted in her seat and pulled out a pen and a collection of Kedar's essays from her carry-on. He wrote every day—in careful ink script—and sent the papers in a bundle whenever he and Mother drove to Las Vegas. He'd need a computer when he left for college. He wrote on topics ranging from Greek mythology to history of aviation: *Why Man Had to Conquer the Air*; *Icarus, The Most Significant Early Aviator*; *The Zen of Flight*; and his most poignant, *The Lightning from God*. Mary had not assigned Kedar a topic since the one last summer, *Holy War is an Oxymoron*.

In his last letter, Kedar had asked Mary to visit him to help him with college applications and to talk to Mother who was insisting that young people needed to go out on their own. He wanted his mother to go to college with him because she shouldn't live in the desert alone. Mary noticed that he called her *his mother*.

Sending Kedar on a suicide mission . . . Mary would never understand why Quill had done that, a holy war of sorts, but morally indefensible. However, without that mission, Mary would not have met Kedar, and Mother would still be without a son. How ironic, how Quill's evil actions had improved the boy's life.

Over the last few months, Quill had affected all of their lives. In fact, all of them were better off- except Quill, of course. Would Jerry accept that and keep his big mouth shut when she told him *exactly* how Quill had evaded the FBI agents? Last summer, Jerry had warned Mary not to cross over to the dark side. Would Jerry forgive her for cutting the line and throwing Fish Eyes back?

GLOSSARY

Alphabet   Phonetic alphabet, used in aviation and by the military

Alpha	Hotel	Oscar	Victor
Bravo	India	Papa	Whiskey
Charlie	Juliet	Quebec	X-ray
Delta	Kilo	Romeo	Yankee
Echo	Lima	Sierra	Zulu
Foxtrot	Mike	Tango	
Golf	November	Uniform	

adler   Eagle. German: der Adler.

Aquila   Eagle. Latin. Constellation containing the star Altair.

ELT   Emergency Location Transmitter radio.

GPS   Global Positioning System: navigation using satellites.

kan-ke-tan-ka: Red-crested woodpecker. Dakota.

ka-po-pa   Make a popping noise. Dakota.

ka-pop-a-pi-da   Carbonated water. Dakota.

ka-pop-a-tatanka   Aquila's name for dream mushrooms

ku-an-shee   Grandmother. Dakota: kuaŋßi.

magneto; mag   Component of ignition system.

na-po-pa   Burst, as a gun shot. Dakota.

o-ji-jit-ka   Rosebud. Dakota: oɲjiɲjiŋtka.

Paha Sapa   Holy place for Sioux Nation. The Black Hills.

po-po-pa   To pop, as in popping corn. Dakota.

ta-tan-ka   Buffalo bull. Dakota: tataŋka.

wam-bdi   Little Eagle. Dakota: waŋmdi.

wam-bdi-u-pi   Eagle feather. Dakota: waŋmdiupi.

zit-ka-da   Small birds. Dakota: zitkadaŋ

Zulu time   Standardized time used in aviation